PRAISE FOR *RATTLE*

'It's a rare debut that has this much polish.
Head and shoulders above most of the competition'
Val McDermid

'An excellent read'
Martina Cole

'Loved it. It made me a paranoid
hypochondriac for a few days!'
Sophie Hannah

'Seriously creepy and very well written. One that'll have
you double-checking your doors are locked at night'
Ali Land

'Dark, stylish and scarily plausible'
Joseph Knox

'If you like Mo Hayder, you'll love this.
Creepy psychopath, well-drawn characters,
original motive and some fabulous writing'
Emma Flint

'Sharp, moving and wholly original.
Rattle is a breath of fresh air'
Tammy Cohen

'A chilling and inventive debut'
Simon Beckett

'Original, vivid, stunningly written . . . A fantastic read'
Debbie Howells

'*Rattle* is such a stunning thriller; a novel that
plumbs the depths of evil yet stuns you with its humanity'
Colette McBeth

'Serial killers don't come much scarier than this
monstrous creation . . . A macabre thrill ride'
Sunday Mirror

'A gem of a scary debut'
The Times

'A thriller to keep you up all night'
Daily Mail

'A highly original and creepy tale that rattles along
with menace and does not let up until the cracking finale'
Daily Express

'Amid the outpouring of crime novels,
Rattle is up there with the best of them'
Marcel Berlins, *The Times*

THE
COLLECTOR

FIONA CUMMINS

MACMILLAN

First published 2018 by Macmillan
an imprint of Pan Macmillan
20 New Wharf Road, London N1 9RR
Associated companies throughout the world
www.panmacmillan.com

ISBN 978-1-5098-1270-7

1 3 5 7 9 8 6 4 2

A CIP catalogue record for this book is available from the British Library.

Typeset in Scala 12/16 pt by
Palimpsest Book Production Limited, Falkirk, Stirlingshire
Printed and bound by CPI Group (UK) Ltd, Croydon, CR0 4YY

Visit **www.panmacmillan.com** to read more about all our books
and to buy them. You will also find features, author interviews and
news of any author events, and you can sign up for e-newsletters
so that you're always first to hear about our new releases.

In memory of Cherry Anthony,
first reader and friend.

'You shall appoint, as a penalty, life for life, eye for eye, tooth for tooth, hand for hand, foot for foot, burn for burn, wound for wound, bruise for bruise'

Exodus 21:24

'The Son can do nothing of his own accord, but only what he sees the Father doing. For whatever the Father does, that the Son does likewise'   John 5:19

SUNDAY

SUNDAY MIRROR

24 February 2013

The parents of missing Clara Foyle will today mark one hundred days since the five-year-old's abduction.

Miles and Amy Foyle will join friends and family at a vigil on Blackheath Common to light candles and release balloons.

Clara, who has cleft hands, vanished on her way home from school in November last year. The chief suspect in her disappearance, 'Butcher of Bromley' Brian Howley, is on the run after escaping police custody.

According to witnesses, including Met police officer Etta Fitzroy, who was briefly held captive by the killer, Howley was a collector of human skeletons with deformities.

He housed the bones in a personal museum at the home of his late father Marshall Howley. The macabre collection is understood to have dated back generations due to a family connection with London's Hunterian Museum, with which the former hospital night worker was obsessed.

Six-year-old Jakey Frith, who suffers from the devastating bone disorder Stone Man Syndrome, was rescued from Howley Snr's house just moments before it was destroyed by fire.

Extensive DNA tests on human remains discovered in the ashes have confirmed that one of the victims was teenager Grace Rodríguez, the so-called Girl in the Woods. Detectives were able to link her disappearance to Howley after it emerged she suffered from a bone condition known as cervical ribs.

They have so far failed to find any trace of Clara Foyle.

1

10.17 p.m.

Saul Anguish was counting out the beats between the jagged spears of lightning and the groans of thunder tearing open the sky.

He was waiting for the rain. Praying for it. Because the rain almost always brought his mother home. And if she didn't come home, she was dead. Not definitely dead. But possibly. Maybe. Saul spent a large chunk of his life braced for this Significant Life Event, the hushed tones of a uniformed stranger who would tell him the body of Gloria Anguish had been found in an alleyway or a deserted corner of the park.

Fat drops peppercorned the sand. He watched them turning the fine grains into damp crumbs, spreading until the jumble of broken-down rocks and shells and glass rubbed smooth over countless decades turned a dirty, unremarkable brown.

As he stood at the window, a watchman, night crept up

behind him, touching the corners of the room with darkness and shadow. Touching his heart.

Saul, no longer a boy but not yet a man, hated this endless waiting for his mother. Because in the gaps of time between worrying and hoping and wanting, slid the Other Thoughts.

The Other Thoughts were itchy and twisty, and even though he tried hard not to scratch at them, he found them impossible to resist.

Saul reached into the pocket of his jeans for the worn twist of pipe cleaner and wool that he and his mother had made all those years ago. The school's specialist learning mentor had searched out Mrs Anguish at the school gates, suggested ever so gently that she and her nine-year-old son might benefit from a series of workshops that Leigh Park Juniors was running: 'Enjoying Your Children'.

In that first session, Saul's mother had twisted the pipe cleaner into a face with arms and legs, and smiled down at her son with bloodshot eyes. His job had been to glue on the black strands of wool for hair, to draw a crooked smile on a pale scrap of felt.

A worry doll. For him to share his secrets. His fears.

The smudge of ink on its face had now been rubbed blank, the pipe cleaner's fluff worn bare in places, exposing the metal beneath. That glimpse of silver made Saul wonder how it would feel to touch his fingertips to electrified barbed wire. To press his soles against the live tracks running through the train station at the bottom of the hill by the boats. To hold his mother's face in the sand until she struggled and stopped moving. Fear for her safety always did that to him. It made him angry and confused and unsure what to feel.

The estuary spread out before him, mud and tide meeting like old enemies. Night had come calling and through its dense curtain, he searched for Gloria Anguish, torn between wanting his mother home and the freedom of never having to watch for her at the window again.

A movement snagged the horizon. A whisper of something. Saul strained into the rainy darkness, trying to read the shape of the night. He fingered the worry doll. Even at sixteen, he still slipped it under his pillow when he slept, although he'd never told his mother *that*.

And then, just as he was wondering whether he should go out and look for her, she was there, stumbling across the wide expanse of beach in front of their rented flat, her coat flapping open, the moon spotlighting her during a break in the clouds.

He did not need to smell the fumes on her breath to know that she was drunk.

Gloria Anguish turned awkwardly, threw a glance down the shoreline towards the distant lights of the refinery, and began to run with an unsteady gait. Saul could imagine that slight sheen across her forehead, the tumbled slur of her apologies when he opened the door and let her in to a tea of congealed baked beans and cold burnt toast.

A few yards from the bottom of the concrete steps that led from the beach up the grassy hill to their flat, Gloria stopped running, just for the briefest of moments. Her shoe had caught on the edge of a small rock and that lull in motion was followed by a loss of balance which sent her sprawling across the narrow strip of sand. Saul waited for her to crawl to her knees, to lever herself upwards, and lurch unevenly home as she had done countless times before.

But his mother lay still, her jaw loose and slightly open, her black hair spread out like seaweed.

Like strands of wool.

The tide, almost home, was lapping at the hem of her coat, like an over-familiar friend. In the time it would take Saul to tie his laces, to run down the stairs of their flat, across the road, past the benches with their memorial plaques and dying roses, and down the steep steps to the beach, his mother's lungs could be filling up with saltwater.

Or perhaps, if he tried really hard, he might reach her just as the bitter liquid trickled into her mouth.

But Saul found his feet were stuck to the stained carpet, that although his eyes were fixed on the shape of his mother, he could not move.

The hands of his watch clicked onwards, each tiny movement a chance squandered. He wondered if her eyes were open or closed.

It was hard to remember, the past all scrunched up in his memory like plastic carrier bags, but the sight of her lying on the sand triggered *something*, half buried like the condoms Posh Dan had hidden under the pier after his shift at the fairground last week.

He squinted, looking beyond the rest of his memories, seeking out that moment amongst the thousands and thousands of others.

And then he found it. The day he had sat his 11-plus exam. A month before his eleventh birthday.

'It's important,' his mother had told him. 'Don't screw it up.' She'd rummaged in her purse then, brushed her thumb across his cheek. 'I'll see you afterwards. I've got enough money to buy us each an ice-cream.'

And he'd listened to his mother, he really had. He'd worked through the papers quickly but diligently. He'd answered all the questions and even thought he'd got some of them right because he'd had a bit of time left over at the end to check his workings-out.

He'd been smiling inside and out as he scanned the nest of parents waiting outside the school hall, could already taste the mint and chocolate, cool and delicious, melting on his tongue, but Gloria Anguish was nowhere to be seen.

He'd still been leaning against the railings when all the other children were long gone, whisked off for pizza lunches and trips to the cinema, and the invigilator had come out carrying her coat and bag,

Eventually, Saul had given up and begun the long walk home.

She had been lying on the bed when he'd let himself in, a boy of not quite eleven in need of his mother. On her stomach, head turned to the side, her hair a black fan. Her eyes had been open, an empty bottle of vodka on the floor. The smell of despair and autumnal heat had drifted in the air.

'Mum,' he'd said. 'Mummy.' He'd shaken her shoulder and patted her back, but Gloria did not answer him. She was somewhere else and even her son's voice was not enough to pull her back.

Saul had seen this before. Not often, but enough. He'd wiped the vomit from her chin with a wet piece of toilet roll, and sat on the edge of the bed until his hunger had become too much and he took himself off to make a jam sandwich. Then he'd carried it back to her room, and stayed with his mother until her eyes closed and day became night, and day again.

Saul's head was nodding against his chest when his mother had finally sat up, the wrinkled sheets imprinted on the side of her face, the dawn's light cold and unforgiving. She had looked at her sleeping son, still in his clothes, a strawberry-red smear on his cheek and guilt had impaled itself in her chest. Guilt and shame.

She had touched him lightly on the shoulder and the boy had opened his eyes, as if he hadn't been sleeping at all, but was merely resting until she awoke.

'Ice-cream?' She had offered him a faint smile.

But Saul was no longer in the mood.

Five years on, he couldn't bear the idea of ice-cream, not even when Cassidy Cranston from the girls' school had licked her cone suggestively at him during a trip to the West End last term. To him, it would always taste of disappointment.

Saul dragged his attention back to the beach. His mother was still lying there, the waves almost upon her. Her leg twitched, a violent gesture, and that seemed to unlock something in him. He bolted from the room, unexpectedly stricken by the thought he would get there too late.

Outside, the rising wind was frothing the waves to a fury. The letterbox rattled. He was halfway down the cliff steps before he realized he was shouting her name, already feeling the bile of betrayal in his mouth.

I'm coming, Mum. Hold on.

The rain was coming down harder now, glazing the concrete steps, misting the glow from the street lamps. Saul lost his footing a couple of times, and grabbed the handrail to stop himself from falling. His eyes followed the tide, too close now. He searched for that first glimpse of his mother as he ran towards the beach and crested the brow of shingle and sand, suddenly terrified he would see the lumpen mass of her body dragged out to sea.

His eyes scanned the stretch of beach where she had been lying. The waves were claiming it, marching on. Soon, there would be nothing left but the inky swell of high tide. Saul swallowed but his mouth was dry. He stared into the water, looking for Gloria. Her black hair. A white plimsoll. But she had simply disappeared.

Water seeped into the fabric of his own shoes, and he stumbled backwards, then hefted his body over the concrete wall that lipped the edge of the beach. He should call the police. Or the coastguard. He should do *something*. But Saul didn't know what. How could he tell a police officer that he had waited so long to help his own mother that the tide had taken her? They might arrest him. What if he went to prison? Cassidy Cranston wouldn't be interested then.

Saul steadied himself by placing his hands on the wall and looked out across the Thames Estuary towards the horizon strung with orange fairy lights. Nausea pushed out every breath into the frigid air. His heart spiralled in his chest. Unsure of what to do next, he headed towards the hill steps, to the safety of the flat. Would it be home without his mother?

But as Saul turned, heavy-shouldered, away from the beach, a man's curse drifted down the pavement towards him.

Saul glanced over to the wrought-iron shelter that stood a couple of hundred yards up the road on a wide expanse of grass favoured by dog-walkers and kids on scooters.

A man with dark hair curling at the edges and a narrow, hard face was bending over a pile of clothes. A pile of clothes attached to a pair of legs wearing white plimsolls.

Saul ran towards it.

Even though he was hunched over and on his knees, Saul could tell the man was very tall. He was vaguely familiar. And he was pushing his hands into the dip of Gloria's chest.

Push. Push. Push. Push.

The man paused briefly, pressed his mouth against Gloria's, blew in four short breaths.

Push. Push. Push. Push.

Saul watched him trying to cajole the life back into his mother. His hands were all twisted, like Saul's late grandfather's, whose arthritis had stolen his clock-making business and his dignity.

The man did not look at Saul. 'Don't just stand there. Take off your coat.' *Push. Push. Push. Push.* 'She's freezing.'

Saul slipped his jacket over his mother, trying to ignore the touch of the rain on his bare forearms. Her eyes were still closed. Saul felt himself slide away, disengage. He could not stand witness to his mother's death, a guilty party.

And then she coughed.

Saul let out a breath and held it, his body still. Waiting. To see what his mother would do next.

She coughed again. Her eyes fluttered. She twisted onto her side, opened her mouth and released a trickle of watery red liquid.

Saul's horror must have shown on his face. The man's dark eyes followed his. 'It's not what you think,' he said, standing up and wiping his hands on his jeans. 'It's just red wine and seawater.'

Saul bent to his mother, who was coughing weakly and

shivering. He put his arm around her and heaved her to her feet.

As they half dragged Gloria Anguish up the steps to the flat, Saul and the man did not speak. Saul had no idea what to say. He didn't like talking to adults. He did not trust them. But this man was not like most adults. He did not fill Saul's ears with meaningless words, trying to make conversation. Silence sat well on him.

The man waited until Saul had opened the front door before he spoke again.

'You should take her to hospital.'

Saul shrugged. 'Maybe.'

A groan slipped from his mother. 'No . . .' She was shaking her head, although her eyes were closed.

'S'all right, Mum. Don't worry about it.'

'Get her into bed, then. Get her warm.'

'Thanks,' mumbled Saul, although when he looked at the sodden heap that was his mother he wasn't sure whether to feel grateful or disappointed.

'Is your father home?'

'Nah.'

'What time is he back?'

Saul chewed on a nail. 'Doesn't live here, does he?'

The man bit down hard on his lip and licked at a tiny bead of blood. His eyes closed briefly as he did so, and a coldness took root in Saul, reminding him it was raining and he was not wearing his coat. The man's dark eyes pinned Saul in place. His scrutiny made Saul uneasy, and it prised a laugh from him. Saul was always getting into trouble for laughing at inappropriate moments. His head teacher Mr Darenth said he had a problem with authority. The man mistook Saul's nerves for mirth and bared his teeth at him in a half-grin. As his cracked lips parted, Saul watched that pinprick of blood bloom again.

'Get her into bed before she freezes to death.' He looked down at Gloria. 'And keep an eye on her. For breathing problems, that kind of thing.'

Abruptly, the man turned and left, limping across the road and down a set of steps which Saul knew led to the Old Town and a row of fisherman's cottages, wind-beaten and dilapidated. They were rental properties, Saul's mother had told him. Money for old rope. She had said it in a sneery type of voice but Saul knew she would have given anything for the lifeline of her own rope, however frayed.

Her clothes were caked in wet sand, which rubbed against his fingers as he helped her up the narrow staircase. The flat was freezing, the gas meter out of credit. In the bathroom, he stripped her, averting his gaze from her protruding ribcage, her small breasts. The shower was broken so he stood her in the bath while he boiled a kettle and handed her a wet sponge to clean the seaweed and sand from her body. There was a large bruise already forming on her forehead.

When she was finished, he handed her one of the old T-shirts she liked to wear to bed and his own grey hooded sweatshirt. She was shaking and, with her thin white legs on show, she looked like a child. Pathetic and weak.

'Saul, I—'

'Just leave it, Mum. I don't want to talk about it.'

She didn't try to speak to him again, but looked longingly towards the kitchen. He could see her mentally opening the cupboard, taking down a glass.

'I've poured it down the sink,' he said.

She laughed guiltily. 'No, no, I was thinking about tea, honestly. Hot and sweet.'

'Get into bed then. I'll make it.'

When he carried the mug through to her room, she was already under the covers, curtains pulled tight to keep out the memories of that night, to obscure the reality of what had nearly been.

He was struck by the contrast of her black hair against the pillow, her wan, tired face.

'Thank you,' she said.

He wasn't sure if she meant the tea or the fact that he was taking care of her again. He turned away without answering, suddenly exhausted by her neediness, the relentless drama.

Later that evening, when the moon was pooled on the outgoing tide, and his mother was finally asleep, Saul, gazing out across the cockle sheds and moored boats, remembered the flash of light in the skylight of the old fisherman's cottage he'd seen a night or two earlier. Like a torch or something.

He blinked, waited for it to come again, but the darkness stayed dark.

Next to the sofa, Gloria's dressmaking scissors were lying on a pile of cheap fabric she'd bought to make dresses to sell at the Thursday market in town.

Saul slipped his hand into his back pocket and pulled out the worry doll. It stared up at him, blank-faced. Frayed and falling apart. Stringy black strands of hair so like his mother's.

Saul picked up the scissors and cut off its head.

2

Ten hours earlier

Detective Sergeant Etta Fitzroy walked down the path and through the cemetery gates. She'd spent more time than most at funerals, supporting the families of the dead: car crash victims; young gang members stabbed in the street; a talented ballet dancer and teenager on the brink of woman-hood, now forever carved into history as the Girl in the Woods.

The last time she had been here, this tiny little cemetery in an under-the-radar corner of the city, not far from home, she had refused herself the luxury of tears. That privilege had belonged to someone else.

Conchita Rodríguez had gripped her hand so tightly as the coffin was swallowed into the frozen earth that Fitzroy had thought her fingers might break. She'd endured the pain; welcomed it, almost. It was a fraction of what Mrs Rodríguez's daughter Grace – reduced to ashes and memories – had endured at the hands of the psychopath Brian Howley.

His name tasted bitter on her lips.

She walked along the verge to the graves on the far side of the lawns, past marble tombstones with names etched in gold leaf and a bank of leftover flowers from an earlier burial that were already beginning to decay.

In a tidy patch of grass, away from the main pathways, was a quieter part of the cemetery. The stones here were much smaller, lined up like children in the playground. There were teddy bears and windmills and brightly coloured plastic flowers, the poignant echoes of what might have been.

Fitzroy averted her eyes, could hardly bear to read the inscriptions of loss and love, although she knew most of them by heart.

RUBY OLIVE JAMESON,
our beautiful girl
born on 15 April 2011,
RETURNED TO GOD'S ARMS
on 14 May 2011.
SLEEP, LITTLE ONE, SLEEP.

OUR PRECIOUS SON
HENRY DONNELLY
1.3.08 – 23.11.10
LIFE IS NOT FOREVER.
LOVE IS.

Past JEMIMA SOPHIE CROSS (aged 7) and ALEX JAMES HARRIS (13) and OLIVIA MAY BARRETT (9) and

TOBY GRAFTON (11) until she reached a plain grey headstone.

IN LOVING MEMORY OF
NATE FITZROY
BORN ASLEEP.
24 February 2008

Fitzroy placed the cloud of baby's breath she'd carried from her own garden on the swell of earth that held her son. He would have been five today. Five. The same age as Clara Foyle.

By now, those tiny fingers would have grown into strong hands that could hold a pencil and catch a ball. They might have picked apples and fired pretend guns, and sliced through the water of a swimming pool. They would have held her own, bigger, hand.

Sometimes, she could hear his voice. A child's giggle, infectious, unstoppable; crying and shouting; singing with joy. The mumbled mouthful of vowels and consonants: *Mummy*.

The sounds of a family made real.

Her family.

Fitzroy fumbled in her bag for a Tupperware box, opened it up and pulled out a small cake. Into soft icing of the palest blue she inserted five silver candles, and placed it on the grave next to the flowers.

Crouching on her knees, Fitzroy cupped her hand around an ancient lighter that her estranged husband David had left behind at the flat when he'd moved out before Christmas, and lit each candle in turn.

Happy birthday Nate, my darling boy.

Head bowed, Fitzroy waited for the wind to blow out each tiny flame, liked to imagine it was Nate's breath carried to her on the currents of air.

Minutes passed. Fitzroy always hated this part of her visits to Nate because it was like saying goodbye to him all over again. Today, she was even more reluctant to leave because she knew what lay ahead.

She thought about the email sitting inside her phone, waiting to be passed on to Amy and Miles Foyle, and how the gleam from this nugget of new information would be dulled by questions she did not have answers to. She checked her watch, pressed her lips to her son's damp headstone.

Time to go.

3

Amy Foyle had always hated balloons. The stench of over-
stretched rubber. That shrivelled, embarrassed emptiness
when they burst. She had wanted Chinese lanterns and a
night-time vigil. But Miles had overruled her. It wasn't fair on
Clara's friends, he'd said. They'd want to remember her too.

As soon as she'd arrived on the Heath, Amy knew it had
been a mistake to invite Clara's class. Children were everywhere. Their little heads weaved from side to side, excited by
the dozens of white balloons restrained in oversized nets
and the weekend sighting of their friends.

Amy's fingers stroked the cool silver of her hip flask. The
urge to unscrew its cap and swallow down its burning contents was ferocious. Even three months on, the other
mothers remained awkward around her, averting their
eyes if they bumped into her in Blackheath Village or in the
playground when she was collecting Eleanor. But she had
promised herself she wouldn't drink today. It was about
respecting Clara. The hip flask was security, that was all.

She scanned the gathering crowds, noting several faces that she recognized. Mr and Mrs Bruton from next-door-but-one. Megan Ambrose, an 'auntie' from Clara's old pre-school. Poppy Smith and her mother, Miranda. Amy bit down on the inside of her cheek.

In another ten minutes or so, there would be a speech and they would release the balloons, and then she could go home and carry on marking out the hours and minutes since her youngest daughter had been snatched.

A girl with exactly the same shade of hair as Clara's wandered past, and Amy had the strangest sensation that her body was peeling away from her mind. She wanted to grab at the child, to spin her around and find herself staring into Clara's eyes. To take her hand, and lead her across the common, back to their home. To explain that something terribly sad had happened, but that it had nothing to do with them.

Amy took a step towards her, and another and another, but the whistle of feedback from the public address system intruded, jerking her back to herself, and she dug her nails into her palms instead. She would not unspool in front of her audience who, she had recently sensed, were becoming weary of this drama. Miles hated it when she spoke like that, but Amy knew. Now the novelty of Clara's disappearance had muted, the masses were growing restless but they still expected to be 'entertained' – fresh sightings, TV bulletins, a nervous breakdown perhaps, or the discovery of Clara's body. Their appetite for bad news was endless.

Miles. She looked for him across the sea of bodies filling up the Heath. He was talking animatedly to a woman she didn't recognize. His skin was the colour of lazy days on the beach, and he had lost weight. He looked – there was no other word for it – good. He had flown in from Spain yesterday but he'd turned down Amy's offer to stay in the home they'd once shared. He didn't want to confuse Eleanor, he'd said. He wasn't ready to return to London yet. Amy had felt like saying that Eleanor was already confused, living with a basket case for a mother and a father who vanished from her life a few weeks after her little sister, but instead she had just nodded and said she understood. The events of the last few months had changed her. Her daughter's disappearance had shown her that no amount of hysteria or bitter accusation would alter that singular painful fact: Clara was gone.

Three months on, the shock of it had not receded, as others had promised, but had become a painful burr lodged in her heart, scratching her afresh with every compression of muscle, every rhythmic pump and beat. Really, what was the significance of a hundred days? Exactly the same as ninety-seven or sixty-three or thirty-one.

As for Him, she did not allow her imaginings to linger down that dark alleyway. Until Clara was found, she would not – could not – allow herself to believe that her daughter was dead.

Someone nudged her from behind.

'I think Daddy wants you.'

Amy looked in the direction that Eleanor was pointing. Miles was waving at them, beckoning them over. He had a microphone in his hand and exuded purpose.

'Are you ready?' He smiled quickly at them both, all business. Amy didn't smile back.

He tapped the head of the microphone and cleared his

throat. Eleanor's hand found her mother's. Amy caught Miles' intake of breath, briefly amplified, before he spoke.

'Thank you, everyone, for coming today and supporting us during a truly testing time for our family.' He glanced over at Amy but she was gazing at the grass, wondering how something that was trodden down and walked over, suffocated by frost and snow, then scorched by the sun, could still be so *alive*.

'It is now one hundred days since our darling Clara was snatched from our lives.' Miles' voice was clear and firm, the audience silent, apart from the occasional *shhh* from an embarrassed parent.

'We know *who* took our daughter but today is not the day to dwell on that. Today is a day to remember our lovely girl, to think about the *where*, to remind everyone out there to keep looking, keep searching for Clara. We believe our daughter is still with us, and until she is found we will never give up on her. Clara, you are our shining light in the darkness, you carry with you our hope and love, and we will find you and follow you home.'

Miles fumbled with the string knot on the bag holding the balloons. Eleanor ran forward to help him. Amy remembered, too late, that she was supposed to bring scissors.

Across the exposed expanse of the Heath, the wind sharpened its knife on her. The crowd was murmuring now, children bored and cold, waiting for the release of the balloons, to chase them across the grass and try to catch them. Amy did not want the children to sully them with their grubby fingers, to burst them and puncture her hope. If Miles was forcing her to have balloons, she wanted them to fly high and free.

23

Ahead of Amy, the section of crowd to her left was looking more restless than the others. She registered low mutterings and a couple of indifferent glances, thrown away like litter. Miles was still struggling to loosen the knot, his head bent, so he didn't see what Amy did; the crowd parting to let through a handful of all-too-familiar faces.

The journalist at the front, a woman called Sarah, looked uncomfortable. Miles had invited them. Important to keep reminding the public about Clara, he'd said. She didn't disagree. She had been bracing herself for the inevitable platitudes and disposable questions. But why was the young woman in front of her wearing that curious expression of sympathy and steel?

The crowd began to clap softly. A local choir Miles had found on the Internet began to sing 'Abide With Me'. Above Amy's head, the balloons drifted upwards, and she was overcome by a sense of dread; that by letting these balloons take flight, they were saying goodbye to Clara.

The children watched and pointed as those white spheres of hope were absorbed by the sky. The volume of the crowd was rising now, the tense silence of remembrance broken up into snippets of conversation about Mrs Foyle's gaunt expression and how Mr Foyle looked so *well*, and poor, poor Eleanor. Thoughts were turning to cups of tea and putting the dinner on and shaking off the sadness of the day. Of holding their own children that little bit tighter.

But Amy was oblivious to this because she was watching that woman journalist exchange the briefest of nods – hardly noticeable if she hadn't been looking – with the paper's photographer. Now the woman was moving forwards, towards Amy, and the other journalists were moving too, slipping their phones into their pockets, holding out their notebooks in supplication.

At the same time, a blur of maroon and navy blue seemed to emerge through the dispersing crowd from the opposite direction. Amy had clocked her earlier, and had been grateful for the respectful way she had hung back, trying not to draw attention to herself whilst lending the family support.

But now Detective Sergeant Etta Fitzroy was almost running towards her, trying to get to her before the journalists did.

'Mrs Foyle?'

Amy closed her eyes.

Opened them.

The journalist was close enough to touch. Amy could see the way her lipstick had bled into the fine lines above her top lip, the scratch on the left lens of her glasses. Her breath smelled of nicotine and lunchtime wine.

'Yes.' She tried to keep her voice steady.

'Sarah Simpson, *Daily Mirror*. How do you feel about the discovery of your daugh . . .'

Amy felt that tilting light-headedness that comes in that fraction of time before the swinging of the axe. Fitzroy was almost upon them, but Amy acknowledged that the detective's efforts were fruitless. She was not going to reach them before the words were out of the journalist's mouth.

'. . . ter's school uniform? I understand it washed up on an island off Essex this morning.'

Amy Foyle had been preparing herself for this moment for one hundred days. For the earth to shudder and break open and tip her into its fractured crevasse. To hear that her daughter was dead.

But this. This she had not expected.

She wanted to shake the answers from them. To demand which island. To find out why the journalists had been told before she had. To ask: what does this *mean*? But all she could think of was an embroidered name label, sewn into a pinafore with tiny, careful stitches.

'Is there anything you want to say, Mrs Foyle?' A camera flash. The click and whirr of a shutter.

'Do you think this confirms she is dead?' A different voice. Male. Young.

'There have been no sightings of her for three months. No trace at all. Do you believe Howley still has her?'

A body in front of her. Shielding her. Fitzroy. Solid. Unflappable.

'Clear off,' she said. 'Show some respect.'

Sarah gave an apologetic shrug but she had got what she had come for. The journalists wandered off in the direction of The Crown to compare notes and file copy.

'I'm sorry,' said Fitzroy, as soon as they were out of earshot. 'I was waiting until this' – she indicated the Heath – 'was over. I don't know how they found out so quickly.'

'Found out what?' Miles was beside her, rubbing his thumb and forefinger together in a circling motion. Amy automatically looked for Eleanor, who was chattering to one of her teachers from school.

'A pinafore dress matching Clara's school uniform and labelled with her name was found this morning on Foulness Island.'

Every part of Miles, the movement of his finger and thumb, the rise and fall of his chest, the open and closing of his eyelids, stilled. 'Where's that?'

'It's part of the Essex archipelago, a haven for wildlife and a handful of residents. About fifty-five miles east of here.'

'And you're sure it's Clara's?'

'We believe so, yes. Obviously, we'll run DNA tests but frankly, I'm not hopeful. It washed ashore on the salt marshes and it looks like it's been in the water for a while.'

Amy watched Fitzroy's lips forming the vowels and consonants that made up the latest chapter in Clara's story. The words slipped away on the rising breeze, and for a second time that afternoon, she was aware of the sensation that she was losing her daughter. That something indefinable was shifting and changing.

'But what does this *mean*?' she said. 'He' – she refused to say his name – 'could have thrown it away weeks ago. It doesn't mean that Clara's body's is going to wash up too. Does it?' She was almost shouting now. 'Does it?'

'True enough,' said Fitzroy, but her eyes were already sliding away, coming to rest on a distant point of the darkening horizon.

In the last weeks and months, Amy had seen enough police officers to last several lifetimes, especially DS Fitzroy, and in that hideaway gesture, that sudden refusal to meet her face-on, Amy understood two truths.

The first: those shiny promises of hope and drive and resolution that had lit the detective's face from the moment that Clara had vanished were losing their lustre.

As for the second – and Amy was as certain of this as she was that her daughter was gone – DS Fitzroy was hiding something.

4

4.47 p.m.

It was only his second day but Saul had already decided that
Conrad Gillespie was a prick.

Perhaps it was the way he ordered him to check the
shop's crappy toilet every hour – it reeked of blocked drains
and bleach – or the smirk as Saul swept urine-soaked dust
from the chinchilla's cage.

But it was a job, and a job meant money.

'Get us a coffee, will you?'

Saul, who was cutting up apples for the mynah bird, considered ignoring him, but decided that he couldn't face
another punishment detail to the toilet so put down his
paring knife.

'Shall I just finish this?' His tone was careful. It had
taken him less than two shifts to discover that Conrad Gillespie did not like to feel undermined.

Cassie had failed to mention that the manager was a
fucktard when she'd tipped Saul off about the job. Mostly,
she had a keen sense for people, but not this time. Perhaps

she'd been blinded by his motorbike and the flashy acces-
sories of a full-time salary. Saul shoved the fruit into a pile
with unnecessary force. Conrad had been a pupil at Saul's
school, a few years above him. He remembered him because
he'd once done a shit in a dustbin for a dare.

'Feed the bird, and then go.' Conrad didn't bother to
raise his eyes from the screen of his iPhone.

Saul transferred the slices onto a plate and carried it over
to the cage. The mynah bird cocked its head and stared,
unblinking, as he slid in a wary hand.

'Fuck you.'

Saul dropped the plastic plate he was holding. It bounced
twice, spilling sticky juice onto the floor. The bird squawked
irritably at the clatter. Saul's face caught fire.

Conrad was pissing himself. 'Always makes me laugh.
My favourite newbie trick.'

Saul wondered whether Conrad would still be laughing
after the 'newbie trick' of a broken nose, but decided his
hands were better occupied picking up the plate if he didn't
want to find himself unemployed.

'Who taught it to speak?'

Conrad didn't even bother to shrug, his attention already
back on his phone.

'Dunno. He belonged to some old guy who carked it. His
daughter gave it to us 'cos she couldn't find anyone else to
take it. It's a bit of liability, to be fair. Have to warn customers
about its filthy mouth.' Conrad laughed. 'Or not. I prefer to
leave the ones with a stick up their arse to discover it for
themselves. One sugar, by the way.'

Saul waited for Conrad to give him some money, but a

customer wandered up to the till, asking if they sold flea collars, and he didn't feel like he could interrupt.

Outside, it was bitter, that point-of-no-return when dusk swaggers up to the day, shoving it out of the way. The late-afternoon air was tinged with woodsmoke and the drifting stink of the estuary mudflats. The stained-glass windows of the church that peered down the cliffs into black water were lit from within, the sounds of choral evensong leaking through the heavy doors.

Saul stopped to listen to those voices carry up into the broad, blank sky. He loved this town, in spite of everything. He never wanted to leave.

The streets were quiet, but as he rounded the corner, past the card shop and the pizza place, past the graffitied metal doors of the public toilets, he could see the coffee shop was still open. Its windows were steamy with the breath of families, the fug of a winter afternoon. He pushed his way in. Lights, chatter and the scent of middle-class money; fresh coffee and expensive cake.

Saul eyed the price list on the wall and counted out the change in his pocket. *Fuckssake.* He didn't have enough for Conrad's cup, let alone one for himself. The barista was struggling with the steam wand, the milk spitting in angry, over-pressured gasps, and there was a pot for tips on the counter top. Saul checked that no one was watching and palmed a shiny pound coin. Needs must, eh?

Back in the pet shop, there was a long queue at the till.

Conrad threw him a look that was shot through with disdain. Saul's comprehension skills were excellent. It read: *What the fuck took you so long?*

'Get to work,' muttered his manager, nodding towards a

man and a boy in a wheelchair, who had just come in through the door. 'You can tell that girlfriend of yours I'll sack her if she pulls another sickie. Go and see if they need any help. And get a move on.'

Saul placed Conrad's cardboard cup on the till point. Conrad could tell her himself. Cassie wasn't speaking to him. Again.

He moved towards the customers, reluctance written in the shuffling of his trainers, the slow-motion swing of his arms. He hated this part, this necessary interaction, all false bonhomie and hustling. The father and son – their rusted hair and matching freckled noses marked them out as such – brought the outside in, the smell of cold on their coats, rolling off their skin.

'It's snowing,' said the boy, and Saul noticed tiny ice crystals disappearing into the wool of his scarf.

'Can I help you?'

Even under the weight of winter wear, it was clear to see that the boy's head was twisted at his neck, his arms peculiarly angled. Saul was embarrassed by it, not sure where to look. He was used to Cassie's sister, but this was different. This father and son were strangers.

If Saul had known the events that would unfold in the hours and days that followed, he would have walked quietly from the shop and never returned. Because there would come a time when he would be forced to make a series of choices; when this man and boy were no longer strangers, but adversaries.

But moments of significance are rarely noted.

And instead Saul found himself wondering if he was going to eat that night, and whether his mother would be sober, and how long it would take for Cassie to calm down, and so barely noticed this father and son who would mark a crossroads in the roadmap of his life.

'We've got a dog.' The kid's voice was like piped music, high and irritating.

'Great.' Saul sounded more sarcastic than he meant to. The man gave him a sharp look. Clearly, he hadn't missed the nuances of Saul's tone. 'I mean,' he stumbled on, suddenly ashamed of himself, 'do you need a new lead, or some treats or a toy, or something?'

The man looked at his son. 'Jakey?'

'A bed.' A chuckle. 'So he can sleep near me, but not with me.' The parrot-fashion chanting suggested to Saul that this had been a subject of contention.

The man smiled. 'That just about sums it up.'

'This way.'

Saul led the pair further into the shop. It smelled dank, of aquariums and sawdust with an undertone of animal excrement.

'Dad, look. Did you see that? Dad?' Like most children, the boy was captivated by the menagerie. The lizards and tarantulas. The plastic containers of roaches, locusts and mealworms that were sold as live reptile feed.

The man crouched next to the wheelchair, head leaning into his son, an arm around his shoulder, drinking down the child's excitement. A spike drilled its way into Saul's heart, and he busied himself with straightening the bags of sterilized soil.

He felt the child's attention shift to him. 'Have you got any pets?'

Saul fixed his gaze on the wheelchair's handles. It was a

complicated question. 'No,' he said eventually. 'But I always wanted a dog.'

The boy – Jakey – beamed.

'We're new here,' said the man. 'We've moved down from London. We're a bit further along the coast.' Chatty. Friendly. 'Bit of a drive for us, but this is a great shop.'

Saul summoned what he hoped was a polite smile.

They walked past the glass cages stacked one upon the other. The vivid slash of colour on the skin of a poison dart frog, the listless comma of a corn snake.

Past the metal bars of the mynah bird's cage.

'Stop, Daddy. I want to look.'

The man pushed his son's wheelchair up to the gleaming prison. The bird was sleek and black, its yellow blindfold of feathers as startling as streaks of lightning. Its glossy eyes fixed them. Saul was just opening his mouth to warn them about its habit of swearing when the bird began to speak.

'You're dead,' it said, hopping on its perch. 'You're dead, you're dead, you're dead.'

MONDAY

5

4.41 p.m.

In the Old Town, where cobbled streets and fisherman's cottages rub worn-down stone against worn-down brick, the man that used to be Brian Howley is searching for someone. His hair is darker now, grazing his shoulders, his pinstripe suit hanging in plastic in the almost-empty wardrobe of his new home. He wears old jeans and a soft black shirt. His beard is flecked with grey, his natural colour pushing through the dye. He knows it needs attending to.

He tells no one his real name. He pays for his new life with used banknotes saved in a suitcase under the bed. Over the years, he has been meticulous in his preparations, exchanging them at the bank as they age like him. But his eyes, scanning each unsuspecting passer-by, are the same dark clots.

The rain-dirty clouds are hanging over the estuary, spilling their polluted contents into the water. To Brian, it looks like someone has taken a lead pencil and shaded in the patch of sky beneath each one. He wonders when the rain will reach the mainland. Twenty minutes. Maybe less.

The boy is about fifteen feet away, chucking chips around the shelter with two others. Brian smells vinegar and the tang of salty air. A black dog chases a stick into the sea, ignoring the bite of the incoming tide. A fishing boat with its dripping net sits on the concrete jetty near the wooden hut selling the day's catch. The cockle sheds, a haphazard collection of buildings, line the cobbled streets. They whisper of history, of the poetry of the seascape. Some have found a second life, as shiny and well maintained as the tourist businesses they now house. Others smell of rotting wood. Briny. Dilapidated. Brian limps over to the bench that overlooks the beach, and sits with his back to the trio. Listening.

'. . . fucking essay on plate tectonics.'

'Dunno why you bother with all that boring shit.'

''Cos I'll get my arse kicked out if I don't.'

'Fuck, yeah. Get kicked out. Then you can come to our school instead.'

'Yeah, do it, Saul,' says another voice. 'Forget about all those posh twats.'

'Gloria would fucking slay me.'

'Ah, the glorious Gloria. How *is* your pisshead of a mother?'

'Pissed.'

The three teenagers laugh; Saul, the loudest. His is a jackal laugh: hungry and mean. He scuffs a trainer against the pavement, circles the ground with his toe. Brian waits for their shouted farewells before he rises from the bench to look.

THE COLLECTOR

Saul is walking back towards the Old Town and the rusting footbridge that crosses the railway track. His hood is pulled over his face, hands digging into his pockets.

Brian likes the way he keeps his head down, eyes locked on the pavement. He likes the way he's not afraid to stand out from his friends, the way his face folds in on the secrets that few but Brian can recognize within. It takes courage to be different, he knows that. But most of all, he likes the way it's just the lad and his mother, because it makes him a target, easy to isolate and separate.

He cannot fight these familiar stirrings, the clean, pure joy of the hunt. He's been waiting, trying to contain his urges with painting and walking on the marshes over at Two Tree, but that sense of duty so carefully fostered by his father is beginning to bleed into the life he is making for himself in this town on the edge of nowhere.

And the boy with the bones is within reach, just a few miles down the coast. New home. Fresh start. The Bone Collector knows this because he has made it so, mining that precious nugget from the house-cleaning company employed by the Friths, and moving himself here too, caught in a riptide, unable to resist.

And now the Bone Collector is perfectly placed. The epicentre. Located close to the boy and the girl, who is hidden, not far, in a place of his childhood.

Biding his time.

Wandering the endless corridor of days since his wife's death, he knows the reaper will one day come for him, just as he did for Marilyn. The stiffness in his joints berates him, nagging at him that he's an old man now.

But with no son of his own, who will rebuild his family's

collection, begun generations ago and destroyed in a few hours by the interfering pig bitch? Who will continue their work when he is gone?

Fragments of that dark night haunt him still. Memories come at him now.

The scent of death in the forgotten hollows of Marilyn's body. The roar of fire in his ears. The clatter of bones as his specimens fall. The smell of his own fear.

He thinks longingly of the Hunterian, and the collection that still inspires his own. Down the tunnel of years, he can hear the orders of the celebrated surgeon John Hunter, whispered to Brian's grave-robbing ancestor Mr Howison; the catalyst behind his family's obsession. But the police will be watching now, and he can visit the museum no longer. Another pleasure denied.

A fury rises in him. He will not allow himself to dwell on these matters. Preparations must be made; a new curator found.

There is time.

There will be time.

He waits until Saul's red tracksuit top disappears, and turns back to the beach.

The newspaper has spread itself across the bench where he left it, as dry as the sand-blasting wind leaching the colour from its pages. He scans the small column of text on the front page, and Clara Foyle stares back at him. There's a comment from the detective.

Detective Sergeant Etta Fitzroy. Her name rolls across his tongue. He conjures up her face, the opposing colours of her eyes. *An eye for an eye.* His fingers twitch.

Seven bones surround the orbital cavity. He wonders if

they will splinter and break when he presses her eye from its socket.

Where is she now? In her flat? At work? Does she look for him each day in the way he searches for her amongst the night-time streets and the news bulletins? Or has she moved on, to other cases, other causes, now she has destroyed his family's legacy? Does she try to hide the scars on her face?

The hate he feels for her fills his mouth. It's in every nerve-ending, every flicker of pain in his arthritic fingers, every moistening of his parched mouth. The fabric of each thought is hemmed with savage, ugly loops of surgical thread, every stitch shaping the patchwork of her death.

He spits on the pavement at her memory.

The sow will bleed.

He limps onto the beach. The sky is closing down with rain. On his knees, he sifts and sifts the sand until icy darts needle his face. At last he finds what he's looking for and slips it into the pocket of his jacket.

TUESDAY

6

Sunday Cranston did not like looking in the mirror. Other people's faces did that job for her. Her family told her she was beautiful but the expressions of strangers, unguarded and slack-jawed, exposed their loving lies.

Actually, what her mother said was that Sunday had a 'beautiful figure'. The omission stung, even though Helen Cranston didn't intend it that way.

Nice body, shame about the face.

In her bedroom, Sunday touched her fingertips to her face, feeling her way across the stretched skin of her cheeks, and the stubs of her ears.

Her watch, loose-strapped and heavy, slid down her arm. She fought against herself, then twisted the face so she could read it. Most mornings, the postman came before nine thirty, and it was a few minutes shy of that.

Cassidy had long since left for school, lifting her hand in farewell without bothering to look behind her, backpack dangling from one shoulder, skirt hitched up to display her

45

slender thighs. Sunday had stood at the upstairs window, watching her younger sister leave, trying to ignore the sharp teeth of her jealousy. Her sister, so accepting of the admiring glances of others, had no clue of what it was like inside a desperate life.

In the sitting room, the television was on, some confessional show about wronged souls pegging out their dirty linen. Sunday followed the subtitles, correcting the occasional mistake and misplaced letter, so used to reading the running together of words, the filling in of blanks. She strained to listen, but her hearing, never good, seemed to have worsened in recent days. She checked her watch again, and headed back into the hallway, hoping but not expecting that today would be any different.

A letter lay on the mat.

A plunge of excitement in her stomach.

The envelope was pale blue. She could see the florid loops and whorls of handwriting. A first class stamp in the corner. Like last time.

Please let it be from him.

She snatched it up, as if some malignant wind would whip it from her hands before she had a chance to savour its contents.

She drank in the sight of her name inked across the flat expanse of paper, pressed the envelope to her lips. A swell of anticipation, dizzying and mouth-drying, surged through her.

Sunday Cranston, who at twenty-five still lived at home with her family, who worked in the cafeteria at the Salvation Army nature reserve three days a week, who had never kissed a boy, had received another letter.

After Saturday's débâcle, she was sure he was never coming back.

He must have posted it almost straight away.

Sunday listened to the silence in her head. *He likes me*, it said. Her face flushed with pleasure and then shame when she remembered what had happened the last – and first – time she'd seen him.

It had taken meticulous planning to persuade her parents and Cassidy to leave the house on the day he had promised to draw her, although neither he nor they had known that.

The night before – Friday – she had gone to bed early, and nerves squeezing her belly, she had lain in the darkness, imagining the moment they would meet.

Next morning, she had groped her way downstairs, eyes screwed up against the light. She had told her family that she didn't feel well, that she needed to sleep off the headache that was spreading, in painful clenches, from her jawline to the back of her head, setting off all kinds of black dots and flashes. That she needed the bliss of complete silence.

Helen and Russell Cranston had tutted in sympathy and bustled her back to bed. They were thinking about heading into town, they said. They would pick up some extra-strong painkillers and do a spot of shopping. They would drop Cassidy at her friend Flora's on the way.

Sunday had struggled to catch the quiet, careful closing of the front door. When the car pulled away, she had leapt out of bed. Showered, a touch of lip gloss, her prettiest dress. She had sat at the bottom of the stairs and waited for the shape of him to appear in the glass of the door.

He had come, exactly as promised. A tall man. Older. Not

at all what she had expected. And yet he had grinned at her in a slow way that she had never seen before.

This was why she had wanted to keep his visit a secret. For once, something just for herself. She did not wish to expose herself to her sister's ridicule or her parents' reasoned concern. He was hers.

He had set down his bag, and asked if she was alone. With another lurch of excitement, glad she'd been able to do as he'd instructed in his letter, she had nodded. His smile was a reward she'd been waiting for most of her life.

And slowly, so slowly, he had traced his fingers across her lips. His eyes were burnt-out stars, long dead, but Sunday saw only a fool's promise of light.

His hand was bent with arthritis, but his skin was warm, and in her parents' sitting room, with its ticking clock and her old school photographs and the fireplace that was never lit, Sunday experienced the most tender of touches from a man who was neither father nor doctor.

The feel of a stranger was something deeply unfamiliar to Sunday.

The memory burned in her still.

She hadn't heard the front door open. All she had seen was a flash of panic across his features, and then he had snatched his hand away, and was picking up his bag and slipping out through the unlocked patio doors into the wet grass.

She had been so stunned she did not think to ask why he was leaving, and by the time she had gathered herself, he was gone.

Cassidy was in the hallway, hanging up her jacket, headphones jammed into neat, pierced ears. She had looked

Sunday up and down, eyebrows raised, a grin spreading across her perfect, symmetrical face.

'Well, you seem to have made a miraculous recovery.'

Sunday, too late, raised a hand to her temple and rubbed at the imaginary pain.

'Not really.'

Cassidy's eyes travelled from Sunday's lip gloss to her dress. 'Nice try, sis. Is he upstairs?'

'I have no idea what you're talking about.'

Cassidy had laughed. 'Oh, come on. The last time I saw you dressed up like that was when Eliot Sullivan was home from uni and his mum asked if they could pop in for a Christmas drink.'

She pushed her face into Sunday's.

'Your lip gloss is smudged.'

Sunday blushed.

'It isn't.'

'Is.'

'How old are you, Cass? Five?'

'Does Mum know?'

'There's nothing to tell.' A diversion was needed. 'Anyway, why are you home so early? How's *Saul*?'

Cassidy's face had closed down then, and she had shrugged and run upstairs, her feet stamping her disdain onto every step.

Aside from a couple of cryptic digs over dinner, Cassidy had let the matter slide, and Sunday had almost given up hope that she would see him again.

Until this morning.

Only when she was safely in her bedroom and propped

up against the soft cushions on her bed did Sunday Cranston allow herself the luxury of opening the note.

Moments later, she closed her eyes, adrift, once more, on the glorious waters of euphoria.

The letter *was* from him.

And this time he was inviting her to dinner.

7

9.26 a.m.

A few miles along the estuary, where the land meets the sea, Jakey Frith was lying on the floor of his new bedroom.

It smelled of paint and freshly laid carpet, but his memories were trickier to gloss over, the stains seeping through, ugly and unwelcome.

His ear was pressed against the vent in the wall, and he was listening for her again, but all he could hear was the wheeze of silence and old pipes.

'Clara?'

He whispered her name even though his six-year-old brain told him that this was a different house in a different town. That it was a long time since he had heard her voice, which he couldn't quite remember except as the sweetest of echoes lighting those hours when his parents slept on, and Jakey, alone in the darkness, stared old terrors in the face.

That Ol' Bloody Bones stalked his days and his nights.

Erdman and Lilith Frith had tried their best to shield him from the fall-out of his abduction; the macabre collection of human skeletons; Brian Howley's escape; the continuing disappearance of Clara Foyle.

They had moved to this seaside town to start a new life.

But the hours Jakey had spent in that house were scored into him, graffiti carvings on the wood of a sapling. When the chaos of his rescue had calmed into something quieter, he had asked about Clara. But no one would tell Jakey the truth, no one except the detective, whose smiley eyes had filled with tears when she had said that Clara was still missing.

Clara's voice had kept him alive, but now she was gone. That thought made him feel like something thick and uncomfortable was stuck in his throat.

When it became clear that Clara was not going to answer him, Jakey shuffled lopsidedly to his bed. It was a new bed with a Spider-Man duvet, and his room was much bigger here, but he missed his old home and his school friends. He missed the familiar shape of the streets and the Heath and the park and the ice-creams. He missed London.

He knew he should go down for breakfast where Lilith would talk about her lesson plans and next week's visit to the old castle ruins at Hadleigh. She'd been a teaching assistant once and had decided to home-school him for a while, just until they were settled. Until they were all sure that this was where they wanted to live.

At least, that was what they had told him. But Jakey had overheard his mum a few nights ago.

'He came to his school, Erdman. His *school*. What if he finds him again?'

'He won't, sweetheart. He's not stupid. He'll be far away from here, buried deep in the countryside somewhere. Hidden away. He's not going to risk getting caught.'

He'll be far away from here.

That was why his daddy didn't believe him when he'd told him he'd seen Ol' Bloody Bones outside their old house.

That was why his daddy wouldn't believe him now.

Jakey's new bedroom had doors that opened on to a balcony which looked across the rooftops to the sea and horizon beyond.

He had been standing there last night, staring up at the banana moon, when a car had slowed beneath his window, its engine idling. The door had opened and a tall man had got out. Jakey had not seen much, just the shadow of a face in the street lamp, but it was enough.

The young boy had stumbled backwards, knocking into the bookcase that Erdman had built that morning. The crash brought his father running upstairs.

'You OK, champ?'

'Yes, Daddy.'

'Sure?'

Jakey had thought about telling him then, but Erdman was shoving the books back onto the shelves, and then the worry lines creasing his brow were smoothing into a smile, and Jakey had thought that his father, who so often seemed sad, was looking happy again, and he didn't want that to change. Never ever.

'Shall I tuck you in?' Erdman had guided Jakey back to bed, drawing the covers around him.

'Orinoco?' He had held out Jakey's stuffed tiger, but he had shaken his head. He still missed Mr Bunnikins, but his soft rabbit was lost somewhere in the past.

As soon as his father had kissed him on the forehead and shut the door behind him, Jakey had shoved off the blanket and limped back to the window. The car and the man were gone.

Jakey had waited five minutes before dragging himself to his bedroom door. Moments later, Scooby, his puppy, was making herself comfortable at the end of his bed, the weight and warmth of her body some comfort against the fear which was stalking him again. He'd kept still, trying not to look at the dark gap beneath his wardrobe, the threatening hulk of Scooby's unused basket, and then he'd slept, his nightmares full of shadow men made from bones.

And now it was morning again. Jakey peered cautiously from his window, parting the curtains to look down on the street below. Empty apart from a few children walking to school, their voices sucked into the wind.

Jakey was worried about Clara. He didn't believe she was dead, even if everyone else did.

Because if Ol' Bloody Bones was here, it could mean only one thing.

That Clara was here too.

And if Clara was here, Jakey was going to find her.

In the kitchen, the television was on. Jakey lingered in the hallway because he knew that his mother would switch it off the moment she saw him.

A man's voice. All shiny and happy. He was talking about a new film about old people *ree-ty-ring* to a hotel in India. He was laughing and so was a woman, and then their voices changed, and they were talking about Clara Foyle. One hundred days since she was taken. More than that. The sound of Clara's mother appealing for information. The same rise and fall as Clara. The sound of voices singing a lament.

And his own name.

Jakey Frith.

And then.

Brian Howley.

Brian Howley.

Brian Howley.

An elastic band was squeezing Jakey's chest, and he could see dozens of black dots in the air around his head, and his breath was stuck, he couldn't push it in or out. A mewl of fear seeped from his mouth.

And then his mother was there, and she was scooping him up and carrying him into the kitchen and his tears were soaking into the shoulder of her dress.

Later, the smell of toast and comfort still in the air, Jakey sat at the kitchen table.

'I'm ready, Mum.'

Lilith, who had her back to him, putting the peanut butter jar into the cupboard, closed her eyes.

'Mum?'

'It's time for lessons now, sweetheart. I thought we could read about the explorer Captain James Cook this morn—'

'You *promised* I could write to her. Please can I? Please, please, please.'

'I'm not sure it's such a good idea.' Lilith pulled out a chair and sat down opposite him. 'It's complicated. She might not want to hear from us. It must be very difficult for her.'

'I want to.'

'I know you do.'

Lilith opened her laptop. She'd hoped to teach Jakey

about explorers and navigation and the discovery of new worlds. To spread the table with sheets of paper and photocopied maps. To lose herself in the ordinary, the workaday.

'Please, Mum.'

But perhaps this would help his recovery. Allow him to move on. Sweep away the clouds he carried with him.

Sensing her indecision, he trotted out a phrase he had overheard the grown-ups use when they thought he wasn't listening. 'It might give me closure.'

Lilith narrowed her eyes.

'Pleaaaasssseee.'

She released a sigh, weary of arguing. 'OK,' she said, even though it wasn't.

The light from her laptop screen made his face glow.

Pushing away her doubts, Lilith sat next to him, her precious boy, whose hand was pinned to his chest but whose heart was full of goodness, and helped him to spell out the letters, one by one.

She prayed he wouldn't get an answer.

8

2.18 p.m.

'I don't know.' The Boss wouldn't meet Fitzroy's eyes.

'But it's a new lead,' she said.

'Is it really? I mean, let's take a look at the evidence, shall we? Clara's uniform washed up on the salt marshes—'

'Don't forget the X-ray he sent to the Friths.'

Fitzroy wanted him to understand its significance, to acknowledge that the glinting black-and-white transparency of Jakey's ribcage that had arrived at the family's home a month ago was a message of sorts. A taunt.

The Boss busied himself with some papers on his desk. Outside, the polluted city sky was the colour of a yellowing bruise. 'Yes,' he said. 'That.'

'Yes, exactly that,' she said, trying to keep her impatience buttoned down, knowing that he would not respond to the anger she could feel straining at the edges. Her gaze strayed to the image of Jakey Frith's chest cavity now pinned to the wall of the Major Incident Room. His twisted bones gleamed in the artificial light. Fitzroy could hear the buzz of traffic on

57

the congested roads outside. It echoed the sound in her head.

'But what does it tell us?' The Boss had sorted his papers into a neat pile and was now busy stringing paper clips together. 'Nothing that we don't already know. That he's out there. That he's possibly still in the country.' He corrected himself. 'Probably.'

'Yes,' she said, her hand clenching into a fist. 'He's still here, which means we can find him.'

The Boss switched his attention to stretching elastic bands into a ball. 'For months, we've thrown everything into trying to find him, Fitzroy.

'Yes, we can try to establish the tidal patterns that brought Clara's clothes to that part of the Essex archipelago; we can – and already have – spent hours scrolling through CCTV footage, but it's like looking for a needle in a haystack.

'This inquiry has already cost hundreds of thousands of pounds and we still have nothing to go on.' He slammed his hand on the desk, making her jump. 'To put it bluntly, we can't afford for it to carry on indefinitely at this level. Not forever. We have to find him, Fitzroy.'

His words built a wall between them. Fitzroy let her wrecking ball fly.

'And Clara?' she said.

At last, he lifted his eyes to meet her own. There was compassion in there, guilt too, but mostly they were the hard, unflinching pebbles of leadership and authority, the taker of difficult decisions, the breaker of bad news.

'Fitzroy, it's been over three months . . .'

She knew then what he was saying, even though he

could not bring himself to speak the words. That five-year-old Clara Foyle, with her dimples and bunches, was dead.

'We don't know that,' she said, despising herself for the pleading note that was creeping in, displaying the flaw that ran through her bones, her inability to stay removed.

'No,' he said quietly. 'We don't.'

'He could be holding her prisoner. You've read the transcripts of the Jakey Frith interviews.' She forced herself to slow down, to present her case in a calm and reasoned way. 'She was still alive when Brian Howley moved her. Jakey heard them.'

The Boss wandered over to the office window and looked down on the hectic mess of south-east London's streets.

'All these people in this city of ours,' he said. 'Going about their lives, to work, to school. Unsuspecting.' He was framed in the cool light of a late winter's day. 'Some will go home victims tonight. Some will become victims as soon as the front door closes behind them. We owe it to all of them to investigate those crimes. To protect and prevent.'

'I know that.' Tears were burning the back of her eyes, but she blinked them away. 'But we can't just abandon her.'

'We won't.' He cleared his throat. 'We're not. I'm not closing this inquiry, Fitzroy. Not at all. Christ, can you imagine the outcry? But you do understand that we need to find both of them. Then we'll nail the bastard to the floor.'

The phone on his desk rang. He picked up the receiver, covered the mouthpiece with his hand.

His lips moved but no sound emerged. *Sorry.*

Fitzroy took the hint.

Outside, the bitter February air coaxed the heat from her cheeks. She drew in lungfuls of cold air, and her anger, molten and loose, solidified into something unyielding, unbreakable.

If The Boss wanted evidence, she would find it. Just as soon as she had worked out where to look.

9

3.45 p.m.

Fairies.

That was her first thought. She made a wish, even though she had long given up hope that wishes came true. She closed her eyes, already knowing they would be gone when she opened them again. Another figment of her imagination.

The cold was vicious. It had teeth that bit into her bones and claws that raked the exposed skin of her face. She burrowed into the duvet, relishing the slow-building warmth from her own body heat.

But she couldn't stop thinking about them.

Fairies.

It was much warmer inside the dirty grey cocoon of her bedding, but she did not stay still for long. Curiosity got the better of her and she lifted a corner of the quilt.

Blinked.

They were still there.

Clara Foyle, five years old and missing for almost fifteen weeks, eased herself into a sitting position. She knew she had to wait a few moments for the stars that danced around her head to wink out before she moved again.

One cleft hand, missing its middle three fingers, scrabbled for a biscuit. Although she would not have been able to explain the scientific reasoning behind it, she had already puzzled out the equation between food and energy. The biscuit would help with the next part of the challenge.

Her mother had always encouraged Eleanor to eat a banana before gymnastics. Perhaps this was why. The memory of her sister pretending to be a monkey made her eyes sting.

She ate with care, knowing, through bitter experience, that crumbs attracted insects and rats. Eyes never leaving the crack in the curtains, Clara levered herself onto her hands and knees, and began to crawl.

The metal cuff around her ankle pulled at the tender flesh. The Night Man had left her hands untethered but he had chained one of her legs to the table in the middle of the caravan.

Clara knew there was just enough slack in the metal links to allow her to reach the bucket in the corner, the mildewed sofa that doubled as a bed, the plastic bags of food and drink on the table that the Night Man delivered every few days.

Any further – the door, for example, or the window with its tempting strip of light – and the cuff would rub cruelly against her ankle bone. She had long since stopped trying to seek freedom but that cold afternoon she was determined to watch the fairies.

The chain clanked as she crawled towards the window, her body trembling with effort, ignoring the stinging sensation of skin rubbed raw.

THE COLLECTOR

A jolt stopped her short, and the chain, stretched taut, would give no further.

Clara grunted in frustration and sank back onto her knees. The lengthening shadows in the caravan warned her that night would soon be upon her, and the finger's width of light between the curtains would fade to a darkness that would overwhelm her.

Since she had been here, the girl existed mostly in a strange kind of twilight. On sunny days, the rays filtering through the fabric of the drawn curtains would flood the room with vivid hues of scarlet and brown. Overcast days were different. Darker. On those days, the shadows simply deepened until she found herself surrounded by the night with all its fears and secrets.

Except for that chink of light.

It kept her going.

And now it was almost within touching distance.

Her fingers strained towards the glass. The white shapes spun and danced, hundreds and hundreds of them. She was close enough now to see they were not fairies at all.

Snow.

Mesmerized, Clara watched the flurries drift past her like feathers.

Is it Christmas?

It must be Christmas.

She pondered the meaning of this new development. She remembered seeing tinsel and fairy lights in the Tesco near her house before she was taken. That felt like a long, long time ago but she *knew* that Christmas hadn't happened yet because Santa hadn't been.

A sensation in her tummy like the swooping of wings.

What if Santa couldn't find her in this place? What if he went to her old bedroom instead? Clara sucked anxiously on a dirty strand of hair. *No, no, Santa had presents for everyone. That was his job.*

She eyed her feet, clad in oversized grubby socks. At home, she and Eleanor had huge red stockings with hand-sewn bells that jingled as they pulled out their gifts. They always had new pyjamas for Christmas. Here, she wore clothes that he brought for her – mainly jumpers and leggings or all-in-one sleepsuits – although they were always too big.

When it was dark, she would lay one of her socks at the end of her bed and in the morning there would be presents.

'Don't you agree, Rosie-pillow?'

Clara picked up the lumpy pillow and waggled it, her voice rising a notch. 'I can think of something better than presents.'

'What, Rosie-pillow? Tell me.'

Silence.

'Please.'

Slower, more thoughtful. 'If Santa comes here – I mean, right here, into this place – you know what that means, don't you?'

Even though she was talking to herself, Clara made an elaborate show of moving her head from side to side.

Her voice became high-pitched and squeaky.

'It means Another Person will be here. It means' – Clara pulled her pillow tightly to her chest – 'that Santa will rescue us.'

The little girl watched the snowflakes fall until darkness closed down the day. Usually, she preferred to climb under

64

the duvet before it went completely dark, hating the shadow shapes in the caravan, the scrabbling sounds of the night coming alive.

But not this time.

Because someone was coming to rescue her.

She could feel it in her bones.

WEDNESDAY

10

The dead bee lay in the middle of the path, too starved from the long winter to fulfil its biological imperative for early spring flowers.

Saul bent to retrieve it, holding the husk of its body in the curve of his palm. The bee's size, and the white flare at the tip told him she was that rarity, a queen. He guessed she had just awakened from her slumber but had lacked the reserves to begin the cycle of seeking nectar and building her nest.

Inside the flat, the silence and stale air reassured him that his mother was not there. He breathed out his relief into the dim light, the curtains still drawn, even though it was past four o'clock. With gentle fingers, he placed the bee on a saucer.

Saul dumped his school bag on the kitchen table, breakfast detritus strewn across its scarred wood. Unopened letters and free newspapers were piled on the work surface closest to the door. Grease spots marked the wall above the hob.

The teenager smelled the remains of the milk, warm,

69

slightly sour, then put the plastic bottle back in the fridge, and shoved the bowls in the sink. The bread in its shiny bag was past its sell-by date but Saul smothered it in jam and ate it anyway. His homework could wait.

Across the narrow strip of landing that ran the length of their home was his bedroom, a boxy space with just enough room for a single bed and a desk.

He kicked the door shut behind him, his black trainer streaking the cheap white paint. His duvet was faded but clean, the curtains open to let in the waning daylight, the books on his desk a tidy stack. The order calmed him. He placed the saucer with the bee on the desk.

On the window was a cracked leather jewellery box with a hinged lid and drawers and compartments. Saul carried it across to the desk, and pulled open the top drawer.

A delicate hint of decay drifted upwards, coating the inside of his nostrils. He began to breathe through his mouth to block out the smell.

The collection of dead bees was nestled in the flocking, the lace of their wings, the distinctive markings on their bodies, each perfectly preserved. Saul placed the queen amongst them.

'There you go,' he said, his voice as soft as snow.

Saul closed the drawer with care and pulled open the one underneath.

Moths.

The scent was stronger here, the decomposition more obvious in the frayed edges of their wings, the dust and dead cells. He would have to do something about that, to find some way of preserving them.

In the bottom drawer, he kept the crickets, the exoskeletons of their pale green bodies masking the rotted mush of their insides. Their black eyes stared without seeing.

Dead bees and moths were easy enough to find, but the crickets were different. Saul caught them alive in jam-jars from the grasses that lined the cliffs. It took hours of patience to locate them. Their camouflage and confusing chorus made it seem like they were everywhere at once.

Satisfied that all was in order, Saul closed up the box of dead insects and allowed his mind to wander. Last September, he had seen the body of a seagull chick, its steel grey fluff, the unmistakable curve of its beak, on the pavement near the school.

He had wondered what it would be like to steal one from its nest and keep it in a box in his bedroom, to squeeze the life slowly from its breast, but when he had nudged the dead bird with his foot, maggots had spilled from its carcass, and he had turned away, revolted.

But the thought had not left him.

His stomach rumbled, the jammy bread not enough to satisfy the hunger that had sprung into action at morning break and stayed with him all day.

He had skipped lunch, feigning his usual indifference, but had walked with Posh Dan to the chippy on the corner, hoping his classmate might buy too much, as he sometimes did, and offer his leftovers to Saul.

When he'd first started at the grammar school, Saul used to have free school meals, but as he'd carried his tray over to where the others were eating sandwiches stuffed with thick slices of chicken from the Sunday roast or expensive Waitrose olives, he'd overheard one of the boys saying they were for 'povvos'.

The next day Saul went without.

His stomach drove him back into the kitchen.

The fridge was empty, except for half a block of butter and the remains of the milk.

The cupboard held a tin of vegetable soup, which he hated, and some gravy powder.

The bread bag was empty.

Saul lifted the lid on the tea caddy, an old Fortnum and Mason tin that had belonged to his grandmother, and groped around inside. There was nothing, not even coins. He remembered seeing a twenty-pound note in there a couple of days ago but his mother must have taken it.

He wasn't sure whether it was that knowledge or his hunger giving him that scooped-out, sick feeling.

Christmas.

Tenner.

Uncle Jimbo.

He was halfway back to his room, reliving that moment of thrilled discovery as he'd pulled the note, greasy with dirt, from his uncle's card, when he remembered he'd spent it weeks ago. And that fucker Conrad had insisted his wages weren't due until the end of next month.

The sound of a familiar voice – shouting – from the street below dragged him, reluctantly, to the window.

His mother was standing on the pavement, her hair a dark veil, lifting in the wind. Her hands were clutching at the air and she wasn't just shouting, she was crying. He could see a wet patch on the fabric of her skirt, and the pocket of her jacket was hanging loose, unstitched, as if someone had yanked it.

A lump of shame and fear settled in Saul's belly, making

itself comfortable, at home. Had she forgotten her key? He didn't think so. Something or someone had upset her.

Saul went into his bedroom and shut the door.

Five minutes later, she was still shouting and then he heard that high, excited sound of shattering glass.

Saul flung open his door and pounded down the stairs before she could do some damage that they could not afford to put right.

Shards of glass were lying on the tarmac drive. Saul arrived in time to see his mother bend down and reach for the broken neck of the vodka bottle. It was clear she had thrown it at the wall of the flat next door.

A ribbon of blood slipped thinly down her wrist.

She stank.

'Mum.' His shout was swallowed up in the backwash of passing traffic.

Gloria Anguish did not give any indication that she had heard him.

The ribbon became a sash.

Fear hardened his tone, shaping it into something ugly and aggressive. 'Mum.' He twisted the splintered glass from her hand. 'Get a grip.'

Gloria turned her eyes on him, and he was frightened by what he saw, which was nothing at all, just a space where his mother – who, in another lifetime, baked brilliant cakes and made his tummy ache from laughing – used to be.

He pushed her towards the concrete staircase that climbed to the back door of their flat, steadying her as she stumbled up the steps. She did not protest, her distress or anger or whatever the fuck it was *this* time cooling in the wind carried in from the sea.

Saul cleaned her up as best he could. She didn't need stitches, just sleep. He washed her face. Pulled off her shoes. He made her drink a full glass of water and put her to bed. He hoped she wouldn't piss herself like last time.

He left her to sleep.

An hour later, he was back. He stood there in the half-light. Five minutes became ten.

A pillow was on the floor. Saul held it to his chest. Watched her breathing through her nose, an abrasive, ragged sound. His fingers buried themselves in the lumpy sponge, whitening his knuckles.

He could hear the cars rushing by on the street below.

The whip of the wind against the windows.

The slowing down of seconds, his feet walking him to the edge of the bed.

So easy.

His mother coughed, just once, and Saul dropped the pillow on the floor.

Gloria's jacket was hanging on the back of a chair. He searched through its pockets, looking for coins, or better still, a note. He did not consider it stealing. It was a matter of necessity. But there was nothing, just a key he didn't recognize tied to a piece of string.

His hunger attacked him again.

Now he *was* going to have to steal something. The flat was in shadow but the shops on The Broadway would still be open, those shiny lights of commercialism. But he would need to be careful. Last time, the manager had trailed him around the small supermarket until he'd left, his hands as empty as his stomach.

Fuck.

He wished his mother was the sort who smelled of flowers instead of stale alcohol and wore clean clothes, not the three-day-old fresh-from-the-floor variety. He envied those with a parent who made them feel as if no dream was out of reach. Gloria used to be like that. But not now. Now, he would settle for a cooked meal. Not all the time. Just once in a while would be nice.

Saul changed out of his uniform. He didn't want to advertise which school he went to in case somebody saw him, and he had to run. An oversized hoodie would do – plenty of room for tins and pills for Gloria, and maybe a couple of bars of his favourite chocolate.

The thought of taking something that didn't belong to him sent hot sparks running down his arms, electrified wires of fear and guilt and anticipation.

The doorbell rang.

Fuck.

He didn't want to answer it. It had to be the neighbour. Saul had meant to sweep up the broken glass, but it had slipped from his mind, and now that sour-faced bitch with her buttoned-down mouth and dull hair and disapproval would be in his face, complaining again.

The bell. Again.

Fuck.

The noise would wake his mother, and that would do no good at all.

Saul dropped to the floor and crawled along the landing on his belly until he could see the glass square of the front door without being seen himself.

A mess of dark hair. Tall. Someone familiar, yet he wasn't sure who.

The head swivelled, and black eyes were staring through the pane of glass, and Saul was being watched, because the man's height gave him that advantage, that view up the stairs and into the flat.

He scrambled to his feet in a warm wash of embarrassment.

The man smiled as Saul opened the door.

'I came to see how your mother is doing,' he said.

A sudden snapshot of Gloria's hands around the jagged neck of the bottle. 'She's fine,' he said.

'No nasty after-effects, then?'

Saul was confused, but he could see the man was waiting for him to answer, and then he realized that he was not talking about this afternoon at all, but the night of the almost-drowning.

'No.'

The man nodded, but didn't seem in a hurry to go. Saul shifted, uncertain, embarrassed. 'Um, thanks for checking,' he said.

Saul's stomach rumbled again, an unwelcome intrusion, just loud enough. The man smiled at him for a second time, and there was something knowing in his stare.

'Have you eaten tonight, son?'

Saul shrugged, his gaze settling on a point to the left of the man's head. It was a tactic he used at school when his teachers were yelling at him, or if he didn't want to see pity or truth reflected back at him in someone's eyes.

When he had composed himself enough to risk another glance, this man, whose name he didn't know, was opening up a black wallet, and pulling out a note with a reddish-pink hue that Saul had never seen before.

'Make sure you have something hot,' he said, pushing it into Saul's unresisting hand. 'Get some shopping in.'

A fifty???

No.

He should say no.

But a fifty.

S.

I.

C.

K.

And then the man was on his way, limping down the path into the gathering night. Saul remembered his manners.

'Thanks, Mr—'

'Silver.' His voice was faint in the darkness. 'Mr Silver.'

In The Broadway, where the march of gentrification was slowly pushing out the independent stores, Saul bought a large kebab, ignoring the hard, suspicious stare of the man behind the counter. The lamb was peppery and delicious.

From the mini supermarket, he piled pasta and chicken and oranges, chocolate and bread and milk into his basket. He stuffed the leftover cash into his jeans. For later. No need to tell his mother.

As he wandered home, his stomach full, relishing the sensation of heavy plastic shopping bags cutting into his hands, Mr Silver was on his mind.

Saul felt a lot of things about a lot of people. But what he felt for Mr Silver was something unfamiliar and surprising in its power.

Gratitude.

11

5.34 p.m.

The man who used to be Brian Howley watches the older boy walk along the cliff edge towards the town. He watches him until he rounds the corner near the library, and is swallowed up by the dusk.

It does not matter that Mr Silver is not his real name. He is known by many names. The Bone Collector. The Night Man. Ol' Bloody Bones.

It is simply a matter of necessity. He must have a name. In this world, a name is everything.

Mr Silver.

He is almost used to it now.

His landlord was the first to ask. Even though he had paid in cash (delivered in an envelope while the nosy bastard was away) for his six-month rental in this house at the edge of the horizon. Even though he had preferred to maintain contact through the anonymity of email.

For the tenancy agreement, his landlord had said.

That day, the sea was still, the sky a flat grey. Behind the cloud, the sun rose, its silvery rays transforming the water into liquid mercury. And the name had slipped from his tongue.

Mr Silver.

An unexpected homage to his late mother, Sylvie.

And now the boy who will become his heir knows it too.

He is lucky, he thinks.

He has always been lucky.

He can still feel the bite of the handcuffs into his wrists, the low singing of the engine, the skid of tyres on tarmac. That freewheeling sense of motion as the car windmilled on its roof. He has read the newspaper headlines. The outcry over the decision to allow the detective constable to drive him back to custody alone.

'A terrible oversight.'

'Short-staffed.'

'Did not follow procedure.'

'Prisoner transport van not available.'

But lucky for him.

He remembers every slowed-down minute of the accident that opened the door on his freedom. The empty roads. The bitter night. The exhausted detective.

He had been going to die in prison.

But life, so often, comes down to the spin of a roulette wheel.

And a fox had run into the road and transformed his fortunes.

The force of the crash on that November night last year had snapped his head forward, but his seat belt had kept him secure, even as the car had rolled over. The scent of rust and light rain had crowded in as slabs of shattered windscreen grazed – but did not pierce – his skin. From his half-twisted position, he had smelled the blood in the car, seen the broken shape of the police officer's body. In that sweet rush of realization, he had forgotten about the fire at his father's home, his blistered palms, the pain in his head from the hammer blow, and concentrated on how to escape.

He remembers silence, the blessed feel of hands pulling him free and laying him on the pavement. Snatches of conversation in a foreign language that he didn't understand. Closing his eyes. The voices softening, moving further away. The tearing sound of metal doors being forced open. A jabber of words, urgent.

They're calling the police, an ambulance.

He had rolled onto his side. The men – his saviours – were bent over the police officer, their backs to him, their attention elsewhere.

Now.

Do it now.

He had levered himself upwards until he was on his knees, the handcuffs slowing his movements, making them lumpen and awkward. Rising unsteadily to his feet, off-kilter and unbalanced, he stumbled into the dark winter dawn. The greatest test of the skills his father had taught him. To move between the shadows, the cusp of night and day. To disappear before anyone noticed.

He had limped as quickly as his bruised body would allow. Did not look back. Head bowed, shoulders down, hands pinned behind his back, he had slipped down the nearest side street, his pace never slackening.

In the distance, he had heard the rising cry of sirens.

They would spread out, the police, until they had found him. To them, he was not a collector, but a killer.

Several streets on, someone had left a pile of clothes in a dustbin sack outside a charity shop. With a wince, he had kicked the bag apart, looking for an old coat. Instead he had found an oversized, hand-knitted jumper.

On his knees again, he had bent over and seized the jumper between his teeth. Ignoring a dizzying whirl of pain, he had staggered upright, carrying the gift of his freedom like a cat with a bird.

Three streets later, he found a place of silence and worship.

His hands, locked against the small of his spine, could not unlatch the heavy wooden door of the church. But his wrists were thin, sparrow-like. He had stood in the porch, fighting against the cuffs, ignoring the drum beat of pain in his head, and concentrated instead on the cruelty of scraping flesh against metal, of working free his hands.

He knew it could be done. The police knew it could be done. One frantic New Year's Eve when he'd worked at the hospital, he'd overheard a couple of them talking. Ankle restraints were harder to remove, they'd said, but a pair of cuffs behind the back was much easier to circumvent than the public realized.

Patience.

Pain.

Patience.

Pain.

And then his wrists were hanging loose, alive with the agony and ecstasy of paraesthesia.

He had pushed his way into the church, ignoring the

pins and needles pricking his arms and the bloodied raw-ness of his skin, and there, in the peace and calm, he had eased his head through the jumper's stretched neck.

Its shapeless bulk was enough to hide, for a while at least, the pinstripe suit that marked him out.

But he'd known he must not linger. He'd known where he was going. Back to the haunts of his youth.

To the girl.

At the nearest station, he had clambered awkwardly over the ticket barriers and caught an early train, the first of the day, trusting that the bleary-eyed guards would pay little heed to him.

His luck had held.

He had swapped trains.

Reached the overground.

There, he had slunk down in his seat, and talked to no one.

When the train had pulled into the station at the end of his journey, when he had caught his first glimpse of the sky and the fields, he knew he was safe.

He had kept his head turned away and slowed his pace as he'd shuffled past the station's CCTV cameras, praying that no one would notice an old man in a baggy jumper, and that if they did, they would simply see a lost soul on his uppers.

He had chosen a house with two cars parked on its drive-way; had watched a man walk in the direction of the station. Half an hour later, a woman and two children, dressed in school uniforms, climbed into one of the cars. His hunch had been right.

He had spent less than twenty minutes inside the property and left with a set of car keys, a duvet and a bag of whatever food he could steal.

His first stop had been the girl.

C.

After he had checked on her, he had collected his suitcase of money, and parked the stolen car in a rarely visited field. He had slept inside it, the duvet keeping out the winter chill.

Days, weeks, had passed by in a blur of fear and cold.

And he had watched and he had waited. He had travelled back to the city. He had found out where the Friths would be moving to. He had found himself a place to live, and to plan.

A seagull's cry drags him back to the present. The cobbles are uneven beneath his feet, the night shading in around him.

Gunmetal.

Plum.

A deepening blue.

Snatches of music spit from the pub. The waves throw themselves against the harbour wall. The cockle sheds are watchful, darkness leaking through the wooded slats, largely unchanged by the march of time. His cottage sits alone at the end of the row. An anomaly. The others are terraces, bricks as glued together as the lives inside, generations of families, fishing folk. He chose this cottage because of its lonely position. Its separation. The view of the water. Thick, thick walls to lock in the sounds of his work.

He is safe here. No one has found him. There is no reason to suspect they will.

Once inside, he switches on the lamps, turns on the oven, spreads the cloth across the small kitchen table. He places the bunch of snowdrops he has picked into a vase with chipped edges.

The glass in the display case lining the hallway glints in the muted light. The empty shelves speak to him of loss, and he is blinded, for a moment, by a flash of the pig bitch's laughing face.

He stands motionless, except for a nerve that indents his cheek. A spike of anger at the destruction of his lifetime's work.

How he longs to fill them again.

A seed of anticipation spreads its roots inside him.

He trusts the older girl will follow his instructions. She has that look about her, of someone seeking to throw off the constraints of her disability, of being ready to strike out alone.

She is looking for new beginnings and so is he.

A slow trudge up the staircase. The cottage is smaller than his father's house, the bedrooms all crooked, sloping floors and low ceilings. He dips his head as he enters the one he has chosen for himself.

In the corner, a ladder is pressed up against the wall. It leads to the boarded attic at the top of house. The hatch is open.

His body is not what it was but he climbs the rungs, a hand, a foot, one after the other. Methodical. The smootheddown wood feels warm against his skin. He ignores the pain in his hip, the dull ache in the back of his skull that still troubles him from time to time, a reminder of the Frith boy's father.

He hefts himself through the hatch. Considers his dilemma. He has tested it, yes, but with sacks of dirty potatoes bought from a farm near Canewdon. He adjusts the swivel hook, pulls at the utility rope. It feels sturdy.

There is nothing to her. It should hold, he thinks. It will hold.

He unfolds the square of plastic sheeting and spreads it across the floor, a metal bucket on a corner, to flatten and hold it in place. The attic smells new.

New beginnings.

It is smaller than the space in his father's house, and draughtier. The rafters sing at night, the wind slipping through the gaps in the roof. But there are dark, dusty corners and it's cold enough to keep the bodies, for a day or two, at least. Room enough to cut flesh from bone, to prepare the feed for his colony in the rooms below. The very best specimens he will display in his cabinets in the hallway downstairs.

His fingers fumble with the tie on the rolled-up wallet he bought two days ago from a cookshop near Ilford. The cream cotton is pristine. Unstained. It is heavy in his hands.

It is hard, he finds, to fill the hours since he was forced to leave his night job at the hospital. Forty years of staying awake while others sleep is not a habit he is able to break so easily. He is not sure that he wants to. But still, he needs to find a way to keep himself occupied.

His father's voice again in his ear.

The devil makes work for idle hands.

If all goes well, she will be here within the hour.

He lowers himself awkwardly to the floor, the wallet spread across his knees. His fingers stroke its contents, testing and flexing each steel point in turn.

He chooses the boning knife.

12

7.46 p.m.

Even after three months, still the letters came. The envelopes were different colours, different sizes and from different parts of the country, sometimes from abroad, but the writing was always the same. Block capitals. Handwritten. Coloured biro. The shaky scrawl of pensioners with too much time on their hands.

Amy Foyle didn't mean to be ungrateful. But lately the tone of the letters had changed. She could have thrown them away without opening them, but as the days blurred into weeks and months, she nurtured a fantasy that she would find some clue within these pages of scrunched-up writing – often without gaps or paragraphs – from strangers who were witness to the most intimate horrors of her life.

There had been two this morning. She took a sip of her wine and opened the first.

25 February 2013

DEAR THE FOYLE FAMILY,
   I SAW YOU ON TELEVISION AND I WANTED TO

WRITE AND TELL YOU THAT YOU ARE IN MY
PRAYERS. MY CHURCH PRAYED FOR YOU ON
SUNDAY. I EXPECT YOU ARE COMING TO TERMS
WITH THE KNOWLEDGE THAT CLARA IS IN A
BETTER PLACE, ESPECIALLY NOW THAT HER
SCHOOL UNIFORM HAS BEEN FOUND. I HOPE
THE POLICE FIND THE POOR LITTLE MITE SOON
SO YOU CAN GIVE HER A DECENT SEND-OFF. WE
HELD A COLLECTION ON SUNDAY. PLEASE FIND
ENCLOSED A CHEQUE TOWARDS FUNERAL
EXPENSES.
  GOD BLESS YOU ALL,
  MRS D. PITT (DORIS)

Amy's hand was shaking as she slipped the letter and cheque back into the envelope. It wasn't the first time that someone had intimated that Clara was dead, but this certainty was new and it frightened her that others, however well meaning, were now prepared to say this to her openly.

'I'm thirsty. Can I have a drink?'

Eleanor was in her nightie, face scrubbed, hair brushed, but although she was too young to carry the same physical signs of trauma as Amy – the strands of silvery-grey hair, that sucked-in look that comes from rapid weight loss – her mother could detect a new wariness in the way she behaved around adults.

She drew her daughter onto her lap.

'Milk?' She nuzzled her head into Eleanor's tummy. 'Or water?'

Eleanor giggled and stroked her mother's hair.

'Hot chocolate.'

Amy frowned at her daughter in mock annoyance. She already knew that in a moment or two she would be frothing milk in their coffee machine and mixing in the sweet powder that Eleanor loved. Since Clara's disappearance, she seemed unable to refuse her eldest daughter anything. She recognized that this was not ideal, that at some point she would have to impose the boundaries that children need for healthy development, but there had been so much loss in Eleanor's life – not just her little sister, but the sudden departure of Gina, their nanny, and the decision by Miles to move abroad at a time when they needed him most – that whether or not Eleanor had hot chocolate or water seemed insignificant in the general scheme of things.

'I'm hungry too.'

'Would you like a banana?'

'Biscuit.'

'Eleanor.'

'Please, Mum.'

Amy placed the drink in front of her daughter, a plain biscuit on a plate, and busied herself with rinsing out the steamer so Eleanor would not see her cry again.

It was the small things that undid her.

Like Clara's Little Miss Sunshine mug.

Sitting there on the shelf.

Brand new.

Unused.

It hurt to remember but it hurt more to forget.

'Look, Mummy, look. Little Miss Sunshine.'

Amy had been distracted that day, looking for a present to buy Miles for their wedding anniversary. She had been irritable, she remembered, because she was irritable almost

every day back then, and certainly with Clara, whose inces-
sant questions, the pulling on the belt of her coat, the *need*
for attention, had driven her to distraction.

Clara had begged her mother to buy it, had even offered
to spend her own money, but Amy had been in too much of
a hurry. There was a long queue and she didn't have time
to wait because Clara had ballet, and Amy was meeting her
friends for lunch, and she had to buy Miles' present *now*
because she was getting her nails done afterwards, and then
Eleanor had to be collected from a party at Pizza Express.
She remembered the outrage she had felt that Gina had
dared to claim a Saturday off on the same day that Miles was
playing golf.

Now, of course, she suspected they had been together,
but she discovered it didn't matter any more.

And so she had snapped her refusal at Clara, who had
asked her mother several times that weekend if she could
please buy that mug, and Amy had eventually tuned her out.

A few days after Clara disappeared, Amy had gone back
to the shop, and she had bought that Little Miss Sunshine
mug. She had imagined the look of joy on her youngest
daughter's face when she saw it. She had imagined her
drinking her breakfast milk from it every day.

But Clara had never come home.

Clara will never come home.

Eleanor wiped the back of her hand across her mouth,
streaking chocolate across her skin. 'That was delicious.'

'Teeth,' said Amy, the heat of grief in the back of her
throat, suddenly grateful for the living, breathing thereness
of her other child. 'Then bed.'

Bedtime was the hardest part of the day. Bedtime and

mornings. Mornings because Amy had no more than a couple of seconds before the weight of Clara's abduction landed, with heavy boots, in her stomach. Knowledge would spread through her like bruising until she twisted her face into the pillow and pulled up her knees, screwing herself into something small and defeated and broken.

Then Eleanor would climb in beside her mother, and the girl would loosen the knots of profound sadness binding her to the bed, and her chatter would lift Amy, and they would go down for breakfast together.

But bedtime was another matter altogether, the routine of stories and bath-time and sweet, sleepy kisses now spoiled, a creeping brown rot on the skin of soft fruit.

One daughter to kiss goodnight.

One daughter lost from sight.

While Eleanor slept, and the long, lonely hours stretched ahead of her, Amy paced the rooms of their expensive house in Blackheath, unable to expose herself to the possibility of Clara's death but blocking out, too, the thought that she was alive and what he might have done to her, *was* doing to her.

These last few weeks, as soon as she was sure Eleanor was asleep, she had found herself falling down the rabbit hole of a desperate new routine.

In the still of Clara's bedroom, she would trace her fingers across the plastic faces of her daughter's dolls propped up on her shelves, and she would choose a favourite and, with tender fingers, dress her in baby clothes she had boxed up years ago.

A tiny pinafore.

Cardigan, cashmere.

Silken shoes.

And then Amy would strap the plastic dolly into the old baby carrier she had brought down from the loft, and she would flit from room to room, talking to the air around her, pretending that the barely there weight at the front of her chest was a child.

Her child.

Clara.

Wandering through the kitchen, still wearing the baby carrier, lips stained from the red wine that she couldn't seem to stop drinking, even though she had promised herself she wouldn't do it any more, Amy was startled by the stranger she saw reflected in her oven door.

Her hair was shorter now, and uneven, where she'd cut at it with a pair of scissors because she couldn't be bothered to go to the hairdresser's.

Narrow, bent shoulders.

A baby carrier with a doll at her chest.

I'm a madwoman; I look unhinged.

But this routine comforted her, it helped her forget, and gave her permission to pretend.

In the silence of the sleeping house, the digital clock on the oven clicked onto another minute. *10.36 p.m.* She should go to bed. Instead she sat down at the table and poured herself another glass. It was still there, the second letter she had all but forgotten about.

After the day's earlier offering, she was tempted to throw it into the bin unopened, and she almost did, but when she picked up the envelope it felt heavier than usual.

When she slit the flap, a pewter token the size of a fifty-pence coin fell out. Amy had seen something like this before in one of the shops in the Village.

Four letters were engraved into the metal.

H-O-P-E.

Her fingers found the letter inside.

Her stomach curled up.

For months, she had avoided all mention of his name, consumed by a complicated mix of emotions; distress and curiosity, and, yes, envy.

But now Jakey Frith was writing to her, his address and a telephone number typed neatly in the corner of the page.

And he was asking to meet her.

13

He slips on a clean pair of gloves and folds her clothes into a neat pile.

Red skirt. Soft jumper. Thick black tights.

Careful. He must be so careful. A misstep here could bring pigs snuffling at his door when he wants only to whet their appetites.

There is still a trace of lipstick on her mouth. When he has finished, it will no longer matter.

She has made an effort for him. It touches him to know this. In return, he will take care of her. It is all he has ever wanted to do. To protect and preserve his family's collection.

Now it is his duty to rebuild.

These last weeks have been difficult, but the work has already begun. He has the beginnings of a new collection.

The young woman lying on the floor.

The hidden girl.

The boy with the twisted bones.

And now Saul.

His apprentice.

His disciple.

He rolls the letters across his tongue. *Saul*, he says again. Meaning 'prayed for; borrowed from God'. It is a sign he would be foolish to ignore.

He tidies away the remains of their meal, sloshing the dregs of the soup from their bowls, careful to roll up the sleeves of the pinstripe jacket he has worn for the occasion. He scrubs at the imprint of her mouth on the glass.

She had been giggly, her cheeks flushed at the secrecy, the *thrill* of it all.

'I didn't tell them.' The words had tumbled from her through spoonfuls of soup. 'I mean, I just said I was going out.'

He had raised an eyebrow, then laid down his own spoon, leaving a streak on the tablecloth. 'I expect you left an address tucked away somewhere. Just in case.' He had smiled, to show it didn't matter.

'I *didn't*.' So naive. So indignant. 'I trust you, Mr Silver.' A coy look. 'I didn't want to spoil the surprise.'

His eyes had met hers, reaching into her, loosening something inside. If she had known the horrors behind them, she would have run. Hard and fast. But she didn't. She misjudged his scrutiny, imbuing his cool interest with warmth, and the confidence that had long eluded her began to flower. Nerves tickling her insides, she had poured more wine into her glass.

'Aren't you having some?'

'It affects my eye, my ability to paint.'

She had giggled again, touched a self-conscious hand to

her hair, to her hearing aid, fiddled with the silver bangle appropriated from her sister's room.

'When shall we start?'

'Supper first.'

'My parents are going to be blown away.' Less sure. 'I hope they like it.'

'They'll love it. What it represents. Your courage and confidence.' He had deliberately stretched the pause. 'Your beauty.'

A softness had lit her face, reminding him of his wife. *Oh, Marilyn.* But it did not weaken his resolve.

She had finished off her wine while he dished up the stew. She poured another refill, misjudging slightly. A drop slid down the outside of her glass.

'So . . .' She had rested her chin in her hand, the words beginning to slur. Five minutes, he estimated. Ten, at most. 'Tell me some more about yourself.'

'Not much to tell.' He had placed a plate in front of her. 'I'm a widower. I like to paint.' A pause. 'And keep rabbits.'

'Any children?'

He had been ladling vegetables into a bowl, his back to her, so she had not caught his expression. 'It's complicated.'

'Complicated is my middle name.' She had given a rueful laugh.

'Potatoes?'

She had blinked, her vision sliding in and out. She reached for her glass, but instead she knocked it over. In the spreading pool of wine, the reflection of a candle. Liquid fire. He looked away.

'Oh. My. God. I'm so sorry.' Her hands had reached for

her napkin, but she couldn't seem to focus on it. She couldn't seem to focus on anything.

As he had mopped up the mess with a tea towel, Sunday Cranston had slid from her seat and onto the floor with a peculiar sort of loose-limbed grace.

She is lying in the same position now, an arm bent beneath her, her cheek pressed to the carpet, exposing her mal-formed ear.

He ignores her while he finishes the pots. *A place for everything and everything in its place.* He rinses the white residue from the soup pan, tips the rest of the drugged wine down the sink, his fingers absently catching the edge of the label. He fills the now empty bottle with hot, soapy water.

Grunting, he drags her body up the stairs. She is slight, but he can only just manage her. Her head makes a soft, dull sound as it thuds against each step. He worries about a hairline fracture of her skull, a crack in the bone of her collapsing cheeks.

On the landing, he stops to catch his breath, takes in great lungfuls of air. He waits for his heart to calm into something steadier. Checks her eyes are still closed. Listens for the whisper of her breath.

In his bedroom, the hatch to the loft is open, the hook already in place. A tarpaulin spreads like water across the floor.

He guides the sharp point of the hook into her chest, splits open the skin, pushes in the metal as deep as it will go.

Her eyelids flicker, the frantic beat of life against death. They slow.

Still.

Once he is sure she is secured, he pulls on the rope, cranks her body through the opening in the ceiling. The rope holds. Her body sways but it does not fall.

Up the ladder he follows, into the roof. To his new cutting room.

The boning knife is surprisingly light, a flash of silver in the half-darkness.

He pierces her heart, just to be sure.

A fog is rolling in from the estuary, blanking out the world. He is learning to read the coastal weather, and these dense winter nights always begin the same way, the day's cool clarity obscured by warmer air carried in on the tide, drifts of cloud that creep and thicken.

Perfect conditions.

The fog deadens the thrum of the engine as he drives through the cobbled Old Town to the beach at Bell Wharf. He parks his car, retrieves the holdall from the passenger seat. He can barely see ahead of him, but he knows his way.

The dampness cools his face, refreshing him, even though he is wide awake. He is at home in the night. He belongs to it.

He walks across the concrete path that leads to the yacht club, places the clothes – *red skirt, soft jumper, thick black tights* – on the wall at the top of the deserted strip of sand. Her boots land further down the beach.

Let the police make of that what they will.

He could burn her clothes, of course. Or hide them at his cottage. But this time he wishes to create a *diversion*. For the sport of it. Only the sharpest-eyed of detectives will find the message he leaves buried here. Because, in spite of everything, he is compelled to let Fitzroy know what he has done.

To draw her closer.

To frighten her.

To see her cower in submisson.

But she will need to be clever.

His fingers brush the first of the fragile skeletons. For the briefest of moments, he becomes a boy of ten again, a boy whose mother and the rabbit she brought home for him have died. Through the dulling of memory, the rubbing down of the years, their deaths have become so entwined he cannot distinguish one from the other. He feels himself shrinking, erased from life, smaller and smaller.

And then he remembers the collection he must rebuild, his purpose, the life that he has chosen and that has chosen him.

A nocturnal bird shrieks across the estuary, and the sound of its cry jolts him back to himself.

And something seems to swell inside him, to fill him up with the joy and glory and the power of it all. He was mighty once and will be so again. And he feels himself growing, as if every atom and cell in his body is bursting with knowledge and strength. And his blood sings as it surges through him. He will build an army of loyal sons, beginning with Saul, and He, the Bone Collector, will become more than himself.

He will be many.

And then the fog breaks, and stars prick the sky, so clear that he can count them, and the moon lays herself down on the black water, and he knows it is a sign from above.

The night is suddenly so full of jewels he is sure it will

not rain, and so he begins to dig at the edge of the tideline, knowing the water will not sneak this far and steal his treasures.

It takes him less than an hour.

Back at the car, he brushes stray grains of sand from his shoes, and smears estuary mud, thick and sticky, across his numberplates. The temperamental clouds have rolled back in again. He pats his pocket. It is still there. One job is done, but now there's another. There is time, he thinks, even in this fog.

He drives through the housing estates that surround the town like a greasy ring of scum, and onto the A13. The roads are empty, the late hour and the weather keeping travellers at bay.

The roads become familiar, the city tower blocks sketched across the skyline, the fog thinning, dispersing.

Loss, heavy and suffocating, tightens its fingers around his throat, choking him.

So much loss.

Because of her.

Etta Fitzroy.

He thinks of the last time he saw her, blood spilling from her broken teeth, the sound of the sirens, the wall of heat from his father's house, flaying his skin and his soul.

And in his memory of the flames lighting her face on that night he lost everything, he sees something else: her triumph.

Marshall, his father, is on his shoulder again.

An eye for an eye, son. A burn for a burn.

THURSDAY

14

1.03 a.m.

'Red or white? Or would you prefer beer? Perhaps a gin and tonic?'

On the stool beside him, Fitzroy slipped a hand beneath her jacket, releasing the top button of her trousers. The relief was intense.

She caught the eye of the bartender. 'Lime and soda, please.'

Dr Dashiell Hall downed a mouthful of his bottled beer, and leaned forward so she could hear him above the thump of music. She could smell his aftershave and beneath that, his maleness.

'You're not still on duty?'

'I'm always on duty.'

'But you must get some time off?'

Was there a subtext in that question? If so, she wasn't sure what it was. Or perhaps he was simply interested in the mechanics of a detective's life. She didn't know him well enough to second-guess him.

She could always ask. But would that seem presumptuous? Did she want to be presumptuous? She wasn't sure how to behave around him. She was still married to David, even though she'd only seen her husband twice in the two months since they'd separated. But she was here, in this bar, at gone one. Which must mean something.

'Of course.'

Oh God, was that too flirtatious? No, he was smiling and now he was saying something about tickets to an exhibition in a couple of weeks.

'I'll have to check the roster,' she said, already wondering who might be persuaded to swap with her if she was on call.

His smile filled her up.

This was the second time she'd been for drinks with Dashiell – and the fourth time he'd asked – since they'd met at the Natural History Museum, at the height of the Clara Foyle madness. He'd identified a rabbit skeleton, and it was his careful forensic examination that led her to *Dermestes maculatus*, the beetles Brian Howley was using to strip the flesh from the bones of his calling cards. Pulling at that thread had revealed his obsession with the Hunterian Museum, and ended with Howley himself.

Dashiell's intellect excited her, but tonight – technically this morning – a bleakness was seeping into her, a sense of having failed Clara, of having failed herself.

She needed Howley to make a mistake.

'I'd love it if you could come,' he said. His finger traced the inside of her wrist.

Fitzroy did not move, could not.

For all her skills as a detective, her ability to read suspects, to recognize the lies in the landscape of their bodies, the sliding-away eyes and over-the-top denials, that fixed posture of someone too anxious to be believed, she had always struggled at reading those she allowed in.

If she was honest, she'd been avoiding him, only suggesting a late-night drink at the end of a long day because she thought it might put him off.

And now this.

The circling of his skin against hers.

The slow-motion pitch and sway in the pit of her belly.

An urge to lose herself in someone else for a few hours.

Fitzroy withdrew her wrist and rummaged in her bag on the pretext of looking for her phone, giving herself a moment or two to collect herself. His next question brought reality crashing down on her shoulders.

'Any news on Clara Foyle?'

He asked that every time they spoke, and her answer was always the same.

'Not yet.'

'You OK?'

'A damn sight better than Clara and her family.'

His concern warmed her, even as she felt, anew, the skewering of Howley's escape. A group of laughing girls left the bar. She wished he would touch her again.

The minutes slid by as they lost themselves in conversation. Dashiell ordered himself another drink. Fitzroy watched his mouth move as he spoke, as he told her about his brother, who was a chef, and his own career ambitions. She enjoyed the way his body stilled as he listened to her, as if he was absorbing her words, and the amusement in his eyes as they met her own.

Dashiell finished his beer, clocked the time. Almost

3 a.m. Two hours had passed since she'd got there. 'Christ, it's late. I should probably go. Shall we get a cab?'

Now there was a question. Did that mean he was hoping to come in? Or was he planning to drop her off first? She tried to remember where he lived. Not that far from her. Dulwich? No, no, he'd moved to the outskirts of Kent recently. Beckenham. A bit of a commute, he'd said.

'Sure.'

On the street, the drizzle planted cold kisses on her face. Fitzroy shivered, and Dashiell slung an arm around her shoulder, drawing her into his warmth. At first, she resisted, holding herself stiff and still, but he moved closer to her, and she let herself relax into him, the rough fabric of his jacket brushing her ear.

In spite of the frigid night air, the starless city sky, Fitzroy would willingly have stood there until the sun rose and fell and rose again. More minutes passed, the streets slipping quietly into Thursday morning. Dashiell muttered under his breath, puffing out clouds which dissolved into nothing.

And then an orange light was barrelling towards them. Dashiell stuck out an arm, hustled her into the road, leaned across her and opened the door.

'Etta?'

She cleared her throat, gave her address, took a break from breathing to see if he would climb in behind her.

He did.

In the cab, his fingers found hers. Another slow roll of her belly. His face, in profile, was serious, the flash and fall of the passing street lamps spotlighting its contours.

Low voices murmured from the radio, and the fuggy

edges of her earlier exhaustion were replaced by a pin-sharp awareness. If he asked to come in, she would let him.

The flats were in darkness, save for the security light which lit the communal front door. Had she remembered to make the bed, to clear away that morning's breakfast plate? Did it matter? He'd said it was late, perhaps he was planning to take the cab home as soon as she'd got out. Oh God, she was too old for this.

She fumbled in her purse, thrust some cash at the driver, suddenly unable to look at Dashiell. Her fingers closed around the leather strap of her bag, and then she was stepping onto the pavement, the cold air a slap.

'Shall I see you up?' His tone was neutral, as unwilling as Fitzroy to expose himself.

For different reasons now, she still couldn't meet his eye.

'Yes,' she said. 'Please.'

As the taxi disappeared, leaving them on the roadside, Fitzroy and Dashiell did not kiss. They did not kiss as they climbed the internal staircase, their fingers touching lightly, or as they pushed through the double doors that led to the third floor, the space between their bodies closing down, heating up.

They did not kiss as Dashiell stumbled on the curling edge of carpet that Maintenance had promised – and failed – to fix, or when Fitzroy steadied him by pressing herself into him.

They did not kiss at all that night because when they arrived at the place Fitzroy called home, both seeking the oblivion of human touch, its front door was standing open, and they found themselves pitching into a new and different kind of darkness.

15

3.26 a.m.

Saul was woken by the voices. No, not voices. A voice. Tearing slowly through each layer of his consciousness.

His instinct was to pull his pillow over his head and try to get back to sleep, but the long, low blare of the foghorn from across the estuary filled up his room, and he groped for his phone, the middle-of-the-night darkness illuminated by the flashgun brightness of its screen.

Saul's brain was not operating at its usual speed, but he was awake enough to register that it was too fucking early. He dropped the phone – lifted by his mate from some prick in a suit for the price of an essay on *The Time Machine* and two weeks' worth of maths homework – back on the thinning carpet, swore softly and stretched out his legs, now so long they hung over the end of his bed. In truth, he had outgrown it a couple of years ago, but his mother couldn't afford a new one.

The air in his bedroom was laced with the breath-fogging iciness of a late-February night when the temperature skidded below freezing and there was no credit on the gas meter. He supposed he could use a bit of Mr Silver's money to top up the card, but he winced at the prospect of the cold bath he'd have to endure first. Or maybe he wouldn't bother. Thursdays meant cross-country, which he despised, but at least there would be the reward of hot water after all that pointless running across muddy fields.

His body was freighted with tiredness, but when he closed his eyes, all he could hear was a voice as familiar as his own. Abandoning the idea of sleep for now, Saul sat up, pulling his duvet up to his neck, insurance against the cold.

Gloria Anguish was trying to whisper, but she'd never been much good at that. Hers was a voice that carried, the volume control fixed slightly louder than most. He caught the word 'cockle' and 'fifteen minutes' and a low laugh, the kind she used when she was called in to school to speak to Mr Darenth, her fingers resting a fraction too long on his sleeve. It gave Saul a squirmy feeling in his stomach, that laugh.

A door shut and he heard her footsteps on the landing outside his room. They stopped, briefly, and he flung him-self back onto the pillow and shut his eyes, willing her not to come in. After a moment or so, from the direction of the kitchen, there came the familiar clink of a glass bottle hitting the rim of a mug.

Disgust, as potent and bitter as the alcohol his mother was using to destroy herself, flooded his mouth. It was a familiar taste.

On his twelfth birthday, Gloria had given him a football and herself a litre of vodka.

'Do you like it, love?' Her eyes were already wearing that glassy, over-bright look he had come to recognize.

Saul had touched his fingertips to the hard leather, not trusting himself to speak. Yes, he had wanted a football, but for his seventh birthday, not his twelfth. He had wanted a ball back when his friends were joining junior leagues, and trading cards, and footie was all they ever talked about.

At twelve, he had wanted a mobile phone or an iPad, or just some money of his own.

'It's . . .' Saul had known it was unwise to tangle with his mother when she had been drinking but he'd found it impossible to disguise his disappointment with faked expressions of gratitude.

Gloria's smile had curdled.

'That cost me eight quid, you ungrateful sod.'

'But I didn't ask for a football, Mum. Can we take it back to the shop?' A note of pleading had crept in, hoping that she'd understand. Her answer was the slam of the bedroom door.

Saul had eaten his birthday tea alone that night.

Another blast from the foghorn intruded into that memory, pushing it from his mind. Saul swung his legs over the bed, goosebumps stippling his bare skin. He pulled on his jeans, and an old jumper with an unravelling hem. He heard the sound of a cupboard opening, glass nudging wood. She was putting a bottle back, he'd worked out that much. He wondered where she had found the money to pay for it.

Her footsteps were taking her back down the hallway now, and Saul pressed himself into the wall, as if she had developed X-ray vision that could burn through his bedroom door.

But his mother didn't hesitate this time. She was at the other end of the flat now, and he could tell by the pattern of creaks that she was walking down the stairs that led to their front door.

A click, metallic and familiar, and then she was gone.

Something inside Saul shifted. *Fuck it.* He had no desire to follow his mother into the night, but she'd been drinking and it was gone three, and she shouldn't be out there on her own. Where the fuck was she going? Duty and distaste tussled for supremacy.

The fog filled up his lungs with its cold breath, obscuring the night. He could not see his mother, could not see much at all except the lumpen shapes of cars under the gauzy throw of the street lights.

The main road that ran along the top of the cliffs and into the town was silenced by the weather; no cars, no people, just the deadening shroud of clouds that hung, static and amorphous, in the air.

Saul rubbed his hands together. *Shit.* Which way had she gone? He was as directionless as the fog, with no hope of finding her in this weather. It wasn't his fault she was an unreliable pisshead who failed to take responsibility for herself, for him. For anything.

He glimpsed up at the windows of the sleeping houses, glossy brick boxes filled with families shuttered against more than freezing fog. Fathers with jobs, mothers, too. Hoovered carpets. Full fridges and iPads. Shiny cars. Birthday parties. Encouragement. Boundaries. The certainty of routine. Unconditional love. A sensation of *something* crept into Saul's consciousness, shutting down the defences he worked so hard to construct. He was never sure how to describe it. Loss? Wistfulness, maybe. A sadness so overwhelming it constricted his gut, pushing hot and unexpected tears up his throat, choking him.

It made him think of that boy in the pet shop, the way his father had leaned into him as they'd looked at the bird. A simple gesture of love and protection.

Saul had popped there yesterday, to see if Conrad would consider subbing his wages. The manager had laughed in his face, said employees worked in 'arrears'. He hadn't given Saul any money, but he had handed him an envelope.

Turns out the boy and his father had been into the shop again.

Inside was a photograph of a puppy. In case Saul was interested. Someone had scribbled 'Scooby' on the back.

He swiped at his eyes. Damn his useless mother. She should learn to look after herself. It wasn't his job to do that. Not again. *No fucking way.*

He had almost convinced himself to go home, had half turned towards the flat, imagined burying himself in his covers, trying to snatch a few hours' sleep before school. If Saul had done that, if he'd gone home at that moment, his life would have taken a different path. A *safer* path. But his mother's laugh – strained, slightly forced – drifted up from the cliff steps, and he jogged towards it, helpless to resist.

His fingers closed around the metal handrail, his feet so familiar with the uneven steps that they found their own way. From the bushes that lined the walkway down to Belton Way, a small shape, black and fast, shot out in front of him.

A rat.

He kicked out with his foot, desperate not to lose sight

of his mother. She rounded the corner, towards the Old Town with its fisherman's cottages and pubs, and he ran to keep up with her. Not too close, but close enough.

The cobbles were hard beneath the worn-out soles of his trainers, but Saul, pinned back in the shadows, could feel nothing except the first drops of rain on his face, as cold and surprising as heartbreak.

His mother was standing in the doorway of a small lock-up, one of the old-style cockle sheds, the too-bright security light exposing her chapped, ageing hands, which scrabbled for the key on a string around her neck. But as he felt his way around that discovery, he was trying to process a new kind of truth. Standing behind Gloria Anguish, a proprietorial hand on her arse, was a man that Saul did not recognize.

Already, he hated him.

The man's other hand slid inside his mother's coat, and she let out a girlish giggle, but all Saul could hear was the last vestiges of his love withering into something ugly and spent.

Saul strode deeper into the Old Town, heading towards the railway bridge shortcut, cursing his stupidity. Never again. From now on, he would let the drunken, disgusting cow sort out her own messes. He wondered what other secrets she was keeping from him.

The fog was thinning slightly and he could see the spread of the beach up ahead. Dust-coloured moonshine was filtering through the clouds, and collecting on the surface of the water. The sand looked like tiny broken bits of metal. It drew him in, a sort of stillness to counteract the maelstrom that was gathering in power and fury inside him.

His trainers sunk into the wet sand as he made his way to the water's edge. He picked up a stone and hurled it into the waning tide. Snatched up another and another, casting out his anger with every throw.

When he was calmer, he turned, intent on heading home, giving himself over to sleep.

But an unexpected patch of colour lit up the monotone shadows of the night. He ventured closer to the wall, his mouth full of sudden feelings.

Folded up was a neat pile of clothing, a red skirt, the softest of jumpers.

Resting on top was a hand-knitted cap and scarf, and a silver bangle. He snatched it up, certain he'd made a mistake. But there was no mistake. He recognized the bracelet because it had once been his mother's but now it belonged to Cassidy Cranston.

The girl he loved.

16

The door stood open, a black yawn. But it wasn't the darkness that frightened Fitzroy, even though she knew that it might have teeth. It was the knowledge that a stranger had polluted the sanctity of her home.

Dashiell pressed his fingers into her forearm, an unspoken gesture that urged caution. He edged ahead, squaring thin shoulders. Fitzroy might have laughed, had the situation not been quite so serious. David had always been happy for her to have courage enough for them both. A man conforming to stereotype – 'Me protect woman' – was oddly comforting, if unnecessary. She doubted that Dashiell had ever had a verbal confrontation, let alone a fight.

Fitzroy stepped deftly past him, reaching into her jacket for the pepper spray she had taken to carrying since Brian Howley had escaped from custody, although she was certain he was long gone. A blade of light from the communal hallway spilled onto her polished floorboards, marking out her path.

Dashiell started to speak, but she pressed a finger to his lips, shushing him. In less than a minute, Etta had slipped from woman on a date to Detective Sergeant Fitzroy investigating a break-in, and now she wanted to catch this bastard in the act.

She listened to the darkness, but all she could hear was the low thrum of her boiler, pumping out heat. She moved forwards into the hallway of her flat, past the old hat-stand that she and David had found at Spitalfields Market; past the bureau stuffed with paperwork; past newly bare walls, their wedding photographs not stolen by this intruder, but taken down by her in the days after David left, until she reached the closed bathroom door.

She pressed her ear up against the wood, found the handle, pushed it down with careful hands, and switched on the light.

Nothing, except the smooth pale lines of her bath, and the smell of still-damp towels.

'Empty,' murmured Dashiell, at her heels. Irritation pecked at her, but she shooed it away. At least he was trying to speak quietly.

Fitzroy repeated the routine; sitting room; kitchen; spare room. But nothing was out of place, not a cushion moved or a piece of furniture upturned. Her laptop sat on the kitchen table, the radio in its usual place on the shelf. David? Had he been here? But then she remembered the jemmied lock.

In her bedroom, the duvet was as smooth as she'd left it that morning, the blinds still pulled against skies that had rolled back around to darkness again. Dashiell was close by, she could hear him breathing, could sense his unease.

In the corner stood a narrow antique wardrobe. David

had hated it when they'd stumbled across it at a market in France, but Fitzroy had fallen in love with its delicate hand carvings, the peeling white wood. When he had refused to buy it, wandering off in search of a beer, she had persuaded the seller and his friend to strap it to the roof of their car, pushing euros into grateful hands. By the time David had returned, red-faced from too much afternoon sun and alcohol, the men had packed up their stall and gone. David had refused to speak to her for the rest of the journey back to England.

The door to that wardrobe was now ajar.

Gesturing at Dashiell to stay where he was, Fitzroy moved quietly across the floor. When she was within touching distance, she gripped the canister of spray in both hands and used her foot to nudge open the painted wood.

The wardrobe, too, was empty, save for her clothes, hanging in a tidy row, Nate's memory box, and the corner of a blue-and-white box, half hidden behind a hat she'd once bought for a wedding.

She released a slow breath, the tension sliding from her neck and shoulders. A heavy cloak of exhaustion took its place, reminding her that she hadn't slept for twenty-two hours.

'There's no one here.'

'No.' Her brain, befuddled by tiredness, could not manage much more.

'Do you want me to stay? I don't mean, you know . . .' He was awkward, looking everywhere but her. 'Just to keep you company.'

He was a good man. Attentive, intelligent. There was

chemistry between them; she knew he felt it too. But, at that moment, sleep was more seductive than he was.

'I'll be fine.'

She tried not to watch his face fall, and considered changing her mind. By the time she had found the words to say that, actually, yes, she would like him to stay, the front door was shutting softly.

'I'll call you,' she said, but she knew he hadn't heard, and didn't know when she would.

She double-bolted the door from the inside, grateful for the extra security she'd installed after Howley's escape. The locksmith could wait until the morning.

Brian Howley.

Was he playing games again? She wasn't sure. It didn't *feel* like his handiwork. He was all about dramatic gestures, cryptic clues. Her flat was empty. She was being paranoid. But then how many burglars broke into a property and stole nothing? Perhaps he – or she – had been disturbed.

Fitzroy stepped out of her clothes, letting them fall to the floor, not bothering to clean her teeth or wipe away her make-up and the grime of a day's policing. Howley was miles away, holed up somewhere. If he had any sense, he'd be abroad. And Clara? She couldn't bear to think about that now. She needed sleep, not nightmares.

The sheets were cool beneath her skin, the pillow an invitation. She closed her eyes, felt herself falling backwards into the darkness, knew, that despite everything, tonight her body would allow her some rest.

Fitzroy stretched out her legs, enjoying the gluey sensation of relaxation after many hours of holding herself rigid.

Her toes slid across the wide expanse of bed and brushed something hard and unexpected.

She jerked her feet up, unable to place the sensation, or the feel of what she'd just touched, but knowing there was a familiarity in it. A streak of adrenaline lit her senses, banishing her tiredness. Fitzroy threw herself from the bed, fumbled for the lamp and bundled the covers onto the floor.

Her breath was sour with the kind of fear that comes once or twice in a lifetime.

Lying on the crumpled cotton was something limp and greyish, smelling of saltwater and decay. She stiffened, the rolling timpani of her heart picking up its pace.

The claw of a dead crab.

Ting.

Fitzroy heard the music in her synapses strike up. Some called it instinct, sharpened at the coalface of policing. But for Etta, the sounds of the orchestra helped her to pluck free the facts, to coax the disparate threads of her investigation into a symphony. And playing now was a song of certainty.

In her mind's eye, she saw Clara Foyle's cleft hands, and she knew that he was back.

17

'Cassidy.'

His cry sliced through the fog.

'Caaaaassssss.'

Saul ran circles into the wet sand, panting out misty ghosts, looking for the girl who made him feel like his life was worth something.

The sea, as dark as ink, slipped further from him, and panic corkscrewed his gut. If she was out there, she'd be dead by now. No one could survive the relentless thrash of the tide, the temperatures that numbed the flesh within seconds at this time of year.

He tried to ignore the drone of static in his head that was drowning out all rational thought. He tried to ignore what the silver bracelet, nestled on top of the clothing, might be telling him. His fingers traced the delicate engravings squeezed across its metal curves; *doubt truth to be a liar, but never doubt I love.*

Saul had longed to give Cassidy something special for

120

her sixteenth birthday, pressing his nose up against the windows of the jewellery stores he couldn't afford. Even when he had cobbled together every penny he had, it wasn't enough. Scrabbling through a drawer in his mother's bedroom, hunting for spare coins, he had come across the bangle, wrapped in floaty paper. His mother still hadn't noticed it was missing.

He had gone without dinner for two nights and written a coursework essay for Posh Dan on *Hard Times* so he could afford to buy Cassidy a slice of cake and a milkshake at a cafe in The Broadway. As she had taken her first mouthful, he had shyly pressed a gift box into her hand.

She had opened the lid and breathed out her delight. 'It's vintage. Saul, it's beautiful.' On reading the inscription, she had rewarded him with one of her special, secret smiles. He could not bring himself to correct her as she had slipped his mother's bangle onto her slender wrist.

But now it was here, a lump of dead metal on a deserted beach. It was cold beneath his fingers when he slid it into his pocket.

Cassie was impulsive, yes, but she wouldn't do *that*. Would she? She'd been so upset after their argument, stormed out of Flora's, hadn't bothered to turn up for work the next day. The soles of his trainers cut grids into the sand, and he was struck by a sense of déjà vu. He pulled up the brake on that train of thought. He would not go there now.

Two spots of light washed clean the beach.

Saul squinted, raised a hand to shield his eyes against the false dawn.

A car door slammed. Footsteps, slow and deliberate, crossed the concrete strip that crowned the sand.

'You all right, son? It's a bit late to be wandering around. You never know who might be about.'

Saul could not see the man's face because the headlamps had rendered him temporarily blind, but he recognized the scratchy-record voice that played across the sand. He wondered why he was on the beach at this time of the night.

Mr Silver answered that question before Saul had time to finish thinking it. 'Couldn't sleep. That's the trouble when you've spent your whole life working nights.' The slam of a car door. 'What's your story?'

'My friend's missing.' Saul swiped at his eyes, a rough movement, but unexpectedly relieved that an adult was here to take control.

Mr Silver did not move off the concrete but stepped delicately towards him, assessed the pile of clothes, Saul's stricken expression.

'Did you see her go in?'

'I didn't see anything,' said Saul, his voice heating up with the injustice of such a question. 'I found this pile of clothes and I—'

'The police?'

It was a simple question, framed in a way that neither censured nor directed, but the answer was there in the fleeting, panicked look that floodlit Saul's features.

'I see,' said Mr Silver. 'You're right, of course. If she's out there, there's nothing we can do for her now, and there's no sense in bringing the police to your door.' A sly look. 'They'll suspect you, you know, you being the first' – he held his fingers in the air like rabbit ears and curled them – '"on the scene".'

His words dropped on Saul like bombs. He and his

mother had spent most of their lives avoiding the authorities. He could not afford to invite them in.

'What shall we do?'

Mr Silver allowed Saul to see him thinking out his answer. In truth, he had known that this was *the* moment as soon as he had heard the boy say 'we'.

'I'll drop you home, son.'

'No, s'all right, I can walk.' Saul's voice was flat. Unconsciously, he groped in his pocket for the key. Empty. He tried the other one, patting himself down. His hands grew more frantic, like the wings of a trapped moth. Nothing on this earth would drag him back to the sheds, to Gloria and that man.

The spare. Under the pot.

The tension eased from his body, but returned almost immediately, there in the stretching of muscles along the back of his neck, the tightening band across his shoulders. The spare key wasn't under the pot. He'd been using it since his mother had lost hers during one of her drunken episodes but insisted she hadn't, claiming his key as her own. There hadn't been the money to get a new one cut. There was no spare key.

Mr Silver watched the drama unfold in Saul's face.

'Everything OK?'

Saul jerked his head towards the shelter, the place where he'd been throwing chips around with his friends a couple of days ago. 'Looks like I'll be sleeping there.' The bravado in his voice sounded forced.

'You can't stay out here all night.' A pause from Mr Silver, carefully timed. 'You'll freeze.' His tone casual, not pushy. 'I've a sofa.' The older man lowered his head, teeth trapping his bottom lip, modest now. 'It's not much, but it's got to be warmer than this.'

The fog was blurring Saul's vision, his sense of danger. He was tired and heartsick, and that made him vulnerable. Briefly, he considered his friends. Half an hour's walk, at least. And there were parents to think about. He couldn't just turn up in the middle of the night.

Go to the police.

For Cass.

Saul hesitated, torn. He was reluctant to seek shelter at the home of a man he barely knew, but already the cold was seeping beneath his jacket, and he did not want to risk seeing his mother. He could imagine her over-bright pretence that nothing had changed, that she hadn't just let that dirty bastard paw at her body, and do fuck knows what else. And he wanted to teach her a lesson. Let her worry about him for a change.

As for Cassidy, every time his mind's eye played footage of her body dragged out by the tide, his heart paused, waiting to see if it was broken. He pictured the grief her mother Helen would be forced to pull on like a new dress when the police came to call.

Go to the police.

But there would be questions. Endless questions.

And he did not want to answer them.

The fog, damp, all-encompassing, crept into his bones, making his mind up for him.

'Ta.' He worried a pebble with the tip of his trainer. 'If you're sure.'

'Come on, then.'

Saul trudged across the sand towards Mr Silver's car, his

footprints taking him further into darkness. He could feel the man's eyes upon him, but he did not look up, weighted down by the ballast of his sorrow.

Less than five minutes later, they pulled up outside Mr Silver's cottage. Saul followed him through the back door into a kitchen that smelled of disinfectant and loneliness, and a thicker odour he could not identify.

Mr Silver switched on an antique lamp which illuminated a small sitting room with a television and a hard-backed chair by the window. There were no photographs on the walls, no personal mementoes at all. An open staircase rose from the corner of the room to the floor above.

Mr Silver disappeared, reappeared with a pillow and blanket, dropping them onto the lumpy sofa.

'You're sleeping here, son. Better get some rest.'

Saul listened for the old man's slow trudge upstairs before he pulled off his trainers and lay down, fully clothed. A black speck tracked its way across the carpet. *Is that a beetle?* Saul hadn't seen one like that before. Sleepily, he considered expanding his insect collection, but didn't have the energy for that now.

His fingers burrowed in his pocket, and found his headless doll. He wondered how long it would take his mother to realize he hadn't come home. He shut his eyes. Just for what was left of the night. He would find somewhere else to sleep tomorrow.

Soon, the sun would bleed into the horizon, pushing itself higher and higher, igniting the sky.

The marking of a fresh dawn.

A new beginning.

18

Last summer

He can hear the sea before he sees it. The lapping of the waves is a song of salvation. He closes his eyes. This was not how he expected the night to end. If he was writing a diary, it would contain a single word: *Fuckssake*.

Even at this hour, even with the breeze sighing across the water, the air remains heavy with heat. The moon is high in a midnight blue sky, hazy and bright. A trickle of sweat slips between his shoulder blades, another slides into his mouth. His tongue tastes saltiness, but his mouth is dry. A smell of dead fish lingers and he half imagines he can see, on the shoreline, the unblinking buttons of their eyes.

It is June. The passion flowers on the neighbour's trellis are in bud, but one or two have already flowered, and are brown and dead. These flowers symbolize crucifixion. There is a message in there somewhere.

The body is wrapped in an old sheet he found in a cupboard. A splash of blood has seeped through the cotton, and he brushes it with his fingers. He cannot tear his eyes from the vibrant staining. Like pollen, he thinks, leaving its mark on everything it touches. He should be crying, or something. But there is a wide, empty space inside him, and he recognizes it as freedom.

He stoops, dragging the body from the boot of the borrowed car. The weight of it strains his back, but he grits his teeth, pushing on. His breath comes in short, heavy bursts, and he is forced to stop what he is doing, leaning against the groyne that splits the sand in two. The darkness hides everything; at least, he hopes that is true. If he is discovered, it is over. For them both.

He can barely believe that it has come to this. But it has, and now it must be dealt with. The only person he can truly depend on is himself, and so this responsibility – like so many others – falls to him. The man of the house.

He wipes a hand across his forehead and tries to ignore the hay fever that does not disappear with the sun; the itch in the eyes, at the back of his throat. Thunderflies. The sucking heat.

Litter decorates the beach, a relic of the folk festival. He thinks of the daytime crowd sliding into something darker, the discarded plastic beakers empty of beer, the faces contorted with alcohol against the backdrop of a jaunty violin and cornet. He thinks of the darkness he has found within himself, that runs through his veins and arteries, hate made loose and liquid.

He tightens his grasp on the sheet, using it as a makeshift carrier to drag the body across the sand and closer to the water. Five hundred yards lie between him and his future.

19

11.16 a.m.

Amy Foyle had brushed her hair seven times that morn-ing, but she ran the bristles through it again. She didn't know why she was bothering. A six-year-old boy would hardly notice what day of the week it was, let alone if her hair looked nice.

Even so, when she had laid down the brush on her dress-ing table, she dusted on some eyeshadow and a coat of pale pink lipstick. Armour came in many guises, and Amy was in need of protection.

Now, an hour and thirty-five minutes later, she was standing outside the address that Jakey Frith had written on his letter. It was a doubled-fronted timber-framed house with a sprawling block-paving driveway, and bedrooms with balconies that peered over the sea.

It was clear the Friths were making a new start.

A wave of nausea overcame her, and she gripped the gate, unsure of why she had journeyed to this place at the end of nowhere. Thorpe Bay. It had sounded pretty enough, and it was; huge houses which ran in neat boulevards down to the water; rows and rows of brightly painted beach huts.

But it was also the edge of the map, a place that tipped into the sea. Amy wondered if Jakey Frith was her own edge of the map. Would she tip into nothingness when she came face to face with the boy who haunted her almost as much as Clara?

She straightened her back and made a quiet promise to herself. She would see what he had to say, and then she would go home. No expectations. Whatever happened, she would not give up on her daughter.

There was no bell, no knocker, just a smooth panel of wood and glass. She knocked, tentatively at first. When no one answered, she rapped hard against the door. A man with rust-coloured hair and a box of Cheerios in his hand opened it. Erdman Frith. He had been all over the newspapers, a hero for rescuing his son. In that splinter of a second, she hated him for not doing the same for Clara.

Judging by the expression on his face, he wasn't expecting her. Or perhaps he wasn't ready to face his own demons.

Amy's tongue stuck to the roof of her mouth along with her words.

'I—'

'It's Mrs Foyle, isn't it?' The warmth in his voice thawed the nub of ice in her heart.

She jerked her head in a facsimile of a nod, wanting to say something but not trusting herself, worried that the act of speaking would oil her grief and jealousy, sending it spilling out and spreading like a black stain.

'Come in,' he said, his manner as easy as an old chair. 'Lilith's in bed with a stinking migraine. It's stress, I think—'

He cut himself off, and his whole body tensed, as if he had made the most terrible faux pas. What right do we have to feel stress, she could almost hear him thinking, when this poor lady has lost her daughter?

She touched his sleeve to show it didn't matter. 'Shall I come back another time?'

'No.' He shook his head. 'Of course not. Jakey's waiting for you. It's just we're running' – he held up the cereal box – 'a little late today.'

The hall was lived-in but spacious. Not on the scale of Amy's grand home, but comfortable, nonetheless. A pair of dirty boots were tangled up with a discarded dog lead, clods of dried mud scattered across the floor. A wheelchair. An umbrella.

And in that clutter of family life was a child's glove, tossed carelessly aside, each tiny, empty finger an emblem of her own loss.

Amy could feel heat at the back of her throat, the usual prelude to tears. She concentrated on her footsteps, one in front of the other, and followed Erdman into the kitchen.

Jakey Frith was sitting at the table, drinking milk from his cereal bowl through a straw. As with his father, she had seen his photograph in the newspapers, had read about his medical condition. Stone Man Syndrome, the body producing layers of extra bone until it encased its sufferers in a skeleton prison.

His head was on the skew, his arms bent into unnatural angles, but his eyes, watching her sideways, were clear and intelligent.

'Mrs Foyle has come to see you, champ.'

'Hello, Jakey.'

130

He let the straw fall from his mouth. 'Hi.'

'Sit down, sit down.'

Amy slid into the chair that Erdman had pulled out for her. A lone droplet of milk lay on the table between her and the boy. His eyes, still watching.

'Tea? Coffee?' A pause. 'Something stronger?'

A weak smile for a weak joke. 'A glass of water. Please.'

Amy listened to the tap running, the clink of glass, the filling of the kettle. She listened for Jakey's voice too, but it didn't come. It seemed she would have to ask.

'You wanted to see me, Jakey?'

The boy's eyes dipped, then lifted to meet hers again. His voice was sunlight and shadow.

'Do you think Clara is dead?'

Amy did not know what she'd been expecting but it wasn't that. The sound of her daughter's name on his lips squeezed the breath from her as surely as if someone had placed their hands around her throat. She was aware of Erdman, a frozen tableau of coffee granules and spoon; of Jakey's unblinking eyes; of the rising whine of the kettle.

'Jakey, I don't think you should—'

She raised a hand to silence Erdman, to show him she was fine.

'I don't know, Jakey, but every day I hope we'll find her. What about you?'

Jakey's eyes flicked in the direction of his father. The kettle was boiling noisily as he heaped coffee into his mug. There was a thump from upstairs, and Erdman raised his gaze heavenwards.

'I'll just go and check on Mum,' he said. 'Be back in a

minute, champ.' He caught Amy's eye and held up two fingers. *Two minutes.*

Jakey waited until he could hear his father climbing the stairs before he answered Mrs Foyle.

'I think Clara is alive.'

A wave of warmth took her by surprise. It was the first time in a long while that somebody had said that as though they believed it, even if he was a child. The residue of the bitterness she felt towards this family dissolved. She searched Jakey's face for answers, desperate to know more.

'Is it true – the police lady said – that you spoke to her?'

Jakey's mouth tightened, and she watched memory play across him. 'Yes.' His fingers twitched against his jumper.

She wanted to grab his bent shoulders, to shake every detail from him. She twisted her hands together beneath the table, forced herself to slow down, to let him take his time.

'What did she say?' A whisper, full of longing.

'She asked if you were coming for her. She was waiting.' Jakey wrinkled his nose. 'She missed you.'

Amy found herself walking in an unforgiving landscape, parched of light. She had known, on some level, that Clara would be wanting her, but to hear the words fall from his lips was a burn on her skin, sucking the hope from her until she was desert-dry. No words would come.

Upstairs, Erdman walked across the landing. Jakey heard his footsteps, moved his head a fraction. There was an urgency in the boy's voice that made the hairs on the back of Amy's neck stand up.

'He's here. That man. I saw him.'

Erdman began to walk down the stairs, each creak marking his approach. Time seemed to crawl for Amy, to trap her between each tick of the kitchen clock.

'Daddy doesn't believe me, but I saw him. I did.'

Jakey's face was thin and pinched. He had been worrying about telling her, she could see that. Perhaps he was afraid she'd dismiss him, like his father. But there was something in his expression that compelled her to lean forward, to mirror his urgency. Because if Brian Howley was here it meant Clara might be too.

'When, Jakey? Where?'

'Outside, on the pavement. Not long ago. I can't remember the day.'

Amy's mind began to race with a thousand possibilities.

'But your daddy told the police, right?'

'Uh-uh. He thinks I'm imagining it.'

A figment of his trauma. That was certainly logical. But Amy wasn't prepared to give up on the gift of hope he'd just handed her.

'But you're telling the truth?' She gripped the table, knuckles whitening. 'Don't lie to me, please don't do that.'

'Cross my heart and hope to die.'

'Sorry about that. Lilith's pillow had fallen onto the beside table and knocked a glass of water on the floor.' And, as if her life hadn't just tilted on its axis, Erdman was back in the kitchen, holding up the empty glass with a rueful smile.

Amy loosened her grip. 'Is she feeling better?'

'Just needs to sleep it off.' He bit his lip, cast an anxious look at the clock. On cue, his phone began to vibrate. He lifted it to his ear. As he listened, his face clouded over.

'Where?' He snatched up a pen, scribbled on the back of

an envelope. 'I'll get there as soon as I can, but Lilith's not well. There's no one to look after Jakey.'

He frowned at the voice at the end of the receiver.

'I know. And I said I'll be there. But I can hardly bring him with me.' A pause. 'OK, OK, I'll sort it. Tell Haskell I'll meet him in half an hour.'

Erdman's phone skidded across the table. Jakey followed its progress, his eyes full of anxiety.

'Go and get your shoes on, champ. Dad's got to work and you're coming with me. That'll be fun, won't it?' He flashed an apologetic look at Amy. 'I'm so sorry. Someone should have phoned you, but Lilith's ill and . . .'

She fixed a smile on her face.

Erdman bumbled on: '. . . you've come all this way, but I've only just got this job. I can't afford to lose it.' He hesitated, torn between his obligation to work and the awareness of how rude he sounded.

'I don't want to.'

'Jakey, don't be difficult, please.'

His son's mouth settled into a thin line of defiance.

'What do you do?' Amy's tone was polite. She tried being angry about her wasted trip, about the energy it had taken to put Eleanor into Breakfast Club and to organize Miles to collect her from school, but since losing Clara, life's irritations seemed so pathetic, so utterly pointless.

'Daddy's a reporter,' said Jakey. 'He writes things in the newspaper.'

A strained silence followed. Amy guessed that Erdman did not want to take his son to work, that it would be inappropriate and inconvenient, and would probably prevent him from doing his job properly. She remembered how

Clara's demands could drive her to the edge of reason, how it would be impossible to keep her quiet if she was in one of *those* moods. An unexpected memory of her daughter, stamping her foot because Amy refused to let her leave the house in a sparkly pair of plastic heels, made her smile. Eleanor seemed so grown-up these days. She missed the company of younger children.

'I'll look after him, if you like. Just until your wife is up and about.' The offer spilled from her lips, surprising her, but she found herself willing Jakey's father to agree.

Erdman stopped shoving his notepad into his rucksack. He glanced at his son, who was staring at Amy Foyle with an unreadable expression on his face.

'Uh, thank you. That's so kind of you, but Jakey will be fine with me, won't you, champ?'

'I want to stay with Clara's mummy.'

Erdman's face was a story with two endings. Doubt wrestling with relief, concern with compliance.

'I'm not sure, sweetheart. I expect Mrs Foyle is very busy.'

Amy wondered whether it was guilt or fear that was holding him back. She was a stranger, after all, whose child was missing. Perhaps he thought she was unstable.

'It's fine. I'm happy to.'

Erdman's phone vibrated again. A text. He scanned it, tapped fingers against its case, anxious to be on his way, but still unsure about leaving his son.

To Jakey. 'You're certain?'

'Yes, Daddy.'

Erdman scribbled his number on a piece of paper and thrust it at Amy. 'Call me if you need me. I'll be as quick as I can.' He kissed Jakey's hair. 'Bye, champ.'

Amy watched him shoulder his rucksack. Check the clock again. Tie the laces of his trainers. She followed him into the hallway, leaving Jakey to finish his breakfast.

'What's the story?' she said. 'Must be urgent.'

'A teenage girl's gone missing, but her clothes have been found on a beach up the road.' He patted his pockets, searching for keys. 'But the cops don't think it's a suicide.'

'They don't?'

'No, she left her sister a message.'

20

Although her personal life had taken its fair share of knocks, DS Etta Fitzroy had not yet slept with a police officer, so it was somewhat disconcerting to see The Boss, perched and awkward, on the edge of her bed.

His shirt strained across his stomach, and in the gap between buttons she noticed a patch of skin and hair. That glimpse of flesh was more intimate than nudity. It made him seem vulnerable, older; herself, a voyeur. She averted her gaze and tried to concentrate on what he was saying.

'It could be coincidence.'

'I don't think so, sir.'

The Boss rose from her mess of sheets, and with delicate fingers, brushed the fabric of his trousers. Fitzroy's insides shrivelled in shame. She'd only changed them a couple of days ago.

But The Boss wasn't looking at her, he was inspecting something between the tips of his fingers.

137

'Sand,' he said. 'Better bag it.'

Fitzroy did as she was told.

Later, while The Boss barked and snapped down the phone, trying to engage the services of a forensic geologist, Fitzroy wondered whether she was making too much of it.

Perhaps it was a joke that had spun wildly out of hand, but, as she reached for the Earl Grey, she couldn't think of a single friend who'd be cruel enough to stage a break-in in the name of humour.

On those days when the continued disappearance of Clara Foyle sent her crawling beneath her sheets, Etta could still taste the raw scent of the bloodied kidney he'd left in her car, could conjure the carefully worded clues he'd planted at the scene of the abductions.

And now there was the claw. With its rotting ocean stink, it fitted a pattern of behaviour she had come to expect from Brian Howley.

She was pouring hot water into two mugs when The Boss materialized in her kitchen.

'Better make it three.'

Fitzroy raised her eyebrows, and lifted down another mug. She knew better than to ask.

The Boss pushed his glasses onto his head and pinched the bridge of his nose. He looked so tired these days, always.

'How's Chambers?'

A good question. She didn't know the answer, not properly. The car accident that had led to Howley's escape had trapped DC Alun Chambers in his own personal hell. A traumatic brain injury. Crush injuries to his chest. Two broken arms.

Physically, he was mending but his wife had confided in Fitzroy that he wouldn't drive again. 'I'm not sure,' Mrs Chambers had whispered, worry slicing up her forehead, 'that he'll ever go back to work'.

'He's still in hospital, sir. His rehabilitation has started, but it's a long road.'

'Quite so.'

The Boss swilled a mouthful of tea, grimaced, and put down his mug. When he spoke, he was all squared shoulders and brisk authority.

'On balance, I think last night's little visit warrants looking into. Let's beef up security at your flat. In the meantime, I'm sending you reinforcements. Have you met DC Tony Storm yet?'

'No, sir.'

'Seconded from Bristol last month. A brilliant officer, I hear. One to watch.'

Fitzroy struggled to keep her face neutral. Perfect, just what she needed. A promotion-hungry glory-seeker who would try and take over her investigation. Let him bloody try.

'Tony's just around the corner. Should be here any moment. I'm sure you'll get on famously.'

A knock at the newly fixed front door.

'Ah,' said The Boss, in satisfaction. 'That was speedy.'

Fitzroy watched The Boss march down the hallway of *her* flat, towards *her* front door. In protest, she turned back into the kitchen and drank her tea, gazing out over the rain-shiny rooftops and chimneys.

She was aware of movement behind her, but refused to look around. DC bloody Storm better get his umbrella out. She was planning to rain on his parade.

'Got any biscuits?'

It was the voice that made her turn, because, rather unexpectedly, it belonged to a woman.

Not Tony.

Toni.

This woman was small and blonde, but she filled up the room. Her cheekbones jutted out at acute angles. She wore a tailored jacket and a messy, fringed scarf. Her brown brogues looked expensive. High fashion made flesh.

'DC Antonia Storm. But call me Toni, everyone does.'

As he hurried to hand her a mug, The Boss was smiling at Antonia Storm in a benevolent, fatherly way. Fitzroy recognized that smile because he used to look at her like that. Before she fucked up the disappearance of Grace Rodríguez and the Girl in the Woods case. Before she let Brian Howley slip from their grasp. The Boss had long been hinting at the possibility of promotion, but he had stopped talking about it since the night that Howley escaped. She wondered if her main competition was right here, drinking tea in her flat.

What was it her mother said? *You'll catch more flies with honey than with vinegar.*

'Detective Sergeant' – she emphasized her rank – 'Etta Fitzroy.' A beat. 'But call me Fitzroy, everyone does.'

Shit. She'd never been good at following advice, but she hadn't intended her mimicry to sound quite so sarcastic.

DC Storm didn't flinch. '"What's in a name?"'

'Ah, a police officer with an education. You enjoy Shakespeare?'

'You recognized it? Congratulations. I heard a rumour that you weren't so great with quotations.'

Fitzroy flushed. Served her right. She and DC Chambers

had made certain assumptions about the quotations that Howley had left behind as calling cards. Wrong ones, as it had turned out. Seems it had filtered down to her colleagues. Fitzroy wondered which other failings of hers were being so openly discussed with this newcomer.

The Boss cleared his throat, and jigged about in a way that suggested he was ready to move on.

'Well, I'll leave you two to get to know each other. I suggest you put your heads together and get to work. If – and it's a big if – this *is* the work of Howley, the shit's going to hit the fan. Let's clean it up before it makes a mess.'

In the silence The Boss left behind him, DC Storm tapped one perfectly polished nail on Fitzroy's granite work surface. Fitzroy could not think of a single thing to say.

Before this awkwardness could translate into unfiltered hostility, she was rescued by the sound of her ringing mobile. *Dashiell.* Perhaps she hadn't put him off, after all.

'Have you seen the news?'

No 'hello', then. No pleasantries. Perhaps he was more pissed off than she'd realized.

'No, I've been sorting out the flat. What's happened?'

'A young woman has vanished.'

'People go missing all the time, Dashiell.'

'In Essex.'

Her ears pricked up. During their conversation in the bar the previous night, she'd told him about Clara's uniform washing up on the mudflats of Foulness Island.

'That's not all.'

'Go on.'

'She's suffering from Treacher Collins syndrome.' He paused, to allow the impact of his words to sink in. 'She's

141

got a facial deformity, Etta. Her clothes were found on a beach.'

Ting.

A missing girl with a facial deformity. Another connection to the coast. And hadn't the Friths moved there? When she'd hung up, Fitzroy fingered the evidence bag containing the crab claw and sand. Finally, she'd thought of something to say.

'Get your coat, Storm. We're off to darkest Essex. And you can bloody well drive.'

21

'Do you think we need a magnifying glass?'

Jakey was staring sideways at her with an expression of such intense seriousness that Amy could not find it within herself to say that, no, she didn't think a magnifying glass would be enough to track down a killer.

Or that she was having second thoughts.

Instead she found herself adopting that tone of false brightness that one uses with children.

'Good idea, Jakey.'

The boy looked at her like she was an idiot. 'I was joking, Mrs Foyle.'

Amy laughed. It was a sound she hadn't made much in recent months, and it warmed her, briefly, before guilt came barging in behind it. She had noticed that about grief. Forgetting for a moment was not only necessary for survival, but part of that long, slow walk to acceptance. But, almost always, she found herself full of remorse, berating herself for that capacity, however fleeting, to feel a spark of something other

143

than loss. But Jakey Frith, it turned out, was surprisingly good company, a bright, sparky child, who despite his condition had plenty to say.

'Call me Amy.'

She didn't believe they were going to find Him, not really. This was some elaborate game to indulge Jakey and make her feel like she was being proactive.

'Shall we go for a walk, get some fresh air or something?'

'I'm not so good at walking any more.' He was matter of fact but that made it more painful to hear. 'My legs have got worse since . . .' He didn't need to tell her. She could tell by the haunted expression on his face.

She kicked herself for not having considered that.

'I mean, I can walk a little bit,' said Jakey. 'But not far. It's OK. We can take my chair.'

Amy helped Jakey to button his coat and do up his shoes. It felt good. Eleanor was older now, she leaned on Amy in different ways. But these snapshots of intimacy reminded Amy of how Clara had still needed her. She liked the way it made her feel. She didn't want it to stop.

She helped Jakey into the wheelchair and opened the front door. The cold air was like a bucket of water, and she hesitated, unsure. But Jakey smiled up at her, and then she was easing gloves onto his hands and tucking a blanket over his knees. She was a mother again.

She didn't tell Jakey's parents where they were going.

22

12.37 p.m.

A tiny river of saliva was running down Saul's cheek as he opened his eyes, and he swiped at it with the back of his hand. His neck ached, and there were deep ridges across his face where he'd slept, hard, against the patterned fabric of the sofa.

Fuck.

Cassidy.

He kicked off the blanket and sat up. The sitting room was empty, but he could smell coffee and frying bacon. He wasn't sure of the time but he knew it was light outside, and that meant he should be at school. Mr Darenth had wanted to speak to him about university. He'd made Saul write the appointment down. *To discuss your options.* But Saul knew exactly what his options were. He didn't have any. Kids like him couldn't afford it.

His whole body was stiff, like he'd slept inside a suitcase. The flat, cool stare of daylight was unforgiving, the furniture in the room tatty and unloved. The face of his mother drifted into his head. He shook her away, but what followed was worse. Cassidy, a body bloated by saltwater, half eaten by crabs, crowned with seaweed hair.

The smell of grease was making him gag. He swallowed, tried to clear the lump of heartbreak clogging up his throat.

He had to get out of there.

His hands groped the carpet, feeling underneath the sofa, behind it. His shoes. Where were they?

The sound of sizzling stopped. The clink of plates. Slow footsteps.

'Here.' Mr Silver handed him a plate. 'Eat.'

He wanted to refuse it, to pretend he wasn't hungry, but the air was full of burned fat and bacon, sending his treacherous salivary glands into overdrive.

'Have you seen my trainers?' he said, between mouthfuls of his sandwich.

Mr Silver took a deliberate bite of his own breakfast and finished chewing before he answered with a shrug.

'But I've got to go.' Saul heard the whine in his voice and hated himself for it. He put down his plate, began to patrol the cramped room, peering behind the armchair, the bureau pushed against the wall.

'I've got to go,' he said again, and this time, Mr Silver rose slowly from his seat, made a show of looking around for Saul's shoes.

'What have you done with them, son?'

Saul could feel the words *I don't fucking know* on his lips, but he swallowed them down. For all her faults, Gloria had instilled in him a sense of old-fashioned propriety. *Don't swear in front of adults or strangers.* But he took them off last night – he *remembered* doing it.

He had to go, to find out what was happening with the Cranstons, to catch his afternoon lessons. To grab some of his stuff from the flat, even if it meant facing his mother. But he couldn't do that in his sodding socks.

'What size are you?'

'What?'

'Your feet. What size?'

'Er, ten.'

Mr Silver disappeared back into the kitchen and re-appeared a few moments later with a pair of polished black shoes. He held them out to Saul. An offering.

'Take them.'

Saul's trainers wore their creases like an old face. These shoes were old-fashioned. They looked like shiny beetles. And they made him feel uncomfortable. Shoes were personal, weren't they? They moulded themselves around the wearer's feet. This was too intimate, like wearing dirty underwear. But he didn't have a choice, not if he wanted to be on his way.

'Look,' said Mr Silver, 'if you must go now, bring these back when you're finished with them. I'll find your trainers for you.'

With a reluctant nod, Saul slipped his feet into Mr Silver's soft-as-butter shoes, and tied up the laces. He wriggled his toes. A perfect fit. Like they'd been made for him.

'I'll see you around,' he muttered, and then the door was slamming and he was gone, hand half raised in thanks.

Mr Silver bent over and picked up Saul's empty plate. He carried it to the kitchen, his movements unhurried.

From the window above the sink, he watched the trawlermen untangle their nets. The tide was out, the anchored boats like floating clouds in the stripped-back sand and mud. Above was a sky running with rivers of orange. A cold, clean day. A life-changing day.

Mr Silver smiled his slow, lazy smile. Upstairs, the body of Sunday Cranston was waiting for him to begin the delicate task of removing the skin from her face. But she was not going anywhere, and he had another task to attend to first.

The fireplace in the sitting room where Saul had slept had remained unused since Mr Silver moved in, but the landlord had left behind a stack of logs and kindling for his new tenant.

Mr Silver did not like fire. His hands stung at the memory of the blaze at his father's house, the loss of his collection, but he wanted to do this. He *needed* to.

With careful fingers, he screwed up newspaper and piled up sticks, pressed a lit match to the tender wood, coaxing it into life. As soon as the flames had taken hold, he pushed in a log, and sat for a while, watching it catch and spit.

A seed of happiness planted itself in his chest. An understanding grew in him, spreading its roots. He could begin again. A new collection. A new family. There was still time.

In the basket by the fireplace, something black and white was buried beneath the haphazard pile of logs. A lucky dip. Mr Silver rummaged inside until he pulled out Saul's trainer.

He threw it on the fire and watched it burn.

23

Last summer

Death is not what he intended. Intimidation, yes. Revenge, definitely. Fear reflected back at him, distorted and ugly like a circus mirror. But not this. A slack-mouthed, colourless mask, lips as pale as tallow, skin waxy and cold.

The lifting breeze is his friend tonight, nudging him along the sand, tousling his hair, which sticks to his forehead in the heat. He grunts, shifts the burden to one arm, then back again. He is strong, but a dead weight would be a struggle for anyone, and it's not like he can ask for help. Imagine what they'd say.

His eyes flick to the borrowed car, which waits patiently on the patch of concrete that borders the beach. There's a light inside. The sunburst of a mobile phone screen. It anchors him, knowing she is in there. That he is doing this for her. For them.

He wonders how long it will take for the body to decompose in the water, to become as ugly on the outside as within. If he fills the pockets with pebbles, will it sink to the bottom of the estuary floor? How long will he have before it washes ashore?

Adrenaline pushes the blood around his veins and arteries, urging him forward. He dare not stop in case he loses his nerve.

He throws another glance behind him. The light in the car has now gone out. She is waiting for him to finish and then they'll be on their way, burying this episode beneath the shifting sands of their memories until there is no trace.

A tiny, glistening jewel of sweat slips into his eye. It stings, but he ignores it. The haze around the moon is shifting, the breeze freshening, drying the dampness on his forehead to a salty residue. His fingers brush the bloodied sheet, the metallic tang of death just detectable beneath the scent of the sea. He hears a faint music, takes a moment before he recognizes the source of the sound.

It's the bells on the cockle boats, ringing in the dead. Their tinny knocking makes him pick up his pace. Before long, the horizon will glow with the promise of the morning. The cleansing power of dawn.

The dead man's feet plough the sand, the unstoppable seep of seawater filling the furrow. He pauses again, the muscles in his arms screaming in protest.

He will never forget the weight of the knife, the cool smoothness of the handle, the leaking hole in the hollow of his chest.

The bells are ringing. The waves are playing their rhythmic song. And beneath it all, he hears, over and over again, the prelude to his father's death.

I'm sorry.

I'm sorry.

I'm sorry.

24

DS Etta Fitzroy was listening to music of a different kind, and it was making her ears hurt.

'What *is* this crap?'

'The driver gets to choose the tunes, everyone knows that.'

DC Storm did not take her eyes off the road as Fitzroy leaned forward and turned down the volume, but there was a sucked-in look to her cheeks that indicated displeasure.

A justification was needed. 'Can't hear the dispatcher.'

One of Storm's eyebrows lifted. 'I didn't have you down as a *conformist*.'

'You say that like it's a bad thing.'

'I heard you were a bit of a rule-breaker, that's all.' She sounded almost disappointed.

'Oh, really?'

'With a decent right hook.'

'For fuck's sake, you've only been here five minutes and you already seem to know everything. Look, if you're talking

152

about the time I hit that guy, I was wrong, OK? I had to jump through a dozen different hoops. I nearly lost my job. I probably should have done.'

'The Boss likes you. He covered for you. Risked his own neck, I heard, and his whacking great pension.'

Fitzroy *hadn't* heard that, but she wasn't about to confide in Storm. Mind you, Storm had clearly heard a great deal since her arrival. Perhaps she was a good listener. Or a gossip. Fitzroy hadn't decided yet. Usually, she made her mind up about strangers within the first few minutes, but Antonia Storm was a difficult woman to gauge.

As the car turned off the traffic-heavy A13, Fitzroy caught her first glimpse of the sea. The wind was merciless, teasing the waves into white peaks. She wound down the window. A blast of cold air slapped her. Above the drone of the engine, she heard the crying seagulls before she saw them, wheeling and cresting the currents, their wings imprinting life on an otherwise characterless sky.

'Bloody hell, shut the window, will you? It's freezing.'

There was no malice in Storm's voice, and Fitzroy found herself enjoying the fact her colleague was undaunted by her reputation. It wasn't that she didn't have friends in the Met, rather that she chose not to seek them out. She had enjoyed the banter she'd shared with DC Chambers, but she knew she had kept him at arm's length, and now they were unlikely to be partnered again.

'Shut it yourself. This car's got electric windows.'

Storm snorted, and did as she was told. Fitzroy felt an unexpected tug of laughter, and covered her mouth with her hand.

'So, we heading to the family of this missing girl? Or

shall we go straight to the scene? Don't you think we'd better clear it first?' Storm was peering at the Sat Nav, trying to navigate the unfamiliar grid of residential roads.

'The Boss has squared it with someone in Essex Police. A DI Thornberry. He's expecting us.'

The women quietened as they drove along the main road that ran the length of a pretty cliff-top green and peered over the estuary beyond. The houses were grand here, but a mish-mash of styles, vast modern monoliths rubbing shoulders with art deco semis. Two trees were framed against the sky, their naked branches touching lightly. It made Fitzroy think of Dashiell, and the phone call that had led them here, to a town just an hour from Howley's former life. He couldn't be here. Surely not. *Surely* not.

The unmarked police car slid down the hill, rounded the corner and headed over the bridge that led to the Old Town, a place of crooked cottages and cobbles.

'Cute,' said Storm. 'Very cute.'

Fitzroy wondered if the residents felt the same way on summer days when sunburnt tourists clogged up the streets with their beer cans and buckets and spades.

The car park by the Mayflower fish and chip shop was practically empty. All action was happening a few hundred yards away, a couple of police cars blocking the entrance to Leigh beach.

Without waiting for Storm, Fitzroy headed towards the knot of uniforms and forensics, who were milling around, lacking direction. What might the collective noun for such a gathering be? A clusterfuck of cops? A psychosis of ser-geants?

'Sorry, I'm afraid you can't do that,' said a young PC as

Fitzroy lifted the police tape and slipped underneath. Fitzroy flashed her badge. 'Where's DI Thornberry?'

The officer reddened, a sign of his youth and inexperience, and pointed towards a squat man with a jaw too big for his face. He was gesticulating at some hapless soul, and when he caught sight of Fitzroy, and Storm, not far behind, he swore under his breath.

'The pride of London, I assume?'

'I wouldn't go that far, sir,' said Fitzroy.

'Look, I don't have time for spoon-feeding today. You're going to have to amuse yourselves.'

His mobile beeped, and then started ringing. Fitzroy was fascinated by the way his irritation began in the creases of his forehead and spread, like ripples on a puddle, across the rest of his face.

'What have you got so far?'

DI Thornberry did not lift his eyes from his screen. 'Did you hear what I said?'

Fitzroy bristled. 'I'm not asking for chapter and verse, but surely a brief rundown of what's been happening is not too much to ask?'

'I think what DS Fitzroy meant to say is that we're investigating a possible link with a known serial killer.' DC Storm shone the full beam of her smile on DI Thornberry. 'You never know, we might be able to help you.'

He grunted, slipped his phone back into his pocket. 'I've got a missing girl who may or may not have killed herself, and a note telling me she was meeting some guy, who may or may not have been the last person to see her alive.'

'Some guy?'

'She didn't say who. Just left a message for her sister

saying she was going on a date and to cover for her if she was late. Her sister didn't find it until this morning, though.'

'But why all the fuss? How do you know she didn't just make a rash decision to stay out all night and is now too embarrassed to face her family?'

'We don't know, not for certain. But there are a couple of things that are ringing alarm bells. She was due at work today, hasn't missed a single day since she started three years ago. She's a sensible girl.'

Privately, Fitzroy thought that didn't stack up. She might have been ill or overslept or decided to stay in bed with her mystery date. Sensible girls could skid off the rails too.

DI Thornberry was still talking, throwing his comments in Storm's direction. 'Secondly, her clothes were found on this beach this morning.'

'Mobile phone?'

Like everyone else, Fitzroy recognized that the secrets to most crimes were served up by forensics, by the hidden worlds in victims' phones and computers.

'Not yet.'

That stopped Fitzroy in her tracks. No self-respecting youngster under the age of twenty-five would let their mobile out of their sight.

'Final calls or texts?'

'We can't tell. It's been switched off for hours. We're waiting for the phone company to get back to us. In the meantime, our techies are having a look at the family computers.' His own phone rang again. 'Sorry, I've got to take this . . .'

'What do you think?' Storm's voice was low. 'Waste of

our time? Smells like suicide to me. Maybe the guy didn't show up for their date and this was the result.'

A couple of weeks after her son was stillborn, Fitzroy had taken to pacing the streets near her south London home, as if the act of moving her body, one foot in front of the other, would force her to keep going, even when her mind was pleading with her to turn off all those broken feelings, not just for a few days, but forever. She had found herself in the grounds of a well-known university, and the rain had started sheeting down, emptying the benches scattered around the quadrangle. She had blindly followed a young woman into one of the buildings and had stumbled, unsuspecting and unchallenged, into a lecture called 'Identifying Different Methods of Suicide: A Forensic Pathologist's Guide'. She had learned, repelled and fascinated, how the instinct not to breathe underwater was so powerful that a drowning victim would not inhale until the point of losing consciousness.

In about ten per cent of cases, the larynx would go into spasm as soon as water touched the vocal cords, overcoming the breathing reflex until the victim suffocated. In the rest, water would gradually fill the lungs, a slow dance of panic and agony.

'I think I'd take an overdose,' the girl in the seat next to Fitzroy had whispered. Fitzroy, who had laid a hand on her empty stomach, had not replied. Her chosen method would be death by self-flagellation.

Drowning was an ugly, brutal, *difficult* way to die, even with rocks in your pocket, and Sunday Cranston had not been wearing any clothes.

Storm was lingering by DI Thornberry, waiting for him to finish his call. She had angled her body towards the inspector in a way he could not ignore, an interested smile on her lips. When she looked up again, Storm was saying something, and Thornberry was laughing and shaking his head.

Even Fitzroy was impressed. She did not enjoy small talk, always groping for the right words or worrying about using the wrong ones. But her new colleague had a knack of convincing others to open up. This was clearly a skill that would come in useful.

Across the estuary, a container ship pushed its way through the distant waves, a hulk of metal and purpose. She watched it until it became lost somewhere in the seascape.

Fragments of information fluttered around her brain, without shape or meaning. Clara's waterlogged school uniform. The rotting crab claw in Fitzroy's bed. Sunday Cranston's facial disfigurement.

Even an amateur could recognize a link between elements of each case, but that didn't mean Brian Howley was involved with this young woman's disappearance. Coincidence, yes. But perhaps Fitzroy was grasping at straws. Most likely, Sunday had simply given up on life, as so many youngsters did these days, crippled by self-doubt and anxiety and a million pressures that became so noisy there seemed only one way to silence them.

Fitzroy glanced across this stretch of beach, automatically combing it for anything that looked out of the ordinary. She remembered the message Howley had left for them at the sweet shop where Clara was last seen alive, and how the initial search had missed it. But all she could see was an old bus shelter daubed with graffiti. A toilet block. A handful of wooden benches. Miles and miles and miles of sand.

Further up the beach, a chattering mob of school children, wearing boots and carrying buckets and spades, began to dig.

This was not her case. There was nothing here for them.

A black fog of disappointment began to descend. Another wasted lead. Was there any point in heading to Foulness Island, where Clara's uniform had washed up? She should, if she was doing the job properly, and for the sake of good order. But she doubted it would yield much, except more disappointment.

As they walked back to the car park, Detective Sergeant Etta Fitzroy could hardly bring herself to say a word. She had no way of knowing that in a cottage less than a quarter of a mile away, the man who was known as Brian Howley and Mr Silver and the Bone Collector was alive and well, and preparing something very special indeed.

25

1.49 p.m.

He watched the sky above the estuary every day, and every
day it offered him something new. Two mornings ago, as he
had made his way to school, there was a strip of fire on the
horizon's edge, igniting the slate clouds hovering above.
Teatime yesterday, rolling grey smudges had towered over
the sky, a mountain above a lake. At dusk, on the night his
mother almost drowned, it was a burning apocalypse, a battalion of altocumulus advancing towards the fading sun.
This horizon changed with the wind. Now, it was devoid of
colour; featureless, blank and as empty as him.

Saul hurried up the road towards the Cranston house,
and every now and then, the heels of Mr Silver's shoes, tied
by their laces to the strap of his rucksack, knocked against
his back.

Inside his bag was the contents of his wardrobe, his
school books, a mobile phone charger, a sketchpad and the
box containing his dead insects. In his pocket was the

remains of Mr Silver's money, his headless worry doll and a fistful of notes he had found in the Fortnum and Mason tin.

He hadn't expected gaining entry to the flat would be quite so easy. When he'd returned to collect his things, he'd been prepared to break a window, but Gloria had left the back door unlocked. *Daft cow.*

The last time he had checked, the tin had been empty, but an unwelcome stab of guilt found him digging down into his jeans for Mr Silver's leftover ten-pound note, just to tide her over. When he had lifted the caddy lid to find it stuffed full of money, his eyes had widened. His mother did not work and spent every penny of her benefits almost as soon as she received them. How would Gloria lay her hands on that kind of cash? His thoughts flitted to the man outside the cockle shed, the memory of his mother's coquettish laugh. Had he lent her some money? Given it to her? Paid her? *Slag.* Saul had bent the pipe-cleaner doll between his fingers until its narrow metal thread had almost broken. Then he had stolen the lot.

Helen Cranston was putting a black plastic sack of rubbish into the outside bin. She was trying very hard to keep to her usual routine because she didn't want to upset her youngest daughter, who could not seem to stop crying since she had discovered her sister's note.

Saul clocked her at the same time that Mrs Cranston saw him, and had no time to prepare himself. He knew she didn't like him, that her husband Russell had never believed him good enough. But Cassidy had never minded about that. She had stroked his face and told him to ignore her parents.

'Mrs Cranston, I . . .' He realized, too late, that he should have brought flowers.

'I suppose you want to see her?' Helen wiped her hands on her coat and looked at him in a way that suggested she hadn't quite decided whether to let him in.

A white heat, instant, all-consuming, flooded Saul; his skin, the back of his eyes, the deep hollow in his stomach. Not because he cared that Helen Cranston treated him like shit on a street corner, but because he was trying very hard not to cry.

If Mrs Cranston was inviting him to see Cassidy, it meant only one thing: her body had been found.

Even the wrought-iron gates squealed their distrust as they opened. He shuffled after her, unable to raise his head, to meet her eyes, to challenge her distaste.

This was worse than the night his father had punched Gloria in the face and fractured her cheekbone, or the sound of pitiful whimpering as he'd turned his temper on the stray dog Saul had befriended and kicked her to death.

This feeling was new, like his chance of a future was falling down around his ears, insubstantial as ash.

Would she be lying in her bed? Or in a coffin? What would she look like? Oh fuck, what would she look like? And Mrs Cranston was being freaky with her creepy, calm voice.

'Shoes off, please.'

Saul kicked off his school plimsolls. He refused to wear Mr Silver's shoes for longer than he had to, and his trainers – his only decent pair – were missing.

He swallowed, and placed his rucksack on the immaculate carpet. Mrs Cranston's lips disappeared.

Footsteps on the stairs.

A blur of colour.

A bolt of warmth.

And Cassidy was in his arms.

Cassie.

His Cass.

Crying and shaking, but alive.

'Sunday's missing.'

Two words, repeated over and over again.

He tightened his grip on her. 'I thought it was you.'

Mrs Cranston, who had been lingering by the cactus garden, looked up sharply.

'What do you mean?'

'I saw – I mean – I . . .'

'What did you see, Saul?'

Saul glanced at Cassidy. Her face was neutral, but she was waiting for an answer. 'Clothes, on the beach. Cassidy's bracelet.'

'When?' Mrs Cranston was shaking his shoulders. 'When? When did you see them?'

Saul's mind emptied. He forgot that Mr Silver had warned him to distance himself, or that it might look suspicious to admit he had been on the beach in the early hours of the morning. He wanted to help, and the truth was all he had to gift them.

As soon as he told them, he knew he had made a serious error of judgement.

Cassidy backed away from him until she was standing next to her mother. Mrs Cranston had pulled herself tall, blown up with outrage and self-righteousness.

'You were on the beach in the middle of the night and

163

you saw Sunday's clothes and you didn't think to *say* anything?'

Put like that, it sounded bad.

'Have you told the police? You need to speak to them. You must.'

Saul did not like other people telling him what to do. And he did not want the police digging into his background.

'And why have you got your rucksack with you? Are you going somewhere?'

Saul waited for Cassidy to speak up for him, to shush her mother and tell her that he had nothing to do with the disappearance of a daughter and a sister. To insist that he would never run away because she loved him and he loved her. But she was looking at him in a way that suggested she was seeing, for the first time, his imperfections and flaws.

'You said you'd make me pay, Saul. The other day. At Flora's house.' Cassidy was speaking slowly, eyes wide. 'Is this what you meant?'

Mrs Cranston covered her mouth with her hand.

Tiny stars began to flash. Saul tried to catch his breath. To mount a defence. He could not think. And then he remembered. A stupid argument. They'd been hanging out in the games room at the bottom of Cassie's best friend's garden. He'd lost his temper because one of Flora's brothers had been flirting with Cassie. Squared up to him. Cassie had thrown her glass of water at Saul and stormed off. She hadn't turned up for work at the pet store the next day.

I didn't mean it, Your Honour. I was angry, because someone had tried it on with my girlfriend. I'd never hurt her. Or her sister. No, Your Honour, you've got the wrong end of the stick.

A bubble of mirth at the awfulness of the Cranstons'

misunderstanding began to work its way up his throat. He didn't want to, knew that he mustn't, but shock and hurt and a million other things were teeming through his brain, and making his blood fizz and his heart jump around.

He laughed.

Mrs Cranston actually gasped out loud, but Cassie didn't say anything, which was far worse. They stood and stared at him, and then Mrs Cranston lunged for the phone.

Saul did not wait. Before she had dialled the first digit, he was pulling on his ratty old plimsolls and snatching up his rucksack. By the third digit, he was opening the front door, and then he was running down the street, running blindly into the February afternoon.

Not to school, too late now.

Not to home, he didn't belong there.

Not to Cassie's.

There was nowhere for him to go. Nowhere at all.

As he ran, past the landmarks of his childhood, past the bus stop where he'd kissed his first girlfriend, the ramp where he'd come off his skateboard, the pair of shiny black shoes *knock-knock-knocked* into the base of his spine. He was crying now, hot, salty tears that slid into his mouth, not just because of Sunday Cranston and Cassie and their mother and his mother, but at the unfairness of a life that fate had chosen for him.

Submerged by a sudden wave of longing, Saul found himself craving the quiet calm of Mr Silver's cottage, and the bacon sandwiches, and the sofa, and his black-and-white trainers.

He picked up his pace.

* * *

From an upstairs window, Mr Silver sees Saul running down the cobbles, distress splitting his face apart.

With careful fingers, he lays down his paintbrush and removes his latex gloves, casting a critical eye over the still-drying, stiffening canvas. Almost finished. As he rinses his artist's palette, he watches the ruby swirls of Sunday Cranston's blood disappearing down the sink.

By the time Saul is ringing his doorbell, Mr Silver has locked up his museum and is waiting in the sitting room to welcome home his *son*.

To begin his instruction in the art of becoming a killer.

26

Erdman checked his mobile for the umpteenth time. *Shitola*. This was not going to plan. He should have been home by now, or on his way, at the very least. He could only assume that Lilith hadn't woken up yet. She'd be having a shit-fit if she had. But the absence of texts suggested she remained blissfully unaware he'd left their son in the care of a woman he'd only met that morning.

The uncomfortable feeling that he'd made a mistake was giving him indigestion, but he didn't know Pete Haskell well enough to ask him to cover for him. 'Can't stand wasters,' the photographer had said on their first job together, the controversial closure of a local prison. Pistol Pete, they called him in the newsroom, because he wasn't afraid to shoot from the hip. He'd worked on the nationals for a while, but now he was in his fifties, he wanted a quieter life. Erdman knew all about that.

The police were saying nothing. One of his colleagues had been sent to the Cranston house, to try and persuade the family to talk. Erdman had been told to wait at the scene in case of an impromptu press conference, but experience told him that the cops were too busy looking for answers to waste time speaking to the assembled media. Only local press for now, but it wouldn't take long for the big guns to rock up if there was heat in this story.

Was there heat? Erdman wasn't sure yet. A missing woman. A pile of clothes. Privately, he thought it smelled like suicide, nothing more. But the sheer weight of police presence indicated they suspected otherwise. There was *something* going on here, and it was his job to sniff it out. Especially as he didn't want to let down his old mate Axel. He'd put his neck on the line, recommending Erdman for this job. Christ, this was why the Friths had moved to this part of the coast to start their new life. Better not fuck it up.

From his vantage point in front of the public toilets and behind the police line, Erdman noticed a couple of officers breaking away from the knot of police clustered on the beach.

Signalling to Pete to stay where he was, he followed the men, who were walking into the Old Town, past the foot-bridge by The Mayflower pub, past the restaurant that wouldn't look out of place on the deck of a cruise ship. One of the officers stopped by a cottage, glorious in the summer with its sentries of flower-filled tubs, but now covered in dead vines.

An elderly lady answered the door. Erdman could see the query on her face, the movement of her mouth, the slow shake of her greying head. For two or three minutes, the officers chatted to her, noting down the odd comment.

House-to-house inquiries.

THE COLLECTOR

It gave Erdman an idea. Perhaps he'd knock on a couple of doors of his own, starting at the opposite end of the Old Town. Technically, he wasn't doing anything wrong. He had as much right to be there as they did. But he knew it irritated the police when journalists got in on the act before them.

Witnesses were always at their most authentic during that first account, especially when taken by surprise. It was human nature to embellish and exaggerate, to convince oneself of a truth during subsequent retellings, once there'd been time to mould the story into a more interesting shape.

Erdman sent a text message to Pete, outlining his plan. It was a tricky judgement call. If he discovered something decent, Pete could fire off a quick headshot, and they would have their exclusive. But if there were developments on the beach, his newspaper wouldn't be there to hear them. Erdman was a newcomer. He hadn't made friends with the rival media outlets yet, and guessed they would not share. But he needed to make his mark. Impress the new boss and all that political shit he hated so much.

Decision made, he waited for Pete to catch him up, and the two men walked briskly past the police officers, eyes forward, casual as anything.

At the end of the cobbles that marked a path through the Old Town, beyond the cockle sheds which, for a century and more, had withstood the harsh weather and the march of time, beyond the pubs and the art gallery and a pretty tea-garden cafe, perched some rundown fisherman's cottages.

The first one they tried looked deserted, and the sound of their knocking echoed through its empty rooms.

The second was lived in – Erdman could see dirty plates

on the table when he peered through the window – but its inhabitants were out, probably at work.

A bit further along was a third cottage. On its own. Left out.

The blinds were half pulled, even though it was gone lunchtime, giving the appearance of heavy-lidded eyes. A suggestion of movement behind the glass, but Erdman couldn't be sure.

He didn't expect much, but it was another place to try.

He knocked on the door. Felt a burst of pain.

A splinter had embedded itself in his knuckle, digging deep in that bony nub of his middle finger.

Erdman lifted his hand to his mouth and sucked away his discomfort. After a couple of moments, he tried again, ringing the bell instead, peering through the slab of mottled glass carved into the top of the door.

He saw another flash of movement. Someone was in there, he was sure of it.

He lifted the brass flap of the letterbox. 'Hello,' he called. 'Any chance of a word?'

His mouth was still level with the letterbox when the door opened, and he straightened up, speaking quickly to cover his awkwardness.

'Afternoon, sorry to bother you. I'm from the *Gazette*, and we're asking local residents about the disappearance of a young woman last night. We wondered if you'd seen or heard anything?'

A boy – Erdman guessed he was about sixteen – with a mop of white-blond hair filled the doorway. He gave Erdman a wary look. There was a familiarity to him, but the connection was weak, a poor signal.

'Sunday Cranston. Ring any bells? She's a local lass.'

The boy's face, as pale as a winter sky, closed down, bereft of emotion. Erdman couldn't help thinking it was an unusual reaction, like someone had turned out a light.

'She's got a sister about your age, I think. Doesn't go to your school, does she?'

Saul slipped his fingers into his jeans pocket and twisted the frayed pipe cleaner. His eyes slid over Erdman and fixed on a point to the left of his shoulder.

'Think you're wasting your time, mate,' muttered Pistol Pete, giving a dismissive snort.

Saul's vision snapped back into focus, skewering Pete. The photographer shuffled his feet, not sure whether to be amused or embarrassed by the teenager's disdainful expression. The boy drew in a breath, as if he had something important to impart.

'Actually—'

He was interrupted by a voice from somewhere inside the cottage, as cold and hard as frost. 'Just tell them to piss off, Saul.'

Saul.

Erdman stored that name in his mental filing cabinet. He'd overheard one of the other journalists discussing Facebook chatter and a lad called Saul that morning, but hadn't a clue who he was. It wasn't a common name. This couldn't be him, could it?

The teenager threw an uncertain look over his shoulder, towards the direction of the voice. Erdman used that brief moment of distraction to signal to Pete. He mimed taking a picture. The photographer winked and lifted his camera.

As Saul turned back towards them, Pete was already firing off his first frame.

The teenager's eyes widened at the teeth-chatter click of the camera. Instinctively, he ducked and lifted his hands to his face, then slammed the door.

'That went well,' said Pete, eyes downwards, scrolling through the series of thumbnail images he'd just taken.

Erdman grunted non-committally, but his antennae for a story were telling him that this Saul, with his cautious eyes and shut-down face, was worth a closer look.

'Why did he do that? Doesn't he need to ask *permission* or something?'

Saul was pacing the tiny sitting room, his face a squabble between outrage and fear.

'What's he going to do with it? Is it going to be in the paper, then? I'll sue the bastards. They can't do this to me. I'm a minor.'

Inside his head, Saul pulled up the face of the photographer with his stupid hair and smarmy grin, saw himself drawing back his fist and hitting him in the mouth. Felt the collapse of bone, the warm slip of blood on his fingers. He saw the man falling to the ground, clutching his chest. Having a heart attack. Dying.

Prick.

PRICK.

He slapped his hand on Mr Silver's glass coffee table, and ignored the spreading sting across the flat of his palm.

'Calm down, Saul.' Mr Silver's voice was cool and even, but there was warning in it. 'Control, son. It's the key to everything. Lose control and you lose yourself.'

Saul, who spent so much of his time buttoning down the ragged edges of his anger, at home, at school, gave a fruit bowl in the shape of a sunflower a half-hearted shove. It was a show of petulance, nothing more. The ashy residue of his temper. But it slid across the smooth surface of the table. Tipped. Fell. An orange flew across the tiles. The handblown green glass shattered into a dozen shiny blades.

Mr Silver stood, his eyes like holes. He did not shout, but there was an unspoken violence in the way he buried the tips of his fingers into Saul's shoulders.

'Stop it, boy.'

'Sorry.' Saul was stammering and he never did that. 'I'll get you a new one.' He couldn't think about the cost, or where he might find one. He just knew he had to get Mr Silver to stop looking at him like that.

'Anger is dangerous, son.' Mr Silver's voice was low, carefully controlled. 'It makes you act without thinking.'

Saul stared at the broken glass on the floor. He wondered if Mr Silver's fingers would leave four perfectly oval-shaped bruises beneath his collarbone.

'But imagine if you *did* think about it. If you could use it and distil it into something even more powerful.' He loosened his grip on Saul and patted him, all benign gesture now.

Saul was doing that thing that teenage boys do. Sort of shuffling his feet and looking down.

'Yeah,' he muttered, because he didn't have a clue what the old man was on about.

Mr Silver smiled. 'Or' – he pushed the shards of glass into a neat pile with the tip of his shoe – 'imagine if you could pass through the world without anyone seeing you.'

173

Saul tried out a laugh. 'What, like you're invisible?'

Mr Silver smiled again. 'Yes, son. Something like that.' He disappeared into the kitchen and came back with a dustpan and brush, which he held out to the teenager. 'It's a skill, see. Blending into the background.'

Saul knelt, and began to sweep up the glass. 'No chance of that with my hair.'

'We'll see,' said Mr Silver softly. 'We'll see.'

He watches Saul for a moment or two, the boy's shoulders bent, cleaning up his mess. Another smile curls up the edges of his face, crinkling his eyes, deepening the parentheses running down to his mouth. A stranger could be forgiven for thinking this is a proud father, watching his son *taking responsibility*.

As Saul tidies up the evidence of his anger, Mr Silver thinks only of a single word. *Yes.*

He does not know that his decision, slippery with the promise of new beginnings, will alter the fates of them all: Saul, DS Fitzroy, Jakey Frith, Clara Foyle and Mr Silver himself.

Outside, the day is growing hostile, sleet weighting down the sky. The wind is in a temper and the clouds run from it. Mr Silver, who has become so used to his new name that he sometimes forgets he was once Brian Howley, is in a hurry.

He can see two men a few houses down the cobbled streets, between the cockle sheds. They carry with them the lustre of respectability, the stiff shoulders of authority. Mr Silver knows what they are. He can smell them.

'Saul.'

The boy appears from the kitchen. His face is pale, his

eyes a clouded blue. He looks worn down by the burden of sorrow. Mr Silver knows what will make him feel better, because this is his son.

'We're going out.'

Saul's mouth hangs open, as if he wants to speak. Mr Silver feels a frisson of irritation. His fingers itch.

'Have you found my trainers?'

Mr Silver does not have time for this particular conversation.

'Wear the black shoes.' He looks down at his own feet. 'Like me.'

Mr Silver jangles the keys in his hand. The van, which he used to transport the specimens C, J and G, is long gone. Now he has a car, small and ordinary. Forgettable.

They must leave by the back door. No need to attract unwanted attention. Mr Silver wants to be on his way before the policemen knock, before their polite queries solidify into suspicion. He does not think the boy will be able to lie. He must extract him. For Saul's own safety.

He watches his guest slip on his coat and pat down his pockets, searching for his mobile phone.

'You can look for it later,' he says. 'We should go.'

There is challenge in the boy's eyes. Defiance. It makes Mr Silver smile.

He will learn.

By God, he will learn.

He does not tell Saul about the claw hammer he carries in his holdall. Or the knife that presses against his ribs, like a lover's hand, or the silent, stolen mobile phone. The boy must be taught how to behave, to fall into line at a raised eyebrow, a held gaze. If that does not work, there are other ways. His father's ways. But not here. Not now.

'Where are we going?' Saul is sullen, grudging.

'Somewhere special.'

The teenager drags himself across the kitchen, his reluctance seeping from him like sweat. Mr Silver, the Bone Collector, waits for him by the sink; flexes his arthritic fingers, a legacy from his father. In his ear, Marshall is whispering instructions. Mr Silver turns on the tap, still smiling. The weight of the hammer in his bag reminds him of his duty.

'Wash your hands, son.'

27

Gloria opened one mascara-clogged eyelid and waited a few seconds before repeating the motion with the other.

There was zero point in trying to get back to sleep now. Zilcho. A big fat nil. However hard she tried, once she was awake, she was most definitely awake, even though her limbs were heavy with dehydration.

Gloria ran a furred tongue around her mouth, trying to guess which it would be today; dry retches that pulled on her stomach muscles until they burned, or a headache that refused to leave her alone, no matter how much water she drank.

A thin light was stippling the corner of the bedroom. Gloria didn't need to check her phone to know it was the middle of the afternoon and she had missed the best hours of market day.

The skin around her mouth had that raw, over-used feeling. Her scalp was tender where he'd gripped a fistful of her hair. She ran her hands over the prominent bones of her body, wincing at the sore spot beneath her ribcage, the bruise along the swell of her breast.

She couldn't do this again, couldn't bear to. She would have to find a way out, but she would need to be cunning. Otherwise, The Secret would leak out, leaving another dirty mess for her and Saul to clean up.

The wind was playing the tiles on the roof, knocking the loose ones together like a madcap xylophone. Again and again, it hurled in from the estuary, forcing the windows of the flat to bend and bow. She wondered if Saul was back from school yet. Didn't he finish early on Thursdays? It wasn't safe to be walking home in this fury of a storm.

Gloria levered herself from the bed and tried to ignore the aggressive lurch in her vision. She forced herself to pause, waiting for her senses to right themselves. Her stomach churned. She was still wearing her smartest silky blouse, the one she wore for job interviews and nights at the casino on the seafront, and a tiny scrap of black gauze that passed as a pair of knickers. She grabbed her ancient dressing gown, the cotton almost worn through in places, and covered herself.

Her belly, so flat as to be almost concave, rumbled but the hunger inside her wouldn't be satisfied by food. She headed towards the bathroom, the tiny salivary glands in her mouth moistening in readiness.

At the back of the cupboard above the sink, between the sponge with a rust stain and some ancient toilet cleaner, was a mouthwash bottle. Gloria loosened the cap and lifted it to her lips. As the liquid hit the back of her throat, she gagged and spat it out. The vodka had been replaced by water.

Muttering under her breath, Gloria dumped the bottle

on the floor and turned her attention to the toilet. The cistern was one of her favourite hiding places. The neck of the bottle was tied to the ballcock to prevent it from clinking against the sides during a flush. With fingers that trembled ever so slightly, she unscrewed the lip, and without bothering to wipe the glass dry, took a cautious sip.

For Christ's sake, Saul.

She pulled in a breath and let it go slowly. She didn't need a fancy-dan counsellor to teach her ways to control her temper. She could manage that all by herself.

Saul's bedroom door was closed but Gloria didn't bother to knock. It was cold in here, the wind sneaking in through the gaps between ill-fitting windows.

His bed was made, and there was a library book on the floor, its spine worn from use, but no sign of her son. There was something about the room that struck her as odd, though.

She stared for a moment, trying to puzzle it out. His clothes – that was it. Usually, there were dirty jeans and jumpers and T-shirts strewn across the old armchair he'd rescued from the pavement outside somebody's house. But this place looked like it was waiting for a hotel guest to arrive.

She opened his drawer, expecting to see the usual tangle of socks and boxer shorts. But it was empty. His phone charger was gone, and so was his rucksack.

If she didn't know better, she'd guess that Saul had run away. The slightly sick feeling intensified, and Gloria only knew one way to make it go away.

With its old vents and crumbling brickwork, the flat was

freezing. Gloria pulled her dressing gown more tightly around her as she entered the kitchen.

She fumbled with the Fortnum and Mason tin. With last night's money, she could buy enough material to make four new dresses, as well as a couple of bottles, possibly more. This time, though, she'd find a much better hiding place for her secret stash. And when Saul came home, as she knew he eventually would, she would tear strips from him layer by painful layer until he swore that he would never tip away her vodka again. Then she would make him his favourite meal. Sausages and mash with lashings of gravy. She smiled. It was a good plan.

At first, she couldn't quite believe what she was seeing. The inside of the tin was the same smooth metal it had always been, with the same stubborn grains of tea sticking to the bottom.

But there was no money.

No loose change, and certainly no sign of the forty pounds she knew she had put in there before taking refuge in her bed.

Gloria wondered if she was still a little drunk.

She flew back to her bedroom, clawing at the pockets of the jacket she'd left lying on the floor, frantically lifting her discarded tights, checking the insides of her shoes and beneath her pillow. She fell to her knees and groped under the bed.

Nothing.

No money left.

A crack opened up inside her, shaded in with disbelief and despair. She couldn't think where it had gone. She must have lost it. But she remembered prising off the tin lid when she'd stumbled in mid-morning. She had the broken nail to prove it. But there was no denying a simple, painful truth: now she had nothing.

Saul took it.

She shook her head, trying to dislodge such a disloyal thought. Saul would never do that. He was her boy. Her protector. He looked after her. There was no way he would steal from her and leave her with nothing. And let's be honest, this wasn't the first time he'd taken off. He'd regularly disappear for a couple of days at a time after The Secret happened. He hadn't done that for months, though. He'd seemed more settled, less jumpy. But even during those dark days when he was prone to vanishing without a word, he'd never helped himself to money. She used to wonder how he fed himself.

In those lost, lonely moments, while he was gone, Gloria would patrol their flat, the alcohol deadening the sense of dread that would score its way into her skin with every passing minute. When it became overwhelming, she would climb into bed, staring at the hairline crack that snaked from the ceiling rose like a trailing stem. And she would simply wait, trusting that Saul would navigate the fog of his grief and regret, and find his way home.

Oh, that sweet moment, the release of hours' worth of pent-up tension in a single exhale of breath at the sound of his key in the door.

Saul took it.

She hummed a wordless little tune to block out the cynical voice that seemed intent on blaming her son. She refused to believe it. There was no way he would take it, not if he had the slightest idea of what it had cost her to earn it.

Gloria did not want to think about that. She knew what it looked like, could reel off half a dozen derogatory names for women like her, who did what she did.

But those who labelled them, who *judged* them, never came close to the truth. This was not about choice. That luxury had been removed from the equation months ago.

She hadn't wanted to have sex with him. He had repulsed her, with his too-big hands and the flabby overhang of his belly which slapped against her when he had laid her on that old mattress and taken what he wanted. The money had been an unexpected bonus, scraps thrown to a maltreated dog. But it was much, much more than that. Because if she didn't go along with his demands, he'd already spelled out what he would do.

The Secret would no longer be secret.

And that would be a disaster.

Christ, she needed a drink.

Except this flat was as dry as the frigging Sahara, and so was her mouth. Gloria ran a glass of water and swallowed three out-of-date paracetamol from the packet she'd bought from Dodgy Boy, who, when he was in a good mood, let her sell her handmade dresses from his market stall in exchange for a couple of quid.

She washed in cold water from the bathroom sink, sponging herself down with an old cloth. She was having trouble thinking straight, the pressing buzz of need clouding her mind. She knew where she could find others like her, who were driven by the same wild desperation. But she hated what it turned her into, begging for a mouthful of someone else's cheap cider, not caring about anything much except the lure of oblivion for a few short hours.

There were always options, of course. But stealing was

risky, even though she was excellent at it. It took a certain chutzpah to brazen out suspicion written in the watchful eyes of those lucky enough to hold down paid employment.

Back in the bedroom, Gloria opened drawer after drawer, seeking out forgotten coins or notes. If there wasn't enough for a bottle of vodka, a can of something would have to do. But aside from some oddments of faded underwear, an old belt, a couple of bits of jewellery and, mystifyingly, a sweet wrapper, they were disappointingly empty, all except the last drawer.

But it didn't contain money.

Gloria withdrew the forgotten passport and, for a tumbling instant, was transported to a different time and place. Her hand was shaking, but this was not the beginning of the *delirium tremens*, merely an ambush of memory.

The gilt-embossed burgundy cover was slightly greasy to the touch. Almost against her will, she flicked through it, letting it fall open at the laminated photo page. His face, so familiar, so terrifying, glared up at her.

Surname/Nom:

ANGUISH

Given name/Prénoms:

SOLOMON FINN

Nationality/Nationalité:

BRITISH CITIZEN

Date of birth/Date de naissance:

11 APRIL /AVRIL 80

Sex/Sexe:

M

Place of birth/Lieu de naissance:

ROCHFORD

Her husband. Saul's father.

Even though he was a two-dimensional presence, locked away behind the glossy sheen and tidy white edges of this photograph, his eyes hooked hers. Accusing. Superior. She remembered when it had been taken. Sol had been making some decent money for a change as a labourer on a new development of flats. Some of the lads were planning a trip to Spain, he'd told her, a rare note of excitement in his voice. They had asked him to go too. He'd never been abroad before, but they were going to stay in a hotel with – *get this* – a bar in the pool that you could swim up to. There had been a taunting defiance in the way he had waved his shiny new passport at her.

She had fought to disguise her disapproval, and tried not to mind that the cost of such a trip would be enough to feed them all for months or buy new school uniform and shoes for Saul ten times over.

But she hadn't tried hard enough, because he'd seen a flicker of those feelings in her face and set about erasing them with vicious words, and when that didn't work, when she'd dared to suggest that perhaps they could go somewhere cheaper as a family instead, he'd slammed her head into the old radiator in their bedroom.

Saul, fresh from the bath and wrapped in a thin towel, had been nine years old.

Naked, he had flown at Solomon, his small hands tugging at his father's forearms, which were heavily muscled from months of hodding bricks and hefting bags of cement.

Fighting against the glare of pain lighting the nerve-endings in her head, Gloria had screamed at Saul to find somewhere to hide. As the familiar print of her bedroom wallpaper began to swarm and jump, the last thing she saw before slipping into the quiet nirvana of unconsciousness was Saul's whimpering, crumpled form hitting the wall.

When she had come to, she was lying on a towel in Saul's lap, a heightened sensitivity to every sensation. Beneath the rough fabric and the weight of her own pain, she had felt the shudders of her son, cold and fearful. It kindled a slow-burning anger of her own.

Later, Saul would relay how his father had stormed off, threatening to leave them, as he always did.

'That's it,' he had shouted, nudging a steel-capped work boot into her unresponsive thigh. 'See how you manage on your own, you silly cow.'

That time, he'd been gone for a week.

By the morning of the fifth day, the watchful expression that Saul always wore had been replaced by a cautious smile. By the evening, when his mother made pancakes for tea, flipping them high into the air, he had laughed.

On the seventh day, Solomon Anguish came back.

When Gloria had first met Sol at a pub near the Kursaal estate, he had been a man with vulpine good looks and an easy charm. A small man with big plans. But disappointment had blunted him, its offcuts evident in this snapshot of a face that was no longer handsome, but narrow and sly.

She closed the passport, and slid it back into the drawer. She should get rid of it. Solomon Anguish was never coming home.

And now to more pressing business.

She ran her tongue around the inside of her teeth, trying to moisten her mouth. She was thinking about something she had seen on the Internet about hand sanitizer, and the way it could be mixed with table salt to separate off the alcohol. It was smaller than a bottle of vodka, easier to slip into her pocket at the supermarket. But she wasn't there yet. Was she?

Her phone vibrated and her heart gave a joyful squeeze.
Saul? Is that you, my boy?

She scanned the text, and the fist around her heart tightened until she could hardly breathe.

Last night was fun. Same time tonight.

Not a question, but an order, and for all her bravado, Gloria Anguish was too frightened to say no.

28

2.48 p.m.

Saul's mother might have been thinking about her son, but her son was not thinking about her.

Grudgingly, he followed Mr Silver out of the back door and into his garden. Four or five hutches were grouped around a patch of grass and a wooden run.

'You keep animals?' Saul didn't have Mr Silver down as the pet-loving type.

'Rabbits.' He was gruff, not looking up as he fumbled with the padlock on the gate.

Saul bent down, peering behind the wire mesh. Bright eyes stared back at him. There was the sound of soft mewling from a nest box at the back of the hutch.

'There's babies in here,' he said, surprised. 'Lots of them.'

'Kits.' Mr Silver was fixing the padlock to the other side of the open gate. A car was just visible on the patch of concrete outside. 'Come on.'

'How many rabbits have you got? It must be hard to keep

them alive when it's so cold outside. Have you got an outside heater? Is there loads of blood when they're born?'

Mr Silver thought the boy asked too many questions.

'Get in the car, son.'

'Where are we going?' The teenager didn't move, sulky now at being put in his place.

Mr Silver's face glowed with an inner light, but he did not answer.

Saul meandered over to the car, not wanting to climb in, but not sure how to refuse. He watched Mr Silver tug on the padlock, making sure it was locked. He didn't know why the old man was so bothered about security. There was jack-shit to steal in his house.

The car edged out of the driveway just as the police officers rounded the bend and knocked on a house a couple of doors down.

Mr Silver let out a long, slow breath.

Saul fiddled with the ancient radio, but turned it off in disgust. He watched the suburban streets blur and fade. He should have gone to school. He was dirtying his clean sheet. Mr Darenth was going to call him in again and lecture him about 'wasting opportunities'. He wasn't sure he gave a fuck any more. He blinked away the memory of Cassidy and Mrs Cranston.

At the traffic lights, Mr Silver stopped watching the road and turned his attention to Saul.

'How's your mother?'

Saul rolled his eyes.

The older man let out a low chuckle. 'That bad?' His fingers were resting lightly on the steering wheel. He flexed them and winced.

'What did you do to your hands?' Saul couldn't stop look-ing at the twisted mess of skin and bone.

Mr Silver didn't speak until the car was moving again. 'Let's just say it was an unwelcome gift from my father.' He changed gear. 'He hit them with a hammer when I was eleven.' His shoe grazed the brake. 'Are you close to yours?'

'My dad?'

'Yes.'

'Nope.'

'But you see him?'

'Not since last year.'

'What's his name?'

'Solomon.'

'And what about your mother?'

Saul unwrapped an old piece of chewing gum he'd found in his pocket. 'She can be—'

'Difficult?'

'You could say that.' Saul savoured the burst of mint flooding his mouth.

'I don't remember much about mine, but my father, he's here.' Mr Silver made a fist and knocked it against his chest.

Saul wasn't sure if he wanted to find out where this con-versation was going. Ordinarily, he would have tried to shut it down, but there was something he was burning to ask.

'When your dad hurt you, did you ever – you know?'

'Cry? Run away?' Mr Silver indicated and the car turned left. 'Get even?'

'I guess.'

'I thought about it.' He laughed. 'I used to wonder what my life would be like without him in it. If he had some kind of accident.' He glanced at Saul. 'If I pushed him in front of a train.'

So Mr Silver had the Other Thoughts too.

'What about you?' Mr Silver's voice was hypnotic, compelling. 'Do you think about death, son?'

He shrugged. 'Dunno.'

'It takes a certain kind of courage to kill, Saul. And not all of us have that courage.' A pause. 'Do you?'

Saul bowed his head. He could not answer.

'*For love is as strong as Death.*' Mr Silver spoke quietly. 'Song of Solomon, chapter eight. And I'm sure you loved your father.'

The streets widened into a dual carriageway, the houses replaced by cheap hotels, and an expanse of grey tide that nudged up against the leaden sky.

A few hardy souls had braved the weather, the wind snatching at their umbrellas. Saul watched them, heads bowed as though in battle, from the warmth of the car.

As the coastal road morphed from the gaudy spangles of the arcades into the more subdued pleasures of Thorpe Bay, the grand houses and pastel beach huts, Saul spotted a figure in the distance, pushing a wheelchair. He sat up straight in his seat, and squinted into the afternoon.

Mr Silver followed the line of his gaze.

The car swerved wildly.

Saul's fingers dug into the sides of his seat.

'Who are you looking at?' Mr Silver's voice was controlled, but Saul noticed his hands were trembling.

'That kid in the chair.' He pointed to the woman and child on the pavement. Beyond them, the boats were blemishes on the skin of the sea's surface. 'I recognize him.'

'So do I,' said Mr Silver, soft as burnt wood ash. 'His father once did me a great wrong.'

Saul shifted around in his seat until he was looking at Mr Silver. Chewed his gum. 'What happened?'

'He stole something from me.' The air in the car seemed to thicken and darken. 'I want it back.'

Saul stretched his legs, and leaned against the headrest, the hinge of his neck tipping him backwards, exposing his throat.

The seascape was like a painting, all dark greys and whites. Blinding. Bleeding into the sky. A lone seagull was wheeling and shrieking. A few flakes of snow began to fall. The bleakness of the scene mirrored the emptiness inside the boy.

'How are you going to do that?'

Mr Silver did not answer immediately, but kept his eyes on the road, the car droning its way steadily along the coast, the weather pressing in, surrounding them.

As Saul watched the small boats thrown about in the water, a wave of tiredness washed over him. 'That boy comes into the shop,' he mused dreamily. Half asleep.

'Does he now?' said Mr Silver. Silence filled the space between them. 'Perhaps you can keep an eye on him for me.' A chuckle, to show he meant no harm. 'I know where they live, it's not far from here.' He did not allow Saul the luxury of protest. 'I can pay you, if you like. Bit of extra pocket money.'

Saul considered this. It was slightly odd, yes. But what harm could it do? All he had to do was follow the boy and his father. Make a note of his movements, perhaps. Report back to Mr Silver. He needed information. Saul needed money. A business transaction. Both would get what they wanted.

He shrugged again, a teenage habit. 'Why not?'

Mr Silver drove on, and soon the estuary was replaced by open skies and fields. Saul tried to resist, but the motion of the car and his broken night soothed him to sleep with persuasive hands.

When he awoke, the car was bumping down a narrow track towards a wooden gate with a weather-beaten sign.

SUNNYSIDE CARAVAN PARK
OPEN APRIL – OCTOBER

Mr Silver parked the car by the gate. The sea was a distant promise, flanked by a strip of sand.

'Stay here.'

Saul rubbed at the ache in his neck and stared out of the window. A few caravans were dotted around a deserted field. Mr Silver was walking towards one in the far corner, a plastic bag in his hand.

Saul watched with interest as the man climbed up a couple of steps, unlocked the door and disappeared inside. He waited a few minutes for Mr Silver to come back, but there was no sign of him. His fingers tapped against his teeth. His legs were stiff from sitting still and he wanted to stretch them. What did he usually do in these moments of in-betweenness? Play games on his mobile, text his friends. But with no phone to distract him, boredom was calling his name.

He opened the passenger door.

Outside, the cool air sharpened his senses. He could

hear birdsong. A woodlouse scuttled across a rotting log. Against the sky, a lone crow spread its wings, a blot of ink on canvas.

Saul climbed over the gate and headed in the direction of the caravan.

29

Mr Silver is always struck by the smell, however many times he visits. It's a curious scent. There's the obvious, of course. But underneath that, something darker.

Fear, perhaps.

Or acceptance.

He opens the caravan door and wonders if *it* will be today. He tries to get here as often as he can, every two or three days, but one must be careful. He does not wish to arouse suspicion. Sometimes, he thinks, it will be a blessing for them both if he arrives to find her statue-still, eyes open, soul departed.

He does not enjoy the kill.

But this afternoon she is awake, dull-eyed and pale as winter ice.

Her hair is thin, exposing white patches on her scalp. There's a smudge of dirt on her chin, a sore at the corner of her mouth. She wears the ragged look of a child who has seen too much.

Her cleft hands rest in her lap, unbound. His eyes linger on their curves.

It excites him in ways he cannot explain.

His own fingers twitch, an unsettled, restless dance. He misses his X-ray machine, with its ability to expose the secrets beneath the skin, to capture the distortions and incursions. No matter. What is done cannot be undone. And black-and-white photographs are no substitute for the purity, for the feel of unsheathed bone.

He croons to her, tries to soothe away her fears.

'Kitty cat?'

She does not answer, but this is nothing new. Her voice has grown rusty from disuse and the realization that no one – except the one she calls the Night Man – is coming. She has given up shouting for help.

A pang of sorrow.

A sense of loss he struggles to shape into words.

One hundred and four days he has let her live, some unnamed compulsion preventing him from doing what must be done. An impulse of tenderness, perhaps. A frisson of what might have been during another life not lived. A daughter. A child of his own.

But now he has Saul.

And she should be dead.

He potters about the van. Tidies the mess of her sheets. Sloshes out the bucket. He has been meaning to move some of his father's things for weeks. He opens the storage hatch to inventory what is there.

Inside, an old bank book, a rusted trowel, an ancient sack full of dust. He leans forward, intrigued by these spoils. His eye is drawn to the symbol on the sack. A skull. Crossed femurs. How fitting. He reads the small print. Acute toxicity. A smile, cruel and quick, cleaves his lips. And the creeping threads of a plan take root.

He finds some old gardening gloves hidden in a drawer, presses a cloth against his mouth and nose, and lifts the bag into his holdall. He scrubs his hands, paying attention to the valley between each finger, until the skin is pink from pressure.

He thinks of the breadcrumb trail he is leaving Fitzroy, tiny morsels, gleaming in the darkness. She is hungry. She will follow them. But she will not find him, or Clara. He is too clever for that. Instead she will find his revenge.

He thinks back to his intrusion into her flat, the glorious moment of discovery, nestled in a blue-and-white box at the back of her wardrobe. A receipt dated the end of last year. A plastic casing, a faded pinkish line in a window, confirming the presence of the pregnancy hormone hCG. He knows what this is. Another new beginning. Like the kitty cats on the ward in his other life.

Before he leaves, he loosens the cap on a bottle of water and slips in a straw. He holds it against her lips. She drinks greedily and her eyes close in a kind of ecstasy. He breaks open the foil-wrapped package of sandwiches he made for her at the cottage. She chews on the bread but does not look at him again.

On the day he took her, that lonely child wandering out of the school gates, he was going to kill her, to cut off her hands and display them in the family museum. But something about her spoke to him, stayed his knife.

Now, as the weeks click down to spring, he knows it is time to act. He can put it off no longer. Last week, when he visited at dusk, he watched a family of badgers make plodding progress across the field and noticed that the grass was freshly mown. Soon, they will come to clean the caravans and prepare the site.

He does not want to kill her, not really.

But it is easier to move a dead body than a missing, living child.

30

Saul could hear voices from inside the caravan. Or, at least, Mr Silver's voice, talking to someone. Saul strained to catch the answer, but there was only the sound of birds, and the rush of uplifting wind.

Curtains covered the dirty windows, obscuring his view. Saul considered knocking on the door, but remembered the way Mr Silver looked at him, those eyes pinning him in place like nails on a cross. He decided to wait outside.

Saul sat on the caravan steps and inspected the shiny black shoes that Mr Silver had lent him. He was used to trainers and the cheap shoes his mother bought from supermarkets, and had dismissed these at first. But they seemed expensive. Smart. He'd never owned a pair like this. Perhaps Mr Silver would let him keep them.

From inside the caravan, the low notes of Mr Silver's voice rang out again. Saul hefted an old tree stump to a spot beneath the window. It wobbled as he stood on it and tried to peer through a slit in the curtains. He wasn't a boy who poked his nose into other people's business – he had enough secrets of his own – but he couldn't help wondering who Mr Silver was talking to.

And he wasn't stupid. He'd noticed the padlock and chains. The idea of those thick metal links blocking the exit – and possibly someone inside – made his insides pitch and swoop. Fear? Or excitement? He wasn't sure.

Saul pressed both palms against the aluminium exterior, and an eye to the narrow strip of glass. The inside of the caravan was mostly in shadow, but there was enough light for him to see. He could pick out a sliver of violently patterned fabric, which he assumed was part of a mattress or a seat, and the corner of a rug or tablecloth.

On top of that was what looked like the tip of the worn ear of a stuffed toy.

Behind Saul, a flock of redwings rose into the sky, full of frantic song. Their sudden departure made him jump, and he lost his footing on the uneven log. Instinctively, he reached out to steady himself, his hands thudding against the wall of the caravan.

The sound of footsteps crossing the floor.

Saul threw himself back onto the steps, trying to regulate his breathing and to hold his body still. His hands were shaking so he sat on them. On some basic level, he knew that Mr Silver would not tolerate his prying.

The door creaked open, its sharp corner catching Saul just above the hip.

'I told you to stay in the car.' Mr Silver's voice had the edge of a razor blade.

Saul clambered to his feet, hands behind his back. His

red jacket was the only splash of colour in the monotone palette of the landscape. 'I wondered where you were.'

'Don't whine.' A whip-crack of words.

'I'm not,' muttered Saul, but the sulky set of his mouth served up a contradiction.

'What did you see?' Mr Silver took a step towards him, the anger spreading from the creases between his eyebrows to the sneering downturn of his mouth, the tense, hard line of his shoulders.

'Nothing.' Saul took a step backwards, holding up his hands to placate the older man, even though Mr Silver had not so much as lifted a finger.

A million questions were racing through his head, like exactly *who* was Mr Silver talking to, because he knew he was talking to someone, and what were they doing in this caravan in a field in the middle of nowhere, and why was he losing it when Saul hadn't done anything wrong? There *must* be someone inside. Someone Mr Silver wanted to keep hidden.

'Don't move this time.'

Mr Silver disappeared back into the van, slamming the door behind him. *Fuck you. Don't tell me what to do.* Saul was halfway to the stile, heading for the road beyond, when he stopped abruptly, turned around and jogged back towards the caravan. Tempted as he was to ignore Mr Silver's order – he *hated* being told what to do – he didn't dare risk his further wrath, not least because he had no phone and no way of getting back.

Saul crouched in the grass, his fingers trailing each vivid blade.

Carbon, nitrogen, phosphorous and oxygen. Chlorophyll and

cellulose formed during photosynthesis. Water and lignin, the main components.

He liked the sciences. Mr Darenth said he showed 'aptitude'. A beetle ran across the grass and Saul cupped it in his hand. He was thinking about introducing a new species to his jewellery box collection. These, with their iridescent wing casings of dented metal, would be perfect. He didn't think it was a Noble Chafer (Order: *Coleoptera*); it was far too early in the season. This looked like an adventurous Green Dock *(*Latin name: *Gastrophysa viridula)*. Its notched antennae twitched before it rolled up like a pea and played dead.

'What have you got there?'

Mr Silver was above him, blocking out the last of the afternoon's light. Saul hadn't heard him lock up the caravan, but he must have done, because he was standing there, jangling the car keys. There was no sign of the plastic bag he'd been carrying earlier, but there was a holdall in his hand, the faintest trace of dust on its leather.

Saul unfurled his fingers. 'I collect them,' he said. 'Insects, I mean.'

The older man delicately moved the holdall into his other hand, away from Saul and the beetle that ran circles around his palm.

A smile danced around the edges of Mr Silver's mouth. 'Then I've got something I'd very much like to show you.'

31

3.48 p.m.

He had come, just as she had known he would.
  Clara had seen him With Her Own Eyes.
  A flash of white hair at the window. A red coat.
  She hoped he had brought her a dolly.

32

3.51 p.m.

The road to Foulness Island was bracketed by salt marshes, lonely dwellings and the North Sea. It felt like the edge of the world.

Fitzroy didn't feel much like talking. The fumes from the car in front of them – and the egg sandwich she'd wolfed down at lunchtime – were making her nauseous. They passed a farm. Fields. A rundown caravan park. She'd read somewhere that this island was owned by the Ministry of Defence and used as a testing ground for military weapons. In a couple of minutes, they'd reach the security checkpoint at Landwick. Foulness only opened to visitors once a month but she'd already let them know they were on their way. She wasn't in the mood for complications.

Some days, when she sat in the courtroom and listened to a drunk driver, impassive and remorseless, who had stolen the life of a child, a father, an auntie, or when she watched a rapist laugh his way through the evidence, full of

203

cheap bravado, she thanked her lucky stars that she was here, doing a job that was worthwhile and relevant.

More often, though, she wondered what was the point in trying to scrub the world of all the filth that polluted its beauty, unable to see beyond the spreading oil slick of hatred and violence. What was the point in seeking a child who would never be found?

Her coat was unbuttoned, and she eased her hand beneath her jumper to the comforting warmth of her belly. There was an unmistakable swelling that was growing more difficult to disguise. She wasn't ready to share, not yet. She wanted to savour her secret a while longer.

And she owed it to David to tell him, although the prospect made her feel . . . what exactly? Would his mouth tighten in that way it always did when he was angry? Or perhaps he would congratulate her, smile in relief and walk away, released from the shackles of obligation and duty.

DC Storm wasn't in the mood for conversation either. Her chatter had faded into a silence that was freighted with awkwardness, lacking, as they did, the intimacy of friendship or the familiarity of everyday colleagues.

Storm cleared her throat, as if the noise would somehow loosen the tension that seemed to have sprung up between them.

'Sorry that Thornberry was being a bit of a tosser.'

It seemed she thought Fitzroy's nose had been put out of joint by the DI's refusal to engage with her. Perceptive as well as smart.

'Not your fault. At least he's speaking to one of us.'

'True, although I still think he behaved like a dick.'

Storm's phone, parked on a dash mount, began to

vibrate. She moved her eyes from the road to the screen and back again. 'Speak of the Devil and he shall appear.' Her sardonic aside was replaced by a more deferential tone.

'Detective Inspector Thornberry. How lovely to hear from you so soon.'

She flicked two fingers in the direction of the mobile before reaching for the gear stick again. Fitzroy tried not to laugh.

The speakers reduced Thornberry's full-of-himself boom to a tinny echo. The snub – by rights, he should have called *her* – was not lost on Fitzroy, who amused herself by picturing him as a Lilliputian, waving his tiny arms to attract attention, stripped of the stature of his ranking, his height.

'Where are you? Not on the way back to London, I hope?'

Storm, uncertain of how much to share, decided to keep it simple. 'No, we're still around.'

'Well, get your arses back to the beach. Pronto.' A gloating sheen to his voice. 'You can thank me when you get here.'

33

4.21 p.m.

From the moment his family had decamped to the Essex edgelands, Jakey had wanted to leave.

Whenever his father drove past the amusement park, the boy would watch the big wheel turn on its axis, slow and interminable, and he would think: *round and round until it stops.*

His childish mind wasn't able to articulate it, but if pressed, he would have said that sometimes it seemed as if he was going round and round – his illness; his parents' anxiety; Ol' Bloody Bones; illness; anxiety; Ol' Bloody Bones – with no room for anything else, no opportunity to vary the journey or the view, until one day, he, too, would simply stop.

Mrs Foyle had walked for miles, pushing him into the wind, past the arcades with their flashing lights and lonely inhabitants, who had nowhere else to go on a winter's afternoon.

Occasionally, she would stop to tuck in his blanket, to

whisper how much she missed Clara and what a treat it was to take him out for the afternoon.

But there was no sign of Ol' Bloody Bones.

None at all.

'Where shall we go?' she had eventually asked him, when it seemed like they had walked for hours.

And they had found themselves outside the amusement park with its over-bright music and its splashy colours and the roar of its rides, and Jakey had been drawn in, a moth to a dangerous, unforgiving flame.

The rollercoaster operator said no.

And he was just the first.

There was no malice, no unkindness, but they were firm.

'I'm so sorry, but it's our health and safety policy. I do hope you understand.'

A knot of small boys, gathered by the ticket booth, were staring at him. The mother carried a Happy Birthday balloon. In one fluid sweep, the boys ran, whooping and laughing, towards the entrance of the ride that had turned Jakey away, and the burn in his chest had become so hot, so intense, that he had to fight his hardest fight to keep the tears inside.

Mrs Foyle had bought him candy-floss on a stick.

But he had struggled to keep his grip on it, and the spun sugar stuck in his teeth, and then Mrs Foyle had looked at her watch and given a little gasp, and said it was time to go.

And Jakey hadn't been on a single ride.

Not one.

Never had he felt so insignificant.

34

4.34 p.m.

The car journey took them back along the coast. Past the grand waterside houses of Thorpe Bay and its beach huts lined up like colourful building blocks, along Southend seafront with its wooden pier that stretched for miles into empty sky. Saul, distracted, kept his eyes on the horizon. For the first time in ages, he wanted to go home.

'Will you drop me at the flat?'

Mr Silver did not remove his eyes from the road.

'Is there something you need, Saul?'

Saul didn't answer. He didn't have to explain himself.

Mr Silver waited for a moment. 'As you wish.'

There was a risk the police might be waiting for him, but Saul only planned to stay long enough to pick up a couple of things and then he'd be gone. Away from Mr Silver, his uncomfortable questions, his strange little secrets. Away from Mr Darenth. Away from his mother, and from Cassidy and her stupid, stupid family.

Along the coast road, in the shadow of darkening skies,

the boy in the wheelchair and the woman were making their way back, hurrying along the length of Marine Parade, towards Eastern Esplanade. Mr Silver saw them before Saul did.

Without speaking, Mr Silver pulled sharply across the pedestrianized zone, the hazard lights on his car pulsing in time with his heart.

'It's that boy again.' He tried to hide the need in his voice. 'Go and speak to him. Find out where's he going.' A beat, filled with impatience. 'Go on.'

Saul slid, squirming, down the passenger seat. 'I can't just go up to him.'

Mr Silver opened his wallet, withdrew a bundle of notes and held them up in front of Saul.

'You'll think of something. Tell him the shop's getting puppies.' A sudden, wolfish grin. 'He loves puppies.'

It was darker now, and there was a kind of rawness in the air that scraped at exposed skin. Saul dug his hands into his pockets.

Amy Foyle had stopped pushing the wheelchair to check her phone. Saul sauntered up. Her eyes met his, but he did not know her name and all he would later remember was her guilty, harried look.

'Hey,' said Saul, and he knocked back his red hood, so the boy could see his white-blond hair.

'You're from the pet shop,' he said. 'How's that naughty birdie?'

'It said a bad word to a customer. She dropped her fish food all over the floor and stormed out. Made a terrible mess.'

The boy – Jakey, his name was – giggled. 'I want to visit him again.'

'We don't know if it's a him. Could be a her.'

'What?'

'Mynah birds are monomorphic, which means both sexes look the same. We'll only know it's a girl if it lays an egg.'

The boy's face lit up like a candle.

'I'll ask my daddy if we can come in at the weekend.'

'We might be getting some puppies soon,' said Saul, inspecting the dirt beneath his nails.

The boy's face clouded briefly, as if someone had blown out the flame, but he rallied. Saul was reminded of those birthday candles that magically relit themselves.

'I love puppies,' said Jakey, almost too quietly for him to hear.

'Me too,' said Saul.

A shy look. 'Did you get the photo?'

'I did. Cheers for that.'

'She's called Scooby. You could help me take her for a walk one day. If you want.'

Saul looked at him, surprised. 'Really?'

'Yeah, that would be epic.' Saul suppressed a smile. The boy spoke again. 'What's your name?'

'Saul. And you're Jakey.'

The boy's cheeks pinked. 'You remembered.'

'So where have you been today?'

'The amusement park.' Jakey's face collapsed. 'But it was too busy. There were queues everywhere. And I wasn't allowed on the rides 'cos of my stupid body.' His words were shot through with venom, but his eyes were full of tears.

'The one up the road?' Saul pointed in the direction they'd just come.

Jakey grunted a miserable confirmation.

'My friend Dan works there. Perhaps I can arrange a VIP tour?'

'What does VIP mean?'

'Very Important Person.'

The boy's face brightened, as if someone had shone a torch on him. 'Can you give Saul my daddy's number? So we can all go together.'

Amy Foyle bit her lip.

'I'm not sure about that, Jakey. I can't just be handing out your dad's phone number.'

'He won't mind,' said the boy. 'I know he won't. Please. Pleeeeaaaasse.'

His lower lip stuck out. Amy bit her own lip again, torn. For the second time that afternoon, Jakey was about to cry.

She checked her watch again, and rocked slightly on the spot in that way that some adults have when they're anxious to leave. Sighing, she reached into her pocket and pulled out Erdman's scribbled number. 'Don't let the boy down,' she murmured, pushing the scrap of paper into his hand.

Saul crouched next to Jakey's wheelchair until he was level with the boy. 'I'll call your dad, I promise.'

The young boy beamed.

'It's getting late, Jakey,' said Amy. 'Your mother will be wondering where you are.' She gripped the wheelchair's handles and started to push.

'See you later,' said Saul.

'Alligator,' said Jakey, grinning. 'Bye.'

Saul watched them disappear into the dusk, a single thought turning over in his mind.

Ding ding. Round one to me.

Back in the car, Saul found his courage. Now that he'd told Mr Silver he wanted to go home, now that he'd done as Mr Silver had asked and spoken to the boy, he found it within himself to voice the question that had been scorching a hole inside him since they'd left the field.

'Was there someone in that caravan?'

As soon as he had let the words fly, Saul's stomach went into freefall, knowing he was speaking out of turn. It was oddly thrilling, like looking down through a bridge made of glass. Part of him was curious, though. More curious than he cared to admit.

Almost excited.

His fingers found the broken doll, bent its pipe-cleaner arm.

But Mr Silver did not rise to the bait.

'All in good time, son,' he said. 'All in good time.'

35

Mr Silver prides himself on being a man of his word. But he does not take the boy back to his mother. Instead he drives him through the Old Town, the cobbles causing the car's suspension to groan and jolt with effort.

'I thought you were taking me home.'

Mr Silver's voice is cool. 'I will. But I thought you would like to collect your things first.'

Something about the way he speaks causes Saul to scratch the hollow at the base of his skull, as if it is crawling with a thousand tiny ants.

'OK,' he mutters, his fingers raking the skin beneath the feathered ends of his hair. 'Cheers.'

Inside the cottage, the evening shadows are painting the rooms with brushstrokes of grey. The boy casts around for his rucksack, gathers up a faded sweatshirt and a dirty pair of socks.

'I'm ready,' he says. 'Dunno where my trainers are. Or

my phone. Can you drop them off if you find them?' He spies a school book on the nest of tables. 'And I'll keep you posted about that kid and his father.'

Mr Silver accepts now that he was foolish to expect Saul to become his overnight. That perhaps he will take a little more persuasion.

'I want to show you something before you go, remember?'

He can tell that Saul is itching to leave by the way his leg jigs with an energy too big to contain within his body. He wants the boy to *want* to stay, but sees that it's too soon. That he has tried to rush him.

But there are other ways and other means.

Saul dumps his rucksack on the sitting-room floor, and offers Mr Silver an expectant look. Mr Silver offers a mock bow in return and obliges by leading him up the stairs. He is still carrying his leather holdall, and its handles cut into his palms.

Three doors on the landing. Two are closed, but one is an arm's-width ajar. Mr Silver indicates this opening to Saul, who pushes against the wood and enters. The room is warm and half shrouded in darkness. A canvas is propped up by the door. There is a mirror on the wall. A faint clicking sound, and the spongy smell of raw meat.

Saul gives the tiniest of gasps, so quiet that Mr Silver almost misses it. The boy's surprise is gratifying.

On vast sheets of plywood balanced across a chest of drawers and an old dressing table rest several perspex tanks. Saul takes a tentative step forward, and another, until he reaches the nearest one. His fingertips press into the surface, leaving behind a greasy confirmation of his presence.

He bends forward slightly, peers into the dim caverns that traverse the unseen divide between life and death.

Saul blinks once or twice, and squints, as if he has made a mistake, and when he looks again, the tableau in front of him will be nothing more than a figment of his imagination.

He watches for a few seconds, and Mr Silver watches him.

This is a test, of sorts. His reaction now will determine his future.

Hundreds of beetles are swarming across a milky grey surface of bone and decaying matter, stripping it down to nothing.

Several of these shiny black dots are clustered around an empty eye cavity.

Saul's face is a changing landscape of emotion. Curiosity, a scientist's eye. Realization. Disbelief.

And something else.

Disgust, he thinks.

The boy takes a stumbling step backwards, his voice high and tight.

'Is that a human—'

'Yes,' says the Bone Collector, and hits him on the back of the head with the wooden haft of a claw hammer.

36

When Fitzroy and Storm arrived back at the beach, the police cordon had widened considerably and was now blocking all public access.

'Talk about shutting the stable door after the horse has bolted,' muttered Storm. She had a point. Several journalists, dog-walkers and Christ knows who else had already trampled over any potential evidence. Coupled with the extreme conditions of such an environment, she didn't reckon their chances.

Behind the tape, Fitzroy could see several forensic officers on their knees, spread out in distinctive spokes, painstakingly sifting through the sand in what she recognized as a wheel search formation. Several small areas at the high-tide mark were roped off and protected by the type of unmarked cardboard boxes favoured by those collecting evidence. Spotlights had been set up at strategic points around the beach as sunset was only half an hour away.

In the distance, she saw DI Thornberry clock them and

start jogging in their direction. It was a far bigger team than Fitzroy had seen in a long while. Surely this couldn't be for that missing woman. Something significant had changed.

She didn't have to wait long to find out what. DI Thornberry was barrelling towards them, his eagerness evident in each sweaty pore on his forehead.

'Wish me luck,' said Storm, sotto voce.

'That was quick.' His hands slid down his knees as he bent to catch his breath. When he looked up, his gaze was fixed on the detective constable, barely glancing Fitzroy's way. She wondered whether getting sacked for gross misconduct would be worth the satisfaction of kicking him in the bollocks.

'We don't mess around.' Fitzroy's smile was saccharine sweet.

Thornberry took out his handkerchief – the scrap of fabric had a faded, yellowing look – and mopped his forehead. A sharp gust of air blew in from the estuary, and Fitzroy clamped her arms to her sides to preserve body heat. Either Thornberry was very unfit or there was something wrong with his endocrine system. The suggestion that he might suffer from excessive sweating gave Fitzroy a tweak of joy.

But her sense of *schadenfreude* was banished by the smug expression on Thornberry's face. He looked like he was privy to a huge secret – but wasn't prepared to share it yet.

'I can't do this justice with words. You'll have to see for yourselves.'

At the cordon, the women avoided the growing swell of reporters, slipped on the plastic shoe protectors procured from the same young constable they'd met earlier that afternoon, and trooped after Thornberry.

Across the sand.

Up the curving rise of the beach.

'There was a whole bunch of school children here earlier,' said Fitzroy. 'That's going to have caused some serious contamination of the scene.'

'Depends on which way you look at it.' Thornberry seemed almost gleeful. 'Without the kids, we might never have discovered them.'

'Discovered what?'

Thornberry beckoned them to follow and walked over to the nearest box. Forensics often used white tents to protect evidence, but Fitzroy, looking out across a forest of cardboard covering a surface area of roughly half a football pitch, could see why that hadn't been feasible, why they had opted for boxes instead. They'd better work quickly, though. Before this evening's incoming tide washed more of the evidence away.

Thornberry slipped on some gloves and lifted up the first, dampening cardboard square and Fitzroy was back in that Blackheath sweet shop, back to those early, adrenaline-fuelled days and nights when following the breadcrumb trail to Clara Foyle was like knocking down the door of a gingerbread house to find the witch had snatched up her prisoners and fled.

Fitzroy swallowed five or six times, dragging in one breath, then another and another. The world seemed to blur at the edges and she experienced a vague tingling around her mouth. She forced herself to slow down, to let the air slide out as well as in, but the shock of what she was seeing made it difficult to focus.

Made it difficult to think of anything at all except a missing girl with dimples.

Nestled in the darkened sand, inside a shoebox and lying on its side, was something that Fitzroy had prayed she would never have to see again.

The delicate bones of a rabbit skeleton stripped of its flesh.

Connective tissues still intact.

A macabre puppet on a string.

A faint aroma of rotting flesh curled its way into her nostrils, and she lifted her eyes to the sweep of sky, its burning sphere half extinguished by the horizon's edge, the clouds smoky with approaching night.

She blinked, forced herself to look once more.

The box inside a box forced an image of Russian dolls.

Except in place of lacquered wood and painted smiles, it was dead children, growing smaller and smaller until they were too far from reach.

'How did you find them?'

'That's what I was trying to tell you. Those school kids from earlier, they were on an outing. They go to a "beach" school, something like that. Anyway, it means regular trips down here' – he spread out the palms of his hands to catch the spits of rain – 'whatever the weather. Apparently they were digging deep holes, to see whose filled up with water first.'

'And they found all these?'

'They found the first three, all within a couple of feet of

each other. Buried in the sand. Up here, on the edge of the high-tide line. Then we got involved.'

'Are they all . . . ?' She indicated the dozen or so cardboard boxes dotted across the beach.

Thornberry nodded, his face grave.

'Yup, all the same.' He paused. 'So far.'

'Do you have any idea how long they've been here?'

His shoulders rose and fell. 'We'll run some tests, but we can't be sure. One of the lads managed to get hold of a field specialist in oceanography. It's feasible they could have been here for at least twelve hours. Or more, apparently.' He mopped his forehead again. 'Sand moves, of course it does, but levels of sand stay pretty stable for longish periods of time, providing there hasn't been a storm.'

'And there hasn't been a storm?'

'Not since Sunday night. There was some pretty impressive thunder and lightning then. Because they were hidden just above the high-tide mark, she says it's possible the saltwater's barely touched them, just enough to dampen them a little.'

So it was likely the skeletons had been buried at some point in the last couple of days. But there had been no guarantees that anyone would dig beneath the sand and unearth them.

She bit her lip.

Unless the missing woman's clothes had been deliberately left on the beach. A marker, of sorts. And he had meant the bones to be found during the search for Sunday Cranston.

Fitzroy crouched down, her eyes following the familiar contours of the mammal's vertebrae, all the way down to its back legs. There it was. Strapped around the bone. A messenger tube of the type favoured by carrier pigeons. And Brian Howley.

Her senses sharpened, the weariness from her broken night's sleep forgotten. The beach, with its promise of summer and ice-cream and laughter, was now awash with an undercurrent of death.

'Have you looked inside?'

Thornberry slipped a hand inside his pocket and produced a clutch of plastic evidence bags. Each had been carefully sealed and labelled.

She flipped the first one over to more easily read the scrap of paper through the bag's transparent side. She recognized his handwriting almost immediately, and although the edges of the ink had begun to bleed from the hours spent in damp sand, the thick black pen was still legible, each waterproofed word marked into the scrap of paper.

Nomen mihi Legio est, quia multi sumus

She didn't know what that meant. The messages he'd left before had been written in English and taken from the Bible, or from the notes of John Hunter, the physician who had founded the Hunterian museum that had so captivated Howley. If she wasn't mistaken, this looked like Latin.

Fitzroy plucked a second evidence bag from Thornberry's willing hand.

Nomen mihi Legio est, quia multi sumus

A third.

Nomen mihi Legio est, quia multi sumus

A fourth.

Nomen mihi Legio est, quia multi sumus

She muttered a prayer before reading the fifth.

Nomen mihi Legio est, quia multi sumus

'Do you have any idea what it means?'

'Cover the skeletons,' Thornberry shouted at forensics and pointed to the darkening sky. Above their heads, the gulls, heading off to roost but distracted by the litter discarded by the waiting reporters, circled and screeched out their approval.

'I do.' Storm had been quiet until that moment, observing the scene unfolding in front of her, but now she stepped forward. 'At least, I think I do.'

Thank Christ for that. Fitzroy prayed she was telling the truth because this was big. Fucking huge. A beach full of identical rabbit skeletons – fourteen, at the last count – all bearing the same message.

Brian Howley hadn't just stepped up a gear, he was driving a whole fucking convoy.

'*I am Legion, for we are many.*'

Storm's voice was low but clear. It cut through the sound of the waves and the relentless cries of that sky army of scavengers. It cut through the shouted exchanges of the forensic team.

It cut through Fitzroy, into the layers of her skin – epidermis; dermis; the fat and connective tissues – until it reached her arteries, which, fuelled by a jolt from her adrenal glands, pumped this revelation around her body in startled bursts.

Storm was still speaking. 'It's from the New Testament. The Gospel of Mark. Chapter five, verse nine.'

'The Bible again.' Fitzroy's nails bit deep into the fleshy bulb of her thumb.

'One and the same.'

222

'Are you sure?'

'Afraid so. I'm the product of a religious upbringing.' Storm smiled but there was shadow in it. Fitzroy wanted to dig deeper, but the words dried on her lips because the younger officer was speaking again.

'*And no man could bind him, no, not with chains . . .*' Storm let her gaze drift across the sea. When she continued, it was with the mechanical tonelessness of an old-fashioned pull-string talking doll.

'*Now there was there nigh unto the mountains a great herd of swine feeding.*

'*And all the devils besought him, saying, "Send us into the swine, that we may enter into them".*

'*And forthwith Jesus gave them leave. And the unclean spirits went out, and entered into the swine: and the herd ran violently down a steep place into the sea, they were about two thousand; and were choked in the sea.*'

Those ancient words, long written down, chilled Fitzroy because she knew there was a message hidden in them somewhere, infused in the ink.

'Thoughts?'

'He's a fucking nutter.' She had forgotten about Thornberry, who was dabbing at his forehead again.

'Thanks for your perceptive insights, Detective Inspector.'

He had the grace to look sheepish, tucked his handkerchief into his pocket and held up his palms in what she suspected was a rare gesture of submission. 'Just a joke.'

'Legion is a reference to the Devil, to evil spirits,' said Storm. 'Bit of a cliché, really.'

Fitzroy, who was intimate with every stomach-crawling

word of the violence meted out by Howley and documented in his case file, did not think it a cliché at all. She thought it a fitting comparison.

'So who's he referring to? Himself? The ghosts of his twisted-as-shit family?' Clearly Thornberry had been doing a spot of his own research.

Fitzroy didn't think so.

For we are many.

'Perhaps he means these skeletons?' Her hand made a sweeping arc across the beach. A forensic officer was walking briskly towards them, and they stopped to watch his progress. When he reached them a couple of minutes later, he touched Thornberry's sleeve, and the men huddled together a little way away.

Storm pulled an apple from her bag and offered it to Fitzroy, who shook her head. Storm took a large bite. 'From what I remember, didn't he leave these little calling cards *after* he'd abducted his victims?'

'What are you saying? That he's kidnapped fourteen people with bone deformities and no one's noticed?'

'Of course not.' A troubled look from Storm. 'But perhaps these are a nod to his undiscovered victims, probably going back years.'

'Or it's a warning,' said Fitzroy. 'He's letting us know exactly what he's planning – mass bloodshed.'

Howley had a fondness for elaborate gestures, she knew that. The kidney. The quotations. And now this disturbing collection of rabbit skeletons. Her knowledge nudged at her now, reminding her that there was always method in his depravity, she just had to puzzle it out.

But why risk this? First the X-ray, then Clara's uniform,

and the crab claw that smelled of saltwater and death. It was almost as if he wanted to be found.

Or perhaps he wanted to frighten her. Well, he'd succeeded in that.

She studied the scraps of paper in the evidence bags again, leafing through each one in turn. After a minute or so, Fitzroy squinted and pulled one of the bags closer to her face.

The words jumped at her.

Nomen mihi Legio est, quia multi sumus

It wasn't her imagination. The s *was* heavier, scratched into the paper.

But why?

Ting.

S

For Sunday Cranston.

A swell of nausea which she fought to keep down. Water. She needed water. She pulled an almost-empty bottle from her pocket, the cheap plastic puckering and sucking in on itself as she drank.

'Are you OK?' A feathery network of lines appeared on Storm's forehead, cracks in her otherwise perfect exterior.

Fitzroy gave one of those brisk sorts of nod that indicated she did not want to be the focus of anyone's attention.

But this was her fault. Another girl was dead because Howley had slipped through their fingers.

A second wave of nausea hit, harder than the first. Fitzroy felt around in her pocket for the crackers she had taken to carrying everywhere, and broke off a corner. It tasted of guilt and cardboard. She did not look up at Storm, but turned her attention back to the evidence bags, thumbing through each one.

Nothing.

No more letters.

No more clues.

Just words.

'Toni,' she said. 'Run through that parable again, the bit about the swine.'

'*And the unclean spirits went out, and entered into the swine: and the herd ran violently down a steep place into the sea, they were about two thousand; and were choked in the sea.*'

Swines.

Ting.

Pigs.

Ting.

Police.

'DS Fitzroy?'

Thornberry was by her side, so close she could taste the burnt-coffee residue of tobacco on his breath. As she met his eyes, several tiny beads of sweat popped on his forehead, but he didn't wipe them away.

'We've found another skeleton.' He sounded uneasy this time, no wisecracks, no swearing. 'You'd better take a look.'

For the third time that day, Fitzroy and Storm followed Thornberry across the beach, the heels of their shoes cutting horseshoes into the sand. Horseshoes were supposed to be lucky, weren't they? Well, Fitzroy wasn't checking her lottery numbers yet.

'It's here,' the white suit said, and lifted the cardboard box.

At first, she couldn't quite work out what she was looking

at. Rabbit bones, yes. The distinctive vertebral column. The bony plate of the scapula. The notched symmetry of the pelvic girdle.

But there was something else.

Tucked into the gap between the rabbit's ribcage and its pubis.

Fitzroy dropped to her knees.

A skeleton in miniature.

A baby rabbit.

Instinctively, her hands fluttered to her stomach.

Thornberry was by her side, fumbling his way into a pair of gloves. He carefully removed the messenger tube attached to the larger rabbit's tibia, unscrolled the square of paper.

Nomen mihi Legio est, quia multi sumus

The 'e's had been been heavily scored into the paper, for emphasis.

E

For Elizabeth or Emily or Eva or Erin.

E

For Emma or Elsie or Esther or Elaine.

E

For Etta.

37

When Saul opened his eyes, he was looking sideways at a night sky the colour of bluebottles.

His head pulsed with a low-level buzzing, convincing him, for a fraction of time, that his skull was full of trapped flies. A bead of cold water slid down his neck.

Mr Silver was sitting in a hard-backed chair next to the sofa that Saul was sprawled across. He held up a dripping bag of peas.

'Put this on it,' he said. 'It will make you feel better.'

Saul's fingers closed around the bag and he swung his legs over the edge of the worn cushion until he was sitting up. The room was a giddying whirl of movement. Gingerly, he did as Mr Silver instructed, relishing the cooling pressure on the back of his head.

'What time is it?'

'Nearly six.' A pause. 'You've been out for a while.'

Saul started to nod but a sickening sort of pain rolled through his skull so he stopped and kept very still.

'What happened?'

'Don't you remember?'

Saul screwed up his eyes. Did he remember? He tried to recreate the events of earlier that day, but the buzzing in his head was getting louder. He thought he might be sick.

'I—'

'The mirror, son. Came right off the wall and slammed into the back of your head. You went down like a ninepin.'

Saul touched his fingertips to the swelling on the base of his skull and winced. He remembered an unexpected blow, the explosion of pain pitching him forward, the feel of perspex against his cheek, the scattering of black specks.

'The beetles—'

'—are safe,' finished Mr Silver. 'You nudged the tank when you fell, but the lid was on securely.' He grinned, pointing to the spider-web cracking in the mirror, now propped against the wall. 'And it didn't break, which means no old wives' tales for you to worry about.'

He took the bag of peas from Saul's unresisting hand. 'On reflection, I think it's best you stay here tonight.'

'Actually, I'd like to go home.'

'Will your mother be there?'

Saul shrugged, triggering another dizzying carousel.

'Exactly,' said Mr Silver. 'You need someone to keep an eye on you.'

'But—'

'Saul. Saul, Saul, Saul. Sometimes we have to do things we don't necessarily want to. For the *greater good*.'

Mr Silver turned his back on the teenager, signalling that their conversation, for the moment, at least, had come to an end.

Saul sank back into the settee. Truth be told, he felt awful. Sick and dizzy. And he didn't want to stay here, especially not now. He could get up and walk out. But he did not wish to test Mr Silver's limits, not tonight. Physically, he was not up to it. Mr Silver was not a man to be messed with and Saul was not prepared to take a risk on which direction the pendulum of his temper would swing.

And something was tugging at him, demanding answers. In spite of everything, he was curious to know who was in that caravan in that field in the middle of nowhere, and he wanted to know why Mr Silver was so interested in that boy.

If Mr Silver was so intent on keeping him here, perhaps he could put this time to good use. Did Mr Silver think Saul hadn't noticed the way he called him 'son' with that peculiar expression on his face?

Mr Silver walked back into the room, a mug of soup in hand. He set it down on the low table, which still held the savage shards of the broken fruit bowl.

'Drink this, son.'

'Thanks, *Pops*,' said Saul lightly.

Mr Silver stilled for a moment and turned back towards the kitchen but not before Saul caught a smile jerking the contours of his face.

When he came back, he was carrying a platter of cheese. He settled in the armchair opposite Saul, shaved off a corner with his knife.

'Do you believe in doing something for the greater good, Saul?'

'S'pose so.'

'But do your actions live up to your ambitions?'

Saul took a mouthful of soup, shrugged.

'Take, for example, a family. The father is a workaholic, the mother, more interested in herself than her disabled child. The child is a lost soul, in need of – but lacking – parental love and attention. What then, Saul?'

'Poor kid.'

Mr Silver clapped his hands together. 'Exactly. *Poor kid*. And so the best, the kindest, course of action would be to remove that child from its parents, into the care of someone who will cherish it. Prize it above all else. Yes?'

'I guess.'

'You guess, Saul?' His voice was a taunt. 'Guessing doesn't come into it. It takes precision and planning. There will always be those who oppose you. Who object to the execution of difficult decisions. But one must have the courage of one's convictions, don't you think?'

Mr Silver's face was aflame with the joy of his own certainties.

'I want you to help me, Saul.' He leaned towards him, his fingertips idly tracing the point of the knife. 'Will you help me?'

Saul was a smart boy. That's why he was at grammar school. That's why he didn't engage in loose and dangerous chatter with his friends. That's why he had survived for so long in the toxic environment of his home.

He reviewed what he knew.

A locked caravan.

A collection of beetles.

A human skull.

A vicious temper.

A mysterious bone-twisted child.

A lonely old man looking for a human connection.

He should be frightened. Fuckssake, he *was* frightened. But he was certain now that Mr Silver had a secret and he wanted to find out what it was. His fingers grazed the worry doll's crooked limbs.

'Yes, sir,' he said. 'I'd be honoured.'

He didn't have to wait long. When Mr Silver re-entered the room with Saul's missing phone in his hand, and a plan on his lips, the boy recognized what he had to do. It was simple, said Mr Silver. Failsafe. Saul was to call the Frith family and persuade them to meet him. Then he would hand his phone back to Mr Silver. For safekeeping, nothing more. To make sure he did not lose it down the back of the sofa again. And Mr Silver would take care of the rest.

A good plan, agreed Saul, his fingers clenching around the silver casing of his mobile.

But first, a photograph.

Together.

Like father and son.

To mark this new beginning.

38

'Turn the lights off when you leave, Erd.'

Erdman Frith grunted his acknowledgement, but didn't look up. He'd spent ages scouring the *Gazette*'s archives, hoping to stumble across some kind of exclusive that would restore the news editor's good faith. He was in the shit for missing the skeletons on the beach. Or rather, he was in the shit because the Press Association's story had dropped on the wires first, before he'd had a chance to phone in this hugely significant development to the newsdesk.

'It makes us all look a bunch of useless pricks, mate,' Arthur Furniss, his news editor, had said, a tad wearily for Erdman's liking. 'Don't do it again.'

But missing the biggest story to hit Essex for years was the least of Erdman's worries.

As soon as he had heard the whispers amongst the waiting reporters, felt the heat of their sidelong glances, his mouth had gone dry and he'd abandoned Haskell and driven home to his family, following the coast road back to Thorpe Bay.

On the way, he'd called Lilith and Mrs Foyle, breaking his own rule about phones and cars, but neither of them had replied. Detective Sergeant Etta Fitzroy wasn't answering either, forcing him to endure the tinny drone of her voicemail over and over again.

When he'd finally got through to the station in Lewisham, to ask whether he should just take his family and run, they'd promised to get someone to call him back.

He was still waiting.

He'd skidded into the drive, the car's tyres crunching on the gravel, and he'd sprinted up the steps, desperate to see for himself that his family was safe.

Lilith's side of the bed was empty but the curtains were still closed. Lego pieces were scattered across Jakey's bedroom floor. He had cried out their names, *Lilith, Jakey,* echoing through the house, but they did not answer.

He'd half thrown himself down the stairs, still calling, and the rise and fall of his voice was a lament.

By the time he had noticed Jakey's wheelchair was gone, he'd searched every room in the house. An hour, he'd waited, fingers twitching, torn in two.

And then he had forced himself to calm down.

Chill out, dude. Jakey's fine. Mrs Foyle's with him. Or Lilith. They've gone to the shops. The signal's shit. Or they're in a noisy cafe. No one's going to take him. Them. He ignored the voice that taunted him. *Except Brian Howley.*

With no idea what else to do, he had driven back to the office.

And he was still here.

Working his arse off.

Of course, Erdman knew how to scramble his way to the top of the greasy pole. To file the mother of all splashes. To enjoy the rare and elusive glory of a 'World Exclusive' story, followed up by every publication across the globe. Christ knows, Furniss had dropped enough hints. But there was no way he was going to exploit his family like that. If he'd wanted to write a first-person piece for a newspaper about Jakey's abduction, he'd have done it months ago, when the letters were piling up on their doormat and their answer-phone had stopped recording messages because it had run out of space. When journalists from every national and international newspaper and every television network had offered the Friths thousands of pounds, imploring them to *share their story*.

No fucking way.

So it was back to the hard grind. To find a way in. And he had the advantage – if he could call it that – of insider knowledge and a burning desire for justice for his son. He would use what he knew.

He scrolled through the events of the day but kept coming back to that haunted, pinched face.

Saul.

Only a first name, but it was a start.

Methodically, Erdman worked through the newspaper's archives, typing in each combination of words in the hope of finding some link, some connection.

'Saul' and 'Sunday Cranston'.

'Saul' and 'Cranston'.

'Saul' and 'conviction'.

He repeated the process with countless combinations.

Nothing.

But then.

'Saul' and 'Leigh-on-Sea'.

Bingo. Three matches.

Erdman called up the first story. It was only three paragraphs.

Thursday, 28 June 2012, Evening Gazette, Essex, England
Type: Article Word matches: 4 Page: 10 Tags: None
Labourer Solomon Anguish has been reported missing after failing to turn up for work.

The married father-of-one, from Leigh-on-Sea, has not been seen since last Sunday.

Anguish, 33, who has been working on a development of flats along Southend seafront, is understood to have a teenage son, Saul.

A statement from property company Waterside Homes said: 'Solomon is a valued contractor. We hope he turns up safe and well.'

Next to the story was a thumbnail image of a man and a boy, taken from Facebook or some other social media site. Erdman compared it to the photograph that Haskell had printed off and left on his desk. The boy's white-blond hair was slightly shorter but he was unmistakable. The connection in his synapses was finally made. The boy from the pet shop. His hunch had been correct. And now Erdman had a surname to work with too.

Saul Anguish.

The other two articles were later versions of the same news story, including an appeal for information from Essex

Police, and speculation about a grudge over money. Erdman also discovered that the boy's father, Solomon, had a previous conviction for assault.

Next, he ran Saul's full name through the database of news stories.

Again, a couple of useful bits of information. Like how he'd scored the highest mark in the county for his 11-plus exam.

And an interview with his outraged mother about how he'd been asked to leave one primary school due to 'behavioural issues'.

And then Erdman's phone began to ring.

39

Journalists called it the Death Knock. That raising of a hand to press the doorbell or rattle the letterbox of a family made vulnerable by grief. Armed with platitudes and a misguided hope – most kept their notebooks hidden in their bags – they would hover on the step, using well-chosen words to persuade and cajole until that crack in the doorway widened into an invitation.

That golden ticket of an interview.

A clutch of childhood photographs.

An exclusive to beat about the heads of their rivals.

Fitzroy did not care for exclusives, nor did she have a name for this joyless aspect of her job, the first visit to a newly bereaved family. But if she were pushed, she would christen it The Hours After, that unending corridor of disbelief and confusion, where time seemed to unfurl itself into individual, pain-filled beats.

The Cranston house was a vision of freshly cleaned

238

brickwork and smart shutters; a middle-class bastion of respectability.

The family had been informed forty-five minutes earlier about the significance of the rabbit skeletons on Leigh beach. The development regarding the letter S – Sunday's initial – being etched into the message had been deliberately withheld from the media.

Storm touched Fitzroy's sleeve. 'Shall I do the talking or will you?'

Her colleague had a lump of couscous in her hair. An hour ago they'd agreed to stop for a brief meal break. Fitzroy had watched in surprise – and envy – as Storm had pulled from her bag a Tupperware box, a sachet of dressing and a fork. She was more used to DC Alun Chambers and burgers from the van on Blackheath Common.

'I prefer to bring my own food,' Storm had said.

Fitzroy's bag of Quavers had lost their appeal.

'You. I'd like to observe the family,' she said. She pointed to Storm's hair. 'But you might want to get rid of that first.'

Helen Cranston was crying as she opened the door. When she saw the police officers, she dabbed at her eyes with a lace-edged hankie, her fingers plucking at the intricate stitching which had begun to unravel, hanging in lonely threads.

'I'm so sorry,' said Storm, and she squeezed Mrs Cranston's restless hand.

'Thank you,' whispered Mrs Cranston, the importance of manners not forgotten, even as death intruded, an impolite and unwelcome guest. In her head, Fitzroy urged Storm to press on. It sounded cruel, but there was mileage in vulnerability, when close-to-the-surface emotion allowed the cracks to show.

'We're from the Metropolitan Police,' said Storm, who remained holding the older woman's hand. 'We'd like to talk to you about Sunday, if that's OK.'

Mrs Cranston was still crying but she didn't make a sound. It was as though someone had once told her that it was fine to feel pain, as long as she did so quietly.

A small man with a bald head and black shirt tucked into his jeans appeared in the hallway. He put an arm around Mrs Cranston, and steered her into the kitchen. Her hand, limp and yielding, slid from Storm's.

The kitchen was one of those open-plan affairs, all shiny surfaces and bi-folding doors that opened into a small, but no doubt perfectly kept, garden.

Fitzroy caught Storm's eye, and gave an almost imperceptible nod. She wanted to begin now, while Mrs Cranston was spongy with emotion, and before their questions hardened into flinty tools, excavating the truth.

'Has Sunday ever mentioned a man called Brian Howley?'

Mrs Cranston's face turned the colour of rancid milk.

'No, no, no.' She breathed out the denial, as if each repetition of that word would build a fortress against a thousand kind of horrors. The whole country and beyond knew that name, as scored into the public consciousness as Ian Brady or Peter Sutcliffe. 'No.'

'Are you absolutely sure?' Storm drew a thin plastic folder from her bag and pushed it across the granite work surface towards Mrs Cranston. It glided gently to a stop in front of her.

Mrs Cranston took in the image of his dark eyes and the brutal edges of his cheekbones.

'No.' She was firmer this time, shaking her head. 'I've never seen this man before. And I'm sure Sunday hasn't, didn't' – she faltered, stumbling over tenses – 'either.'

The kitchen door opened and a teenage girl slouched in. She was wearing a T-shirt and a pair of faded jeans, but she shimmered with youth, all dewy skin and clear eyes. When she saw the room was full of faces she didn't recognize, she took an uncertain step backwards.

'These are police officers, Cassidy,' explained Mr Cranston, speaking for the first time. His voice was surprisingly deep for a man of such reduced stature.

Cassidy mumbled something – Fitzroy didn't catch what it was – and turned to leave.

'Miss Cranston,' she said. 'Did your sister ever mention a boyfriend?'

'It's *Cassidy's* boyfriend you should be looking at.'

'Mum.' A mix of embarrassment and outrage.

'His name is Saul Anguish,' said Helen. 'Write that down.'

Fitzroy did as she suggested.

'And Sunday?' said Storm. 'Was she seeing someone?'

'No.' Mr Cranston's bark was short and sharp. 'Sunday doesn't have boyfriends.' A pause, then these words, delivered with unconscious cruelty: 'Have you *seen* my eldest daughter, officer?'

Cassidy's cheeks pinked. Fitzroy knew that didn't necessarily mean a thing. The girl was at that unfortunate age where conversation with adults could be an awkward and uncomfortable ordeal. Perhaps she was ashamed of her father's brusque tone or the implication of his words. But when Cassidy's eyes flicked in the direction of her parents and away again, all in a fraction of a moment, Fitzroy suspected she had found a way in.

'How about you show us Sunday's bedroom? If that's OK with you, Mr and Mrs Cranston.'

Mrs Cranston had stopped crying but her eyes, with their livid web of capillaries, were testament to her ongoing agony.

'Take them upstairs, Cassie. There's a darling.'

Fitzroy kicked off her shoes at the bottom of the staircase. Like everything else in this house, the carpet was pristine and she felt bad about sullying it with grime from the outside world. Storm followed suit. Seeing her colleague in striped socks made her look vulnerable. Fitzroy enjoyed the fact that Storm's perfect put-togetherness didn't extend as far as her feet.

The door to Sunday's bedroom was closed. Cassidy Cranston pushed against it, biting her lower lip. Fitzroy's first impression was that the room belonged to someone much older than Sunday's twenty-five years.

A floral bedspread; chintzy curtains with pelmets and tie-backs; a vase of blousy fabric peonies. The only concession to her youth was a poster of a Hollywood actor on the wall. One corner was peeling away. Fitzroy recognized the young star but she couldn't name him.

'Saul wouldn't hurt my sister.' The words tumbled out of Cassidy, as if she couldn't hold them in. 'We had an argument, that's all.'

'Did he threaten you? Or her?'

'No. I mean, he was angry because he thought I was flirting, but he wouldn't hurt Sunday. I know he wouldn't.'

'Was Sunday seeing someone?' Fitzroy's tone was gentle. 'Someone your parents didn't know about?'

Cassidy's face was a quarrel between conscience and loyalty. She sank into her sister's bed, her fingers finding their way into her mouth. She pulled at the skin around her nail with her teeth.

'I think so.'

'Do you know who he is?'

Cassidy shook her head. 'She pretended to be ill. I came back early and she was all glammed up. She wouldn't tell me who it was, though. Just asked me not to mention it to Mum and Dad.'

'Has she had a boyfriend before?'

'Never – at least, not one I know about.'

The strings section in Fitzroy's synapses began to play; a gentle melody, barely a whisper. If this mystery boyfriend was Sunday's first, there would be some trace of him in this room. She remembered her own early romances; the jealous hoarding of every ticket stub and scribbled note. A sharp whoosh of relief. They would find him.

Storm had already begun, opening drawers and sifting through underwear. Cassidy opened her mouth when Storm held up a lacy bra, and shut it again. The wardrobe; the drawers under the bed; the space between the mattress and the bed-frame. Handbags; jewellery box; the pockets of her dressing gown, hanging on the door. By the time Storm peeled back the rug in the middle of the floor, she was beginning to look defeated.

Fitzroy sought out the places that Storm had overlooked.

243

The cistern in the tiny en suite; a sunglasses case; even the flat buckle of a belt (she'd once found a stash of cocaine wedged inside the loosened metal mechanism). Half an hour later, the women had still found nothing.

Frustrated, Fitzroy straightened up, scanning the room for clues she may have missed. Her vision snagged on the poster of the actor. She gazed at it for a moment or two, and walked purposefully towards it.

Taking the curled-up corner between her fingers, she pulled the rest of it off the wall, leaving behind four lumps of Blu-Tack. Two pieces of paper landed on the carpet.

'How did you . . . ?' Storm was staring at Fitzroy with something that looked suspiciously like respect.

Fitzroy pointed to the wall. 'The paint was darker underneath, it hadn't been faded by the sun, so I knew this corner of the poster must have been stuck down until very recently, which made me wonder whether Sunday had fiddled with it.' She held up the letters that had been hidden behind the glossy photograph. 'Looks like I was right.'

But Storm wasn't looking at the letters. She was looking at the back of the poster that Fitzroy had placed on Sunday's bed.

Written in the lightest touch of pencil was a name – *Mr Silver* – and an address.

40

8.23 p.m.

He listens to the boy. Occasionally, the rhythm of his breathing speeds up or slows down. Mr Silver knows this is when he's feeling pain. It will pass. He knows this because he has lived through pain himself.

'Not long now, son.' He enjoys the feel of that word on his tongue. *Son.* He wants to say it again and again, to wrap it around the boy, binding them together with words and deeds. Is it true that blood is thicker than water? Perhaps. But the boy's father is gone; his mother is a drunk. The family ties are severed.

Mr Silver will be his family now.

And if you drink from the same glass, your bond is shared.

If you spill the same blood, your bond is shared.

He longs to hear the boy call him father once more.

His hands rest lightly on the wheel, and the road unfurls in front of him. As he drives, the Bone Collector replays the last two hours in his head. All being well, the Friths will walk into the trap set by Saul. All being well, the detective will walk into the trap set by him.

It is possible the specimen *S* will have to be sacrificed for the sow. But he is prepared to take that risk. Because, this time, the detective is the greater prize.

He smiles, and the night grows a little darker, and stars stud the sky, cold piercings that witness the ugly wonder of every birth and death. Before. Now. Always.

His son pulls his coat a little tighter.

My museum, thinks Mr Silver, is taking shape.

Soon, *C* will join the collection. And, when he is sure it is safe, *J*. And the others. Their time is coming. He has his son to assist him now.

Nomen mihi Legio est, quia multi sumus.

I am Legion. For we are many.

We. My son and I.

But Mr Silver has learned much from last year's mistakes. The police will not ambush him again. Not this time. The tables will turn.

He considers what he discovered in the caravan the last time he took Saul there, hidden in a space below the floor. Still indebted to Marshall, even though he has been dead two years now. His father. Always helpful. Always collecting. He smiles again, and he tastes the blood on his lips. And he wants more. Always more.

His son is staring out of the window, lost in thoughts of his own. This evening, he will teach him the tenets of duty and privilege.

He does not know when the police will find the fisherman's cottage. Only that they will.

Yes, he will be sorry to lose his new specimen S.

It puts him in mind of another S, another lifetime.

But now Saul is beside him, and he sees something in this quiet boy in his passenger seat that reminds him of himself. Their shared love of insects. That hunted expression. A reflection of loss, of death, and a knowledge that the shadows in this young man's eyes are a sign that he has borne witness to darkness too.

The coast road is deserted. He knows it is quiet during this part of the night as he has travelled it many times before. An owl brushes the overhanging trees. The car is silent, except for the breathing of his son. The field is around the next bend. He stops the car at the level crossing, waits patiently for the passing train.

Even now, the sound of the wheels on the tracks takes him back to his mother.

Saul feels his gaze upon him. Turns. Smiles.

In his heart, the Bone Collector feels the soaring wings of happiness take flight.

41

2 July 1955

The train stuttered and swayed, and she closed her eyes. She had been awake for most of the night, but she ought to get some rest. If she was to be convincing, she would need to keep her wits about her. He had a way of sniffing out the truth.

It was half an hour until the train was due in to Charing Cross. Her mouth dried up. She had no desire to go back, except to collect her son. But it would not be for long. This time next month, they would be far away, living with her sister, and she would never have to see her husband again.

The train rolled on, clanking and rumbling its way down the tracks. Her gloved hands were folded in her lap. The cardboard box rested on the seat next to her. She could kill for a cup of tea. Or something stronger.

Even now, she couldn't believe what she had done. Father Michael would be horrified, and she daren't contemplate what the others would make of it, all that finger-pointing and gossiping. Well, let them talk. She would not be around to hear what they said.

THE COLLECTOR

The motion of the train brought to mind the rocking of a baby in its crib. It was peculiar the way one's brain worked, but the imagery did not upset her. She had long accepted there would be no more children. This was a truth she held tightly to her chest. Despite her insistence on a nursery, it was all a pretence. She wanted nothing more to bind her to him. She was looking for escape.

Her son loved watching the trains. He often stood on the bridge, his mouth open to catch the steam, laughing as it billowed in his face. It made her laugh too, to see him happy.

He didn't laugh as much as he ought to. Ten-year-old boys should be roaming the fields and paddling in streams, not studying anatomical drawings and whispering in corners with their fathers. She drew in a breath to steady herself. Two weeks. That was all. And then they'd be gone.

She glanced at the bundle of fur in the box. She hoped it would make their leaving a little easier on her son.

The woman let her mind drift. A light sheen of sweat decorated her top lip. Her breath deepened, head nodding. The train swayed gently. The sun glinted on the tracks. A perfect summer's day, as ripe and as sweet as the berries growing in the fields of a nearby farm.

It happened without warning.

A horrific sound of rupturing metal.

Her eyes flew open.

Spinning light and shadow. Flashes of cornfields and the vast sky, an inappropriate swathe of cheery blue.

The world capsized.

And then it was raining suitcases, and the contents of her bag were spilling across the floor and a man was shouting and everything was upside down.

She hit the floor of the train, which was actually the roof, and landed heavily on her shoulder, something soft and yielding breaking her fall.

She recoiled when she realized it was the prone body of an elderly man, especially as, in the confusing aftermath of the crash, her own hands had pushed into the cushion of the man's belly as she struggled to find her balance and heave herself to her feet.

The carriage was in disarray.

Passengers and luggage and hat-boxes strewn across the place. And blood. Lots and lots of blood.

Oh, heavens, she thought, the carriage has flipped over. The train has come clean off the tracks.

She bent over the man whose body she'd landed on. His eyes were closed, his chest as still as the air outside.

As they had waited to board the train that morning, the same chap, with his Brylcreemed hair and smart jacket, had confided he was on the way to London to visit his son, returning home from overseas for the first time in three years. His eyes had been alight with the promise of their reunion.

She had told him about her own son. 'His name's Brian and he's ten.'

The old man had smiled at her, indulgent. 'That's a terrific age.' He had fumbled in his pocket and handed her half a crown. 'Here, give this to him from a happy old fella to a young 'un.'

She had flushed, embarrassed. 'No, no, I couldn't possibly.'

'I insist,' he said, and placed the coin in her gloved hand, folding over her fingers and patting them. 'Today is a special day for me, seeing my son. I want to share it.'

She stroked the man's dry hand, her sorrow spilling over at the knowledge that no such reunion would take place now.

250

A silence settled over the carriage, inserting itself into that eerie bracket of time immediately after impact but before the realization that something truly awful had happened.

It didn't last long.

Sobs began to compress the gaps of quiet, constricting them with pain and shock and disbelief. Barely able to comprehend the horror, she lifted her hands to her ears. She was still wearing her gloves, but the pale fabric was now rusted with something dark.

The shouting fellow took her elbow and guided her to the disfigured mess of the door. A dripping cut by the inner sweep of his eyebrow made him look like he was weeping blood. She felt in her pocket for a handkerchief, but he brushed it away impatiently.

'The train's derailed,' he said. 'We need to get out as quickly as possible.'

He crouched amongst the debris and yanked on the window sash, but it wouldn't give so he took off his shoe and hit it, hard, against the glass. Once. Twice. The sound made her flinch.

He shrugged off his sports jacket and wrapped it around his hand, feeling blindly through the teeth of broken glass for the door handle to the carriage.

The floor shifted suddenly, and she screamed.

The man's eyes lifted heavenwards, and he stilled for a moment, watching and waiting.

'It's OK,' he said. 'It's just the wreckage settling.' He eyed her. 'Is your hand all right?'

She peeled off the sticky glove. A deep gash bisected her palm. 'I'm fine.'

She threw a glance behind at the old fellow. He hadn't moved, but something dark and red was trickling from his ear. Nausea forced her to press herself towards the broken window. A light breeze cooled her hot skin, and brought with it the cry of sirens.

'Nearly there,' said the man, and pushed violently against the door. Taking him by surprise, it lurched open and he half fell through it, onto the fields below.

'Sir, are you OK?' she called.

He scrambled to his feet.

'I'll live.' He extended his hand towards her. 'Down you come, Mrs . . . ?'

'Howley. I'm Sylvie Howley.'

His warm fingers closed around her wrist, the second time in twenty-four hours she had been touched by a man who wasn't her husband. She blushed at the unfamiliar feel of him, and pulled away as soon as she was safely on the ground.

The train was a mangled snake of metal, spilling across the cutting and into the farmers' fields beyond. A body was face down on the tracks. A cow was chewing grass, unmoved by the tableau of death unfolding before it. The scent of manure and burning filled the summer skies.

She turned away from her rescuer and bent over, her thin frame wracked by dry heaves.

He patted her awkwardly on the back.

'It's a shock,' he murmured. 'A terrible shock.'

And so how could she tell him that it wasn't the crash, but her husband's reaction to the certainty of her lateness that was making her sick with fear.

Joyce Manning from number 30 waddled down the road as quickly as she could manage, which wasn't very fast for a woman of her ample girth.

She hammered on the door of number 17. 'Mr Howley, come quickly.'

Mrs Manning waited for a fraction of a second before she

knocked again, several loud raps which echoed down the quiet street and made the curtains twitch. She hoiked up her girdle, and tried to quieten her wheezing. Droplets of sweat rolled down her flushed cheeks. She was unused to this amount of physical effort.

The door opened a slit.

'What is it, woman?' said Marshall Howley. He was wearing a white vest and dabbing at his lips with a napkin.

Mrs Manning's mouth dried up. She swallowed audibly, and then the words tumbled out in a rush.

'My Sandra, she works at the Big House up on Lindemanns Lane, the one with the stone lions, and they've got one of those televisions, and there's been a dreadful train crash, one of those big old express engines, the Folkestone to London train.'

She drew in another lungful of air, exhaling words in her haste to speak.

'And my Sandra, well, she saw Mrs Howley, sir. Near the wreckage. She had a blanket around her and she was drinking something, hot tea, I expect, but she was standing up, and she didn't look too badly hurt. It must have been an awful shock for her, poor love, but I thought you'd like to know. I didn't want you and the young lad to worry when she wasn't home on time. Fear the worst, you know. It's probably on the wireless by now.'

She smiled, wallowing in the satisfaction of delivering Important News.

'My wife is in Teddington with her sister. She took the trolley-bus there two days ago. I dropped her off at the stop myself. She's due back' – he checked his wristwatch, his voice slow and deliberate – 'in ten minutes.'

Mrs Manning, never one for reading signals, shook her head in disagreement, as stubborn as a mule.

'No, no. It was definitely Mrs Howley. Sandra recognized her. Clear as day, she said. Ran all the way home to tell us.' She gave a chuckle. 'Wants her father to buy her a television now. I told her what's what, I did. I said, "The radio's plenty good enough for the likes of us, young lady."'

She would have gabbled on, oblivious to the implications of what she was suggesting, but Marshall's expression was hardening, his dark eyes watching her with something approaching disdain.

She caught the change, and it made her stumble, change tack.

'Perhaps they were having a nice day out.' She faltered. 'Before she came home.'

He continued to stare at her.

Mrs Manning lowered her gaze, feeling a coldness penetrate her bones, despite the heavy heat of the day.

'Well,' she said. 'Perhaps Sandra made a mistake, after all. I'll leave you to it, shall I?'

She could feel his unforgiving eyes upon her as she hurried back up the street, past Mr Hope, who was watering his rhododendrons and Mrs Driver, who called out at her to stop for a cuppa.

Even when she was back inside the safety of number 30 with its familiar wallpaper and three flying ducks, the exertion making her pant like an overheated animal, she couldn't shake off the sense that in doing a good turn for Mr Howley, she'd done a serious wrong to his wife.

42

The house was in darkness when Amy turned in to Pagoda Drive. Twelve hours ago, it would have seemed ridiculous, wasteful even, to switch on the carriage lamps that bracketed her front door, the pale morning skies offering plenty of protection against the distant night.

But now she was facing those shadows on her own, Amy wished she'd had the foresight to light her way.

Even at this late hour, the street was busier than usual, cars lining the quiet residential enclave. A van had parked across her driveway, forcing her to find a space halfway down the road.

Head down, Amy hurried through her gates and up the garden path, fingers closing around her keys. No lights, no warmth, no welcome.

With Eleanor staying over at Miles' flat, and Clara gone, the house was exactly that. A house. Home was people. Never before had this simple truth been so apparent. This was bricks and mortar, nothing more, the sucked-out shell of her former life.

'Mrs Foyle,' someone shouted, and she turned on the doorstep, stupidly surprised. Then car doors were opening, and late-shift journalists, who had been waiting for her return, were sliding from the relative warmth of their vehicles into the cold, fresh night. Photographers were running towards her. A cameraman was filming.

Flash.

'Have you heard?'

Flash.

'Heard what?'

Flash.

The journalist looked awkward, embarrassed even. 'That Howley may have killed again?'

Flash.

Another voice. Brusque. Crass. 'Have you got a message for Sunday Cranston's mother?'

Flash.

'What would you say to Howley, if he's watching?' A third voice from the back of the crowd.

Amy froze on the step, unprepared for the ambush. The day after tomorrow, those same newspapers and TV bulletins would be full of that image of her. A startled expression on her face, artificial light accentuating every pencil line of grief and loss. But not for the reason that she – or the headline writers – could have predicted. But Amy, alone and lonely, had no inkling of that now.

She fumbled with the lock and slammed the door behind her.

Amy did not stop to take off her coat or remove her

shoes. She headed straight for the kitchen, pulling open cupboard doors in an unconscious echo of Gloria Anguish. Except Amy did not have to scrabble around for relief. Expensive wine was easy to find in the Foyle household.

With a careless hand, she poured Ribera del Duero into a glass. The liquid sloshed over the rim, staining the table-cloth, seeping into the cotton fibres, spreading until it had covered a large part of the fabric.

Where once she would have leapt into action, blotting the stain, pouring salt or white wine in a frantic rescue mission, Amy made no move to clean it up.

She pulled out a chair, sat down and stared at the brimming glass.

She imagined her fingers closing around its stem, lifting it to her lips, drinking it down in one fluid motion, the firm tannin, the complex notes of mulberry and blackberry filling her nose and her mouth. Refilling her glass and repeating. Refill, repeat. Until the world blurred into oblivion.

The *look* on Lilith Frith's face.

Jakey's mother had been waiting on the pavement outside the Frith house when Amy had pushed the boy's wheelchair around the corner and into the home straight. Underneath the street lamp, in its unforgiving orange glow, her face had looked – there was no kinder word for it – old.

Mrs Frith had been wearing slippers, and as she ran up the street towards them, one slid from her foot, but she made no effort to retrieve it, and kept on running. Amy could empathize with that.

That desire to keep on running.

But lately she had been wondering how long one could do that with no prospect of a finishing line?

'Where have you been?' Lilith's cry had been the sound of fear and hurt.

'I'm sorry, we got distracted and I didn't realize –' Amy had lifted a hand to indicate the falling night. 'I'm sorry,' she'd said again, knowing it was not enough.

'Why on earth didn't you leave me a message? A note?'

Amy had no answer to that. Or rather, not one she could share.

'I didn't know where you were,' Lilith had said then, calmer, but only just. 'I've been everywhere, looking for you. The park. The beach. I even tried the library. I've only just got back.' Amy could read what she was not saying in the button-down of her lips, the flint in her eyes. *You, of all people, should have known better.*

'It's OK, Mummy,' said Jakey. 'Amy did a good job of looking after me.'

Lilith's jaw, clenched and tight, had loosened.

'I'm sure she did.' She had sounded more controlled then, softening her voice for her son. To Amy: 'Thank you. I appreciate you taking care of my son whilst my husband was at work.' She had turned her attention back to the boy. 'Right, it's getting late, Jakey. You need something to eat, and then bed.' She helped him out of his wheelchair, guided him inside.

'Bye,' he had called.

Lilith had begun to collapse the wheelchair. Briefly, their eyes had met, and it seemed to Amy as if she wanted to say something else, but then her gaze had slid away.

'I'm sorry, Mrs Frith. Truly.'

Lilith had nodded in mute acceptance of her apology. Amy had wanted to say something more, to fill up the silence with her sudden, guilty sorrow. But there had been a stiltedness between them, these two mothers with so much in common, that couldn't be smoothed away.

'I'll be off then,' Amy had said.

'Yes,' said Lilith. 'I hope . . .'

But she never did say what she hoped.

And Amy had left.

The part of her that had wanted to shake Lilith for her clipped voice, her brutal dismissal, to shout *'At least you have your son'*, was silenced by the knowledge that some sadistic streak in her had wanted Lilith to worry, that she had been oh-so-aware of the passing hours, that she had heard the click in her own behaviour, sliding from appropriate to inappropriate.

That she had wanted to mother this young boy who had been the last to speak to her daughter.

That he had felt like a connection to Clara, however tenuous.

And then she had checked her phone. Seen the news that Brian Howley had likely struck again.

And here she was, inside this moment.

Just her.

The glass.

The strength of her will.

And for all her privilege, her wealth, underneath the veneer that money can bring, Amy wasn't so different from Gloria at all.

She picked up the glass and drank deeply, all her heartache, all her mistakes, all her dark nameless fears.

Then she picked up the empty glass and threw it against the wall.

43

Saul could smell earth, rich and deep and meaty. There were worms beneath, turning the soil. Armies of beetles and ants and grubs. He could imagine them all, each committed to their tasks, conditioned by nature. The freshening wind carried with it the promise of snow.

Mr Silver had parked the car by a stile leading into The Field. But this time, he did not instruct Saul to stay inside. Instead, he opened the passenger door and stood back. Saul accepted the invitation.

His head swam as he leaned to unbuckle his seat belt, the throbbing at the base of his skull roaring into life. He gripped the headrest for support, and Mr Silver offered his arm. A courtly stroll across a field. As if it were the most ordinary thing in the world.

Two or three flakes began to fall, captured in the sudden blaze of torchlight.

Up close, the caravan looked the same as last time. The same patch of rust on its bottom left flank. The same crooked step. The sinewy muscles in Mr Silver's arm tensed as he fumbled with the torch. The key found its way into the lock.

'For the greater good, son.' Mr Silver's eyes were shining black stones in the darkness.

Saul drew in a nervous breath and didn't let it go. His heart was knocking in his chest. They had stopped for dinner, and he could feel its heavy weight in his belly. He was aware of the misted moon and the rustle of leaves, and the smell of something deeper, something fetid.

Light flooded the caravan.

He did not know what to expect. He could not know.

There. It. Was.

A wisp of child. Asleep beneath a duvet. Hair so filthy it was impossible to tell its colour and dirt-smudged skin and arms like spindles.

Saul was a statue. He did not know whether to move and wake it up, or whether to leave it lying there. Although it was wrong, the unpalatable truth was he felt a frisson of disgust at this young child. He could not tell if it was a girl or boy. He had no experience of youngsters. He could not think how it had got here.

The child whimpered and rolled onto its side. In the low light of the caravan, Saul saw its hands, like two pairs of forceps. They reminded him of a pseudoscorpion (Class: *Arachnida*) or an earwig (Order: *Dermaptera*).

Something in Saul's memory tickled him, like a spider walking across his brain. Something about hands.

It had been a rare day of calm, during that strangely flat time in the holidays, between Christmas and New Year. Saul and Gloria had walked along the desolate sweep of the beach, the salted wind blowing into their faces and snatching their breath and their hair.

When they'd got back to the flat, Saul had changed into his jogging bottoms while his mother had loaded up plates with thickly buttered turkey sandwiches and pickled onions and leftover Pringles that she'd spent weeks saving up for. They had eaten it on their laps in front of the telly, and there had been mugs of sweet tea and whisky, and oranges for pudding and a little pile of jewelled wrappers from the box of Quality Street an elderly neighbour had given them. He remembered his mother watching a documentary and talking about a missing child.

It's wicked. She's got cleft hands, bless her.

Gloria had sounded outraged, as if it was fine for children with ordinary hands to go missing. Saul had thrown a cushion at his mother, and she had laughed and he remembered what it felt like to be happy.

There'd been other stories too, in the newspapers, on the radio and the TV news, and her name was ingrained in the nation's consciousness. Even a teenager like him had heard of Clara Foyle.

He looked at the child, lying on the floor. It was yawning and blinking.

Slowly, it lifted its eyes to his, beseeching him.

Could this be her?

Mr Silver had a small silver padlock key in his hand.

'It's time,' he said.

44

Fitzroy did not expect a result. That was the brutal truth and it was a relief to admit it. There had been too many false leads, too much time squandered in that wasteland of hope.

Clara Foyle was never coming home.

Brian Howley was gone.

It could take them years to find him, if ever.

But as she stared at the cottage on the crooked, cobbled street, a single light in an upstairs bedroom, the moon riding high, Fitzroy heard Storm mutter a prayer. So that's what it had come to, exhorting an unproven deity. She could not muster the energy to feel affronted. They needed all the help they could get.

Fitzroy did not have a search warrant. Nor had she told DI Thornberry what they were doing. She still had not decided whether this was a mistake. Technically, she was on his turf, but this was part of the Met's own investigation. Even so, the simple truth was she did not expect to find Brian Howley.

She was looking for a man called Mr Silver because she was hoping that Sunday Cranston might have confided in him some truth that would lead her to the Bone Collector. He was not under suspicion himself, although he was a potential witness.

Pressing a finger to her lips, she pushed her ear against the front door, seeking out the sound of voices or the rumble of a radio or television. It was late to come calling, but this was important.

But it was impossible to hear anything except the drunken catcalls of the smoking pub-goers down the street, drowning out all else.

She knocked sharply.

Five seconds.

Ten.

No reply.

'What do you think?'

Storm shrugged, and peered through a window. The blinds were half drawn but it was too dark to see properly.

'Asleep?'

Fitzroy didn't think so. She'd glimpsed a rectangle of hardstanding around the back when they'd pulled up outside the cottage. The patch of oil gleaming in the headlamps suggested a car or van had been parked there recently. Perhaps its owner would come home soon.

She rapped on the door again.

When no one answered, she jerked her head in the direction of the back of the cottage. Fitzroy and Storm walked around the side of the property until they reached the concreted drive, bordered by overgrown bushes, an ancient wheelie bin and a couple of wooden crates. A street lamp highlighted a brick wall, with crumbling cement and telltale subsidence cracks, and a gate secured with a large padlock.

Even though she knew it was a waste of time, Fitzroy rattled the gate. It was an outlet for her frustration.

Storm placed a restraining hand on Fitzroy's. 'Let's go,' she said. 'We can come back first thing.'

As the women started to walk back towards their car, a narrow streak of brown-and-white fur was squeezing its body beneath the wooden slats of the gate. Had they seen it, they might have mistaken it for a rat, much like the one Saul Anguish had seen on that night his mother almost drowned.

But Fitzroy and Storm were bickering about who was going to drive back to London. Fitzroy, tired and irritable, who hated driving in the dark and only did so when there was no other choice, pulled rank. Storm, unfazed, nudged her in the shoulder.

'Tomorrow's a new day. After a bath and bed, everything will seem brighter.'

But the women never got the chance to find out the truth of that statement because events were about to move very quickly indeed.

A scream speared the darkness, riven with pain and a thousand nameless fears.

Fitzroy swung around. 'What the—?'

A second, louder scream interrupted her, broken up into a series of staccato whimpers.

And then Fitzroy and Storm were running back in the direction of that padlocked gate, and Storm was fumbling for her torch and the older detective was taking aim at the gate with her foot.

Oh my God it's a baby a very young child aim for the weakest part of the door by the lock don't kick the lock you could break your foot thank God the hinges don't open towards me don't jump the instructor said not your shoulder might dislocate use a well-placed forceful kick there it is again it's the scream of a baby a thin reedy cry it's dying oh God it sounds like it's dying.

With all the power she could muster, Fitzroy kicked at the gate. The wood splintered but it did not break. She repeated the motion and all the while, the cries were growing fainter, like life was spilling out into the night air and could not be pushed back in, only carried away to the cold stars above.

The gate made a sickening cracking noise and gave way.

Fitzroy held up her palm at Storm.

Wait. Wait.

They listened.

The tiniest whimper of pain.

As if they had been partners for years instead of hours, the women stepped over the broken gate and into the garden, and in a single, smooth motion, split up and spread out, seeking the source of the cries while trying not to expose themselves to danger.

Storm was the first to piece it together, the thin beam of her tactical flashlight picking out the familiar shapes of a garden. An old rattan chair. A wrought-iron table.

Several pairs of unblinking eyes.

She swung the torch back and forth, just to be sure.

'Fitzroy, over here.'

The detective was by Storm's side in the time it took for her to clear her throat.

Ting.

'Rabbits,' she breathed.

Both of them knew what it meant.

'But the screaming . . . ?'

Storm jerked the flashlight inside one of the hutches.

Three rabbits were huddled in the corner, twitching with nerves and fear. In the centre, a large rabbit lay on its left flank amidst the hay, limp, beaten, two neat puncture wounds in the scruff of its neck, eyes brilliant with the closeness of death.

A stoat stood on its hind legs, the sharp points of its teeth stained with its kill.

But although the scene was disturbing, Fitzroy understood it was the natural order of things. That the stoat was acting on an instinct it couldn't deny, even if it tried.

Brian Howley didn't have that excuse.

She stared at the blank windows of the cottage.

She had to get inside.

45

10.37 p.m.

The mattress was lumpy and smelled musty, unloved. When Erdman rolled over, the springs creaked and dug into his back. The pillow was full of feather quills that pricked his cheek.

The spare room.

There'd been a time, not so long ago, when he'd slept here almost every week, trying to dodge the masonry of a marriage falling down around his ears. They'd rebuilt, he and Lilith, brick by painful brick, the foundations of their relationship more solid than they had realized, strengthened by a steel core that had surprised them both. They had survived, their love for each other salvaged by the most horrific of ordeals. The irony had not escaped them. They did their very best not to waste their time arguing these days. But he'd gone too far. He should have checked before leaving Jakey in the care of Amy Foyle. Even he would admit that.

When he'd got home from the office, Jakey was asleep,

and Lilith had flown at him, hitting him until he'd been forced to grab her wrists.

This had been a first in the Frith marriage.

'What's happened?' he'd said, although he already knew.

'You should have asked me first.' Her face was streaked and blotchy. 'You left our son with someone we don't know, you stupid fuck. Someone potentially unstable. I didn't know where they were.' She started sobbing. 'And the news. He's been all over the news.'

Erdman didn't need to ask who 'he' was.

She had turned her back on him then, her voice clipped, shutting down.

'Belinda Chong called.' It was a while since he'd heard the name of their family liaison officer and it brought with it a rush of memory and pain. 'There's a police car outside, just for tonight. They're sending someone to collect us tomorrow. I'm going to pack. I suggest you do the same.' Those were the last words she had spoken to him that evening.

A shiny smudge from the street light outside marked his curtains. He wasn't tired. Not remotely. But when Lilith switched to Ice Queen mode, the atmosphere became so frigid that even this draughty bedroom without a TV and abysmal mobile reception was preferable to being in her company.

At least she was asleep now. Gentle snoring was coming from their bedroom; a migraine and its medication always knocked her out. In a minute, he would go downstairs for a glass of whisky and some telly. He wouldn't sleep tonight. Howley was in the darkness somewhere, laying out his skeletons for the dead.

Tomorrow they would move to a safe house.

Tomorrow he'd speak to Fitzroy.

They had a lot to discuss.

Alone in bed, he allowed himself to mull over the phone call again, replaying the conversation in his head.

The question was: Could he trust that boy from the pet store? There was something uncomfortable about him, something that Erdman could not put his finger on. Their exchange had been stilted and awkward. Unexpected. But if he was telling the truth . . .

His fingers touched the hard wood of the baseball bat under his pillow.

His job tonight was to protect his family.

'Daddy . . .'

A small shadow with the twisted limbs of a tree was framed in the doorway.

Erdman, lying on top of the duvet, sat up and switched on the lamp.

'What's up, champ? Bad dream?' He didn't voice the thought that came before all others. *Where does it hurt?*

Jakey limped towards him. Erdman resisted the urge to leap from the bed and scoop him up. It was good for his son to keep moving. It was just so damn hard to watch him struggle.

'He's out there, Daddy, I know he is.'

Erdman didn't know what to say. He didn't want to lie to his boy, his champ. He had watched the glow of his innocence dim in the last three months. All he wanted was to chase the shadows from his eyes, to cleanse and purify the darkness. But Howley *was* out there. He wouldn't lie, not again.

'Yes, champ. He is.'

Jakey bit his lip, as if to say *I knew it*.

'I'm going to die, aren't I?'

Erdman had heard this question before, but Jakey's eyes were fixed on him with an intensity that made him feel like the boy was asking something important of him, only he wasn't sure what. He swung his legs over the edge of the bed.

'We all die, champ.' It was the best he could muster, but it sounded weak, even to him.

'You said I must always tell the truth, Daddy. So if I have to, you should too.'

Jakey's words were scorched with irritation. Such impatience was rare for his son and it forced Erdman to sit up and take notice. He weighed his own words with care.

'Statistically, it's likely that me and Mum will outlive you, but that doesn't mean it *will* happen.' Erdman hoped that Jakey wouldn't see through the smokescreen of language to the truth.

'So does that mean I'm going to die first, or Mummy and you?'

'Jakey—'

'Daddy! Just tell me. Are you saying that I'll die before you?'

Erdman forced himself to meet his son's unflinching gaze. Jakey didn't want platitudes or woolly reassurances. He was asking his father to be honest with him.

'Yes, champ. That is what I'm saying.'

'And it could be soon?'

Erdman did not want to have this conversation. He did not want to discuss the potential complications of pneumonia, or the effects of rapidly accelerated bone growth on the existing organs within his son's hardening cage of a body, or the restriction of movement that would imprison him physically and psychologically.

He did not want to shine a light on the darkness that he carried with him every waking moment, and sometimes when he slept.

Terrible, sweat-drenched nightmares of losing his boy.

Nightmares that would come true.

'It's possible, sweetheart.'

Jakey let out a long, loose breath. If Erdman had been pushed on the issue, he would have said it sounded like relief.

'That's what I thought,' said Jakey. A squall of expression – sadness, stoicism, defiance – clouded his young face, like the changing sky.

This was too much for Erdman. He was off the bed in an instant, drawing his child into his arms, the sharp ridges of Jakey's bones pressing into his own skin.

'We can't know the future, champ. Probabilities, that's all we've got to go on. You might well live to be a ripe old age.'

Jakey's eyes blazed. Erdman didn't need his son to speak to hear the sentiment. He knew what that look meant.

Don't humour me.

'But I probably won't.' His eyes were narrowed now, watching his father, and Erdman was hopelessly lost, trying and failing to gauge what his son was driving at. But if Jakey was ready for the truth, it was his responsibility to step up to the plate.

'No,' he said softly. 'Probably not.'

'Ol' Bloody Bones wants to kill me –'

What could he say to that? Surely there was a time when

even the truth was too much. He sank back on the bed, Jakey on his lap.

'– but I'm going to die anyway –'

Erdman watched his son's face. It was lit from within, as if he was experiencing a new dawn. Jakey smiled up at his father. It was surprisingly tender. A creeping sense of unease began to prickle Erdman's skin.

'– so if I give myself to him –'

No.

'– then he would come for me –'

Nononononononono.

'– and it might lead the police to Clara.'

Erdman gave a violent shake of his head, as if the movement would somehow dislodge the sheer ludicrousness of his son's suggestion. Jakey offering himself up as bait? Not in his lifetime.

'No, champ, that's not going to happen.' A beat. 'Was this Mrs Foyle's idea?'

Jakey's bottom lip pushed itself out into a familiar gesture of stubbornness.

'No, it was mine. And if you don't help me, Daddy, I'll do it by myself.'

Erdman lay down on the bed and tucked himself around his son, the boy's back pressed into his chest, his hair tickling his nostrils, the still of the house about them. He listened to Jakey breathe, his gorgeous, living son.

'It's too dangerous, sweetheart. Too much to go wrong.'

Jakey didn't move except to trace a pentagon with an 'S' in its centre on his father's forearm.

'You saved me, Daddy. Like a superhero, like Superman.

I'll never get to be a daddy like you, but, just for one time, I want to be a superhero.'

A lump lodged itself in Erdman's throat, one he couldn't swallow away. He didn't dare speak because he knew that tears would spill from him instead of words.

'I thought, Daddy, that as I'm going to die anyway, I might as well do something brave.'

Trying to hold himself steady and silent whilst weeping was harder than Erdman expected. As an overwhelming sadness took hold, he tensed, creating a vacuum between their bodies. It was just as well that Jakey had his back to him. A face full of snot and tears was not the look of fatherly reassurance that Erdman was striving for.

To buy himself time, he stroked his fingers through the mess of Jakey's hair. He was aware of his son relaxing into him, closing the gap between them. He needed to pull himself together and say something.

No fucking way.

That's what he wanted to say. Not say, *shout.* From the rooftops. *You're six and this is stupid and you're not doing it.*

But there was something about the quiet conviction in his son's voice, the desire to do something honourable that was breaking Erdman up inside. Because it was so fucking brave and his boy was still a baby, and yet he had the courage to do this, more courage than a man five times his age.

'Jakey, I—'

'I'm doing it, Daddy.'

Erdman couldn't manage to say anything else, and so he nodded instead, and Jakey felt the movement and rested his cheek against the squashy underside of his father's arm.

Eventually, Erdman found courage enough of his own to speak.

'What did you have in mind?'

'I don't know, Dad, but he's near, I know he is. I've seen him, remember.' A pause. 'You'll help me, won't you? Promise you will.'

Erdman couldn't bring himself to challenge Jakey. He now knew his son had been telling the truth all along.

Jakey pulled himself up into a sitting position. 'Please, Daddy.'

Erdman kissed the forehead of his son. His skin smelled of toothpaste and washing powder, but his eyes were knowing, a maturity born of the darkness he'd endured.

'We'll see, sweetheart.' That non-committal parental staple.

Jakey's whisper cut him down.

'Ol' Bloody Bones is going to kill her, Daddy. He's going to kill Clara.'

'You don't know that, sweetheart.'

'I do, Daddy. I know these things. I do. And I think it might be tonight.'

46

When Saul was ten years old, a friend of his mother, seeing his love of the natural world, bought him a butterfly garden.

It came in a box with a pop-up net and three pound coins Sellotaped to the outside so he could send off for caterpillars and witness the miracle of metamorphosis.

When the tiny wriggling shapes arrived through the post in a plastic cup, it was one of the best moments of his life.

Every morning for a week Saul marvelled at the way the caterpillars doubled, tripled, quadrupled in size. He watched in wonder as they shed their exoskeletons and spun silky webbing, attaching themselves to the lid of the cup. He made notes in his book about the process of pupation. He waited, with infinite patience, for the chrysalids to harden. With gentle fingers, he transferred them to the safety of their new habitat, zipping up the net to keep them safe.

For eight days he waited, leaping out of bed the second he opened his eyes, rushing to his room when he got home from school.

276

And, one warm afternoon in May, the first butterfly emerged.

At first he thought the scarlet staining was blood, that the butterfly had somehow hurt itself. He had yelled for his mother, hysteria making him shrill.

Gloria appeared in the doorway, rubbing her hair with a towel. She flicked through the booklet that came with the kit.

'No,' she said, 'not blood. It's' – she pointed to the word – 'that stuff.'

Saul had peered over her shoulder. 'Meh-co-nee-um.' His eyes scanned the text. It was nothing to worry about, a natural part of the transformation.

The relief was vivid.

He cut up a wrinkled apple he found in the fridge and collected fallen blooms from next door's front garden, daubing the petals with sugared water. His heart filled with joy as he watched the butterfly's proboscis seek out his homemade nectar.

By bedtime, two more had emerged.

The next day, Thursday, the fourth of the butterflies – its wings expanding to display its painted colours – had wriggled free.

The fifth butterfly arrived while Saul was at school.

One of its wings was crumpled and half formed, entangled in silk that had clung to the pupa, dragging the husk of its home behind it. Saul freed it, reviving it with drops of the sweetened water from a pipette. It could not fly so he placed it amongst the petals.

Saul could hear them as he lay in bed, the delicate

brushing of their wings. He would release them at the weekend, when he'd had a day or two to enjoy them.

That Sunday, he was first up. The air was heavy with heat. He carried his habitat downstairs and opened the front door of the flat. Their fragile wings beat against the netting.

From upstairs drifted his father's voice. Saul couldn't hear the words but he could tell by the cadence – ugly, aggressive – that Solomon Anguish was in a foul temper.

A collection of butterflies is called a kaleidoscope.

He whispered to himself so he wouldn't have to listen to the sounds of his father's anger.

Also, a flutter. A swarm. A rabble. A flight.

Heavy boots thudded down the stairs. Saul could taste blood in his mouth. He had bitten down on the inside of his cheek and its salted rustiness made him gag.

His father swore loudly and appeared in the doorway. He was wearing shorts and yesterday's T-shirt, accessorized with a corrugated forehead and a mean mouth.

'What the fuck you staring at?'

Saul dropped his eyes but it was too late.

His father's gaze fell greedily on the butterfly habitat in Saul's hand. He snatched it from his son and gave it a shake. The butterflies rose in panic.

'Don't.' Saul's cry leaked from his mouth before he could stop it.

'Why are you pussying around with shit like this, Saul?' Another, more violent shake. 'Go and watch the telly or something.'

Saul could feel the heat rising inside him.

'Dad, don't.' He tried to grab at the flimsy net. 'You'll hurt them.'

His father smiled and unzipped the mesh lid. One of the butterflies – a Painted Lady (Latin name: *Vanessa Cardui*) – crawled trustingly onto his hand.

Solomon slowly lifted the butterfly until it was right under his son's nose. With the flat of his other hand, he crushed its delicate body.

Saul, skinny, small for his age, flew at his father, but it was like a paper dart hitting a brick wall. His father batted him off, laughing. Disturbed by the sudden flurry of movement, three of the butterflies spiralled madly around the net.

Solomon captured and killed them all. Then he walked down the garden path, whistling as he left.

Saul could not have known then, in that moment of acute loss, that another ten-year-old boy, over five decades before, had been in thrall to *his* father; that the same boy had lost the rabbit that was the last living piece of his mother; that life and death, that murder, moved in patterns; that behaviour echoed and repeated down the long valley of time.

All he understood was the pain of the now.

The discarded habitat had fallen on its side, fruit and flowers, already decaying, spilling onto the grass. Saul, crying, snot running down his face, gathered up the broken parts of his butterflies. His mother had an old jewellery box. He would keep the pieces in there until he decided what to do with them.

He lifted up a faded bloom. He was about to throw it in the bushes when it twitched, making him jump. Hidden beneath its petals was the butterfly with the deformed wing.

It was half dead but had somehow escaped the cruelty of his father.

It was still alive.

Its weakness had become its strength.

Clara Foyle reminded him of that butterfly.

47

Saul did not want to touch the child, but Mr Silver was making shooing gestures at him so he bent over the small figure sitting on the floor until their faces were close together.

'Er, hi.'

The child did not move. He could see that it – she – was shackled to the table. A strong odour drifted up from her body and Saul's mouth twisted into a bitter lemon shape.

Mr Silver was swinging the key in his left hand.

'Here.' He threw it to Saul, who caught it, an instinctive reaction.

The child watched him. Her eyes dominated the thin triangle of her face. He wanted to ask her if she was OK, but it seemed like a stupid question. Instead he turned his attention to her weeping ankle.

'I'm just going to undo the padlock. It might hurt a bit but then the pain will go away. Is that all right with you' – he hesitated – 'Clara?'

The shooting-star flash in her eyes confirmed his hunch had been on the money.

'Very good, Saul,' murmured Mr Silver. 'Very sharp indeed. I see that your grammar school education hasn't gone to waste.'

Saul removed the metal clasp from Clara's ankle. He wasn't sure what he had been expecting, perhaps an attempt to run, that's what he might have done in her shoes, but the girl did nothing. She sat on the floor, dull eyes fixed on some invisible point, lost in a place he didn't want to visit.

'*Time and tide wait for no man*,' said Mr Silver.

He placed his holdall on the table, unzipped it and pulled out a blue tarpaulin.

Saul looked at the tarpaulin and then at the girl. Her cleft hands were folded in her lap, her feet, bare, the skin on her ankle, a raw mess.

A damaged butterfly.

He tried to process what was happening.

Clara Foyle.

Her name was familiar but the details of her abduction remained frustratingly elusive. He wished he'd paid more attention to the news, to that documentary his mother had been glued to at Christmas.

He risked another look at Clara's hands.

Remembered the beetles in Mr Silver's cottage.

The sly, greedy expression in his eyes.

He was half sickened, half thrilled by his proximity to a man he suspected of snatching this child. He groped his brain for some snippet of information, some sense of who he was dealing with.

A sudden vision of Clara's father rose from a trapdoor in

his subconscious memory. A doctor. Weeping. Addressing the camera. Offering a reward.

All of it – the smell of the caravan, the injury to his head, the realization that his presence in the caravan may well implicate him – smacked into Saul with dazzling ferocity.

'I think I'm going to throw up,' he said, stumbling towards the door.

Mr Silver followed him outside.

'It's quite usual to feel this way, Saul.' He smiled and his teeth were pearls in the darkness. 'It gets easier after a while, especially the surgery.'

What surgery?

Mr Silver waited for Saul to finish and held open the door.

'Come along, son.'

Wiping his mouth on his sleeve, Saul trudged back into the caravan. A queasiness had settled on him, and he experienced a fierce longing for his shitty bedroom with its threadbare furnishings and comfortable familiarity.

Mr Silver had slipped on a dark jacket with delicate stripes in its fabric and was now removing a thick cotton wallet from the holdall. Saul's gaze flicked to the girl. She hadn't moved at all. Part of him wanted to shake the malaise from her, to slap her into life. She was pitiful, pathetic. Her skinny frame reminded him of Gloria. A prick of irritation made him wonder if he was more like Mr Silver than he'd realized.

A sense of disassociation overtook him. Like he was a distance from this place, a million miles away. But he *was* interested. He *wanted* to see what would happen.

On the table, the wallet lay open. Six knives with their blades exposed.

Mr Silver was muttering to himself, *proximal phalanges* and *preserve the scaphoid*. Saul did not have the faintest inkling what he was talking about, but he knew about knives and he knew they meant trouble.

'Saul?' Mr Silver's voice was courteous. 'Are your hands clean?' He indicated the knife wallet. 'Would you care to do the honours?'

'I—'

'Choose a knife, boy.'

Clara's head jerked up. Her eyes flicked from Saul to Mr Silver and back again. Very slowly, she began to inch away from them, moving backwards on her bottom, her feet scrabbling on the dirty floor.

'Why do I need to do that, Mr Silver?'

Saul was a clever boy. He understood how to play for time, to slow down a situation that was speeding into a car crash. Mr Silver withdrew a meat cleaver from the knife wallet and dragged the tip of his finger along its sharpened edge.

'I prefer to work on specimens that are deceased. It is about preservation, son, and that requires a certain degree of skill. The hands must be intact.' His smile was congenial. 'Do not fear it. You will learn.'

Clara was whimpering, her eyes fixed on the blade.

Mr Silver handed it to Saul. 'Careful,' he said. 'It's sharp.' He folded his arms. His manner reminded Saul of a teacher. Encouraging but appraising. The older man lowered his voice and pointed to a spot high up on his own neck. 'A clean incision between the atlas and the axis should do it.'

The weight of the meat cleaver in Saul's hand was as heavy as his heart. This was not an exam question where more than one answer was correct. There was no room for doubt. Mr Silver wanted him to kill.

Saul imagined the blade splitting Clara's neck. He wondered if she would cry out or if it would cut off the sound before she could make it. It would be easy to overpower the child, weak from a lack of sunlight and all those nutrients required to make young plants grow.

The cold was making his hands numb. A slip and he could lose a finger, a toe. The child was crying openly now, and she was pressing a pillow against her chest. That flash of irritation again. As if a pillow would act as protection against a blade.

'Go on, Saul.'

He took a step towards her, the meat cleaver hanging by his side. Time seemed to slow and still, every second a freeze-frame. All his senses were enhanced. An owl screamed in the distance. Tiny ice crystals in the air made his lungs burn with cold. He caught the muffled timbre of male voices.

Male voices?

Laughter and a subdued curse.

And then there was a knocking at the caravan door.

Mr Silver mimed putting his hand across his mouth and pointed to Clara. Saul crouched beside her and did as he was told. Her breath was warm and tickled the back of his palm. A musty blanket landed on top of them both, blinking out the light.

Another round of knocking.

The sound of Mr Silver's footsteps crossing the caravan, the door creaking open and an unfamiliar, confident, well-spoken voice filling up the space.

'Hello, so sorry to trouble you at this time of night, but

our bloody car's broken down. We think it's the battery, and we saw your light on across the field and we wondered if you had any jump leads.'

'No.'

'Um, OK. Well, do you have a torch we could borrow? It's pitch dark out here and we're in the middle of nowhere and can't see a thing. We'll drive by in the morning and drop it off. If we can get the bloody thing fixed, of course.' A tentative laugh. 'Or we could come in. Warm up a bit.'

'No.' Saul caught the kink in Mr Silver's voice, but didn't think the men had noticed. 'I think there's a spare torch in my car.'

The caravan door shut.

Saul let his hand slip from Clara's mouth and shrugged off the blanket. The child would not let go of her pillow, clasped it in her broken-butterfly hands. Carefully, he placed the meat cleaver on the floor.

Two sets of eyes stared at it.

A childish lilt.

'You're not Father Christmas, are you?' Almost to herself. 'So *who* is going to save me?'

Saul did not answer straight away. This child could not understand that he was more concerned with saving himself. His soul was already a dirty swathe of grey. Carrying out Mr Silver's bidding would turn it black.

The lights of the caravan caught the edge of the blade, making the steel glint and flash. There was cruelty in him. He wanted to scare her, to make her cry, to squeeze some fight into her.

He leaned over and whispered in her ear.

48

'We need a warrant, Fitzroy.'

'There's already a warrant out for Howley's arrest.'

Storm gave her a look that said Don't Be Stupid. But there was no need to spell it out. Neither of them knew who lived here. With nothing concrete linking Howley to this property, the evidence was circumstantial at best. An address scribbled on the back of a poster. Some pet rabbits in hutches. A missing girl. It might be enough to persuade the on-call magistrate. Probably. But even in emergency situations, these things took time. Always time.

She didn't want to land Storm in the shit.

But she didn't want to wait.

She was done with waiting.

'Go and sit in the car.'

Storm pressed her lips together tightly, but she didn't move. She could read the need in Fitzroy's face and its savagery frightened her.

A hard frost was settling, making the air snap with cold.

287

Fitzroy's shoes cut shapes into the grass. She assessed the back of the property. He wasn't the type to leave out a spare key. But a small pane of glass in the back door could be easily broken.

She could say she thought she heard a child screaming.

Which was sort of the truth.

Just not all of it.

To ask Storm to lie for her went against all she believed in. But could the younger woman be trusted to stay quiet? Fitzroy couldn't make the mistake of getting it wrong. Much less trouble this way.

'Toni . . .' she said. 'Go back to the car.'

Storm picked up a loose stone from the rockery, judged its weight with her left hand.

'For the record, this is a bloody ridiculous idea, but I'm not letting you go in there on your own. Just don't get caught, all right? I want to keep my unblemished record, if nothing else.'

Fitzroy did not want this on her conscience. But as she was preparing to harden her tone into an order, Storm dragged an evidence bag from her pocket, wrapped it around the rock and smashed it into the back-door window.

The sound of Storm's flawless years of service fracturing into a dozen irreparable shards filled the night.

'For fuck's sake,' said Fitzroy. 'You could've warned me.'

Storm gave a small, neat smile. 'I've worked on enough burglary cases to know we need to make it look like we're in a hurry.'

Fitzroy opened her mouth and shut it again. That was the last thing she had been expecting. She hadn't pegged Storm as a rule-breaker, quite the opposite.

Storm wrapped the same plastic bag around her hand and thrust it through the broken window pane, twisting the back-door key in its lock.

'Don't want to make it easy for them, but I've got to leave *something*, otherwise it'll look too damn suspicious.' She rubbed the cuff of her coat against the jagged glass, leaving behind a handful of fibres. 'Zara's finest. There'll be thousands of coats like this out there.'

Storm had a point. If there was a police investigation into this break-in, if an innocent party lived here, Storm didn't want to make it too easy for Essex Police, but if, somehow, it *was* linked to them, if they were forced to own up to what they had done, it had to look realistic, as if they were reacting to an emergency, with no thought to the forensic trace they might leave.

Fitzroy squared her shoulders. 'Let's go.'

The house was silent but there was death in its walls. Fitzroy could smell it as soon as she crossed the threshold. A distinctive perfume that coated her tongue and filled her nostrils, that clung to her clothing, her hair, the cells of her skin. The bloodied scent of a life violently ended.

By the expression on Storm's face, she could smell it too.

'Should we call for back-up?' Storm's whisper was drowned out by the drum in Fitzroy's brain. 'I think we should.' She was already reaching for her radio.

Fitzroy shut her eyes and listened to the sounds of the house, the pattern of the beats. Although she had never been here before, she knew this place. It was filled with the echoes of that cold November night when that psychopath Howley had carried her into his museum and left her for dead. The rattle of bones. The quiet weep of the missing and the dead.

A tear pooled on her lashes, drawn from the hot well behind her eyes.

There it was again. That irrational urge to protect the lost, to preserve the dignity of the victims. She knocked Storm's radio away.

'I want to see what we're dealing with first,' she said. 'Then we'll call The Boss.'

In the sitting room, Storm switched on the lights.

A fireplace.

Cold ashes in a cast-iron grate.

In one case Fitzroy had worked on, a devoted husband had beaten his elderly father-in-law to death with the blunt end of a poker. As they had settled down to watch a Sunday night film, he had laid a fire for his unsuspecting family and burned the fragments of his victim's shattered skull. Fitzroy made a mental note to get forensics to test the dusty residue.

A half-open rucksack, decorated with badges.

The glimpse of a dog-eared science textbook.

A set of headphones.

Either a student lived here. Or had been taken.

Fitzroy bolted towards the stairs.

'Shut up.' A hiss from Storm. 'You're like a herd of elephants.' An intake of air, as if steeling herself. 'Look, we need back-up, Etta.'

Fitzroy was being unprofessional, she knew that. There was a protocol to these situations designed to safeguard them both. In that breath of time, Fitzroy should have known better. She should have considered all that had gone before her, all that her impulsive nature had already cost.

Instead she began to climb the stairs.

49

11.03 p.m.

The man with many names is full of false smiles as he waves them off down the lane and into the night, the single strand of torchlight strobing wildly like his heart.

'Tomorrow is fine,' he calls out softly, already knowing he will not see them again, that he and Saul will be long gone by the time the sun has risen and the men come knocking on the caravan door. He can see them scratching their heads, too polite to do more than simply go away again. Perhaps they'll leave the torch on the stoop. Perhaps they won't come at all. Whatever happens, it does not matter. The specimen C will be dead by then.

The vast sky above his head is scarred by thousands of stars that scintillate through the turbulent atmosphere. Those luminous balls of exploding gas remind him he is nothing more than a speck on this earth, that the universe will continue to turn when he is bone dust and worm-food. The knowledge that his new collection will outlive him is a comfort. The end days are coming. He can taste them.

The clouds – now swollen with snow – have drifted eastwards. The moon is a blessing, her cold, hard stare lighting a path for him across the field.

Her unforgiving gaze falls upon the caravan. A shambling mess of a holiday home. He can hear his father's laughter in the whisper of the trees that border the old place, feel the absence of his mother in the caress of the air currents that make their branches tremble.

Months, he has waited for this.

Torn between life and death.

But now the decision has been made.

It is time for C to write her place into his family's history books.

For Saul to draw his first blood.

The old man sets off back across the field. In his heart, he is not a killer, but a collector, alight with the simple thrill of bringing home the freshest of specimens for his museum.

The moon watches him go, and the wind begins to mourn.

50

11.15 p.m.

Fitzroy was in desperate need of a handkerchief. Preferably doused in Olbas oil. But as she hadn't so much as seen a handkerchief since she was eleven and rebelling against her mother's insistence that she stuff one up the sleeve of her school blazer, she would have to improvise.

She tugged the neck of her cardigan across her nose and mouth, but even the nylon fibres could not protect her from the stink of death that filled the narrow spaces of this fisherman's cottage.

The stairs creaked. The memory box in her mind sprang open, belching out flames and smoke and the stripped-down skeletons of tortured children. A cruel reminder of another house. Another staircase. Another hallway. She slammed it shut. But the vision didn't go away.

Because, three months down the line, Fitzroy found herself again standing in an upstairs hallway. With three doors. An open loft hatch.

A steel hook.

There was a symmetry here, and its familiarity frightened her.

She threw a look at Storm. The younger officer's eyes were watchful. Scared, even. Fitzroy sought and found the reproof, barely concealed beneath the fear. A temptation to slip back down the stairs and into the cleansing night air tugged at her. One more plea from Storm and she would do it, she would go outside and call for help and, fuck it, she would let The Boss and Thornberry take credit for it all.

But Storm did not utter a sound, and the moment slipped, unremarkably, from possibility to regret. Of course, Fitzroy could not know that yet.

By silent agreement, the women inched along the hallway. Fear has its own peculiar taste. When Fitzroy was a girl, it had been winter greens and the sickly slur of unrequited love. As a wife and would-be mother, it became the desperate bitter metal of rising oestrogen. As a police officer, in the here and now, it was dank and sour, the unhappy combination of past horrors and those hidden in a future as yet unknown.

What lay behind those doors?

Fitzroy motioned to Storm to close in behind her. Her own fingers grazed the handle. At her feet, dark spots pockmarked the pale carpet. She dropped to her knees. Coffee? Or blood spatter?

Stretched across the carpet, close to the mouth of the door, something taut and thin and barely visible. Fitzroy traced its length, her mind alight with the *ting-ting* music of her synapses. She frowned, feeling her way through all her knowledge of policing, all the courses and cases and years of on-the-job training.

A tripwire.

By now, Storm had slipped ahead of her, already opening the door, already too late to react to Fitzroy's half-strangled, half-shouted cry to get out.

Storm did not see the beetles in their tanks or the spider-webbing cracks in the glass of the mirror. She did not see the bloodied portrait of Sunday Cranston leaning up against the wall, or the knife flung carelessly on a chest of drawers.

The elegant dorsal of her foot had triggered a trap, and as she glanced upwards, her lips slightly parted, a bag split open and a pale snow began to fall.

51

11.17 p.m.

How many minutes had Mr Silver been gone? Twenty? Thirty?

But just when Saul thought the old man was never coming back, the door to the caravan opened and he was standing in the shadows, a look of wolfish hunger on his face.

Mr Silver moved forward with purpose across the small square of space and selected from the wallet a knife, thinly bladed.

Saul crouched down, an animal assessing his prey, damp fingers reaching for the handle of the meat cleaver that lay discarded on the floor.

Silver's black eyes met Saul's blue ones.

Tacit agreement.

Saul began to rise.

Clara scrabbled across the caravan, her bare feet sliding on the shiny plywood, cleft hands fumbling behind her back for the catch on the door, trying to get as far from them as she could, eyes darting from Saul to Silver.

Silver to Saul.

Saul to Sliver.

A barely discernible mewl slipped from between her lips.

Saul moved towards the huddled shape of the girl, intent written on his face, cleaver raised above his head like a trophy, determined to reach her before Mr Silver did.

His senses were alive with the white-water thrill of it all.

The ragged catch of Clara's breathing.

The shuffle of Mr Silver's shiny black shoes.

The stale-air odour of wet weekends and Calor gas.

The astringent scent of fear.

Clara covered her eyes. Mr Silver offered up his invitation. 'Now, Saul. Go on, son . . .'

The boy sucked in the tainted air, blew out a shaky breath. He manoeuvred himself so that he faced the girl on the diagonal, half twisted to allow Mr Silver an unobscured vantage point.

To ensure there was no room for doubt in the older man's mind.

As Saul brought down the blade, he could hear the faintest whine of displaced air.

And Clara's teeth – miniature pearl-hued daggers – broke open the skin of his forearm.

Saul shouted, louder than he'd intended, and staggered against the door, dropping the cleaver, narrowly missing his foot.

Two jagged half-circles were already rising to a bruise on his arm.

A mirror image.

A branding.

He threw himself wildly into the door, shouting again at the pain, surprisingly intense, streaking up his arm.

Mr Silver was moving towards them, darkness and shadow, the brutal lines of his cheekbones carving up his face into two symmetrical scars.

Saul stumbled again, his body backing up against the hard frame of the caravan door, blocking Mr Silver's view of its handle and the frantic twitching of his fingers; a prayer running through his mind.

Clara, in her pyjamas, was a blur of motion, a flash of quicksilver.

In the melee, Saul was aware of two things.

A hiss of outrage from Mr Silver.

And the coldness of an open caravan door.

52

Last summer

He has never seen a dead body before.

The need to hurt him, yes, he understands that. To make him beg. To apologize. But not this. A man with a knife sticking out of his chest, seeping blood and, he half imagines, the blackened wisps of his soul.

And yet.

A dart of unexpected pleasure.

To see his father reduced to an empty husk of bone and flesh. To see those hands, scarred from violence, stilled. Those eyes, mocking, cruel, closed forever.

The thud had woken him. He had stumbled from the sweat-drenched sheets of his bed, following the sound. Expecting to calm her, to offer paracetamol and a glass of water, to heave her back into bed.

It is dark in the hallway, and she is the silent star of a black-and-white movie, the smudge of her face in the night, the ghostly shape of her dressing gown, the gape of her open mouth.

And, Jesus Christ, the blood.

Thick and black.

She has pressed her dripping palms against the walls, to her face, down the front of the white towelling robe.

He has been studying Lady Macbeth at school, and at the sight of her, wringing her blood-stained hands, the words rise to a murmur on his lips.

'*Who would have thought the old man to have had so much blood in him.*'

Her eyes are wild with the shock, the animal brutality of it all.

'What have I done?' A whisper rising to a shout. 'What have I done?'

'Shhhh.' He places a finger to her lips and jerks his head towards the wall that joins their flat to the one next door. 'Get in the shower.'

His father is lying on the kitchen floor.

He has heard somewhere – probably from one of his old crowd – that it is dangerous to remove a knife from a wound. That it might worsen the blood loss, a single misplaced attempt to help that actually hastens death.

He drags the blade from the older man's chest.

A bubble of blood and fluid seeps from his mouth. It bursts, and tiny droplets leave their mark on his bottom lip, an official stamp of Impending Death.

He is bleeding out. Medical term: exsanguination.

He crouches by the prone figure whose life is leaking out on the linoleum.

The man's skin is clammy but surprisingly cool for the swimming-pool heat of the night. A gasp for breath, as if he is trying his hardest to stay on this earth, as if he can cling on to his humanity by sheer willpower.

The boy's fist curls in the damp, bloodied mess of the dying man's white-blond hair.

His father's fingers twitch and dance like puppet strings, his face a twist of pain. His mouth is moving now, he is trying to speak.

'Saul,' he says. 'My Saul.'

53

11.24 p.m.

Clara almost stumbled at the first hurdle. Her bare foot caught on the step, and she lost her balance, pitching forward into the frozen darkness.

The Night Man was not far behind; she could taste the smell of him. He was in the memory of the nosebleed she'd had at school, and the dead mouse Gina found under a floorboard last Halloween, and the fear that had become her way of life.

But after looking in the other direction for so long, fate had turned her kindly gaze on Clara, and the Night Man ran his foot into the edge of the cleaver Saul had dropped on the floor.

It caused barely a nick, penetrating the leather just enough to draw six tiny beads of blood, but the unexpected lightning bolt of pain was enough to stop him in his tracks. That thirty seconds or so bought Clara time to scramble to her feet and stagger towards the hulk of bushes that enclosed the field.

rungrassruncoldmoonrunfeetcoldruntreesrunrunrunfind mummyhiderunrun

She was ambushed by her senses. A stream of thoughts filled her young mind, tumbling one after the other like the clowns she'd seen with Eleanor at the circus. It was a long time since Clara had breathed in clean, cold air and the rush of it went to her head, filling her with a giddying burst of energy.

She lumbered past the shadowed humps of other caravans, trying to force life back into muscles atrophied by months of captivity, and ignored the rustle of a prowling fox. Once upon a time, the shapes and sounds made anonymous by darkness had held unspoken terrors. The tap of branches at her bedroom window. The bogeyman hidden under a pile of clothes in the corner of her room. Death hiding in the vacuum beneath her bed. Now these held no fear.

She had seen fear.

It had hollowed-out eyes and thin, dry hands that stroked her own.

It had the face of a skeleton brought to life.

She could hear footsteps behind her, not within grasping distance yet, but close enough. Her legs were weak, trembling, but she pushed herself on. She ran harder. Faster.

Her five-year-old heart was a flying bird, a runaway train, a beating drum.

Harder.

Faster.

The trees and bushes beckoned to her. They represented safety. Refuge.

Clara threw herself beneath the twigs and leaves and the tumbled mess of a bush in the south-west corner of the field.

Being small, she squeezed herself into its heart, ignoring the sticks scratching her cheeks and pulling at her hair.

She had the briefest of seconds to catch her breath before she could see his shiny black shoes, could hear the dry rasp of his voice, like driftwood over the night air.

'Where are you?' he sang. 'I'm coming to find you.'

She rolled out from beneath the bush and emerged the other side, into another field.

notimetostoprunningkeeprunningrunrunrun

The stink of farmyards rose in her nostrils as her bare feet sank into something soft and disgusting. But Clara didn't care.

Because that smell meant animals. And animals meant people.

The night was darker than any kind of night she had seen before. In Pagoda Drive, she was used to street lights and the comforting glow of the lamp in the hall. Even the Night Man had left the caravan curtains slightly open to allow the moon to peek in. But here, in this field, the blackness was unfamiliar. For once, she liked it. It kept her hidden.

She could hear him, crashing around the bushes. He was too big to crawl underneath them, and she sensed he was trying to scale them, those prison gates of greenery. A pang of satisfaction. Let him see what it felt like to be trapped.

But if he made it over, he would certainly catch her. During a break in the clouds, and a streak of cold moonlight, she saw the whole field stretch ahead of her, no trees, no bushes, nothing at all, not even sheep or cows. No place for a game of hide-and-seek.

He could run faster than she could.

THE COLLECTOR

Clara scrunched her toes against the frigid earth and made a decision.

Beyond the field's edge, where black sky became black everything, was a house. And it had a light.

54

Thirty-nine miles away, as the crow flies, Amy was easing the hard plastic limbs of Clara's doll into a set of pyjamas decorated with giraffes.

Today had been a bad day. Her cheeks burned with the memory of her confrontation with Lilith Frith. It had been foolish of her not to consider the impact of her vanishing act. Not foolish, idiotic.

Amy pressed her lips to the doll's face. A heady scent rose up to welcome her, a sweet-smelling combination of talcum powder and love. It ignited a lightning storm of memories. A gift-wrapped box. A circle of indulgent smiles. The sound of tearing paper.

Clara's chuckle.

If only memory was physical. If only she could reach out and touch each of those moments from the past, coaxing them back into flesh.

With gentle fingers, Amy finished buttoning up the doll's top. With Eleanor staying overnight at her father's, there was no longer any need to maintain the pretence of normality.

Amy climbed between the cold sheets of her bed and drew the dolly into her chest, closing her eyes and her heart against the nightly barrage of taunts, the mental images and whispered voices.

'Goodnight, Clara.' She kissed its cold fingers. 'I'll see you in the morning.'

She had no way of knowing that in a field on the edge-lands of the Essex coast her youngest daughter was running for her life.

55

11.29 p.m.

When she was a girl, she had always loved to watch the snow fall, seeking perfection in the chaos of each blurry-edged flake.

But try as she might, Detective Constable Antonia Storm could not detect any beauty in the blizzard of pale powder that was falling from the torn sack above, settling in her hair, her nostrils, the damp inside of her mouth.

Fitzroy's face was an oval of worry in the shadows of the hallway. She was mouthing something, but all Storm could hear was a roaring in her ears.

Instinctively, she ran her tongue across her coated lips and tasted an unfamiliar, chemical bitterness. She swallowed, trying to force saliva into her mouth; her tongue was thick and sticky, and that bitterness slid down her throat.

Her nostrils were filled with powder too, and she tasted it again, at the back of her throat, the way one does with the hot richness of a nosebleed.

Storm tried to process what was happening, but the

younger officer could not organize her thoughts into the neat furrows she was used to. Her mind was a sludge of confusion, coalescing into the muddied awareness of a single idea: *This is not good.*

Fitzroy was edging towards her, a hand over her own nose and mouth. 'Get out.' She was shouting now, from beneath the useless shield of her fingers. 'Move, Toni. Run.'

The powder was sand in the back of her throat; a mouth filled with sawdust; lungfuls of dust. The skin on her face, her eyelashes, the delicate hairs of her eyebrows were decorated with fine grains. Storm's eyes lifted heavenwards, the puckered, empty sack dangling above her head confirming what she already knew. A set-up. A trap. Laid by the Bone Collector. She had blundered straight into it.

Her eyes itched.

Her skin burned.

Storm leaned into the wall, weakened by a sense of regret, a longing to remake the past.

'Toni, come on.' Fitzroy stretched out her hand towards her colleague, willing her to move, to bridge the distance between them, her own nose wrinkling at the faint chemical scent in the air.

'Don't touch me.' The words cost a great deal of effort.

A hurt bewilderment lit Fitzroy's face as Storm lurched towards the door, threw it shut. There was a bolt across the top, slightly crooked, as if it had been fitted in a hurry, and the younger woman slid it into place, locking herself in.

She held herself still, allowing the horror to settle upon her. In the dim light, her gaze drifted around the room.

Perspex tanks.

A skull.

A bloodied face etched into canvas.

So Fitzroy's hunch had been an accurate one. Turns out her reputation was deserved. She was an excellent officer.

'Open the door.' A pause. 'Please, Toni. I'm getting help, OK. They'll be here soon, I promise. But you've got to open up in case you pass out or something.' Another burst of hammering. 'Come *on*.'

Storm heard the creak of guilt in Fitzroy's plea. She wanted to say that she didn't blame her, that she must be stupid if she thought Storm hadn't noticed the gentle curve of her belly, and everything it meant. She wanted to say she was trying to protect her, even though they barely knew each other. She wanted to say that she had been looking forward to changing that.

She wanted to tell Fitzroy all of these things, but there was a spiteful pain in her head and the taste of sickness in her mouth.

The drumming on the door was becoming louder, more frantic.

Stop.

She didn't know if she had spoken aloud. Her head was full of a strange ringing, a thousand bells chiming and dimming into the distant call of music carried on the wind.

Fire. My head feels full of fire.

The pain was so great that Storm screwed up her eyes and kneaded her knuckles into the hollows of her temples, sliding down the wall until she was in a sitting position, legs splayed in front of her like an oversized doll.

Her left leg jerked.

Once.

Twice.

A staccato movement.

Staccato: Italian, past participle of staccare, meaning detached, music cut short crisply.

Life

   cut

      short

         crisply.

'Toni, can you hear me? Open the door.' Pleading. 'Please.'

Storm could not wrench her gaze away from her leg. Her thigh jumped again, two, three times. A muscle in her cheek tightened. In her mind's eye, she could visualize the pages of handwritten notes she had made during one of her police training courses.

The symptoms of a myoclonic seizure include twitching and muscle spasms. There are many different types of seizure. Some sufferers may experience an aura a few seconds beforehand. It can manifest as an odd smell or taste, a feeling of detachment or strange lights.

Metal filled her mouth.

She blinked.

The room became a carousel, a listing ship. Storm had always prided herself on having a clear head, but now it was full of rippling images. She seemed to be swimming through water.

Music – violins and a cello – began their lament. She inclined her head, trying to locate their source, not quite aware that they were serenading her from some faraway point in her mind.

Loud thumps from behind the door. Fitzroy was kicking it again.

She. Mustn't. Come. In.

'Stop.'

This time her voice was so loud that the banging ceased immediately. She had seconds, probably. Thirty or so. She could recognize the signs. Her little brother James had always spoken of a burning smell. Although he hadn't spoken for twelve years now. If she died, would he be waiting for her in Heaven?

An old line of scripture began running through her head.

Fear thou not; for I am with thee: be not dismayed; for I am thy God: I will strengthen thee; yea, I will help thee; yea, I will uphold thee with the right hand of my righteousness.

Twenty seconds.

A kind of peace settled over her. So God didn't care that she had abandoned Him. He was here when it counted, after all. Her mother would be pleased.

Storm moved a fraction, leaning into the wall. Her body – which had served her well for thirty-one years – was burdened with the weight of her knowledge.

Five seconds, seven at best.

Now she could not remember how she came to be in this room, or why. She could not remember much at all, except how it felt to be a child, when love was all Heinz tomato soup and Rich Tea biscuits, all long summer days and goodnight kisses from her mother. Church pews and Sunday school.

A rising heat.

Storm had now lost the ability to articulate her thoughts, but if she had been able to speak she would have told Fitzroy that they had made a stupid mistake, and while the cost to

Storm was not yet clear, she did not want Fitzroy to pay for it with the rest of her life.

The dark room, with its clicking beetles and its smell of death, receded.

Storm's body began to convulse.

56

11.43 p.m.

Christopher Cherry was worrying about money. Or more specifically, his lack of it. Which was why he was staring at his bank statements in the study instead of snoring in his bed.

He should have gone upstairs hours ago. The cows wouldn't milk themselves in the morning, and his wife wouldn't milk them either. Joan was a stickler for fairness. She sorted the chickens and pigs, ran the caravan park side of things, and maintained that blasted website, an alien language to him. His job, or at least one of them, was to see to the cows. Only once had he seen her down in that barn, but he didn't fancy getting pneumonia again just so Joan would oversee the milking.

He breathed in, feeling the cold air expand in his lungs before releasing it in a troubled rush. The figures were an ugly mess. Doubling feed costs and falling milk prices had meant a catastrophic year. He would have to let two or three of the lads go. A crying shame, especially as Jerome had just taken out a mortgage.

Bed, then.

He sniffed the back of his hand, a habit from childhood he found impossible to break. The smell of his warm, tobacco-edged skin was a comfort in these trying times.

Christopher, a heavyset man, heaved himself from the chair and turned out the light. His left foot had just pressed itself into the first creak of the staircase when the hallway was filled with the flare of the security light.

Damn foxes.

He was bone tired, but his conscience wouldn't let him rest until he'd checked the hen house. Not two months ago, they'd lost thirty-eight chickens in a single night. A fox had embarked on a killing frenzy, tearing the heads off each animal, but stealing only one. The waste had enraged Christopher, but Joan had calmly insisted on electric netting. It was no good if the battery had shorted, though.

Shrugging on the battered wax jacket that had outlived two tractors, he grabbed a torch and pushed his socked feet into a pair of boots.

The night air smelled cold. The scent of rain was called petrichor, the earthy dampness that comes from droplets of moisture touching dry soil or asphalt. But if there was a name for the scent of ice, he didn't know it. Perhaps it was the absence of smell that gave crisp nights such as these their own distinctive stamp. He couldn't even pick up the coastal seasoning of salt.

A light covering of ice had turned the grass outside his farmhouse into brittle shards. With every step, his boots sent tiny, broken pieces flying. He cast around in the darkness, seeking the burning eyes of the fox, its telltale *yip yip*.

As he rounded the corner, heading towards the chicken house at the edge of the south-west corner of his smallholding, something small and white bolted towards him.

His first muddled impression was that it was a stray animal of some kind. A sheep wandered in from a neighbouring farmer's field, perhaps, or a dog who had failed to navigate its way home.

But his confusion was short-lived because he saw, almost immediately, that it was a young child.

The wind lifted, rustling the leaves on the trees. For a moment, it sounded like applause. The child's lips were moving but he could not hear what it – no, *she*, he guessed from the tangle of hair – was saying.

Instinctively, he leaned towards her, and she recoiled, as if he was going to hurt her. He held up his palms to show he meant her no harm.

'He's coming,' she said. Her voice sounded like it had been spread thin over too many days of disuse.

Christopher took in the pyjamas and bare feet, the dirty face. 'Are you lost?' A concerned pause. 'Have you run away?'

A shake of her head so violent he worried she would hurt herself. 'No. Yes. I have run away. From the Night Man. He's coming.' There was an insistence in her that belied her years. He thought she might cry, but she was throwing looks over her shoulder, twitching with nerves or fear, he wasn't sure which.

Christopher Cherry didn't have children. He was a good man, he lived a plain, uncomplicated life, and he didn't like trouble. But all his years in dairy farming, dealing with businessmen as greasy as the butter that came from his milk, had given him an instinct for liars, and he knew, as surely as Joan's hens would lay eggs tomorrow, that this child was telling the truth.

He hunkered down in the darkness, careful not to get too close.

'What's your name?'

'Clara Edith Foyle.'

'And does he scare you, this Night Man?'

She swallowed, nodded. *Yes. Yes. Yes.* Another look over her shoulder. Christopher pulled himself up to his full height and scanned the dark horizons of his fields.

'In that case, I think we'd better call the police.'

Inside the refuge of the farmhouse, he switched on the lights and reached for Joan's cardigan, which she'd left hanging on the back of a kitchen chair.

With its over-long sleeves and hem that came down to her knees, it made Clara look even younger than she was.

'Stay there,' he said.

Teeth chattering. 'I want to stay with you.'

'Come on, then. Let's go and wake Joan. She's my wife.'

To her credit, Joan, who slept with her mouth open and a full face of cold cream, did not seem fazed to see a small child in her bedroom. She slipped on her glasses and listened to her husband's account without interruption.

To Clara: 'Hello, pet.'

To Christopher: 'Call the police.' A brief pause. 'And get the gun.'

Less than three minutes later, Joan, in her chenille dressing gown, was filling the kettle and warming soup. Clara sat quietly at the table, but every few seconds, her eyes darted to the black square of the window.

'We'll get you something to eat and drink, and then perhaps you'd like a little lie-down, just until the police get here. You look exhausted, pet.'

While Christopher was in his study, dialling 999, Joan handed Clara a mug of warm milk.

'You like milk, don't you?' Joan smiled, encouraging. 'Every child likes milk. And it might help you sleep.'

The sound of broken crockery shocked them both.

Clara looked at her hands, as if she could not believe them capable of such deliberate destruction.

But still she did not cry.

FRIDAY

57

12.01 a.m.

'Hello, this is Essex Police. What is your emergency?'

'Um, I've got a young girl here. Found her on my land. She's frightened, says she's running from someone. Says he's coming after her.'

'What is your address, caller?'

'The Old Blue House, Foulness Island, SS3 9XN.'

'And do you need an ambulance?'

'Not sure. She's very thin and jumpy, but she seems all right. Um. She says she's that missing girl, um, Clara Foyle. You know, the one off the telly. Says he's been keeping her against her will, so you might, um, you know, need to check her over.'

'Visible injuries?'

'None that I can see, but from what she's told us, she's lucky to be alive. Hurry now, won't you? She says he'll be here soon.'

58

12.01 a.m.

'Hello, this is Essex Police. What is your emergency?'

'Where *are* you? I need the fire service and an ambulance. I called fifteen minutes ago. I'm a police officer. My colleague, she's—'

'What is your address, caller?'

'The Old Town, Leigh-on-Sea. I don't know the postcode. Near the pub. The house has a name. Seawings, I think.'

'And do you need an ambulance?'

'Yes, yes, that's what I'm trying to tell you. Is it on its way? It should be on its way. Quick. Please. Sorry. Quickly. She's ingested something, a poison, a chemical. I don't know. Please, just hurry up. She needs specialist medical help. I'm trying to think. Activated charcoal, is it? I can't think.'

'Visible injuries?'

'I can't see her; the door, it's locked but – oh, God, I'm sorry, I'm sorry – I heard her fall down. I think she might be dead.'

59

'Pink or red?'

Gloria held up the lipstick to her reflection. She mostly saved red for the men whose attentions she craved. But tonight was different. Tonight was a special occasion. 'Red it is, madam.'

After she had applied a layer so thick it smeared against the jut of her two front teeth, she selected a bra and knickers. The lace was a rough caress against her skin.

Where the hell was Saul? He was in the shit, no doubt about it. But knee-deep or neck?

The flat was silent. No music. No shriek from the seagulls. Just the clink of the bottle against her lipsticked enamel. She balanced it carefully on the sink, between the toothpaste and her make-up bag, and fluffed out her hair.

Thank fuck for clever hiding places.

She'd found the vodka a couple of hours ago, wrapped in newspaper, stuffed up the chimney breast. So clever that even she'd forgotten she'd hidden a bottle up there too, which had to be a first in the history of the fucking universe.

She took another swig, tipping back her neck until her throat was exposed, relishing the burn of liquid heat through her veins.

Fucking elixir of life right there.

Since that night last summer when all this shit had begun, she had forced herself to turn away from what she had done, but now it was time to remember, and to end it. Anything else was too much of a risk, especially as today was turning into all kinds of fucking weirdness. Starting at tea-time, when those bastards had almost banged down the door.

She'd tried to ignore them, but one had shouted through the letterbox, the boom of his voice a grenade in the still of the flat.

'Saul, are you in there? It's the police. We need to speak to you.' When no one had answered, he'd tried to talk his way in with threats. 'It'll be easier on you if you do as we ask. Don't want to be arrested, do you?'

Alarmed, she had locked herself in the bathroom until they'd gone. When Saul's mobile defected to voicemail, she'd switched on the local evening news to see if that might give any hints as to why the police were soiling her doorstep, seeking out her son.

Sunday Cranston?

The kid with the face.

That's Cassie's sister, isn't it?

But what's that got to do with my Saul?

He's not involved.

Is he?

Can't have the police sniffing round.

Get rid.

Tonight.

Get rid.

In the hours after the Incident last summer, Gloria and Saul had agreed to bury their shared secret as deeply as the memories of that awful night. But for her, even as she'd tried to forget the whole goddamn mess, the truth never went away, floating to the surface like oil, polluting everything around it.

Blood feels like warm water on your hands.

Guilt stalked her. It was in every tumbler of alcohol, every fractured sleep, every raised voice and broken bottle. Not for herself, mind, but for Saul. For the burden she had laid upon his shoulders.

The last Sunday in June. Eight months ago. Remembered in a series of snapshots, a nightmarish photograph album, capturing the final moments of Saul's father.

Solomon had returned home late from the folk festival, reeking of beer and ill-temper, opening cupboard doors and slamming them shut. Gloria had tiptoed along the hallway and closed the bedroom door on Saul, asleep and unaware, before she'd opened up the confrontation.

'What the hell is wrong with you?'

'Fuck off, Gloria.'

Another bang. He'd been pulling out mugs and glasses, shoving them back in with careless hands. Then he had prised the lid off the Fortnum and Mason tin before tossing it on the floor.

'Where is it?'

'What?'

'My fucking money.'

'You've spent it, Sol.'

'You've stolen it, you lazy piece of cunt.'

A hard, sarcastic laugh. 'No, you've pissed it away.'

In less than five seconds he had crossed the room, forcing his fingers around her neck, shutting down her windpipe, shoving her into the gap of wall between the door and the counter top.

'Don't speak to me again, bitch.'

Gloria could not have done so, even if she'd wanted to. He had squeezed her throat so tightly that she had nothing left to push out her breath. Little black flowers had burst open in front of her eyes.

'Say sorry.'

Again, she had not answered. Could not. Even though she had wanted to taunt him, to laugh at his contradiction.

His grip had tightened, and her vision had grown ragged at its edges, dimming into a blur of loose shapes and impressions. She had longed to drink down air, but there was nothing left, just her dry, empty lungs.

'Say it.'

Her right hand had been flailing, scrabbling blindly for something.

Anything.

Unopened letters had slid in a blizzard to the floor.

Her fingertips had grazed a leaking pen that belonged to Saul, a torn packet of playing cards, the polished wood of the knife block.

Upwards.

To a familiar, comforting shape.

326

In one fluid motion, she had pulled the knife from its home and buried it in his chest.

Solomon's eyes had widened slightly, as if she had surprised him with a kiss, or his favourite meal, or a cold can from the fridge. He had stumbled backwards, only a step or two, but it was enough to ease the pressure on her neck. She had drawn in a new breath. Another. And another.

Her throat had been raw, bruised. One of her old boyfriends had liked to strangle her during sex, but never like this. She had tried to swallow but the inflammation was shards of glass with a burning tequila kick.

Solomon had weaved gently, the knife sticking out, a rude, unexpected presence in the region of his heart. Ironic, she had thought, to have landed there when she could have chosen any part of his anatomy, when once her own heart had been so full for him.

He had knelt before her.

Get away from me. Away from me.

She had kicked him in the face.

Solomon had fallen backwards then, his knees twisting beneath him, his head hitting the floor with a crack that split the small-hours silence of the flat. Beneath his body, a vat of spilled Bloody Mary.

Gloria's face had collapsed. With small, frantic movements, she had tried to scoop up his blood with her hands, tried to force it back into his chest, even though it was hopeless, even though his breathing had accelerated into the rapid-fire rasp of heavy blood loss, even though his skin had cooled too quickly for the overripe midsummer heat.

fuckfuckfuckfuckfuck

She had stumbled around the kitchen, a moth repeatedly

bumping into a light, grasping at her hair, placing her blood-ied palms against her cheeks.

In the corner, by the toaster and tucked beneath the curl-ing pages of a food magazine, had been the corner of a pale brown envelope. 'Solomon Anguish' had been scrawled on the outside in biro. It had bulged with cash-in-hand prom-ise.

Into the hallway she had careened, frantic with horror at what she had done, her husband's blood clumping together the strands of her hair and drying in the grooves behind her nails.

And then Saul's bedroom door had opened, and her son, her precious son, had become complicit.

In the weeks that followed, they never spoke of it. Gloria had tried, especially in those moments when Saul's face had pinched itself shut, to crowbar her way in. But her son had closed himself off and would not discuss it.

And then matters had quickly taken a turn for the worse, and now, eight months on, she could no longer talk about it, even if Saul were to bring it up. Because her memories of that night had since become lost in all those other nights when the animal who had let them borrow his car – he no longer deserved to be called a friend – had forced her into doing things she did not want to do.

To buy his silence.

Except Saul knew nothing about that, and never would.

Another mouthful. Heat. Fire.

Dutch courage.

And so, a few hours ago, when the early-evening news bulletin was over, Gloria had dragged free the cushions they had stuffed up there to keep out the winter draughts and plunged her hand into the chimney.

Her fingers had run along the bricked ledge, seeking out the slippery feel of the plastic bag. The vodka had been a glorious and unexpected prize, yes, but she had been looking for something else.

The bag was nothing special, from Sainsbury's. Its ordinariness had made her feel odd inside, like this was perfectly usual behaviour for a Thursday night. Her hand had been dusted with soot.

She'd unrolled it, two, three times, and made herself calm with a mouthful of vodka.

Almost half the bottle had gone by the time she felt ready to retrieve the bag's contents.

The knife she had used to kill her husband was still spotted with his blood.

And tonight she would use it to kill another man.

60

2 July 1955

The faces of the firemen were black with soot. One of them, a youngster, had white tracks running down his cheeks. In his arms was the body of a child, and he was crying as he carried her from the wreckage into a council depot shed.

The men had laid tarpaulin on the floor to protect the bodies from the grease. Elsewhere, she could see a broad back topped with dusty hair pinning sheets to the windows to shield the dead and stop the gawpers. That gesture made Sylvie's chest hurt. A lady in slippers and a housecoat whose garden backed on to the railway line was washing the faces of the lost, dipping her greying cloth into a bowl of water.

Her tenderness was too much, and Sylvie turned away, searching out the man who had helped her, but he had melted into the swelling crowd. Men were shouting, families weeping. Blue skies filled with clouds of grief.

Her hand hurt, but there were others who needed medical attention more than she did. Someone had given her tea but she had only managed a sip, and the blanket was too hot. She tried to fold it, but the pain made things awkward.

'Here, let me.' The woman placed the folded fabric square on the grass. 'You should get that seen to, you know.'

'I'll live.' Sylvie didn't mean to sound short, but the shock was easing off and fear was creeping in to take its place. Marshall didn't like her being late.

'Is someone coming to collect you?' The woman had a face that spoke of hard work and hard living.

'No.' In truth, she had no idea how she was going to make her way back to London. Perhaps she could ask one of the policemen for help.

'Where do you live?'

Sylvie told her, and the woman's face broke into a smile. 'My husband's aunt lives there.' She looked behind her. 'Freddie, Fred, come over here.' A man with a beard wandered over.

'This lady's from Bromley, near Daisy. We could . . .' She signalled at him with her eyes. His shrug said suits me. The woman turned back to Sylvie. 'We'll drive you, if you like. We stopped because we wanted to do something. Let us help.'

Sylvie bent and picked up her box. She didn't want to get in the car with strangers. She didn't want to make conversation and be polite. She didn't want to do anything, except get as far away from home as possible.

But she was too tired and too scared to argue.

61

12.07 a.m.

If a bird hits the window of a house, it's an omen of the death of a stranger. If it dies, a loved one will too.

Mr Silver smiles down at the limp form of the barn owl, its neck twisted against the frozen earth, talons pointing towards the dark skies above. He marvels at the imprint of its feathers on the glass. A ghost of itself.

According to folklore, someone in this family will die tonight.

He licks his cracked lips, tastes the familiar blood.

He will kill the man first.

Mr Silver does not enjoy taking life for the sport of it. But he will lose this precious specimen if he does not act.

The tall man who carries death with him moves silently around the perimeter of the farmhouse. The lights are blazing now, sprung into life by the arrival of the child. He calculates how far they are from the closest town, how long it will take for the police to arrive.

He will aim for the hollow of the neck at the angled

junction of the mandible, just below the ramus. He will cut through the outer layer of the adventitia, the muscular middle of the media until his blade reaches the intimacy of the intima. He will do this on both sides, and the man will bleed out in minutes.

Death, done properly, takes hardly any time at all.

62

'Mr Silver . . .'

Saul's voice was a long, low call across the fields. He stood on the caravan step, surveying the darkness. *Fuckssake.* He didn't know what to do. His head ached from earlier and the bone-numbing cold was making his teeth hurt.

Not for the first time he wished he was at home. His shitty little bedroom with its shitty single bed and its shitty faded duvet cover. Who the fuck had a single bed at sixteen? None of his friends, that's who. Cass had a king-size double bed and her own wide-screen TV and a cool-as-shit record player that cranked out her dad's old Bowie albums. And Posh Dan's room was off-the-scale massive with a whole fucking in-house entertainment system. Christ, there was even a cinema room downstairs. But while he'd always been envious of the glossy, Instagrammed lives of his peers, their iPhones and MacBooks, all he wanted now was his own shitty little room, and the gentle clink of Gloria's bottle hitting the rim of her glass.

A rattling hiss filled the darkness. Like a breath drawn in and spat out again. Saul froze. What the fuck was that? He was a townie, brought up against the urban scenery of high-rises and shopping centres and motorways. Only time he'd been to the country was a trip with the school to an outward-bound centre when he was eleven. But this was creepy shit. Logically, he knew it had to be an owl or something, but it sounded like the rasp of a dying man.

Saul peered across the field, but could see very little except the dim humps of the hedges. Mr Silver and the girl had taken off before he'd realized what was happening, and he was fucked if he knew which direction they'd gone. He glanced back into the caravan. At the mattress. The lumpy pillow. The pile of food wrappers and the stink of piss. Mr Silver had been holding her hostage for some time.

An acid, nauseous feeling burned inside him. By being here, his fingers touching the handle of the caravan door, the shedding of fibres from his clothes, the distinctive white strands of his hair, he was implicating himself in a whole world of shit.

Saul ran back into the caravan, snatched up the knife wallet and stuffed it into his jacket's inside pocket. The toes of his shiny black shoes nudged into a pile of child's drawings, sent them scattering like leaves across the floor.

Detailed drawings. Dozens of them. Ugly, deformed images, all in a childish scrawl. A skull with sharp teeth. A hand with seven fingers. A skeleton with tree branches twisting out of its torso.

Saul stared at the pictures, his mouth filling with something bitter, a kind of poison. His face, his arms and legs were all pricking, like someone was driving dozens of pins into his skin. A heavy weight settled over him. If he'd been superstitious, he'd have said this intensity of feeling, this certainty that something awful was about to happen, was a premonition of death.

But he didn't need to be a psychic to know one thing. If Mr Silver caught her, he would kill her.

Clara Foyle, darling of the newspaper headlines, bleeding, broken, lying on the frosty grass, a knife in her neck.

A buzzing sound, like a swarm of bees. Saul looked up, trying to locate its source.

Mr Silver's holdall.

Saul's missing mobile phone and a set of car keys.

Now here was an opportunity.

He took a quick photograph and stepped into the frozen night.

63

12.09 a.m.

Jakey was lying on his father's lap, watching television. Every now and then, his eyelids would drift shut and jerk open, as if he could stay awake through sheer force of will.

Erdman, who could not endure another episode of *Mighty Morphin Power Rangers*, was on his mobile phone, scrolling through the countless news stories that had sprung up about Howley.

The shape of an idea was forming in his mind, but he wasn't sure if it was going to work. He had tried to call the boy, not a minute ago, but he hadn't answered. Of course he hadn't. It was gone midnight. He would probably be asleep.

Where was Fitzroy when he needed her? He tried her number again. For the millionth time that day. She didn't answer. No shit, Sherlock.

Jakey's eyes closed again, and this time they stayed closed. Erdman held himself still. In a few minutes, when he was sure that Jakey was in a deep sleep, he would carry his son upstairs. His dreams of saving the world could wait until morning.

He switched off the television and the room slipped into silence.

A car drove past, and the deadened sound of its tyres told Erdman the snow had started again. He yawned. He should probably sleep himself. Tomorrow would be a difficult day.

He eased himself from the sofa with difficulty. Jakey was getting heavier, older. But he would never grow up. He would never have a family of his own. That thought filled Erdman with an acute sadness. And not just for Jakey. For himself. For Lilith.

He watched his son settle further into sleep, the softening of his muscles, the slackness at his mouth.

And then the rectangle of metal and plastic that was Erdman's mobile phone began to throb.

He stared at it, as if he couldn't quite believe it. There it sat. On the sofa arm. Flashing. Vibrating. And then he came alive and snatched it up before the caller hung up.

The words were tumbling out of the boy's mouth at a frantic, frightened pace.

'Slow down,' said Erdman. 'Start again.'

As he listened, the idea that had been the blurriest of shapes came sharply into focus: a final, desperate throw of the dice.

He let the boy finish, and then it was Erdman's turn to ask questions.

'You mean now?' A pause. 'I'll bring Jakey.' And another. 'Yes, of course. I'll ring her now.' Erdman's left hand was buried in his hair. 'OK, where?' Silence. 'We'll meet you there,' he said.

His own heart hammering, Erdman immediately tried to reach Fitzroy again.

'Come on,' he muttered. 'Answer your damn phone.'

When his glance landed on his son, Jakey was awake and watching him.

'I'm ready, Daddy,' he said.

64

The sound of sirens always reminded Fitzroy that the city was a living, breathing entity. Millions of voices. Millions of hearts. All different. All human.

The blare of emergency might trigger a baby's cry that would spark the row that would lead to the divorce. Or cause the drunken teenager to stumble before he stepped off the kerb, that moment's hesitation saving his life by the width of a wing mirror.

The butterfly effect.

But here, in this old fishing town, amongst the cobbles and the understated beauty of the estuary, the approaching scream of the ambulance was as discordant as gunfire.

Fitzroy's career was as good as over.

She looked up at the swathe of sky, the moon's pale face in the water. It reminded her of another sky, another moon. A hotel room on a fume-choked road. A need for human touch. Both of them had been embarrassed afterwards, not by the act itself, but their mutual abandonment of sense and

340

reason. The loss of control. The heat and chemistry and filth of it all.

They had agreed to keep their distance.

Technically, she'd still been married to David.

But once was all it had taken.

The spark of creation.

He still didn't know. When Dashiell had asked to meet her for a drink, she'd planned to tell him then, but that moment had been lost in the darkness of that night.

Life versus death.

The beginning and the end.

Antonia Storm was lying in Howley's house, unconscious or dead. And it was Fitzroy's fault. Another black mark by her name. The death knell.

She would be suspended, almost certainly. Sacked, probably. No pension, no prospects. She could lie, of course, but that was not a natural fit for her, and it would be a thousand times worse if Storm survived, and her truth was not the same as Fitzroy's.

Clara Foyle would never be found if Fitzroy was taken off the case.

A twist of pain in her stomach.

The ambulance was creeping its way along the cobbles, washing down the walls of the fisherman's cottages with its electric blue lights.

She stepped into the road and waved her arms.

Her responsibility was to stay here. With her fallen colleague. To get herself checked over. Nobody knew what that powder was or whether she had ingested it. If it would have any effect on the baby. Or anyone else.

She should stay.

She would stay.

A short distance behind the ambulance, she could see the hulking shape of a fire engine. It had parked down the road, too wide to make it up the narrow street without damaging the cars parked on either side.

Two firefighters in protective suits were running towards her, followed by the rest of the crew. Just ahead of them, the paramedics were pulling in.

Fitzroy's phone was ringing again, from a number she didn't recognize. From the number that had been ringing her all afternoon. She didn't answer. Couldn't bear to speak to anyone she knew, to say the words out loud and transform the horror of what had just unfolded into the formality of investigations and disciplinary hearings. To speak to the coroner's office. Storm's family.

The fire crew reached her. They would need to quarantine her, they said. Just to be on the safe side. She was fine. She felt fine, but she told the Incident Commander what she knew, watched him confer with his team, watched them don their breathing apparatus and enter the house.

They would need to decontaminate Storm before she could be treated. Precious minutes lost.

'Did you breathe in the chemical?' The Incident Commander was organizing his team, setting up safety cordons. They may have to evacuate the residents. Just to be on the safe side. That fucking phrase again. What was life without risk?

One of his crew was gesticulating at him, and he held up a finger to Fitzroy. Loose, wet snow had begun to fall.

Her phone started to ring again. Same number. *Fuck off.* Duty won.

'Yes.'

She was brusque, distracted, not listening properly. Her focus was on the fire crews and the impotent presence of the paramedics. *Hurry*, she willed them. *Hurry.* The local police would be here soon. The Boss was already on his way.

'DS Fitzroy?'

'Yes.'

The voice was familiar, but she couldn't place it, even though she knew its deep tone, its warmth. Even though she had faced down death with this man.

'It's Erdman, Jakey Frith's dad.'

Relief. She wouldn't need to explain herself to him.

'Your number – it's changed.'

He sounded surprised. 'It's my work phone.' A pause. 'I did leave several messages.'

Guilt, again.

'How's Jakey?'

'Well, you know . . .' His words were stitched through with weariness. She could almost see the slump of his shoulders as he spoke. Perhaps Jakey's condition had worsened, or the boy was struggling to cope in the aftermath of his abduction. Or both.

'It's late, Mr Frith. What can I do for you?'

He did not beat around the bush. 'Howley.'

Suddenly, she could not breathe.

'They're moving us to a safe house tomorrow.'

'Good.'

'Are you close to getting him?'

She didn't know how to answer.

'Tell me.' His plea was soft.

'No.'

She was too heartsick to try and defend their inabilities, their failings. If Howley had planned to return to the cottage tonight, he would not do so now. She'd endangered her colleague and fucked up their strongest lead.

'I thought not.'

What could she say to that?

'Which is why I'm ringing you.'

The first of the squad cars was barrelling down the road at speed. A woman peered out of her window and then at Fitzroy, and she was filled with an urge to shout at her, to ask her what she was looking at. To hurl a rock through the pretty, leadlight glass.

'Go on.'

'You're at his house now, aren't you?'

'How the hell do you know that?'

'Someone at the newspaper got a tip from a contact. He's on his way with a photographer.'

'Shit.' She dug her nails into her palm.

'But I think I might be able to help.' He was hesitant, unsure.

'What do you mean?' She was alert suddenly.

'There's something you need to know. It involves me. And Jakey.'

Ting.

A police officer was talking to the Incident Commander, and they were pointing in her direction. Both of them turned away when they saw her looking.

'What do you mean?' she said again.

'We've got an idea. A way to lure him in.'

'How?'

'Jakey.'

'No.'

'It will work—'

'No.'

'—but it needs to be tonight.'

'No.'

'He's going to kill Clara.'

She stopped. The whole world stopped.

'She's still alive?'

'Yes.'

'How do you know?'

The steadiness of his voice astonished her. How could he sound so calm when everything she knew was tipping and shifting beneath her feet?

'Let me explain, Fitzroy. And then you can make a decision. You owe us that, at least.'

She could not sanction this. Would not. It was irresponsible, absolutely fucking stupid.

But the orchestra in her head was picking up its instruments and tuning up. Preparing for the crescendo, the fortissimo. The finale. Yes, she was in the shit. But this was the opportunity of a lifetime. She'd already fucked her career, but perhaps she could save Clara. Bring down Howley too. She would listen, that was all. No promises.

'How soon can you pick me up?'

To the officer who had drawn the short straw of keeping an eye on her, Fitzroy called out that she needed to relieve herself. He nodded, then looked away, embarrassed.

When she was certain that no one was watching, she climbed over the sea-wall and onto the beach below. She began to run.

With every footstep, every imprint in the sand, Fitzroy thought about how she had almost ignored Erdman's call. How the events of the next few hours might change everything.

How a single conversation could alter the course of the future.

Everybody's future.

The butterfly effect.

65

Clara was wolfing down a bowl of soup – her first hot food for three months – when the lights in the farmhouse went out.

She whimpered because the darkness wasn't the kind of darkness usually associated with winter nights. This was a darkness with shadows that hunted, and shapes that slid noiselessly through the realm of death. This was the Night Man's darkness.

'Don't worry, pet,' soothed Joan, who put down the bread knife and passed Clara a thick slice covered with salted butter.

'Christopher.' Joan's cry drifted around the kitchen, down the hallway, into the sitting room and up the stairs. And again, much louder, hemmed with impatience: 'Christopher!'

She rummaged in the drawer for some candles, turning to offer up a reassuring smile to Clara, although the child

347

could not see her in the darkened kitchen. 'It's just the fuse box. Christopher will have them on again in an insta—'

At the sound of breaking glass, Joan faltered, the words on her lips dissolving like wisps of woodsmoke. Clara whimpered again, and Joan went to her, suddenly afraid for them both.

The child began to shudder, a series of violent tremors that caused her whole body to shake. To Joan, who had placed a motherly arm around her bird-like shoulders, it felt like Clara was being manipulated, by the jerk of strings, into a dancing skeleton.

'It's him,' whispered Clara. 'He's here.'

Joan, a practical, no-nonsense woman, had met death before. She'd watched her mother Maud succumb to dementia. At the time, it had seemed to Joan that the executioner had slipped his black hood over her mother until only her eyes were recognizable.

And it was Joan who had been the one to load the decapitated bodies of the chickens into a wheelbarrow after what she had privately named 'The Night of the Long Teeth', and she had been the one to bury Elkie, Christopher's dog, under the willow while her husband had wept between puffs of his pipe.

But Joan had never experienced anything like the creeping cold that was stealing beneath the doors and up through the cracks in the floorboards, bringing with it the smell of spoiled meat. Nor the thick darkness that seemed to catch in her throat, making her cough and gag.

Her mother, who had worked in a care home for the elderly before she'd been sentenced to wander the lost corridors of her childhood, had recounted stories of how the nurses could sense death coming. A thrumming vortex of energy.

Maud had always said it was astonishing how patients suffering from Alzheimer's, from the effects of a stroke, suddenly managed to speak with clarity after months of struggling to communicate. That they emitted a sheen, a kind of joyful radiance that helped to create the phenomenon known as terminal lucidity.

But Joan didn't think joy had anything to do with it.

It was *fear* that loosened their tongues at the point of earthly departure, and fear that painted their eyes with that glazed, stunned look.

Because they had seen Him.

The Grim Reaper.

Death.

Joan finally understood what her mother had meant. Because on some instinctive level, she knew that death was here, in her farmhouse.

'Christopher,' she called again, fear sharpening her words into knives, all hard edges and steel, slicing up the silence.

But Christopher, with his 12-bore shotgun and his broad, comforting bulk, did not reply.

To the left of the island in the centre of the kitchen was an old wood-panelled door set into the stone flags. It had a circular handle, which Joan was now grasping.

'We must hide,' said Joan. 'In the cellar.' When Clara did not move, she grabbed the girl by the shoulders, propelling her out of the chair. 'Quickly.'

But the ice in Clara's veins was freezing her to the spot,

slowing her breathing and making her shudder. Her teeth were chattering again. She *could* not move.

And then the smell of death was in the kitchen and it was tainting the air and Clara screamed, because she knew that smell.

The Night Man.

The cellar, a damp trap home to half a dozen bottles of Christopher's home-brewed wine and a battalion of mice, was on the opposite side of the kitchen to the worktop. Joan realized this too late. The bread knife would remain decorated with crumbs, too far away to be of any use.

Like Clara, Joan could taste the air. It flooded her mouth with memories of the jar her mother had kept on the windowsill and filled with coppers for the breast clinic. On summer days, the scent of those coins would linger until the warmth had gone out of the sun.

But that memory was blotted out by the looming shadow of something larger. Another scent that Joan recognized immediately, as any farmer would. Despite Christopher's mutterings, she cared what happened to their cows, even arranging a tour of their local abattoir.

This smelled the same but different.

Blood.

Fresh.

Heat flushed through her body, and then a chilling numbness that tiptoed its way across her skin before lodging its weight in the pit of her belly.

Where had that iron-earth smell come from? Their cows? Christopher? She resisted the urge to scream his name and pushed Clara roughly behind her back, so her own body was shielding the child.

'Give her to me.'

The voice was courteous, laden with age and something darker that spoke of decades touched by deeds too grim to contemplate. It was a voice that demanded attention. It was fear and death and pain parcelled into the dusty timbre of a psychopath.

The lights flickered, came back on.

In that breath of a moment, Joan saw him. The man in the kitchen was much taller than her husband. He was wearing a suit and the white of his shirt was stippled with dark red spots.

The skeleton of a small mammal hung loosely from his gloved hand. In the other, a scalpel and a shotgun.

The kitchen was silent now except for the rhythm of three sets of breathing and a sound like a dripping tap.

Joan glanced at the floor.

Droplets were falling from the hem of the stranger's jacket, strafing the flags with ruby rain. The fabric of his suit, which she had glanced at and unconsciously noted was black, had been saturated into a deeper kind of darkness.

Drip.

Drip.

Drip.

Joan didn't know it, of course, but the blood belonged to her husband who was lying in the hallway with a sliver of glass driven through his eye and into his brain, and another drawn with fine precision across his throat.

The Bone Collector, the Night Man, the man who walked with death, observed Joan and the thin legs of Clara Foyle, just visible behind her.

'Give her to me,' he said again, and his voice was a threat, and a promise and it creaked with knowing.

Joan did not move.

He took a step towards her.

Smiled.

Threw his scalpel at her head.

Joan ducked, dragging Clara to the floor with her. The child yelped. He strode towards them, unhurried. He checked his watch. Another two minutes, maybe more.

He cocked the gun, pointed it at them both.

'Your life for hers.' His words were softly spoken, gentle, almost. A caress.

Joan imagined her conscience as a sheet of paper, torn into halves. If she refused him, they were probably both dead. But if she made it easy for him, there was a chance he would spare her.

A traitorous stream of thoughts flooded her mind.

She did not ask for this. She was fifty-five, still youngish and healthy. This man did not want her. If it had not been for the child, bringing darkness to her door, their paths would never have crossed.

She owed it to Christopher to fight for her own life.

Joan Cherry rose slowly to her feet, hoisting Clara with her. When both of them were standing, she shoved the child in the centre of her back, forcing her to stumble towards him.

The look of betrayal and bewilderment on Clara Foyle's face would turn out to be Joan's last memory.

In three swift steps, the Night Man was across the kitchen. He picked up Joan's wooden hammer, the one she used for tenderizing her casserole meat, and swung it at the soft hollow of her temple.

'I said, "*Your* life for hers." Thank you for your sacrifice.'

The hammer blow inflicted serious damage to her pterion, the thinnest part of her skull, but it did not kill Joan. Fear did. The effect of the flood of adrenaline on the cardiac myocytes of her heart was to send calcium ions rushing in, causing the muscle to contract and triggering the abnormal rhythms that tipped her into cardiac arrest. She was dead in less than a minute.

And now it was just Clara and the Night Man.

As it always had been.

As it always would be.

The Night Man showed Clara the scalpel.

'It will be like falling asleep, my dear.'

He crouched beside Clara, and gathered the child into him. Pressing the blade to her throat, he watched the frantic flutter of her pulse.

Flick.

Flack.

Flick.

Flack.

All these years, all the heartbreak, the loss and love and duty and privilege, and it came down to this: a single, beautiful moment. Clara's hands were in her lap. They trembled. He ran a thumb along the cleft, rode the swell of his admiration, his wonder.

But the seconds were ticking down, and he understood that he had neither the time nor the inclination to shoulder the weight of her body; that, in order to make his escape as easy as possible, he would need to detach her hands.

In that moment of reflection, the Bone Collector made a mistake.

By looking away from Clara, by allowing himself to be seduced by her deformity, he missed the briefest flash in her eyes, and so he was not prepared for the child, who had always been so malleable, so pliable, to find within herself the courage to orchestrate her own escape.

But Clara had tasted freedom, and now she wanted to gorge on it. As the Night Man drew back his arm to bring down the scalpel with the necessary force, Clara bared her teeth and hissed, a feral animal held against its will.

The Night Man, still confident of his superior strength, patted her shoulder and tightened his grip on her waist.

Using all her strength, Clara lifted her right hand, jamming her thumb into the Night Man's eye. How ironic that the very specimens he coveted would turn out to be his downfall.

He let out a cry, his hands instinctively rising to his face, and then she had twisted out of his grip, and she was scrambling out of the kitchen, into the hallway and towards the front door of this unfamiliar house.

Straight past the still-bleeding hump of Christopher Cherry's body.

She screamed.

The Night Man was already on his feet, his shiny black shoes echoing on the stone floors, and her hands were fumbling to reach the door lock which was just out of reach for a five-year-old girl when he followed her into the hall.

He did not run, the Night Man, the Bone Collector. He did not need to. He knew how to bend the darkness until he was it and it was he.

THE COLLECTOR

Clara was standing on her tiptoes, still straining for the lock when the dark hallway was filled with the sweeping theatrics of light. For a moment, Clara stopped what she was doing, and wondered if she was already dead, but then the lights passed, and there was the sound of car engines and doors slamming and voices.

The *blim-blam* of a knocker.

Clara looked around the hallway and dragged the shoe-rack towards the door, ignoring the falling boots and slippers that would never be worn again, and clambered onto the unstable structure.

Her hand closed around the lock mechanism and finally, finally, she opened the door to a man and a woman in police uniforms.

The little girl looked behind her to where the Night Man had stood. The hallway was empty. She thought she heard the squeak of his shoes in the darkness, but she couldn't be sure.

'Hello,' said the female officer, reaching out a hand to steady the child. 'Are you Clara Foyle?'

Her voice was gentle. Like the warm water of a bath, the spring sun, the touch of her mother's hand.

Finally, Clara let herself cry.

66

Saul had been about to cross the ice-tipped grass when he saw a battalion of headlights advancing up the lane at the bottom end of the field.

Blue lights danced above the hedgerows before disappearing. For all his brains, Saul didn't need to be a genius to puzzle it out. *The fucking Feds are here.*

He closed his eyes, as if by shutting out the world he could erase all the memories of his past, and rewind to the time when he was a boy again, and the responsibilities he carried on his shoulders like lumps of rock were still weighted in the soil, not yet unearthed.

If the lights were flashing but the sirens were off, it meant the police did not wish to announce their presence. As if his thoughts had taken flight across the snow-leaden skies, the flashes of blue silently strobing the trees winked out, although he could still hear the tyres as they rumbled over the uneven camber.

The car keys were heavy in his hand.

Saul had never driven before although he'd watched in envy as some of his friends were given lessons for their seventeenth birthdays, a gift that would be well beyond his reach when he left sixteen behind. Gloria didn't have a car, never had. She begged a lift if she needed one. His old mates used to nick them, but Saul was too clever for that kind of shit. Posh Dan kept bragging he was going to take them out in his dad's Audi when he passed his test. No fucking danger of that.

But Mr Silver's car parked across the field by the stile presented an opportunity. A way out. For both of them. *How difficult could it be? Fuckssake. It was just a steering wheel and a couple of pedals.*

The car was unlocked when he slid into the driver's seat.

Mr Silver's shoes were starting to pinch, so Saul loosened the laces and eased them off, throwing them into the passenger's footwell. He flexed his feet, enjoying the feel of his sock-clad soles against the hard metal of the pedals.

Saul slipped the key into the ignition and twisted it.

The car flared briefly into life, lurching forward before the engine stalled.

Fuck.

Saul plundered his memory for some recollection of the basics of driving, but all he could think about was Gloria's fuckwit friend from Luton who'd filled his car up with the wrong sort of petrol and had to fork out several hundred quid to have the tank drained and flushed.

Truth be told, he didn't have the faintest idea of how to drive.

He tried again, his feet playing randomly against the pedals.

The car gave a violent jerk, throwing him forward.

He tried to guess which way Mr Silver had gone. The silent stream of police cars were all travelling in the same direction. It was not too much of a stretch to assume Mr Silver and Clara had gone that way too. If he was to play a knight in shining armour, he had to effect a rescue.

He tried again, but the car did not move.

Ten minutes passed. Fifteen. He was getting colder, more desperate. If he didn't leave soon, the police would find him, and then he'd be truly fucked. He'd have to abandon the plan. Hitch a ride.

He turned the key in the ignition again, one foot pressing on the accelerator, the other on the clutch, his hand grasping the gear stick in the way he had seen Mr Silver do it.

And by some miracle, the car burst into life.

Saul revved the engine, the sound breaking open the night.

And so it was that a minute or so later Mr Silver appeared like a shadow from the fields of darkness, holdall in his hand, and opened the door.

The dome light in the roof of the car spotlit his entrance, a star in the Mr Silver Show.

Saul wriggled out of the driving seat, back to passenger again.

'Hurry,' he said to the older man. 'The police are here. I saw them.'

He tried not to notice the damp, raw smell leaking from Mr Silver as he rested his gloved hands on the wheel. The bones of a small animal skeleton on his lap. But he could not ignore Mr Silver's eye, which was completely filled with blood.

The car slid quietly onto the road.

'Where's . . . ?' Saul did not know how to finish his question. He tried another. 'Is your eye . . . ?' He wanted to ask Mr Silver what had happened to Clara, and could he see to drive safely in the dark, and what about the police? He wanted to ask if Mr Silver had doubled back to the caravan to collect his holdall or to collect him, Saul, his *son*. But Mr Silver was as still as stone apart from the movement of his fingers on the wheel as the car bumped up the lane.

Outside, snow was falling.

Inside, a bloody tear streaked down the valley of Mr Silver's cheek.

67

12.37 a.m.

To avoid any awkward conversations with The Boss, Fitzroy
had switched off her mobile phone and all other methods
of communication. She had texted him, to explain what
had happened to Storm, and he had replied soon afterwards,
already on his way. By her estimate, he would arrive in
Leigh-on-Sea in the next ten minutes. But if he couldn't
speak to her, he couldn't suspend her.

And so Fitzroy, who spent far too many nights watching
the darkness reduce into morning, turning over and over the
details of this case, had no way of knowing that fifteen weeks
after her abduction Clara Foyle had been found alive.

All she knew for certain was that Erdman Frith was carrying his son across the sand to meet her in the darkest hour
of the night.

And that according to Mr Frith, who had never lied to her
before, Clara's life was at stake.

How he knew this, or what she was going to do with this
information, was, at that moment, unclear.

Fitzroy tried to smile at them both, but the gesture felt forced, as if she was pretending to be the same person she had been before Brian Howley had visited death on them all.

'It's good to see you again,' said Mr Frith.

'Don't lie,' she said, and when he grinned, a part of her thawed, a little less terrified of the future. 'Hi, Jakey.' She bent to touch his hand.

She looked at them both. Father and son. Same eyes. Same rusted hair. Same determined set of their jaw.

'Convince me,' she said.

Mr Frith handed her his mobile phone. She studied the first photograph on the screen. Two faces. A boy with snow-white hair. An older man. Strip away the beard and the dyed black hair, and his eyes were those familiar black clots.

A second image.

The inside of a caravan. A dirty mattress. A worn soft-toy rabbit.

From his pocket, Mr Frith pulled out another photograph. The same boy was standing on a mat, just inside a cottage in the Old Town. Fitzroy knew that cottage. She recognized its front door.

Ting.

'The boy is called Saul,' said Mr Frith. 'He says this man is called Mr Silver. He's bringing him to us. But we need to go now.'

The orchestra was playing now, full volume. Fitzroy wanted to ask how this had happened, and how he could have kept this from her, and then she remembered the missed calls, and the artificial light of the caravan photograph, and the time on the text message, not twenty minutes earlier.

And then Mr Frith was half running back across the beach, Jakey in his arms, and she was following them, and there was no time for questions, no time for much at all.

Inside Mr Frith's car, her fingers reached for her own mobile phone. Its blank screen was an accusation. Whatever it cost her – and the price would be heavy – she would not repeat the mistakes of the past. This was too big for her now.

The Boss answered immediately.

68

The Bone Collector is concentrating on the road ahead of him. The vision in his left eye is blurred, his heart sick with loss.

The boy was stolen from him, and now the girl is gone too.

Specimens *J* and *C*.

He thinks he might break apart if he speaks, and so he does not, even though he feels Saul's eyes upon him, watching him. Even though his son is waiting for his father to take the lead.

The countryside rolls by until he rounds the bend, glimpses the sea. The snow has stopped. He takes a long, slow breath, uses the time to reorder his thoughts. His son leans forward and the radio cracks open the silence. Music, chatter, and the sudden voice of a male announcer.

A piece of breaking news for all you night owls out there. There are unconfirmed reports that a female Metropolitan Police officer has been seriously injured in a chemical spillage in a house in Leigh-on-Sea's Old Town. Properties nearby are being evacuated.

More as we get it.

The Bone Collector does not speak. He does not breathe. He does nothing except to rest his shoe lightly on the accelerator.

Vengeance is mine, I will repay, sayeth the Lord.

Fitzroy has found what he has gifted her.

Something catches in the back of his throat. He cannot return to the fisherman's cottage now. This has cost him dearly. The specimen *S.* His colonies.

Gone, too, the fourteen sets of medical notes he had stolen from the Royal Southern Hospital when he fled on that November night last year.

And his rabbits, oh, his rabbits, the soft down of their coats and the perfect symmetry of their skeletons.

A sense of loss engulfs him.

So much loss.

69

2 July 1955

'Please, you must let me have your address and I will send you a postal order for the cost of the petrol.' She inspected her gloves, an unexpected pricking behind her eyes. 'And thank you. I don't know what I would have done without you.'

The woman smiled over her shoulder at her passenger. 'It's no trouble, honestly. Now get home to your family, they must be terribly worried – and don't forget that.'

She pointed to the cardboard box on the back seat with an indulgent grin.

The sun was already beginning its slow descent as Sylvie waved off her Good Samaritans, a few houses up from her own front door. She couldn't risk Marshall seeing her in the company of strangers and she didn't need a wristwatch to inform her she was horribly late.

The rabbit was still, sleeping after the trauma of the day. She hefted the box off the ground. The movement made the wound in her hand open, but the pain was an irritation compared to the cauldron of nerves in her belly.

The curtains at Mrs Manning's house moved as she walked past. Sylvie had done a reasonable job of wiping the grime from her face, her clothing. She'd spent most of the car journey planning what she would say to Marshall.

'I fell over, and cut my hand on a rock. It needed looking at so I missed the trolleybus.'

'I was looking at the tomatoes, and I slipped and put my hand through the greenhouse. It needed looking at so I missed the trolleybus.'

'I dropped a plate and was tidying up the mess when I cut myself. It needed looking at so I missed the trolleybus.'

The box was awkward in her arms. It had been a stupid idea, but she'd come this far and it was too late to abandon it now. She imagined the joy on Brian's face. He had never quite recovered from the death of the rabbit she had chosen for his sixth birthday. This would ease the pain of separating him from his father.

'Coo-ee, Mrs Howley . . .'

Sylvie kept her eyes forward, pretending not to hear the street's resident nosy parker. She quickened her pace.

'Mrs Howley.' Barely time to exhale before her name was called again, more sharply. 'Sylvie.'

Sylvie composed her face into a neutral expression. Mrs Manning was advancing towards her, apron on, hands floury. Her neighbour's bulk and unexpected speed made her look like a great ship, swaying from side to side.

'Joyce.'

Mrs Manning was wiping her hands on her apron, causing dusty clouds to rise. 'Making a pie,' she said, unnecessarily.

'I'm sorry, I can't stop. I'm in a bit of a hurry this afternoon.'

'Yes, well.' Mrs Manning looked down the street, towards the Howley house. 'That's why I wanted to catch you.'

Sylvie waited for her neighbour to elaborate, but she didn't have the chance because at that moment her own front door was opening and Marshall was standing there, arms by his sides, pinning her to the pavement with the weight of his stare.

Mrs Manning followed Sylvie's gaze, and visibly started when she noticed Mr Howley. She gave a little gasp.

'I'm sorry,' she muttered, head bowed, before scurrying back inside.

Marshall was grinning at her as she walked up the garden path. It's going to be all right, she thought, the tight band squeezing her middle loosening just enough for her to smile back.

'Bloody hell, Sylvie, where have you been?'

'I fell over, and cut my hand on a rock. It needed looking at so I missed the trolleybus.' That would explain the dirty residue on her coat and gloves, at least.

His eyes narrowed. 'What's in the box?'

'A rabbit.' Her smile widened. 'For Brian.'

Marshall rubbed the stubble on his chin. It made a rasping noise. 'You mollycoddle that boy.'

But he didn't offer to take the box from her, and that simple omission reminded her that in two weeks' time she would be leaving him.

'Did you have a good time with your sister?'

'It was lovely to see her,' she said, busying herself by placing the box on the step. 'We went to the Royal Botanic Gardens. At Kew.'

Slowly, she lifted her gaze, testing out the strength of her lie. 'What did you like best about it?' He was still smiling, but *was now slightly bent over, fiddling with the metal buckle on his belt.*

In the swollen heat of the afternoon, that moment between them seemed to liquefy into something loose and uncertain. A crossroads, of sorts. A sealing of fate.

'All of it. It's spectacular.'

He cocked his head, impaled her with his eyes. 'But there must have been something that stood out for you.'

Sylvie's body tensed, as if she had been sculpted from molten glass into something brittle and easily shattered. She plundered her memory, seeking out some titbit from the wireless or a newspaper, some throwaway comment she might have stored away that would rescue her now. A fly buzzed lazily around her head.

But her mind was as blank as Marshall's stare.

'No,' she said, 'Not really.' And she knew it sounded weak.

He nodded his head then, the flatness of his expression morphing into a look of such undisguised disappointment that her first thought was: he knows.

But then Marshall spoke again.

'It's just that I've always wanted to go there.' He pushed open the door for her, and stepped aside to let her pass. 'Come inside and I'll make us both a cup of tea.'

Sylvie let out a laugh and the air was filled with releasing tension. She bent to pick up the box, so bloated with relief that she did not notice her husband's uncharacteristic chivalry.

'Where's Brian?' The smile lingered on her lips as she passed through the front door. 'I thought he'd be pleased to see me.'

'He's downstairs,' said Marshall. 'Tidying up the cellar. Why don't you go and say hello.'

He shut the door behind them, and took off his belt.

70

'Where are we going?'

Saul's voice leaks into the darkness of the car. There's an intimacy between them now; he feels it. He knows his son feels it too.

But he does not answer Saul's question because he cannot.

He does not know.

He is at sea.

Adrift.

He has lost another collection. Another home.

And then, as if he reads his mind, his son throws him a life rope. 'I know where we can go,' says Saul, smiling.

He tells him about the plan. About the meeting. About what he has arranged. 'It is time for him to give us back what he stole,' says Saul.

The *us* is not lost on Mr Silver. It is all he can hear. And, just like that, his son saves him.

The boy is still out there.

369

The One.

Mr Silver *must* collect. For himself, for his son.

He has nowhere to go.

Except there.

71

1.07 a.m.

Amy was asleep and then she was not. She lay on her side, not moving, wondering what had woken her and straining to decipher the sounds of the night. But all she could hear were the internal rhythms of her heart, the turnstile mechanics of the four valves – tricuspid and mitral, aortic and pulmonic – as they allowed her blood to pass through before shutting off the exit.

Lub-dub. Lub-dub. Lub-dub.

The darkness was thick and heavy. A floorboard in the landing creaked, once, twice, and then her ears were filled with a rushing sound, and not for the first time, she wished that Miles still lived at home, that there was a lover to wake, to chase away the terrors that plagued her, translating the nightmare of reality into frequent dreams of death.

Amy sat up, mouth dry, wondering where she had put her phone. As she reached across the covers to the table by her bed, her arm brushed hard plastic. The doll fell onto the carpet with a dull thump, and the creaking on the landing stopped.

She held her breath.

Waited.

Her fingers found the silenced handset.

Eighteen missed calls.

At the same time, the light in her bedroom snapped on.

Miles was standing there, his hair sticking out at crazy angles, wearing an old jumper and shoes that didn't match. His tan had faded, even though it was only four days since she had seen him.

He was crying.

For Amy, the room shrunk at dizzying speed. Heat, white, burning, scalded the back of her throat. There was only one reason her estranged husband would appear in her room in the middle of the night, only one explanation that would not wait until morning.

He was taking off his glasses and wiping his eyes with his sleeve.

Amy could not bear the weight of his pain, the terrible confirmation that life is a series of chances, of kinks and quirks. The knowledge that nothing is promised. That the child who giggled, and irritated, and wet the bed, and who squeezed all her love into every cuddle, could have gone while she was looking in the other direction.

'No.' She was shaking her head. 'Not my girl. Not my Clara.'

But then Miles' wet face was breaking open into sunshine, and a smile lit every part of him. He was radiance. He was joy.

'You didn't answer your phone.'

Amy did not move, not a breath, not an eyelash. She was tethered to the bed, weighted down by her own uncertainty. She *thought* she knew what Miles was suggesting, but she couldn't face getting it wrong, if she had somehow misinterpreted him.

And then he said it, the words spilling from his mouth like water to someone parched and close to death.

'They've found her, they've found our little girl. She's alive and she's talking and she's asking for us, Amy. She's alive.'

And Amy, who had rehearsed this moment in her head for so long, found that she could not speak, that she could not cry, that she could not react at all, as if all emotion, all hope and energy, had been sucked from her.

Miles was pulling clothes from the wardrobe. He threw some trousers and a pale blue cashmere jumper on the bed. 'Get dressed, you need to get dressed. We're meeting the police at the station. They're bringing her there. They need to interview her, find out what happened. She needs to be thoroughly checked over' – his face darkened for a moment – 'but we can stay with her while they do it.'

'They've found her?' Amy croaked out the words as if she could hardly keep up with what Miles was telling her. She hadn't moved from the bed, the shape of her legs visible beneath the duvet.

He sat down next to her, took her trembling hands in his. 'Yes, my love. Clara's coming home.'

Clara's coming home.

Clara's coming home.

Clara

is

coming
home.

Galvanized into action by his words, Amy shot from the bed and sprinted downstairs to the kitchen. Two minutes later she was back upstairs, placing the Little Miss Sunshine mug on her missing daughter's bed.

Back in her own room, she pulled on knickers, a flimsy bra, not bothering to hide herself from Miles, forgetting that it had been months since he had seen her naked. As she slipped into her trousers, she glanced up at her husband. He was looking at her with a kind of wistful hunger.

She snatched up her jumper, self-conscious, warming under his gaze. She was too skinny, the events of the last few months stealing from her an appetite as well as a daughter.

A sudden thought occurred to her.

'Where's Eleanor?'

'She's safe, with my mother.'

'Does she know?'

He couldn't quite meet her eyes. 'Best to let her sleep.'

He didn't say it, but the *just in case* hung in the air between them. She understood. He would need to see Clara, to touch her before he believed in the truth of her rescue. To assess the damage.

She bit her lip. 'Do you think Clara's been . . . ?' She tried again. 'Did they say if he had' – her eyes filled – 'hurt her?'

Miles was rummaging through the drawer for her socks. 'They didn't say much, just to meet them at the station.' He held up her phone and waggled it. 'They'd have told you the same if you'd answered this.'

374

She smiled at him then, and for the first time in months, there was genuine warmth in it.

There was still an awkwardness between them, neither quite sure how to behave around the other. A distance that she didn't know how to bridge, or whether she wanted to.

Miles cleared his throat.

'I know it's possibly too much, but I was wondering, I mean, Clara will be expecting both of us to be at home, and so would it be OK if I stayed here for a few nights, just until she's settled?' Miles' voice broke. 'I mean, I'm her daddy, and I wasn't there when she needed me, but this is a chance for me to make it up to her. I'm going to be there every god-damn day she needs me.'

And Miles started to sob, the pain and the hope and the giddying trauma of the last fifteen weeks overwhelming him, drowning him until he could barely breathe, and he collapsed to his knees.

Amy held out her arms then, and Miles buried his face in her stomach, and Clara's parents, whose marriage, whose lives had been thrown into shadow by the sheer scale of their loss, took their first tentative steps into the light.

72

1.09 a.m.

The coat was too big for her and kept slipping down, but no one seemed to notice. Clara didn't care. The merry-go-round of faces, inspecting her, talking at her, slyly glimpsing her reactions to the simplest of questions, made her want to hide. All these strangers. The noise. The attention.

A small, treacherous part of her craved the quiet of the caravan.

Someone had placed a sheet covered with flowers over the old man. Christopher, his name was. It was the same as the one she'd seen on his bed when she'd followed him upstairs. There had been blood on the floor, lots and lots of it. Clara had been ushered away when they caught her looking.

'Is Joan all right?' she had asked each of the faces, but all of them had stopped talking when she'd said that except the coat lady, who told Clara she would be going in a car to London soon.

That coat lady – Clara couldn't remember her name – had tutted at the sight of Clara's pyjamas and taken off her own jacket, placing its winter weight on the girl's shoulders. She was now whispering down the phone to someone, but Clara picked out one of the words.

Tror-ma-tysed.

She didn't know what that meant, but it made her think of the red sparkling drink that Poppy's mother had promised they could have with their sausages and chips on the day the Night Man took her.

What if everyone has forgotten me?

Clara wanted to ask if her mum and dad were coming, but the coat lady was still talking and she had an edge to her voice that her own parents sometimes had, and that made Clara feel a bit funny, as if she might have disappointed them somehow. As if they would be angry with her for leaving the playground and buying those strawberry bonbons.

As if they wouldn't want her back.

At the thought of bonbons, her mouth watered and, instinctively, her hand slipped into the square at the front of her pyjama top.

The sweets were long gone, but Clara had often hidden food in her pockets, and it was a habit that was hard to break.

No food this time, but her hand brushed against something soft. She withdrew it, a smile on her lips.

A pipe cleaner with two arms and two legs and no head.

The big boy had made her bite him.

The big boy had told her to run.

She stroked its legs.

He had brought her a dolly, after all.

73

1.11 a.m.

'I'm starving,' said Saul, as they drove past the gaudy lights of Southend seafront. 'Shall we stop for some chips? They'll be here soon.' A sharp intake of breath. 'Now. We need to stop now. I think I see them.'

Such was his desperation, Saul almost shouted the words, and for a moment, he thought he had blown it, that Mr Silver was going to ignore him and all would be lost, but a few seconds later the older man slid the car into a parking space close to the amusement park. The fairground was in darkness, most of the kiosks that lined this part of town shut for the winter, except one, known for its love of twenty-four-hour deep-frying.

The lights of the arcades flashed on and off. Blinking. Preening. The shadows they cast transformed the hulking metal rides of the fairground into shape-shifters, sliding in and out of view.

These desolate structures would keep his secrets. Saul was counting on it.

'I'll go and have a recce,' said Saul, slipping on the discarded shoes, their polished sheen catching the light.

Mr Silver accepted with a brusque nod, his gaze fixed on the rear-view mirror. 'Be quick.' These were the first words he had spoken since Clara's escape. 'Don't want them to get fed up with waiting and leave.'

The cold air was a relief to Saul, who was finding the atmosphere in the car suffocating. It slapped at his face, his ears. It held the promise of snow. The smell of hot fat drifted towards him. His mouth began to water.

He risked a look at the stand. A couple of people were queuing up. Saul spotted a wheelchair, a familiar rusted head. A figure in a woollen hat, a scarf.

Fuckssake. This was actually happening.

He doubled back, opened the car door and leaned in, his breath coming in cloudy gasps.

'That boy, Jakey Frith, it's him. He's here. And so's his father.'

Mr Silver turned to him, and the older man's eyes were obsidian holes, and his body was trembling with a kind of suppressed energy.

'Where exactly?'

Saul pointed in the direction of the stand.

'They're there, exactly as we arranged. If Dan's done what he promised, I'll take them into the fairground. Meet us inside, at the old Crooked House.'

And then Saul was gone, disappearing into the night.

74

1.13 a.m.

A sign from God, he thinks, and a laugh slides from his lips.

A voice drifts towards him from that distant place, the past. His memory serves up a housecoat and rollers, and he tastes the gingerbread, still warm from her oven. It must be fifty years ago, or more, since he has seen her.

'Well, Brian, if you believe in God, you must surely believe in the Devil.'

It is a long time since he has thought of their old neighbour Mrs Manning, but he can still conjure up the creak in her voice as their families walked to the church at the end of their road. Every Sunday morning, regular as clockwork, they would meet Mrs Manning and her daughter on the corner. He can still see the flushed cheeks bulging beneath her best hat, sweat beading her upper lip and the antidote of his mother's fragrant presence.

But all that changed the moment his father informed the street that Sylvie had abandoned her family without so much as a by-your-leave, leaving all her belongings behind.

THE COLLECTOR

From then on, Mrs Manning sat ahead of them in church and made the sign of the cross whenever she saw them.

But surely this, the presence of the boy just when he is suffering the loss of the girl, is a sign.

Not from God, but the Devil himself.

His son has done well.

His naivety is touching.

The Bone Collector unfolds himself from the car and removes his holdall from the boot.

His claw hammer, a rope and a metal shank.

Into the breast of his jacket, he slides two knives.

In his hand, he carries the skeleton of a rabbit.

75

2 July 1955

'I'm home, my love.'

Sylvie called down the cellar steps and waited for Brian to reply. He hated being parted from her. But his silence suggested otherwise.

'Go and see the boy,' said Marshall, chivvying her along. 'He's got a surprise for you.'

His voice was so full of warmth that she half turned towards him. It had been a long time since he had spoken to her like that, years since he had made her feel more than just a skivvy. His black eyes were shining like tiny beetles.

A blade of guilt carved neat markings into her heart. A boy needed his father and she was preparing to tear him away.

'How lovely,' she said instead, even though she rarely ventured into this dank hole beneath their home. But it was easier to turn her back on Marshall than to witness the rusty spectacle of his love. He was so close to her she could feel the heat from him. She could not afford to weaken.

* * *

382

Brian had his back to her when she entered the cellar. A tank filled with insects which were busy, hard at work on something. A chicken bone, she guessed. In the corner stood an anatomical replica of a human skeleton, a hook hanging from its vertebrae. Marshall hadn't said anything about buying one of those – goodness, it looked almost real, but she guessed it must have cost an awful lot of money.

The heat down here was intense, an underworld of mildew and rotting flesh. She cupped her palm over her nose. The smell made her stomach roil.

'Hello, Brian,' she called, and started towards him. Brian's shoulders were shaking, but before she had a chance to ask him what the joke was, a noose of leather jerked her back, pulled so tightly around her neck that she did not have the breath to gasp.

Her fingers worked uselessly, trying to get some kind of purchase, trying to claw back some air.

Slowly, Brian turned around.

And here was the punchline.

Her son was not laughing.

But weeping.

Then Marshall's face was close to hers, his black eyes bulging as he drew his belt strap tighter still.

She could smell his breath, could taste the whisky–tobacco flavour of his anger.

'Lying bitch.'

She wanted to explain, to tell him that this was why she was leaving him. The violence. The anger. This peculiar cellar and its effect on her son. She wanted to say sorry and to ask him to stop.

She would get down on her knees and beg if she needed to.

Please.

Please.

Except that she could not say it aloud, could not push enough of the air out of her lungs, and propel it up through her trachea and into her voice box, to create enough energy for her vocal folds to vibrate and produce sound. No, it was simply a word that bounced around the echo chamber of her thoughts.

Please.

Plea

Pl

And so Sylvie Marshall, mother, wife, sister, lover, never got the chance to kiss her son a final time. Never got a chance to begin her new life. Never got the chance to be more than she was.

Marshall killed her in the cutting room and then he made Brian take her apart, organ by organ, and when her body was a few days old, he let his beetles feast on her, and she became the first specimen labelled S.

The first kill that Brian witnessed.

The first evisceration.

A couple of hours later, when Brian had finished the task his father had set him, he went upstairs, heartsick and lonely, rigid with the shock of what he had done.

The heat had broken and the night sky had begun to weep with rain. His mother's coat was hanging in the hallway, a cardboard box nudged up against the wall.

Brian peered inside.

His eyes widened, and a shadow of a smile played across his lips, the thinnest glimmer of light on this darkest of days.

He ran to the kitchen for a bowl of water, rummaged for a leftover cabbage leaf that hadn't been used. He would care for this one, keep his temper and not kill it like before. It would serve as a reminder of Sylvie, a living tribute. Something to love.

Ten-year-old fingers dragged themselves through the gleaming fur, stroked soft ears, chucked it under its chin.

But the rabbit did not twitch its whiskers, did not wrinkle its nose, did not so much as blink.

It did nothing very much at all.

And it seemed to Brian as if the death of this rabbit represented all his feelings about what he had done to Sylvie. What his father had done, and would continue to do.

The evisceration of his mother. Her empty eyes, which, moments before, had gazed at him with love. The smell of warm raw meat, and the coconut in her hair.

A stone, hard and smooth, stuck in his throat, and he wept for his mother, for himself, for the poor dead rabbit.

When he had finished crying, when he had pulled himself together and his father was smoking and singing in the bath, Brian carefully carried the box back into the cellar.

The thing that used to be his mother was lying on a concrete slab, empty-eyed, hollowed out. Drying. In preparation for the colony.

Brian picked up the lifeless form of the rabbit and tucked it under her arm.

76

1.16 a.m.

The rollercoaster had been there for years, lording it over the estuary edgelands, its metal loops making cut-outs of the sky.

Having never been so close to an amusement park at this hour of the night, it was a revelation to Fitzroy that the lights on the rides were turned off. Fun dictated by the flick of a switch.

Without the flashing riot of colour, the clamour of music, the blare of electronic voices and thrill-seeking screams, the park barely existed at all.

Deserted.

Dark.

A playground for the damned.

The wind played its music on the Ferris wheel, making its carriages rattle and dance. The clanking of metal was the sound of sharpened knives and chains.

The darkness spoke to Fitzroy. Taunting her. So much to go wrong.

So much to lose.

The tide was on the move again, almost at its peak, and the whisper of water was like the breath of fear on her neck, making her skin prick. She glanced behind her, alert and watchful, and the ghosts of all the lost children gazed back at her.

'Remember what I told you?' Fitzroy's low voice carried to Erdman and Jakey. 'Do not deviate from the plan.'

She slid into the shadows then, into the wall of shrubs bordering the park's high fences and tucked her curls into the hat, pulling her scarf over her face. Edging backwards, she bumped into something solid and unyielding, and let out a scream. Just a bin. But she was a cat on a hot tin roof.

Erdman buried his hands in his coat pockets. Not because he was cold, although the snow had just started again, but because of what might happen in those moments in front of him, as yet unlived.

Because what he most wanted to do was rip at the skin around his cuticles, to tear at his nails. To feel pain. To shred himself apart. Because his son's life was at stake and he couldn't allow himself, not even for a breath in time, to lower his guard.

Right on cue, the boy from the pet shop appeared.

He grinned at them both. 'Ready?'

'Yessss,' said Jakey.

Saul pushed against the metal gates at the east entrance of the park. They shut with a clang, like the quiet tolling of funeral bells. Locking them in.

And into darkness they walked.

* * *

The fairground.

A big wheel. Two rollercoasters. The helter-skelter with its lollipop stripes.

A child's paradise.

Or its tomb.

For a second or so, Erdman glimpsed the giant wheel moving on its own. His mouth dried, and he swallowed, his eyes following the sway of carriages.

The metal spokes of the ride pressed against the skin of the sky, and he thought he saw the shadow of a tall thin man, and he was riding the wheel, leaning over the edge, and his skull was a gleam in the darkness and he was laughing, but his teeth were sharp and his eyes were empty holes.

And Erdman's courage broke apart, a thousand pieces scattering at his feet.

'Let's go home, champ,' he said. 'It's too dangerous.'

But Jakey struggled to pull himself upright in his wheelchair, and although no stranger would have seen it, Erdman noticed the slight upwards tilt of his chin, and the defiance in it.

'No, Daddy,' he said, and there was a strength in his voice, a purpose.

And Erdman glanced back over his shoulder, and the Ferris wheel was still, no bogeyman's face, no teeth and bloodied smile, just the stare of the moon.

Beyond the prison of fences surrounding the fairground, the pier stretched into the black emptiness of the sea. Erdman could smell its briny promise. Fear stroked its fingers down his back.

'Come on,' said Saul, heading towards the control room. As agreed, the door was unlocked. 'Some mates of mine broke in here once,' he said conversationally. 'Climbed the fence and rode the rollercoaster for twenty minutes before the security guards called the police.' He laughed. 'Got let off with a caution.'

He studied a panel on the wall and snapped on one of the floodlights. He turned to Jakey, a grin still on his lips. 'Do you reckon we've got enough time for a private tour? What do you want to see first?'

Erdman tried to read the older boy's expression. Was this some kind of elaborate hoax? Nothing more than a joke to him? Saul seemed relaxed while his own nerves were stretched thin as wire. His body tensed. This was never going to work. He hoped Fitzroy was nearby, but the place was deserted. He prayed she had kept her promise.

'The rollercoaster is a bit of a no-no, obviously. But what about the helter-skelter?' Saul's face fell as he looked at Jakey. 'Too risky, right?' A pause. 'I know,' he smiled, and his teeth gleamed in the darkness. 'The Crooked House.'

The skies had split open and steady snow was falling, feathers shaken out of stuffed clouds. There was a peculiar kind of silence that came with it, muffling everything, softening the sharp edges. He had forgotten weather like this. The abrupt disappearance of the ordinary. The place seemed too big for them. Too exposed.

'I don't think we shou—'

'Please, Daddy. Please.'

Erdman scanned the darkness. No sign of anyone. 'Just for a minute then,' he relented. 'No more than that.'

Erdman had just lifted Jakey from his wheelchair and was halfway up the stairs, Saul a couple of footsteps behind them, when there was a flash of something from across the expanse of the fairground.

Saul and Erdman, who had both caught it in their peripheral vision, turned together in one fluid motion.

The snow was coming down, much heavier now, blurring the cut of his black pinstripe jacket and dulling the sheen on his shoes. But there was no mistaking the tall man who cut through the darkness, walking towards them with deliberate steps, greed carved into the hollows of his face.

'And I looked, and behold a pale horse and his name that sat on him was Death,' murmured Saul. 'And Hell followed with him.'

77

1.21 a.m.

Shit, thought Erdman.

78

Shit, thought Fitzroy.

The fairground's security had done their bit, reacting quickly to phone calls, unlocking the gates, allowing the Metropolitan Police access to the pleasure park.

A team of ten officers – some drawn from DI Thornberry's hard-pressed Essex force because of the short notice – were in place at strategic points, out of view but with a clear sight-line of what was supposed to be the epicentre of the action.

Stay in the open, she had warned Erdman and Jakey. *Keep out of dark corners, the shadows, the buildings.*

We cannot guarantee your safety if you don't follow our advice.

And now they were heading into a closed-off house with no CCTV cameras, and no line of sight.

Ting.

The mournful strings, the gentle timpani of the 'Dead

392

March' struck up their chorus. The funeral lament of Handel's *Saul*. The irony did not escape her.

Fitzroy had kept watch until the wheels of Jakey's chair had disappeared before she'd slipped through the frozen darkness to the discreetly placed security office at the rear of the park, a block of concrete in her stomach. She had volunteered to watch Howley via the closed circuit television cameras, to feed information to The Boss until the moment presented itself when he would give the signal to move in. It was a gamble with high-risk stakes, but she'd always been one to try her luck.

Losing the bet was too awful to contemplate.

A brief doubt flared. Fitzroy had agreed the boy would tell Howley that his friend Dan, a ride operator at the park, had lent him a stolen set of keys. That all three of them would keep to the wide-open spaces. But what if Saul had drawn them into the Crooked House deliberately? This was not part of the strategy they'd agreed. Did that mean it was some kind of set-up?

Rapidly, she reassessed.

'The exits,' she hissed to the night shift security guard whose job it was to patrol the grounds and monitor the banks of CCTV cameras, pointing at the leaning building. 'How many?'

His face was blank. He was used to kids climbing over the fences and drunken stag parties. This was a whole new ballgame. He rubbed his chin, his answer so painfully slow that Fitzroy wanted to shake some urgency into him. 'Dunno. Two?'

'But you don't know?' she pressed him, demanding the certainty of facts.

He gave a hopeless shrug.

Fitzroy bit her lip.

She glanced again at the screens.

The tall man was walking towards the Crooked House with slow, deliberate steps. He was broader than she remembered, his hair much darker, the shadow of a beard. Was it him? She thought so, but she wasn't certain.

To move now or wait?

Indecision.

The state of mind that made her stumble.

Ting.

The majestic pomp of trombones, the softer call of flutes. The music played on and on, getting louder and louder until it drowned out everything around her except him.

And the rabbit skeleton in his hand.

She ran.

79

It is oddly fitting, the Crooked House.

It is here they came, he and Marshall, after his mother Sylvie died. He remembers it now. They stayed in the caravan. Visited the pier. Ate warm doughnuts and played on the slot machines and climbed its rickety stairs. A popular weekend destination for Londoners. It is old, this funhouse, he thinks. Like me. But it is still standing.

He wonders if the Crooked Man with his unseeing eyes and flyaway hair, his shaving brush and his paintbox, is still there.

Saul has done as he was asked. He has proved his worth. The Bone Collector has found his rightful heir. That knowledge fills him with a sense of peace.

He watches them, sees the fear carved into their faces as they disappear inside.

Yes, he thinks, it is oddly fitting.

A crooked boy in a crooked house.

80

The stairs leaned so far to the right that Saul had to close his eyes to stop himself from feeling dizzy.

It was dark inside, and he didn't know where the switches were. Didn't know how to turn on the animatronic displays, didn't know how to light their way out of this darkness.

Jakey Frith could not run.

He had somehow forgotten that.

Or maybe, somewhere deep in his subconscious, that oversight had been deliberate. Now the Friths were boxed into a house with crooked floors and crooked windows.

And Mr Silver was coming with his knives.

81

1.31 a.m.

'Ol' Bloody Bones is here.'

Erdman had heard the same squeal of the door's hinges, and he placed his hand over Jakey's mouth, off balance, disorientated, desperately trying to navigate the lurching stairways of this fucked-up house.

His son was trembling, and his fear was like an infection, spreading to Erdman, distracting him, sending him off-kilter, shutting him down.

Don't deviate from the plan.

That's what DS Fitzroy had said. But going inside this house had not been part of the plan. Stay in plain sight, she had warned them, after the fairground's security staff had unlocked the gate. And they had done the opposite.

'Daddy's here, champ.' A murmur against Jakey's ear. 'But we must stay quiet, or he'll find us.'

In the silence of the Crooked House, the sound of a heavy bag hitting the floor, of a zip being unfastened. The dull clunk of steel and savagery.

'It's over, Mr Frith. Give the boy to me.'

'Do it, Daddy,' said Jakey.

Erdman clamped his hand over Jakey's mouth again.

But his son wriggled so violently, so unexpectedly in Erdman's arms that he loosened his grip, and before he knew it, his boy was limping away from him, into the dead of darkness, towards the Bone Collector.

Jakey Frith was braver than most, and this was his sacrifice.

But had he known what the Bone Collector was planning, even this bravest of boys would have faltered.

Because the Bone Collector was about to slit his throat and let him bleed out. He would carry his body away in the holdall.

But Saul had suspected.

And the Bone Collector had underestimated his heir.

82

Mr Silver was standing in the sloping hallway, next to a mechanical doll with dead eyes and a head that span in slow-motion circles, but was now as still and watchful as the night.

Saul did not know this because he could barely see ahead of him. The floors in the house made it difficult to get a sense of himself. All he could hear were the ragged sounds of breathing, and the exchange between Mr Silver and Jakey.

And now, long, low whimpers that were filled with fear and reminded him of what it was to be six again.

To be afraid.

The light and shade in Saul seemed to ebb and flow. He was death, he was life, a traumatized boy and a damaged teenager. A son. An orphan.

This was the moment.

Because there was no going back from it.

This was what he had wanted when he had contacted

Erdman Frith and told him all about the man called Mr Silver who was obsessively interested in him and his son.

And Mr Frith had inhaled sharply.

Asked him to prove it.

And so he had sent him a picture of himself and Mr Silver.

But then Mr Silver had introduced him to Clara Foyle.

And Saul had known then that he did not want to follow this path.

And he had helped Clara Foyle to escape.

And he had found his phone.

And he and Mr Frith had come up with this plan.

He had lied to Mr Silver. He had lied when he'd told him Dan would open the gates.

To make it seem convincing.

But where were the police?

Mr Frith had promised the fucking police.

And then.

The whine of a blade.

The intake of breath.

And he had to act. Saul knew that Mr Silver would not let this boy live, that this child's death would leave another stain on his conscience, and he fumbled with the knife wallet he had snatched from the caravan, and he ran into the darkness, towards the sounds of fear.

And then floodlights and shouted voices were filling every window of the Crooked House. And Saul saw the flash of quicksilver and Jakey's twisted face, and the agonized expression of Erdman Frith.

And before he had time to think, he pressed the blade into the hollows of Mr Silver's spine and killed the devil on his back.

83

1.33 a.m.

Oh, Saul, he thinks.
My son.
My betrayer.

84

1.34 a.m.

Fitzroy was first inside the house, senses roaring with the success of the chase, the adrenaline spilling through her like liquid. Something fluttered inside her, and she placed a hand on her belly to calm her baby.

To calm herself.

The Boss and the rest of the team were fanning around the Crooked House, covering exits, eyes fixed on the prize inside. Brian Howley, the collector of bones, would not escape them again.

He was lying on his stomach, his head turned to the side, a knife in his back. The sloping floors gave the illusion he was trying to claw his way upwards, to escape. A hand was flailing uselessly, trying to free the hilt of the blade, but he could not reach it.

Erdman Frith was holding his son in his arms. The boy – Saul Anguish – was standing a short distance away, listless arms by his sides. She blinked. The uneven floors were playing havoc with her sense of perspective. All three were skewed. A floating tableau.

Fitzroy ran back through the corridor of the tipped-sideways house. 'Paramedics!' A shout, shot through with urgency. She wanted justice, not the get-out clause of death.

Fitzroy's mind rolled back to that night at his father's house, when Brian Howley had taunted her with that child-hood rhyme about the little girl with the little curl.

Now it was her turn.

She crouched next to him, reading the approach of death in the clamminess of his skin, the rasp of his breath, the dark blood that was leaking from him. She cuffed his wrists behind his back, and the metal hung loosely around them like too-big bracelets. She did the same with his ankles. She was taking no chances this time. Fuck the rules. Her mouth was by his ear, and she tasted the rotting core of him.

'There was a crooked man who walked a crooked mile.
He found a crooked sixpence upon a crooked stile.
He bought a crooked cat, who caught a crooked mouse
And they all lived together in a little crooked house.'

His eyes flickered and opened, and then she was falling into the black hole of his deeds, the evil he had wrought on all of his victims.

He was trying to speak. To confess, she suspected. She leaned closer to catch the words spilling from his lips, still chapped, in bubbles of blood.

'You were hurt.' His voice was the creak of a thousand childhood nightmares. 'I heard it – the radio.'

Fitzroy permitted herself a smile.

'Yes. Except that wasn't me, it was my colleague. And she isn't dead, although I'm sure that's not what you intended.'

She grinned, her face up close to his. 'Never mind. We'll release the details of her heroics in the morning. Along with a press release confirming your arrest.'

He did not react, not a flicker in his dead eyes, not a rise. Nothing.

And then his lips were moving again.

'You weren't *supposed* to die.' Every word an effort. 'That insecticide, aldrin, it's very bad for babies.' A smile stretched the skin across the hard edges of his bones. 'Causes birth deformities.'

The world tilted beneath Fitzroy's feet as she remembered the clouds of powder drifting towards her, and the rush to capture Brian Howley instead of taking care of herself. Her baby.

Fucked up again. Silly girl.

He closed his eyes, but he was still trying to speak, to tell her something else.

'I was going to collect it.' He spoke slowly, just to make sure she understood him. 'Your baby, I mean.'

And never before had Fitzroy wanted to place her hand over the mouth of a suspect, and take from him his life in the way he had stolen hers; her career, and now her child.

And her hand was pressing down over his mouth, his nose.

Harder.

Harder.

And his eyes were closing, and she could feel him smiling against the skin of her palm.

And then Erdman was pulling her off, and DI Thornberry was there, and other officers she didn't recognize, and the paramedics, who had been on standby, were telling her to move, move, move.

She ignored them all, leaned over him one last time, suddenly desperate.

'How did you know?'

A faint smile. Even as adversaries, they had always been peacocks. Strutting about. Showboating their superiority. Outsmarting and undermining each other.

It had been his undoing, and the look in his eyes told her he knew that too.

'The pregnancy test. In your wardrobe.'

And he laughed.

'And the fourteen skeletons at the beach, what did you mean by those?'

His face closed down, and he moved his head, seeking out the boy he had called his son.

'Saul.' An insistent rasp. 'Come.'

'Don't get too close to him,' said Fitzroy, sharp, alert for trickery.

Saul lumbered forward. 'Yeah.'

That boy had courage, thought Fitzroy. She hadn't asked who had placed that knife between Howley's shoulder blades, but she could guess by the awkward way he was holding himself, the anxious flashes in her direction.

'Closer.'

Saul knelt down beside him.

'It's OK, son,' said Howley, barely audible. 'You are braver than me.' He drew in a breath, every inhalation a struggle. 'I wanted to kill my father too, but I never found the strength.'

Saul threw another worried glance at Fitzroy, fear ironed

into his face, but she shook her head, to say it doesn't matter now, to let him talk.

Outside, a blizzard. The floodlights projected the frenzy of flakes onto the walls, thousands of shadows crawling across the paintwork like beetles. The Crooked House was cold and growing colder.

And Jakey Frith, whose face had been buried in the safety of his father's shoulder, leaned forward and stared down at Ol' Bloody Bones, lying on the floor.

And then the lights were flickering, and those who were looking at the Bone Collector would say that it seemed as if he was merging with the darkness and shadows, like the black scratches and dust on an old cine-film, moving in and out of focus.

And Fitzroy – with her rational detective's mind – would later tell herself that it was impossible, that of course he had not vanished for a moment or two, it was tiredness and the effects of the pesticide on her brain.

Because when she looked down again, he was still there, knife in his back.

Saul brushed the Bone Collector's hair from his face, a final gesture.

And the older man gave a quiet cry of recognition, like he was saying goodbye.

Or hello.

And the peaks and troughs of his breathing flatlined into the kind of freedom that Brian Howley had never known in life.

Finally, the bogeyman was gone.

85

One month later

'Come in.'

The Boss was sitting behind his desk. His office felt familiar to Fitzroy and a long way away, like a memory of a place that had once been important to her.

'You wanted to see me, sir?'

Even now, she couldn't bring herself to call him by his name. Probably never would.

'I did.'

Fitzroy sat down without being asked. Her belly was nicely rounded now. There was no denying it. A couple of uniforms had offered surprised congratulations, and she had smiled, and thanked them.

The Boss had fresh lines in his forehead, and a letter in his hand. She recognized its signature.

'Change your mind, Etta. You're a decent cop.'

'Thank you, sir. Means a lot to hear that from you.'

'Or take a leave of absence. Come back when you're ready. After the baby's born, if you like.'

'That's generous, sir, but I've made up my mind.'

The Boss tapped his pen against the desk, adjusted the photograph of his three grown-up children and gave a rueful grin. 'Family first, eh?'

'Something like that.'

Easier to say that than opening up with the truth. That she had stared into darkness, and its shadows still lingered. That policing had been her vocation, but she needed to do something different now, before it swallowed her up. That the necessary chains of law and order were too constricting. That she could no longer bear to gamble on the lives of her colleagues. That she wanted to spend time with her sister Nina and her nephew Max. That, in the finding of Clara, she had found herself.

She valued her life.

Her sanity.

The promise of a new beginning.

'Toni Storm's coming back next week. I'm considering promoting her. What do you think?'

Fitzroy felt a warmth inside her. 'I think it's an excellent idea, sir.'

The Boss nodded a couple of times, satisfied by her response. 'She was playing the hero and it damn nearly killed her.' His grimace twisted into a smile. 'And created a fuckload of paperwork.' Serious again. 'But without her we'd never have found the remains of Sunday Cranston. And she was the one who made the crucial link, you say? Found the house, the evidence? Worked out that Howley was Mr Silver?'

'That's right.' Fitzroy concentrated on making her lie sound as natural as possible. A debt paid.

'Fourteen skeletons on the beach, fourteen hospital files stolen from the Royal Southern, all victims of bone deformities. Ms Cranston was the first.' He softened his voice. 'And your baby . . .'

He could not bring himself to finish that sentence. Cleared his throat.

'It would have been the biggest mass killing since Harold Shipman. If he'd got the chance to carry them out.' The Boss looked out of the window, onto the streets of Lewisham. 'I owe you an apology.'

'What for?'

'I thought Clara Foyle was dead.'

'We all did, sir.'

'Not you, Etta.' He turned away from the glass then, intent, curious. 'What do you make of the boy?'

'Saul Anguish?'

'His fingerprints were all over the cottage and the caravan. He was wearing Howley's shoes, for Christ's sake.'

'I believe him, sir. And his mother. Classic case of grooming.' She shifted, a roar of heartburn in her chest. 'What do you think will happen to him?'

'That's for the CPS to decide. I imagine the courts will be lenient, if it goes to trial. He's got the Friths as witnesses. That'll win the sympathy vote, for starters.' The Boss shrugged. 'He killed a psychopath who was on the run, and orchestrated the escape of a child who'd been held captive for months. There'll be a nationwide outcry if they send him to prison.'

'Still no trace of his real father?'

'Nothing. There's a story there, I'm sure of it. But whatever it is, they aren't telling.'

'And his mother seems to have made a full recovery.'

'The scars will take a while to heal, but she's a strong woman. Must run in the family. Not everyone would have the strength to fight off a rapist. She's been charged with manslaughter and carrying an offensive weapon.'

'Bail?'

'Yes, and several women's charities have taken up her cause. Her attacker had previous convictions for sexual assault.'

'It's odd, though, isn't it,' said Fitzroy, 'how both of them were caught up with those deaths on the same night?'

She couldn't bring herself to meet his eye, to share her hunch about Saul and his mother, to replay Brian Howley's words.

You are braver than me. I wanted to kill my father too, but I never found the strength.

Too.

Three little letters that might just have given the game away.

Did Howley, in the confusion of death, believe himself to be Saul's father?

Or was he alluding to something darker?

She pushed that thought away. In her mind's eye, she could see the frightened boy in the almost-man that was Saul. The hunted look in his eyes. The scars criss-crossing his mother's hands, and the ones she couldn't see.

Saul deserved a new beginning too.

Dashiell Hall was waiting outside the offices of the Metropolitan Police's Homicide and Serious Crime Command, lounging against the wall. He was reading an article on the epidemiology of wildlife diseases.

'Hey.' A smile. Tentative, but hopeful. 'How did it go?'

'He wants me to retract my resignation.'

Dashiell's smile collapsed. 'Are you going to?'

'And miss the chance to move to New York? It's not every day your . . .' she hesitated at the unfamiliar word '. . . boyfriend gets offered a job at The Smithsonian.'

His smile reinstated itself, and he pulled her towards him.

Etta wasn't giving up. Never that. The desire to find the truth in the horror of the everyday burned within her, but its flame was dimmed for now. She would turn up the gas again when she was ready.

But for now, there was no rush.

It was still so shiny and untarnished, this sense that Dashiell was on her side, that he wanted the same life as she did. But she was getting used to it, to seeing her own happiness reflected in his.

It was nothing short of a miracle.

In the hours after Howley's death, she had called Dashiell because he deserved to know about the baby. He deserved to know the truth.

He had listened without interruption, without dictating her next move, without saying very much at all.

'It might be damaged,' she had said, and the tears had spilled down her cheeks, but she had told him that she would keep the child that was growing inside her.

If it survived.

When she had arrived back at her flat, hours and hours later, after Howley's body had been removed, after the debrief and the questions and the endless medical checks, he was waiting for her.

He had unfolded himself from his car, and he had run a bath and made scrambled eggs, and he had put his arms around her and never left.

Aldrin, a pesticide now out of production and banned in this country, had been stored in the Howley family's caravan on Foulness Island for decades.

It was toxic, horribly so, but they were praying the years had dulled its potency.

The news from the scans had been positive so far, but there were no promises, the doctors said. No promises at all.

And Etta Fitzroy, former detective sergeant, estranged wife, girlfriend, sister, lover, mother-to-be, could live with that.

She could live with anything if she still had hope.

86

Now

A kitchen. A mother is standing at the work surface, mixing batter for Yorkshire puddings. Her hair is tied into a loose ponytail, and she is singing under her breath.

The smell of roasting meat fills the house.

A man wanders into the room, pulls a bottle from the shelf. 'Wine?' he says.

The woman – Amy Foyle – shakes her head, sips her glass of water. 'No, thanks, not tonight.'

Her husband – Miles – drapes a casual arm over her shoulder, and peers into the bowl.

'Want me to finish that?

She turns to him, and laughs. It is such a lovely sound that he laughs too. 'Since when have you been interested in cooking?' she says.

He grins, sheepish. 'I just want to help.'

'You are,' she says softly. 'By being here.'

Amy and Miles sleep in separate bedrooms, but in the

evenings they turn off the television and they talk to each other, and they count their blessings.

At the table sit their two girls.

Eleanor is doing her homework. It's junk modelling, making instruments out of recycled boxes and cartons. Her tongue is sticking out.

'Where's the glue?' she says. 'And the black pen?'

The youngest girl is thin, but her cheeks have plumped out in the last two weeks. She pushes the glue stick towards her sister.

'Can I help you?' she says.

The older girl looks up. Her sister Clara has barely spoken since coming home, has drifted around the house like a ghost, screaming at shadows.

It takes time, says her mother.

Miles and Amy are both still, both watching, breath caught at the back of their throats, waiting to see what happens next.

'Sure,' she says, and passes her an empty milk bottle. 'Can you fill this with the rice? I want to make another shaker.'

Clara does what her sister asks, and she is absorbed in the activity, forgetting about everything except the passing of the uncooked grains into the mouth of the washed-out plastic container.

She picks up the lid, screws it as tightly as her five-year-old cleft hands allow.

Shakes it.

The sound is like rain and the wind in the trees.

On the table is a tatty toy rabbit that belongs to a boy Clara knew once upon a time. The police lady gave it to her when she cried out for it, and her mother has washed it and sewn up the torn seam. Jakey Frith is coming to visit in the morning. Their mothers have been talking on the telephone. The children have not seen each other yet, but both have asked to. Clara will give it back to him, and she knows he will be happy. She knows that both of them will always fear the night, but that the pull of light is stronger. Always.

She shakes the bottle again and again until Eleanor joins in.

Clara throws back her head and laughs, takes a sip of juice from her Little Miss Sunshine cup.

It tastes sweet.

87

Now

Saul is cleaning out the mynah bird's cage when the bell above the shop door rings.

'Fuck you,' says the bird conversationally.

Saul traces a finger down the curve of its breast feathers. He has grown quite close to it. In recent days it has started to mimic him. He enjoys the sensation of its beating heart, the rattle in its ribcage. He is thinking of asking Conrad if he can keep it.

Of trying to breed a pair.

'How's my hero today?' asks Cassidy Cranston. She's in her work uniform and she kisses him on the corner of his mouth. 'Mum sent you this.'

Another packed lunch. Smoked salmon. Bagels. Fresh juice. The Cranstons have been lavish with their attentions since discovering he killed the man who stole Sunday's life.

Sometimes it is a little too much.

But Saul is the toast of the town. His picture has appeared on the front page of newspapers. The school is creating a prize in his name. There has been talk of a Special Commendation from the police, and an article has been cut out and pinned on the noticeboard in the store's staff room. No one has yet drawn on devil's horns.

Mr Foyle has paid him the first half of the £100,000 reward.

Cassidy has gone from ignoring him to ringing him all the time. Some days she cries. Some days she is stronger. Some days she asks questions he prefers not to answer.

Were you scared you were going to die?

Did you try and escape?

Did you kill Brian Howley for me?

Some days Saul prefers the company of the bird.

He does not believe that Mr Silver – he cannot think of him by any other name – wished to kill him. He was armed with two knives, yes. One for Erdman and one for Jakey.

But he does know one thing: that Mr Silver wanted to own him, in the way that he was owned by his own father, and the generations before him.

No one will own Saul.

He was intrigued by Mr Silver. He was an anchor in the shifting outflow of Saul's life. He offered stability. Shelter.

But he will never share with Cassidy that truth.

That he had seen the painted canvas of her sister's face. That he had been tempted by the nature of Mr Silver's work. The glory of it all.

That he had yearned for his own father figure. That he had trusted him.

Until a single, broken moment.

'The mirror, son. Came right off the wall and slammed into the back of your head. You went down like a ninepin.'

Saul knew then that Mr Silver's promises were full of dust. Because Saul had been bending over, looking at the beetles, fascinated, seduced. And he had caught a movement in the shiny reflection of the tank, and he had seen Mr Silver coming for him, a hammer in his hand, in that snatch of time before it all went black.

And Saul had vowed then to seek vengeance.

'I see that your grammar school education hasn't gone to waste.'

Saul was a clever boy. He had known he would be implicated in Sunday's disappearance. In Clara's abduction.

And that documentary had come back to him in flashes of memory. The girl with the hands. Her heartbroken mother. Mr Foyle's offer of a reward.

He is good at pretending.

Pretending to be frightened.

Pretending to be honest.

Pretending to be a victim.

Bending himself to fit the truth of those around him.

And so he had double-crossed Mr Silver. He had double-crossed them all.

The mynah bird hops on its perch, watching Saul. He gives it fresh water and shuts the cage door.

Next, he checks on the insects.

A locust (Family: *Acrididae*) is lying on its side. Saul's heart soars. He is lucky the other locusts haven't eaten it yet. He cannot risk leaving it there.

Saul checks that Conrad is not watching, and slips it into a matchbox.

* * *

THE COLLECTOR

There is spring in the air as Saul makes his way home from work.

Banks of narcissi line the cliffs, and he gathers up a bunch to take home to Gloria. She has promised to bake him a cake.

His mother is in the sitting room, making dresses for the Thursday market. The flat's windows are open, and the breeze, fresh and briny, is fluttering the curtains.

Gloria's hair is washed, and she is wearing a skirt he hasn't seen before. It's a long time since he's seen her sewing but her needle flies through the fabric.

'Guess,' she says, through a mouthful of pins.

He narrows his eyes, makes a pretence of sniffing the air. 'Victoria sponge?'

She grins, and the pins indent her lips. 'That's right.'

Saul has not asked his mother what happened that night, and she has not told him.

All he knows is that Gloria has seemed lighter in the days and weeks following Mr Silver's death.

The drinking has slowed down. No more late-night wanderings. She's more present, more like her old self. It pleases him.

Saul leaves his mother sewing, and opens the door to his bedroom, flings his bag on the floor and lifts down his jewellery box. The familiar musty smell of decay fills his nostrils.

He removes the matchbox from his pocket and unsleeves it, lets out a breath at the sight of the dead locust.

Careful now, or the wings will tear and fall apart.

With a kind of reverence, he eases out the bottom drawer,

and, using his tweezers, lays the insect to rest with its cricket cousins.

Saul loves this jewellery box.

And what he loves most is its secret compartment.

He fiddles with the spring-loaded mechanism, carefully flips open the false bottom. Lying against the velvet flocking are two new worry dolls.

Two pipe-cleaner bodies.

Two pale faces made from felt.

But Saul has not used wool for their hair. Not this time.

The first doll is crowned with strands as blond as Saul's own. Close inspection reveals rubied spotting on the platinum shafts of keratin.

His father had always been so vain about his hair.

The second doll's is much darker, dyed threads of black with glimpses of silver.

It is fitting, he thinks, those glimpses of silver.

He straightens their crooked limbs, and tidies the stolen snippets of hair. Locks them away behind the safety of the box's wooden lid.

His trophies.

Because Saul likes to collect things too.

ACKNOWLEDGEMENTS:

Every book has a story behind it. And the story behind *The Collector* is one of friendship, quiet dignity and loss.

Perhaps you noticed the dedication at the beginning. *Cherry Anthony*, it says. *First reader and friend.* You might throw it a cursory glance. Wonder briefly. Move on, to other stories, other lives. Her name won't mean anything to you, reduced to anonymity by the flat blackness of printing ink. You'll almost certainly forget.

I will never forget.

To me, Cherry was twenty-six years of deep, enduring friendship. She was loyalty and compassion, integrity and great judgement; a lover of words and punctuation. She was books-for-Christmas-and-birthdays and long telephone calls, daydreams and laughter.

Cherry was the first (and only) reader of the early tangled mess of a manuscript that became my debut novel *Rattle*. It was she who encouraged me to send it off to agents. And she – as potty about books as I am – was the friend I rang first with news of my publishing deal.

But for every word of *The Collector* I wrote, for every week that passed, for every character and plot twist I shared with her, it seemed as if my much-loved friend, who carried herself with such dignity and poise, was becoming weaker.

And a few days after I typed 'The End', Cherry closed her eyes for the last time.

I was in Amsterdam with a group of old school friends when her husband called me with the news. Those lovely friends, some I have known for almost forty years – Keely Buckle, Carole Marchant, Liz Cherry, Anna Bobin, Sarah Mayhead and Steph Lister – supported me through those first hours when it felt like my grief would overwhelm me.

Thank you for being in my life.

And thank you to all the friends who have danced with me, drunk with me and been in my corner, buying my books, including Tracie Couper, Emma Chong, Jo Darwin, Catherine Smith, Hannah Wilson, Jon Clark, Tony Mitchell, Jason Shelley, Emma Inmonger, Nicola Methven, Sinead Coles, the Barlow & Fields crew (Des, buying six hardbacks was above and beyond the call of duty, but thank you), and for all the support from the School Mums massive, especially Kim Loakman, Linda Wellard, Julia Barrett, Claire Cosgrove, Jacqui Waller, Anne-Marie Cumberworth, Jo Cobbold-Clarke, Zoe Pryor-Bennett, Kelly Collins, Julia Irwin, Kerry Farnall, Sam Smith and Louise Foster. If I've forgotten you, I'm an idiot, but I'm also very, very grateful.

As my second novel is published, this talk of friendship seems rather fitting, because the crime-writing community I find myself a part of feels like coming home.

It has been an unexpected joy and privilege, in my fourth decade, to discover a new Band of Brothers (and Sisters). To all the bloggers and reviewers, the buyers and booksellers and librarians, the Twitter compadres and the many talented authors who have extended the hand of friendship, thank you for your welcome.

Grateful thanks must also go to my wonderful editor Trisha Jackson, and to the publishers and translators of my books in other countries, as well as Francesca Pearce, Saba Ahmed, Phoebe Taylor, Amy Lines, Amber Burlinson and the team at Pan Macmillan. To the fabulous Sophie Lambert, and my agency C+W. And to my family, who are with me on every step of this journey.

Thank you to the police officers who have offered advice, and to oceanographer Dr Britt Raubenheimer for her expert guidance on the impact of tidal patterns on sand. Any mistakes are my own. This novel is set in the Essex town of Leigh-on-Sea, which I know well. At times, I have played with the geography. Any mistakes are deliberate.

My final thank you is for Cherry.

I miss her every day, but I have found comfort in the familiar pages of all the books she has gifted me over the years. I have reread the stories she wrote. I have turned over the Shakespearean words of encouragement she scribbled in my notebook not long before she fell ill: *Though she be but little, she is fierce.*

And as this adventure called publication continues, I will be forever grateful to her for persuading me that it was worth trying. For teaching me that when life's rollercoaster curves and banks from dazzling heights to stomach-twisting lows, as it surely must do, it will *always* be worth trying.